Isaac Asimov, one of America's great resources, has by now written more than 330 books. No other writer in history has published so much on such a wide variety of subjects, which range from science fiction and murder novels to books on history, the physical sciences, and Shakespeare. Born in the Soviet Union and raised in Brooklyn, he lives in New York City with his wife, electric typewriter, and word processor.

Martin H. Greenberg, who has been called 'the king of anthologists', now has some 130 to his credit. He is also co-editor, with Bill Pronzini, of The Mammoth Book of Short Crime Novels and The Mammoth Book of Short Spy Novels. Greenberg is professor of regional analysis and political science at the University of Wisconsin – Green Bay, USA, where he also teaches a course in the history of science fiction.

Charles G. Waugh, a professor of psychology and mass communications at the University of Maine at Augusta, USA, is a leading authority on science fiction and fantasy who has collaborated on more than 80 anthologies and single-author collections with Isaac Asimov, Martin H. Greenberg, and assorted colleagues.

Also available in
ISAAC ASIMOV'S MAGICAL WORLD OF
FANTASY

COSMIC KNIGHTS

GIANTS

Also edited by Isaac Asimov,
Martin H. Greenberg and Charles G.
Waugh

**THE MAMMOTH BOOK OF
SHORT SCIENCE FICTION NOVELS**

**THE MAMMOTH BOOK OF
CLASSICAL SCIENCE FICTION**

INTERGALACTIC EMPIRES

SUPERMEN

Isaac Asimov's Magical World of Fantasy

SPELLS

Edited by Isaac Asimov,
Martin H. Greenberg
and Charles G. Waugh

Robinson Publishing
London

Robinson Publishing
11 Shepherd House
Shepherd Street
London W1Y 7LD

First published in the UK by Robinson Publishing in 1988

Collection copyright © Nightfall Inc.,
                      Charles G. Waugh and
                      Martin H. Greenberg, 1985

Cover illustration © Julek Heller

ISBN 0 948164 63 8

Printed by Wm. Collins & Sons Ltd., Glasgow

CONTENTS

ACKNOWLEDGEMENTS

Grateful acknowledgement for permission to reprint material is hereby given to the following:

'The Candidate' by Henry Slesar. Copyright © 1961 by Greenleaf Publishing Company. Reprinted by permission of the author.

'The Snow Women' by Fritz Leiber. Copyright © 1970 by Ultimate Publishing Company. Reprinted by permission of Richard Curtis Associates, Inc.

'Invisible Boy' by Ray Bradbury. Copyright © 1945 by Ray Bradbury, renewed in © 1973 by Ray Bradbury. Reprinted by permission of Don Congdon Associates, Inc.

'The Hero Who Returned' by Gerald W. Page. Copyright © 1979 by Gerald W. Page; reprinted by permission of the author and the author's agent, James Allen.

'Toads of Grimmerdale' by Andre Norton. Copyright © 1973 by Dell Publishing Company. From FLASHING SWORDS, Vol. II. Reprinted by permission of Larry Sternig Literary Agency.

'A Literary Death' by Martin H. Greenberg. Copyright © 1985 by Martin H. Greenberg.

'Satan and Sam Shay' by Robert Arthur. Copyright © 1942 by Robert Arthur; copyright renewed. Reprinted by permission of the agents for the author's estate, the Scott Meredith Literary Agency, Inc., 845 Third Avenue, New York, NY 10022.

'The Witch is Dead' by Edward D. Hoch. Copyright © 1956 by Columbia Publications. Reprinted by permission of Larry Sternig Literary Agency, Inc.

'I Know What You Need' by Stephen King. Copyright © 1976 by Stephen King. From NIGHTSHIFT by Stephen King. Reprinted by permission of Doubleday & Company, Inc.

'The Miracle Workers' by Jack Vance. Copyright © 1958 by Street & Smith Publications, Inc. Reprinted by permission of Kirby McCauley, Ltd.

Introduction

CURSES!

by Isaac Asimov

If you have an enemy and are desperately anxious to get rid of him, the most straightforward thing to do is to get a big club and bash him over the head. That's it!

But what if he's bigger and stronger than you are? Or what if he isn't, but he has a big family that will get after you once you've done your job? Or what if you live in a society that has a large and interfering police department that will then pursue and arrest you?

You're stuck with the next best thing. You must confine yourself to *wishing* he were dead. Naturally, if you believe in the existence of gods or demons, and if one of them happens to be a friend of yours, perhaps you can persuade said god or demon to do the job for you. You would use some magic chant, or perform some magic ritual, or both, in order to cajole or force the god or demon to oblige. You must, in other words, cast a "magic spell"—where "spell" is an old Teutonic word for "chant" or "tale."

Of course, the magic spell doesn't have to bring death. Death is, after all, not much of a punishment. A moment of dizziness, a pang or two, the coming of blackness, and then—nothingness. What kind of punishment is that? Most people find that rather dull and unimaginative, and definitely unsatisfying. That is why a lot of thought has gone into inventing and describing hell (or its equivalent) as a place where people you don't like can be consigned after death, in order that they may be tortured in horrible ways not just for a rotten tri!lion years, but *forever*!

Or else, the victim of a magic spell can be left alive in order to suffer something that will make them feel a lot worse than just dying will. For instance, suppose you order a man

7

and a woman not to eat a certain kind of fruit, because if they do, you will kill them. "In the day thou eatest thereof, thou shalt surely die," you say solemnly.

And then the man and woman go ahead and eat the fruit, and you decide that for a serious infraction of the rules like that, death isn't enough. So, since you're omnipotent, you break your solemn word and say to the man, "In the sweat of thy face shalt thou eat bread," and to the woman you say, "In sorrow thou shalt bring forth children." In other words, the man is condemned to lifelong hard labor and the woman to the repeated pangs of childbirth. What's more, all the descendants of these two are condemned to the same punishment!

Isn't a magic spell like that much better and more satisfying that just bashing people over the head?

It's no surprise at all, then, that throughout history, magic spells have delighted humanity. It got so that nobody could die of disease, or have an accident, without everyone else in the community suspecting that a magic spell was the cause. After all, what else could possibly bring about such things? And as though that weren't fun in itself, there would then be the additional pleasure of finding someone you didn't like—an ugly, old woman who's no good to anyone is the best bet— accusing her of casting the spell and torturing her to death.

Those were the good old days.

In theory, to be sure, magic spells don't have to bring misfortune. They don't have to be "curses," in other words. They might be used as "blessings" to ensure good fortune, or to neutralize misfortune. Such things are indeed sometimes described, but very little interest is aroused in them.

I suppose the psychology of that is not very difficult to understand. If things are going well with you, there's no need to feel that magic is involved. After all, things *ought* to be going well with you. You're a wonderful person, as you yourself will testify (and who knows you better than you do), and wonderful things should naturally happen to you. And as for wishing good fortune on someone else and blessing them, what the devil have *they* done to deserve it?

Thus, in the Gilbert and Sullivan play, *The Sorcerer,* John Wellington Wells (who is the sorcerer of the title) is describing his stock-in-trade. "We have some very superior Blessings, too," he says, "but they're very little asked for. We've only sold one since Christmas. . . . But our sale of penny Curses, especially on Saturday nights, is tremendous. We can't turn 'em out fast enough.''

There you are. Would William Schwenk Gilbert lie?

So popular were magic spells, in fact, that even though they were seen everywhere in real life, that wasn't enough. They penetrated literature as well. Think of all the folktales populated by wicked witches, and offended fairies, and haughty enchanters, and devious sorcerers, all of them with an inexhaustible fund of assorted curses to hurl at those unfortunates who have committed such terrible crimes as forgetting to invite them to a christening.

Of course, in our present disgustingly secularized times when humanists and suchlike scum abound, and when belief in gods and demons and magic spells (whether blessings or curses) are frowned upon by vicious modernists, there is a sad falling off in the good old customs. Witches are hardly ever burned anymore (though there's a move on among the pious, I understand, to burn Liberal Democrats who refuse to vote right).

Fortunately, however, magic spells and the hearty curses of yore live on in our modern fantasies, and just to bring you all a breath of fresh air, we are supplying you with a dozen or so stories of this kind for your pleasure and delectation.

What's more, the fact that Martin, Charles, and I have edited this collection gives us certain powers. It is only fair to warn the critics, therefore, that if any of them are so shortsighted as to say bad things about this book, their word processors will go down at the first stroke of a key. And if they use a typewriter, a toad will leap out of their machine each time they complete a sentence.

(At this point I wanted to describe the blessings that would be showered upon them if they gave us a good review, but Martin and Charles insist that critics don't understand kindness and can only be dealt with severely.)

THE CANDIDATE

by Henry Slesar

The winner of an Emmy and an Edgar, Henry Slesar (born in 1927) is most noted for his accomplishments in television and the mystery field. However, he has also written about 100 works of science fiction and fantasy, many of which are excellent. One of his great strengths, mastery of the O. Henry ending, is illustrated by the story below.

"A man's worth can be judged by the caliber of his enemies." Burton Grunzer, encountering the phrase in a pocket-sized biography he had purchased at a newsstand, put the book in his lap and stared reflectively from the murky window of the commuter train. Darkness silvered the glass and gave him nothing to look at but his own image, but it seemed appropriate to his line of thought. How many people were enemies of that face, of the eyes narrowed by a myopic squint denied by vanity that correction of spectacles, of the nose he secretly called patrician, of the mouth that was soft in relaxation and hard when animated by speech or smiles or frowns? How many enemies? Grunzer mused. A few he could name, others he could guess. But it was their caliber that was important. Men like Whitman Hayes, for instance, there was a twenty-four-carat opponent for you. Grunzer smiled, darting a side-long glance at the seat-sharer beside him, not wanting to be caught indulging in a secret thought. Grunzer was thirty-four; Hayes was twice as old, his white hairs synonymous with experience, an enemy to be proud of. Hayes knew the food business, all right, knew it from every angle: he'd been a wagon jobber for six years, a broker for ten, a food-company executive for twenty before the old man had brought him into

10

the organization to sit on his right hand. Pinning Hayes to the mat wasn't easy, and that made Grunzer's small but increasing triumphs all the sweeter. He congratulated himself. He had twisted Hayes' advantages into drawbacks, had made his long years seem tantamount to senility and outlived usefulness; in meetings, he had concentrated his questions on the new supermarket and suburbia phenomena to demonstrate to the old man that times had changed, that the past was dead, that new merchandising tactics were needed, and that only a younger man could supply them. . . .

Suddenly, he was depressed. His enjoyment of remembered victories seemed tasteless. Yes, he'd won a minor battle or two in the company conference room; he'd made Hayes' ruddy face go crimson, and seen the old man's parchment skin wrinkle in a sly grin. But what had been accomplished? Hayes seemed more self-assured than ever, and the old man more dependent upon his advice. . . .

When he arrived home, later than usual, his wife, Jean, didn't ask questions. After eight years of a marriage in which, childless, she knew her husband almost too well, she wisely offered nothing more than a quiet greeting, a hot meal, and the day's mail. Grunzer flipped through the bills and circulars, and found an unmarked letter. He slipped it into his hip pocket, reserving it for private perusal, and finished the meal in silence.

After dinner, Jean suggested a movie and he agreed; he had a passion for violent action movies. But first, he locked himself in the bathroom and opened the letter. Its heading was cryptic: Society for United Action. The return address was a post-office box. It read:

Dear Mr. Grunzer:
Your name has been suggested to us by a mutual acquaintance. Our organization has an unusual mission which cannot be described in this letter, but which you may find of exceeding interest. We would be gratified by a private discussion at your earliest convenience. If I do not hear from you to the contrary in the next few days, I will take the liberty of calling you at your office.

It was signed, Carl Tucker, Secretary. A thin line at the bottom of the page read: A Non-Profit Organization.

His first reaction was a defensive one; he suspected an oblique attack on his pocketbook. His second was curiosity: he went to the bedroom and located the telephone directory, but found no organization listed by the letterhead name. Okay, Mr. Tucker, he thought wryly, I'll bite.

When no call came in the next three days, his curiosity was increased. But when Friday arrived, he forgot the letter's promise in the crush of office affairs. The old man called a meeting with the bakery-products division. Grunzer sat opposite Whitman Hayes at the conference table, poised to pounce on fallacies in his statements. He almost had him once, but Eckhardt, the bakery-products manager, spoke up in defense of Hayes' views. Eckhardt had only been with the company a year, but he had evidently chosen sides already. Grunzer glared at him, and reserved a place for Eckhardt in the hate chamber of his mind.

At three o'clock, Carl Tucker called.

"Mr. Grunzer?" The voice was friendly, even cheery. "I haven't heard from you, so I assume you don't mind me calling today. Is there a chance we can get together sometime?"

"Well, if you could give me some idea, Mr. Tucker—"

The chuckle was resonant. "We're not a charity organization, Mr. Grunzer, in case you got that notion. Nor do we sell anything. We're more or less a voluntary-service group: our membership is over a thousand at present."

"To tell you the truth," Grunzer frowned, "I never heard of you."

"No, you haven't, and that's one of the assets. I think you'll understand when I tell you about us. I can be over at your office in fifteen minutes, unless you want to make it another day."

Grunzer glanced at his calendar. "Okay, Mr. Tucker. Best time for me is right now."

"Fine! I'll be right over."

Tucker was prompt. When he walked into the office, Grunzer's eyes went dismayed at the officious briefcase in the man's right hand. But he felt better when Tucker, a florid man in his early sixties with small, pleasant features, began talking.

"Nice of you to take the time, Mr. Grunzer. And believe me, I'm not here to sell you insurance or razor blades.

Couldn't if I tried; I'm a semiretired broker. However, the subject I want to discuss is rather—intimate, so I'll have to ask you to bear with me on a certain point. May I close the door?''

"Sure," Grunzer said, mystified.

Tucker closed it, hitched his chair closer, and said, "The point is this. What I have to say must remain in the strictest confidence. If you betray that confidence, if you publicize our society in any way, the consequences could be most unpleasant. Is that agreeable?"

Grunzer, frowning, nodded.

"Fine!" The visitor snapped open the briefcase and produced a stapled manuscript. "Now, the society has prepared this little spiel about our basic philosophy, but I'm not going to bore you with it. I'm going to go straight to the heart of our argument. You may not agree with our first principle at all, and I'd like to know that now."

"How do you mean, first principle?"

"Well . . ." Tucker flushed slightly. "Put in the crudest form, Mr. Grunzer, the Society for United Action believes that—*some* people are just not fit to live." He looked up quickly, as if anxious to gauge the immediate reaction. "There, I've said it." He laughed, somewhat in relief. "Some of our members don't believe in my direct approach; they feel the argument has to be broached more discreetly. But frankly, I've gotten excellent results in this rather crude manner. How do you feel about what I've said, Mr. Grunzer?"

"I don't know. Guess I never thought about it much."

"Were you in the war, Mr. Grunzer?"

"Yes. Navy." Grunzer rubbed his jaw. "I suppose I didn't think the Japs were fit to live, back then. I guess maybe there are other cases. I mean, you take capital punishment, I believe in that. Murderers, rape-artists, perverts, hell, I certainly don't think *they're* fit to live."

"Ah," Tucker said. "So you really accept our first principle. It's a question of category, isn't it?"

"I guess you could say that."

"Good. So now I'll try another blunt question. Have you—personally—ever wished someone dead? Oh, I don't mean those casual, fleeting wishes everybody has. I mean a real, deep-down, uncomplicated wish for the death of someone *you* thought was unfit to live. Have you?"

"Sure." Grunzer said frankly. "I guess I have."

"There are times, in your opinion, when the removal of someone from this earth would be beneficial?"

Grunzer smiled. "Hey, what is this? You from Murder, Incorporated, or something?"

Tucker grinned back. "Hardly, Mr. Grunzer, hardly. There is absolutely no criminal aspect to our aims or our methods. I'll admit we're a 'secret' society, but we're no Black Hand. You'd be amazed at the quality of our membership; it even includes members of the legal profession. But suppose I tell you how the society came into being?

"It began with two men; I can't reveal their names just now. The year was 1949, and one of these men was a lawyer attached to the district attorney's office. The other man was a state psychiatrist. Both of them were involved in a rather sensational trial, concerning a man accused of a hideous crime against two small boys. In their opinion, the man was unquestionably guilty, but an unusual persuasive defense counsel, and a highly suggestible jury, gave him his freedom. When the shocking verdict was announced, these two, who were personal friends as well as colleagues, were thunderstruck and furious. They felt a great wrong had been committed, and they were helpless to right it . . .

"But I should explain something about this psychiatrist. For some years, he had made studies in a field which might be called anthropological psychiatry. One of these researches related to the voodoo practice of certain groups, the Haitian in particular. You've probably heard a great deal about voodoo, or obeah as they call it in Jamaica, but I won't dwell on the subject lest you think we hold tribal rites and stick pins in dolls . . . But the chief feature of his study was the uncanny *success* of certain strange practices. Naturally, as a scientist, he rejected the supernatural explanation and sought the rational one. And of course, there was only one answer. When the vodun priest decreed the punishment or death of a malefactor, it was the malefactor's own convictions concerning the efficacy of the death wish, his own faith in the voodoo power, that eventually made the wish come true. Sometimes, the process was organic—his body reacted psychosomatically to the voodoo curse, and he would sicken and die. Sometimes, he would die by 'accident'—an accident prompted by the secret belief that once cursed, he *must* die. Eerie, isn't it?"

"No doubt," Grunzer said dry-lipped.

"Anyway, our friend, the psychiatrist, began wondering aloud if *any* one of us have advanced so far along the civilized path that we couldn't be subject to this same sort of 'suggested' punishment. He proposed that they experiment on this choice subject, just to see.

"How they did it was simple," he said. "They went to see this man, and they announced their intentions.They told him they were going to *wish him dead*. They explained how and why the wish would become reality, and while he laughed at their proposal, they could see the look of superstitious fear cross his face. They promised him that regularly, every day, they would be wishing for his death, until he could no longer stop the mystic juggernaut that would make the wish come true."

Grunzer shivered suddenly and clenched his fist. "That's pretty silly," he said softly.

"The man died of a heart attack two months later."

"Of course. I knew you'd say that. But there's such a thing as coincidence."

"Naturally. And our friends, while intrigued, weren't satisfied. *So they tried it again.*"

"Again?"

"Yes, again. I won't recount who the victim was, but I will tell you that this time they enlisted the aid of four associates. This little band of pioneers was the nucleus of the society I represent today."

Grunzer shook his head. "And you mean to tell me there's a *thousand* now?"

"Yes, a thousand and more, all over the country. A society whose one function is to *wish people dead*. At first, membership was purely voluntary, but now we have a system. Each new member of the Society for United Action joins on the basis of submitting one potential victim. Naturally, the society investigates to determine whether the victim is deserving of his fate. If the case is a good one, the *entire* membership then sets about to *wish him dead*. Once the task has been accomplished, naturally, the new member must take part in all future concerted action. That and a small yearly fee, is the price of membership."

Carl Tucker grinned.

"And in case you think I'm not serious, Mr. Grunzer—"

He dipped into the briefcase again, this time producing a blue-bound volume of telephone-directory thickness. "Here are the facts. To date, two hundred and twenty-nine victims were named by our selection committee. Of those, *one hundred and four* are no longer alive. Coincidence, Mr. Grunzer?

"As for the remaining one hundred and twenty-five—perhaps that indicates that our method is not infallible. We're the first to admit that. But new techniques are being developed all the time. I assure you, Mr. Grunzer, *we will get them all.*"

He flipped through the blue-bound book.

"Our members are listed in this book, Mr. Grunzer. I'm going to give you the option to call one, ten, or a hundred of them. Call them and see if I'm not telling the truth."

He flipped the manuscript toward Grunzer's desk. It landed on the blotter with a thud. Grunzer picked it up.

"Well?" Tucker said. "Want to call them?"

"No." He licked his lips. "I'm willing to take your word for it, Mr. Tucker. It's incredible, but I can see how it works. *Just knowing* that a thousand people are wishing you dead is enough to shake hell out of you." His eyes narrowed. "But there's one question. You talked about a 'small' fee—"

"It's fifty dollars, Mr. Grunzer."

"Fifty, huh? Fifty times a thousand, that's pretty good money, isn't it?"

"I assure you, the organization is not motivated by profit. Not the kind you mean. The dues merely cover expenses, committee work, research, and the like. Surely you can understand that?"

"I guess so," he grunted.

"Then you find it interesting?"

Grunzer swiveled his chair about to face the window.

God! he thought.

God, if it *really* worked!

But how could it? If wishes became deeds, he would have slaughtered dozens in his lifetime. Yet, that was different. His wishes were always secret things, hidden where no man could know them. But this method was different, more practical, more terrifying. Yes, he could see how it might work. He could visualize a thousand minds burning with the single wish of death, see the victim sneering in disbelief at first, and then slowly, gradually, surely succumbing to the tightening, constricting chain of fear that it *might* work, that

so many deadly thoughts could indeed emit a mystical, malevo-
lent ray that destroyed life.

Suddenly, ghostlike, he saw the ruddy face of Whitman
Hayes before him.

He wheeled about and said, "But the victim has to *know*
all this, of course? He has to know the society exists, and has
succeeded, and is wishing for *his* death? That's essential,
isn't it?"

"Absolutely essential," Tucker said, replacing the manu-
scripts in his briefcase. "You've touched on the vital point,
Mr. Grunzer. The victim must be informed, and that, precisely,
is what I have done." He looked at his watch. "Your death
wish began at noon today. The society has begun to work.
I'm very sorry."

At the doorway, he turned and lifted both hat and briefcase
in one departing salute.

"Good-bye, Mr. Grunzer," he said.

THE CHRISTMAS SHADRACK

by Frank R. Stockton

Trained as a wood engraver, Frank R. Stockton (1834–1902) drifted into writing, eventually receiving great popular acclaim for marvelous fairy tales such as "The Griffin and the Minor Canon," "The Bee Man of Orn," and "Old Pipes and the Dryad." His stories, like the one below, are usually filled with much charm and civility.

Whenever I make a Christmas present I like it to mean something, not necessarily my sentiments toward the person to whom I give it, but sometimes an expression of what I should like that person to do or to be. In the early part of a certain winter not very long ago I found myself in a position of perplexity and anxious concern regarding a Christmas present which I wished to make.

The state of the case was this. There was a young lady, the daughter of a neighbor and old friend of my father, who had been gradually assuming relations toward me which were not only unsatisfactory to me, but were becoming more and more so. Her name was Mildred Bronce. She was between twenty and twenty-five years of age, and as fine a woman in every way as one would be likely to meet in a lifetime. She was handsome, of a tender and generous disposition, a fine intelligence, and a thoroughly well-stocked mind. We had known each other for a long time, and when fourteen or fifteen Mildred had been my favorite companion. She was a little younger than I, and I liked her better than any boy I knew. Our friendship had continued through the years, but of late there had been a change in it; Mildred had become very

18

fond of me, and her fondness seemed to have in it certain elements which annoyed me.

As a girl to make love to, no one could be better than Mildred Bronce, but I had never made love to her—at least not earnestly—and I did not wish that any permanent condition of loving should be established between us. Mildred did not seem to share this opinion; for every day it became plainer to me that she looked upon me as a lover, and that she was perfectly willing to return my affection.

But I had other ideas upon the subject. Into the rural town in which my family passed the greater part of the year there had recently come a young lady, Miss Janet Clinton, to whom my soul went out of my own option. In some respects, perhaps, she was not the equal of Mildred, but she was very pretty: she was small, she had a lovely mouth, was apparently of a clinging nature, and her dark eyes looked into mine with a tingling effect that no other eyes had ever produced. I was in love with her because I wished to be, and the consciousness of this fact caused me a proud satisfaction. The affair was not the result of circumstances, but of my own free will.

I wished to retain Mildred's friendship; I wished to make her happy; and with this latter intent in view I wished very much that she should not disappoint herself in her anticipations of the future.

Each year it had been my habit to make Mildred a Christmas present, and I was now looking for something to give her which would please her and suit my purpose.

When a man wishes to select a present for a lady which, while it assures her of his kind feeling toward her, will at the same time indicate that not only has he no matrimonial inclinations in her direction, but that it would be entirely unwise for her to have any such inclinations in his direction; that no matter with what degree of fondness her heart is disposed to turn toward him, his heart does not turn toward her; and that, in spite of all sentiments induced by long association and the natural fitness of things, she need never expect to be to him anything more than a sister, he has, indeed, a difficult task before him. But such was the task which I set for myself.

Day after day I wandered through the shops. I looked at odd pieces of jewelry and bric-à-brac, and at many a quaint relic or bit of art work which seemed to have a meaning, but nothing had the meaning I wanted. As to books, I found none which satisfied me, not one which was adapted to produce the exact impression that I desired.

One afternoon I was in a little basement shop kept by a fellow in a long overcoat, who, so far as I was able to judge, bought curiosities but never sold any. For some minutes I had been looking at a beautifully decorated saucer of rare workmanship for which there was no cup to match, and for which the proprietor informed me no cup could be found or manufactured. There were some points in the significance of an article of this sort, given as a present to a lady, which fitted to my purpose, but it would signify too much: I did not wish to suggest to Mildred that she need never expect to find a cup. It would be better, in fact, if I gave her anything of this kind, to send her a cup and saucer entirely unsuited to each other, and which could not, under any conditions, be used together.

I put down the saucer and continued my search among the dusty shelves and cases.

"How would you like a paperweight?" the shopkeeper asked. "Here is something a little odd," handing me a piece of dark-colored mineral nearly as big as my fist, flat on the under side and of a pleasing irregularity above. Around the bottom was a band of arabesque work in some dingy metal, probably German silver. I smiled as I took it.

"This is not good enough for a Christmas present," I said. "I want something odd, but it must have some value."

"Well," said the man, "that has no real value, but there is a peculiarity about it which interested me when I heard of it, and so I bought it. This mineral is a piece of what the ironworkers call shadrach. It is a portion of the iron or iron ore which passes through the smelting furnaces without being affected by the great heat, and so they have given it the name of one of the Hebrew youths who was cast into the fiery furnace by Nebuchadnezzar, and who came out unhurt. Some people think there is a sort of magical quality about this shadrach, and that it can give out to human beings something of its power to keep their minds cool when they are in danger of being overheated. The old gentleman who had this made was subject to fits of anger, and he thought this piece of shadrach helped to keep him from giving way to them. Occasionally he used to leave it in the house of a hot-

tempered neighbor, believing that the testy individual would
be cooled down for a time, without knowing how the change
had been brought about. I bought a lot of things of the old
gentleman's widow, and this among them. I thought I might
try it some time, but I never have.''

I held the shadrach in my hand, ideas concerning it rapidly
flitting through my mind. Why would not this be a capital
thing to give to Mildred? If it should, indeed, possess the
quality ascribed to it, if it should be able to cool her liking for
me, what better present could I give her? I did not hesitate
long.

"I will buy this," I said, "but the ornamentation must be
of a better sort. It is now too cheap and tawdry-looking."

"I can attend to that for you," said the shopkeeper. "I can
have it set in a band of gold or silver filigreework like this, if
you choose."

I agree to this proposition, but ordered the band to be made
of silver, the cool tone of that metal being more appropriate
to the characteristics of the gift than the warmer hues of gold.

When I gave my Christmas present to Mildred, she was
pleased with it; its oddity struck her fancy.

"I don't believe anybody ever had such a paperweight as
that,''she said as she thanked me. "What is it made of?"

I told her, and explained what shadrach was, but I did not
speak of its presumed influence over human beings, which,
after all, might be nothing but the wildest fancy. I did not feel
altogether at my ease, as I added that it was merely a trifle, a
thing of no value except as a reminder of the season.

"The fact that it is a present from you gives it value," she
said as she smilingly raised her eyes to mine.

I left her house—we were all living in the city then—
with a troubled conscience. What a deception I was practicing
upon this noble girl, who, if she did not already love me, was
plainly on the point of doing so. She had received my present
as if it indicated a warmth of feeling on my part, when, in
fact, it was the result of a desire for a cooler feeling on her
part.

But I called my reason to my aid and I showed myself that
what I had given Mildred—if it should prove to possess any
virtue at all—was, indeed, a most valuable boon. It was
something which would prevent the waste of her affections,
the wreck of her hopes. No kindness could be truer, no regard

for her happiness more sincere, than the motives which prompted me to give her the shadrach.

I did not soon again see Mildred, but now as often as possible I visited Janet. She always received me with a charming cordiality, and if this should develop into warmer sentiments, I was not the man to wish to cool them. In many ways Janet seemed much better suited to me than Mildred. One of the greatest charms of this beautiful girl was a tender trustfulness, as if I were a being on whom she could lean and to whom she could look up. I liked this; it was very different from Mildred's manner: with the latter I had always been well-satisfied if I felt myself standing on the same plane.

The weeks and months passed on, and again we were all in the country, and here I saw Mildred often. Our homes were not far apart and our families were very intimate. With my opportunities for frequent observation I could not doubt that a change had come over her. She was always friendly when we met, and seemed as glad to see me as she was to see any other member of my family, but she was not the Mildred I used to know. It was plain that my existence did not make the same impression on her that it once made. She did not seem to consider it important whether I came or went, whether I was in the room or not, whether I joined a party or stayed away. All this had been very different. I knew well that Mildred had been used to consider my presence as a matter of much importance, and I now felt sure that my Christmas shadrach was doing its work. Mildred was cooling toward me. Her affection, or to put it more modestly, her tendency to affection was gently congealing into friendship. This was highly gratifying to my moral nature, for every day I was doing my best to warm the soul of Janet. Whether or not I succeeded in this I could not be sure; Janet was as tender and trustful and charming as ever, but no more so than she had been months before.

Sometimes I thought she was waiting for an indication of an increased warmth of feeling on my part before she allowed the temperature of her own sentiments to rise. But for one reason and another I delayed the solution of this problem. Janet was very fond of company, and although we saw a great deal of each other, we were not often alone. If we two had more frequently walked, driven, or rowed together, as Mildred and I used to do, I think Miss Clinton would soon have had every opportunity of making up her mind about the fervor of my passion.

The summer weeks passed on and there was no change in the things which now principally concerned me, except that Mildred seemed to be growing more and more indifferent to me. From having seemed to care no more for me than for her other friends, she now seemed to care less for me than for most people. I do not mean that she showed a dislike, but she treated me with a sort of indifference which I did not fancy at all. This sort of thing had gone too far, and there was no knowing how much further it would go. It was plain enough that the shadrach was overdoing the business.

I was now in a state of much mental disquietude. Greatly as I desired to win the love of Janet, it grieved me to think of losing the generous friendship of Mildred—that friendship to which I had been accustomed for the greater part of my life and on which, as I now discovered, I had grown to depend.

In this state of mind I went to see Mildred. I found her in the library writing. She received me pleasantly, and was sorry her father was not at home, and begged that I would excuse her finishing the note on which she was engaged, because she wished to get it into the post office before the mail closed. I sat down on the other side of the table, and she finished her note, after which she went out to give it to a servant.

Glancing about me, I saw the shadrach. It was partly under a litter of papers, instead of lying on them. I took it up and was looking at it when Mildred returned. She sat down and asked me if I had heard of the changes that were to be made in the timetable of the railroad. We talked a little on the subject, and then I spoke of the shadrach, saying carelessly that it might be interesting to analyze the bit of metal; there was a little knob which might be filed off without injuring it in the least.

"You may take it," she said, "and make what experiments you please. I do not use it much; it is unnecessarily heavy for a paperweight."

From her tone I might have supposed that she had forgotten that I had given it to her. I told her that I would be very glad to borrow the paperweight for a time, and putting it into my pocket, I went away, leaving her arranging her disordered papers on the table and giving quite as much regard to this occupation as she had given to my little visit.

I could not feel sure that the absence of the shadrach would cause any diminution in the coolness of her feelings toward me, but there was reason to believe that it would prevent them from growing cooler. If she should keep that shadrach, she might in time grow to hate me. I was very glad that I had taken it from her.

My mind easier on this subject, my heart turned more freely toward Janet, and going to her house, the next day, I was delighted to find her alone. She was as lovely as ever and as cordial, but she was flushed and evidently annoyed.

"I am in a bad humor today," she said, "and I am glad you came to talk to me and quiet me. Dr. Gilbert promised to take me to drive this afternoon, and we were going over to the hills where they find the wild rhododendron. I am told that it is still in blossom up there, and I want some flowers ever so much—I am going to paint them. And besides, I am crazy to drive with his new horses, and now he sends me a note to say that he is engaged."

This communication shocked me and I began to talk to her about Dr. Gilbert. I soon found that several times she had been driving with this handsome young physician, but never, she said, behind his new horses, nor to the rhododendron hills.

Dr. Hector Gilbert was a fine young fellow, beginning practice in town, and one of my favorite associates. I had never thought of him in connection with Janet, but I could now see that he might make a most dangerous rival. When a young and talented doctor, enthusiastic in his studies and earnestly desirous of establishing a practice, and who, if his time were not fully occupied, would naturally wish that the neighbors would think that such were the case, deliberately devotes some hours on I know not how many days to driving a young lady into the surrounding country, it may be supposed that he is really in love with her. Moreover, judging from Janet's present mood, this doctor's attentions were not without encouragement.

I went home; I considered the state of affairs; I ran my fingers through my hair; I gazed steadfastly upon the floor. Suddenly I rose. I had had an inspiration; I would give the shadrach to Dr. Gilbert.

I went immediately to the doctor's office and found him there. He too was not in a very good humor.

"I have had two old ladies here nearly all the afternoon, and they have bored me to death," he said. "I could not get rid of them because I found they had made an appointment with each other to visit me today and talk over a hospital plan which I proposed some time ago and which is really very important to me, but I wish they had chosen some other time to come here. What is that thing?"

"That is a bit of shadrach," I said, "made into a paperweight." And then I proceeded to explain what shadrach is and what peculiar properties it must possess to resist the power of heat, which melts other metal apparently of the same class; and I added that I thought it might be interesting to analyze a bit of it and discover what fireproof constituents it possessed.

"I should like to do that," said the doctor, attentively turning over the shadrach in his hand. "Can I take off a piece of it?"

"I will give it to you," said I, "and you can make what use of it you please. If you do analyze it, I shall be very glad indeed to hear the results of your investigations."

The doctor demurred a little at taking the paperweight with such a pretty silver ring around it, but I assured him that the cost of the whole affair was trifling and I should be gratified if he would take it. He accepted the gift and was thanking me when a patient arrived and I departed.

I really had no right to give away this paperweight, which, in fact, belonged to Mildred, but there are times when a man must keep his eyes on the chief good and not think too much about other things. Besides, it was evident that Mildred did not care in the least for the bit of metal, and she had virtually given it to me.

There was another point which I took into consideration. It might be that the shadrach might simply cool Dr. Gilbert's feelings toward me, and that would be neither pleasant nor advantageous. If I could have managed matters so that Janet could have given it to him, it would have been all right. But now all that I could do was to wait and see what would happen. If only the thing would cool the doctor in a general way, that would help. He might then give more thought to his practice and his hospital ladies and let other people take Janet driving.

About a week after this I met the doctor; he seemed in a

hurry, but I stopped him. I had a curiosity to know if he had analyzed the shadrach and asked him about it.

"No," said he, "I haven't done it. I haven't had time. I knocked off a piece of it, and I will attend to it when I get a chance. Good day."

Of course if the man was busy, he could not be expected to give his mind to a trifling matter of that sort, but I thought he need not have been so curt about it. I stood gazing after him as he walked rapidly down the street. Before I resumed my walk, I saw him enter the Clinton house. Things were not going on well. The shadrach had not cooled Dr. Gilbert's feelings toward Janet.

But because the doctor was still warm in his attentions to the girl I loved, I would not in the least relax my attentions to her. I visited her as often as I could find an excuse to do so. There was generally someone else there, but Janet's disposition was of such gracious expansiveness that each one felt obliged to be satisfied with what he got, much as he may have wished for something different.

But one morning Janet surprised me. I met her at Mildred's house, where I had gone to borrow a book of reference. Although I had urged her not to put herself to so much trouble, Mildred was standing on a little ladder looking for the book, because, she said, she knew exactly what I wanted, and she was sure she could find the proper volume better than I could. Janet had been sitting in a window seat, reading, but when I came in, she put down her book and devoted herself to conversation with me. I was a little sorry for this, because Mildred was very kindly engaged in doing me a service and I really wanted to talk to her about the book she was looking for. Mildred showed so much of her old manner this morning that I would have been very sorry to have her think that I did not appreciate her returning interest in me. Therefore, while under other circumstances I would have been delighted to talk to Janet, I did not wish to give her so much of my attention then. But Janet Clinton was a girl who insisted on people attending to her when she wished them to do so, and having stepped through an open door into the garden, she presently called me to her. Of course I had to go.

"I will not keep you a minute from your fellow student," she said, "but I want to ask a favor of you." And into her dark, uplifted eyes there came a look of tender trustfulness clearer than any I had yet seen there. "Don't *you* want to drive me to the rhododendron hills?" she said. "I suppose the flowers are all gone by this time, but I have never been there and I should like ever so much to go."

I could not help remarking that I thought Dr. Gilbert was going to take her there.

"Dr. Gilbert, indeed!" she said with a little laugh. "He promised once and didn't come, and the next day he planned for it, it rained. I don't think doctors make very good escorts, anyway, for you can't tell who is going to be sick just as you are about to start on a trip. Besides, there is no knowing how much botany I should have to hear, and when I go on a pleasure drive, I don't care very much about studying things. But of course I don't want to trouble you."

"Trouble!" I exclaimed. "It will give me the greatest delight to take you that drive or any other, and at whatever time you please."

"You are always so good and kind," she said, with her dark eyes again upraised. "And now let us go in and see if Mildred has found the book."

I spoke the truth when I said that Janet's proposition delighted me. To take a long drive with that charming girl, and at the same time to feel that she had chosen me as her companion, was a greater joy than I had yet had reason to expect, but it would have been a more satisfying joy if she had asked me in her own house and not in Mildred's, if she had not allowed the love which I hoped was growing up between her and me to interfere with the revival of the old friendship between Mildred and me.

But when we returned to the library, Mildred was sitting at a table with a book before her, opened at the passage I wanted.

"I have just found it," she said with a smile. "Draw up a chair and we will look over these maps together. I want you to show me how he traveled when he left his ship."

"Well, if you two are going to the pole," said Janet with her prettiest smile, "I will go back to my novel."

She did not seem in the least to object to my geographical researches with Mildred, and if the latter had even noticed my willingness to desert her at the call of Janet, she did not show it. Apparently she was as much a good comrade as she had ever been. This state of things was gratifying in the highest degree. If I could be loved by Janet and still keep Mildred as my friend, what greater earthly joys could I ask?

The drive with Janet was postponed by wet weather. Day after day it rained, or the skies were heavy, and we both agreed that it must be in the bright sunshine that we would make this excursion. When we should make it, and should be alone together on the rhododendron hill, I intended to open my soul to Janet.

It may seem strange to others, and at the time it also seemed strange to me, but there was another reason besides the rainy weather which prevented my declaration of love to Janet. This was a certain nervous anxiety in regard to my friendship for Mildred. I did not in the least waver in my intention to use the best endeavors to make the one my wife, but at the same time I was oppressed by a certain alarm that in carrying out this project I might act in such a way as to wound the feelings of the other.

This disposition to consider the feelings of Mildred became so strong that I began to think that my own sentiments were in need of control. It was not right that while making love to one woman I should give so much consideration to my relations with another. The idea struck me that in a measure I had shared the fate of those who had thrown the Hebrew youths into the fiery furnace. My heart had not been consumed by the flames, but in throwing the shadrach into what I supposed were Mildred's affections, it was quite possible that I had been singed by them. At any rate my conscience told me that under the circumstances my sentiments toward Mildred were too warm; in honestly making love to Janet I ought to forget them entirely.

It might have been a good thing, I told myself, if I had not given away the shadrach, but kept it as a gift from Mildred. Very soon after I reached this conclusion, it became evident to me that Mildred was again cooling in my direction as rapidly as the mercury falls after sunset on a September day. This discovery did not make my mercury fall; in fact, it brought it for a time nearly to the boiling point. I could not imagine what had happened. I almost neglected Janet, so anxious was I to know what had made this change in Mildred.

Weeks passed on, and I discovered nothing, except that Mildred had now become more than indifferent to me. She allowed me to see that my companionship did not give her pleasure.

Janet had her drive to the rhododendron hills, but she took it with Dr. Gilbert and not with me. When I heard of this, it pained me, though I could not help admitting that I deserved the punishment, but my surprise was almost as great as my pain, for Janet had recently given me reason to believe that she had a very small opinion of the young doctor. In fact, she had criticized him so severely that I had been obliged to speak in his defense. I now found myself in a most doleful quandary, and there was only one thing of which I could be certain—I needed cooling toward Mildred if I still allowed myself to hope to marry Janet.

One afternoon I was talking to Mr. Bronce in his library, when, glancing toward the table used by his daughter for writing purposes, I was astounded to see, lying on a little pile of letters, the Christmas shadrach. As soon as I could get an opportunity, I took it in my hand and eagerly examined it. I had not been mistaken. It was the paperweight I had given Mildred. There was the silver band around it and there was the place where a little piece had been knocked off by the doctor. Mildred was not at home, but I determined that I would wait and see her. I would dine with the Bronces; I would spend the evening; I would stay all night; I would not leave the house until I had had this mystery explained. She returned in about half an hour and greeted me in the somewhat stiff manner she had adopted of late, but when she noticed my perturbed expression and saw that I held the shadrach in my hand, she took a seat by the table, where for some time I had been waiting for her, alone.

"I suppose you want to ask me about that paperweight," she remarked.

"Indeed I do," I replied. "How in the world did you happen to get it again?"

"Again?" she repeated satirically. "You may well say that. I will explain it to you. Some little time ago I called on Janet Clinton, and on her writing desk I saw that paperweight. I remembered it perfectly. It was the one you gave me last Christmas and afterward borrowed of me, saying that you wanted to analyze it, or something of the sort. I had never used it very much, and of course was willing that you should take it and make experiments with it if you wanted to, but I must say that the sight of it on Janet Clinton's desk both shocked and angered me. I asked her where she got it, and she told me a gentleman had given it to her. I did not need to waste any words in inquiring who this gentleman was, but I determined that she should not rest under a mistake in regard to its proper ownership, and told her plainly that the person who had given it to her had previously given it to me; that it was mine, and he had no right to give it to anyone else. 'Oh, if that is the case,' she exclaimed, 'take it, I beg of you. I don't care for it, and, what is more, I don't care any more for the man who gave it to me than I do for the thing itself.' So I took it and brought it home with me. Now you know how I happened to have it again.''

For a moment I made no answer. Then I asked her how long it had been since she had received the shadrach from Janet Clinton.

"Oh, I don't remember exactly," she said, "it was several weeks ago."

Now I knew everything; all the mysteries of the past were revealed to me. The young doctor, fervid in his desire to please the woman he loved, had given Janet this novel paperweight. From that moment she had begun to regard his attentions with apathy, and finally—her nature was one which was apt to go to extremes—to dislike him. Mildred repossessed herself of the shadrach, which she took, not as a gift from Janet, but as her rightful property, presented to her by me. And this horrid little object, probably with renewed power, had cooled, almost frozen indeed, the sentiments of that dear girl toward me. Then, too, had the spell been taken from Janet's inclinations, and she had gone to the rhododendron hills with Dr. Gilbert.

One thing was certain. I must have that shadrach.

"Mildred," I exclaimed, "will you not give me this paperweight? Give it to me for my own?"

"What do you want to do with it?" she asked sarcastically. "Analyze it again?"

"Mildred," said I, "I did not give it to Janet. I gave it to Dr. Gilbert, and he must have given it to her. I know I had no right to give it away at all, but I did not believe that you would care, but now I beg that you will let me have it. Let me have it for my own. I assure you solemnly I will never give it away. It has caused trouble enough already."

"I don't exactly understand what you mean by trouble," she said, "but take it if you want it. You are perfectly welcome." And picking up her gloves and hat from the table, she left me.

As I walked home my hatred of the wretched piece of metal in my hand increased with every step. I looked at it with disgust when I went to bed that night, and when my glance lighted upon it the next morning, I involuntarily shrank from it, as if it had been an evil thing. Over and over again that day I asked myself why I should keep in my possession something which would make my regard for Mildred grow less and less, which would eventually make me care for her not at all? The very thought of not caring for Mildred sent a pang through my heart.

My feelings all prompted me to rid myself of what I looked upon as a calamitous talisman, but my reason interfered. If I still wished to marry Janet, it was my duty to welcome indifference to Mildred.

In this mood I went out, to stroll, to think, to decide; and that I might be ready to act on my decision, I put the shadrach into my pocket. Without exactly intending it, I walked toward the Bronce place and soon found myself on the edge of a pretty pond which lay at the foot of the garden. Here, in the shade of a tree, there stood a bench, and on this lay a book, an ivory paper cutter in its leaves as marker.

I knew that Mildred had left that book on the bench; it was her habit to come to this place to read. As she had not taken the volume with her, it was probable that she intended soon to return. But then the sad thought came to me that if she saw me there, she would not return. I picked up the book; I read the pages she had been reading. As I read, I felt that I could think the very thoughts that she thought as she read. I was seized with a yearning to be with her, to read with her, to think with her. Never had my soul gone out to Mildred as at that moment, and yet, heavily dangling in my pocket, I carried—I could not bear to think of it. Seized by a sudden impulse, I put down the book; I drew out the shadrach, and tearing off the silver band, I tossed the vile bit of metal into the pond.

"There!" I cried. "Go out of my possession, out of my sight! You shall work no charm on me. Let nature take its course and let things happen as they may." Then, relieved from the weight on my heart and the weight in my pocket, I went home.

Nature did take its course, and in less than a fortnight from that day, the engagement of Janet and Dr. Gilbert was announced. I had done nothing to prevent this and the news did not disturb my peace of mind; but my relations with Mildred very much disturbed it. I had hoped that, released from the baleful influence of the shadrach, her friendly feelings toward me would return, and my passion for her had now grown so strong that I waited and watched, as a wrecked mariner waits and watches for the sight of a sail, for a sign that she had so far softened toward me that I might dare to speak to her of my love. But no such sign appeared.

I now seldom visited the Bronce house; no one of that family, once my best friends, seemed to care to see me. Evidently Mildred's feelings toward me had extended themselves to the rest of the household. This was not surprising, for her family had long been accustomed to think as Mildred thought.

One day I met Mr. Bronce at the post office, and some other gentlemen coming up, we began to talk of a proposed plan to introduce a system of waterworks into the village, an improvement much desired by many of us.

"So far as I am concerned," said Mr. Bronce, "I am not now in need of anything of the sort. Since I set up my steam pump, I have supplied my house from the pond at the end of my garden with all the water we can possibly want for every purpose."

"Do you mean," asked one of the gentlemen, "that you get your drinking water in that way?"

"Certainly," replied Mr. Bronce. "The basin of the pond is kept as clean and in as good order as any reservoir can be, and the water comes from an excellent, rapid-flowing spring. I want nothing better."

A chill ran through me as I listened. The shadrach was in that pond. Every drop of water which Mildred drank, which touched her, was influenced by that demoniacal paperweight, which, without knowing what I was doing, I had thus bestowed upon the whole Bronce family.

When I went home, I made diligent search for a stone which might be about the size and weight of the shadrach, and having repaired to a retired spot, I practised tossing it as I had tossed the bit of metal into the pond. In each instance I measured the distance which I had thrown the stone and was at last enabled to make a very fair estimate of the distance to which I had thrown the shadrach when I had buried it under the waters of the pond.

That night there was a half-moon, and between eleven and twelve o'clock, when everybody in our village might be supposed to be in bed and asleep, I made my way over the fields to the back of the Bronce place, taking with me a long fish cord with a knot in it, showing the average distance to which I had thrown the practice stone. When I reached the pond, I stood as nearly as possible in the place by the bench from which I had hurled the shadrach, and to this spot I pegged one end of the cord. I was attired in an old tennis suit, and having removed my shoes and stockings, I entered the water, holding the roll of cord in my hand. This I slowly unwound as I advanced toward the middle of the pond, and when I reached the knot, I stopped, with the water above my waist.

I had found the bottom of the pond very smooth, and free from weeds and mud, and I now began feeling about with my bare feet as I moved from side to side, describing a small arc; but I discovered nothing more than an occasional pebble no larger than a walnut.

Letting out some more of the cord, I advanced a little farther into the center of the pond and slowly described another arc. The water was now nearly up to my armpits, but it was not cold, though if it had been I do not think I should have minded it in the ardor of my search. Suddenly I put my foot on something hard and as big as my fist, but in an instant it moved away from under my foot; it must have been a turtle. This occurrence made me shiver a little, but I did not swerve from my purpose, and loosing the string a little more, I went farther into the pond. The water was now nearly up to my chin, and there was something weird, mystical, and awe-inspiring in standing thus in the depths of this silent water, my eyes so near its gently rippling surface, fantastically lighted by the setting moon, and tenanted by nobody knew what cold and slippery creatures. But from side to side I slowly moved, reaching out with my feet in every direction, hoping to touch the thing for which I sought.

Suddenly I set my right foot upon something hard and

irregular. Nervously I felt it with my toes. I patted it with my bare sole. It was as big as the shadrach! It felt like the shadrach. In a few moments I was almost convinced that the direful paperweight was beneath my foot.

Closing my eyes and holding my breath, I stooped down into the water and groped on the bottom with my hands. In some way I had moved while stooping, and at first I could find nothing. A sensation of dread came over me as I felt myself in the midst of the dark solemn water—around me, above me, everywhere—almost suffocated, and apparently deserted even by the shadrach. But just as I felt that I could hold my breath no longer, my fingers touched the thing that had been under my foot, and clutching it, I rose and thrust my head out of the water. I could do nothing until I had taken two or three long breaths; then, holding up the object in my hand to the light of the expiring moon, I saw that it was like the shadrach—so like, indeed, that I felt that it must be it.

Turning, I made my way out of the water as rapidly as possible, and dropping on my knees on the ground, I tremblingly lighted the lantern which I had left on the bench, and turned its light on the thing I had found. There must be no mistake; if this was not the shadrach, I would go in again. But there was no necessity for reentering the pond; it *was* the shadrach.

With the extinguished lantern in one hand and the lump of mineral evil in the other, I hurried home. My wet clothes were sticky and chilly in the night air. Several times in my haste I stumbled over clods and briers, and my shoes, which I had not taken time to tie, flopped up and down as I ran. But I cared for none of these discomforts; the shadrach was in my power.

Crossing a wide field, I heard, not far away, the tramping of hooves, as of a horseman approaching at full speed. I stopped and looked in the direction of the sound. My eyes had now become so accustomed to the dim light that I could distinguish objects somewhat plainly, and I quickly perceived that the animal that was galloping toward me was a bull. I well knew what bull it was; this was Squire Starling's pasture field, and that was his great Alderney bull, Ramping Sir John of Ramapo II.

I was well acquainted with that bull, renowned throughout the neighborhood for his savage temper and his noble pedigree—son of Ramping Sir John of Rampo I, whose sire was the Great Rodolphin, son of Prince Maximus of Granby, one of whose daughters averaged eighteen pounds of butter a week, and who, himself, had killed two men.

The bull, who had not perceived me when I crossed the field before, for I had then made my way with as little noise as possible, was now bent on punishing my intrusion upon his domains, and bellowed as he came on. I was in a position of great danger. With my flopping shoes it was impossible to escape my flight; I must stand and defend myself. I turned and faced the furious creature, who was not twenty feet distant, and then, with all my strength, I hurled the shadrach, which I held in my right hand, directly at his shaggy forehead. My ability to project a missile was considerable, for I had held, with credit, the position of pitcher in a baseball nine, and as the shadrach struck the bull's head with a great thud, he stopped as if he had suddenly run against a wall.

I do not know that actual and violent contact with the physical organism of a recipient accelerates the influence of a shadrach upon the mental organism of said recipient, but I do know that the contact of my projectile with that bull's skull instantly cooled the animal's fury. For a few moments he stood and looked at me, and then his interest in me as a man and trespasser appeared to fade away, and moving slowly from me, Ramping Sir John of Ramapo II began to crop the grass.

I did not stop to look for the shadrach; I considered it safely disposed of. So long as Squire Starling used that field for a pasture, connoisseurs in mineral fragments would not be apt to wander through it, and when it should be plowed, the shadrach, to ordinary eyes no more than a common stone, would be buried beneath the sod. I awoke the next morning refreshed and happy and none the worse for my wet walk.

"Now," I said to myself, "nature shall truly have her own way. If the uncanny comes into my life and that of those I love, it shall not be brought in by me."

About a week after this I dined with the Bronce family. They were very cordial and it seemed to me the most natural thing in the world to be sitting at their table. After dinner Mildred and I walked together in the garden. It was a charming evening and we sat down on the bench by the edge of the pond. I spoke to her of some passages in the book I had once seen there.

"Oh, have you read that?" she asked with interest.

"I have seen only two pages of it," I said, "and those I read in the volume you left on this bench, with a paper cutter in it for a marker. I long to read more and talk with you of what I have read."

"Why, then, didn't you wait? You might have known that I would come back."

I did not tell her that I knew that because I was there she would not have come. But before I left the bench I discovered that hereafter, wherever I might be, she was willing to come and to stay.

Early in the next spring Mildred and I were married, and on our wedding trip we passed through a mining district in the mountains. Here we visited one of the great ironworks and were both much interested in witnessing the wonderful power of man, air, and fire over the stubborn king of metals.

"What is this substance?" asked Mildred of one of the officials who was conducting us through the works.

"That," said the man, "is what we call shad—"

"My dear," I cried, "we must hurry away this instant or we shall lose the train. Come, quick; there is not a moment for delay." And with a word of thanks to the guide, I seized her hand and led her, almost running, into the open air.

Mildred was amazed.

"Never before," she exclaimed, "have I seen you in such a hurry. I thought the train we decided to take did not leave for at least an hour."

"I have changed my mind," I said, "and think it will be a great deal better for us to take the one which leaves in ten minutes."

THE SNOW WOMEN
by Fritz Leiber

*Winner of over a dozen major awards in fantasy and
science fiction, Fritz Leiber is best known for stories
about Fafhrd, the barbarian, and his friend and
fighting companion, the Gray Mouser. The novella
below, which takes place before the two have teamed,
is one of the series' best.*

At cold corner in midwinter, the women of the Snow Clan
were waging a cold war against the men. They trudged about
like ghosts in their whitest furs, almost invisible against the
newfallen snow, always together in female groups, silent or
at most hissing like angry shades. They avoided Godshall
with its trees for pillars and walls of laced leather and tower-
ing pine-needle roof.

They gathered in the big oval Tent of the Women, which
stood guard in front of the smaller home tents, for sessions of
chanting and ominous moaning and various silent practices
designed to create powerful enchantments that would tether
their husbands' ankles to Cold Corner, tie up their loins, and
give them sniveling, nose-dripping colds, with the threat of
the Great Cough and Winter Fever held in reserve. Any man so
unwise as to walk alone by day was apt to be set upon and
snowballed and, if caught, thrashed—be he even skald or
mighty hunter.

And a snowballing by Snow Clan women was nothing to
laugh at. They threw overarm, it is true, but their muscles for
that had been greatly strengthened by much splitting of
firewood, lopping of high branches, and pounding of hides,
including the iron-hard one of the snowy behemoth. And they
sometimes froze their snowballs.

The sinewy, winter-hardened men took all of this with immense dignity, striding about like kings in their conspicuous black; russet, and rainbow-dyed ceremonial furs, drinking hugely but with discretion, and trading shrewdly as Ilthmarts their bits of amber and ambergris, their snow diamonds visible only by night, their glossy animal pelts, and their ice herbs in exchange for woven fabrics, hot spices, blued and browned iron, honey, waxen candles, fire powders that flared with a colored roar, and other products of the civilized south. Nevertheless, they made a point of keeping generally in groups, and there was many a nose a-drip among them.

It was not the trading the women objected to. Their men were good at that and they—the women—were the chief beneficiaries. They greatly preferred it to their husbands' occasional piratings, which took those lusty men far down the eastern coasts of the Outer Sea, out of reach of immediate matriarchal supervision and even, the women somtimes feared, of their potent female magic. Cold Corner was the farthest south ever got by the entire Snow Clan, who spent most of their lives on the Cold Waste and among the foothills of the untopped Mountains of the Giants and the even more northerly Bones of the Old Ones, and so this midwinter camp was their one yearly chance to trade peaceably with venturesome Mingols, Sarheenmarts, Lankhmarts, and even an occasional Eastern desert man, heavily beturbaned, bundled up to the eyes, and elephantinely gloved and booted.

Nor was it the guzzling which the women opposed. Their husbands were great quaffers of mead and ale at all times and even of the native white snow-potato brandy, a headier drink than most of the wines and boozes the traders hopefully dispensed.

No, what the Snow Women hated so venomously and which each year caused them to wage cold war with hardly any material or magical holds barred, was the theatrical show which inevitably came shivering north with the traders, its daring troupers with faces chapped and legs chilblained, but hearts a-beat for soft northern gold and easy if rampageous audiences—a show so blasphemous and obscene that the men preempted Godshall for its performance (God being unshockable) and refused to let the women and youths view it; a show whose actors were, according to the women, solely dirty old men and even dirtier scrawny southern girls, as loose in their morals as in the lacing of their skimpy garments, when they went clothed at all. It did not occur to the Snow Women that a scrawny wench, her dirty nakedness all blue goose bumps in the chill of drafty Godshall, would hardly be an object of erotic appeal, besides her risking permanent all-over frostbite.

So the Snow Women each midwinter hissed and magicked and sneaked and sniped with their crusty snowballs at huge men retreating with pomp, and frequently caught an old or crippled or foolish, young, drunken husband and beat him soundly.

This outwardly comic combat had sinister undertones. Particularly when working all together, the Snow Women were reputed to wield mighty magics, particularly through the element of cold and its consequences: slipperiness, the sudden freezing of flesh, the gluing of skin to metal, the frangibility of objects, the menacing mass of snow-laden trees and branches, and the vastly greater mass of avalanches. And there was no man wholly unafraid of the hypnotic power in their ice-blue eyes.

Each Snow Woman, usually with the aid of the rest, worked to maintain absolute control of her man, though leaving him seemingly free, and it was whispered that recalcitrant husbands had been injured and even slain, generally by some frigid instrumentality. While at the same time witchy cliques and individual sorceresses played against each other a power game in which the brawniest and boldest of men, even chiefs and priests, were but counters.

During the fortnight of trading and the two days of the show, hags and great strapping girls guarded the Tent of the Women at all quarters, while from within came strong perfumes, stenches, flashes and intermittent glows by night, clashings and tinklings, cracklings and quenchings, and incantational chantings and whisperings that never quite stopped.

This morning one could imagine that the Snow Women's sorcery was working everywhere, for the weather was windless and overcast, and there were wisps of fog in the moist freezing air, so that crystals of ice were rapidly forming on every bush and branch, every twig and tip of any sort, including the ends of the men's mustaches and the eartips of the tamed lynxes. The crystals were blue and flashing as the Snow Women's eyes and even mimicked in their forms, to an imaginative mind, the Snow Women's hooded, tall, and white-robed figures, for many of the crystals grew upright, like diamond flames.

And this morning the Snow Women had caught, or rather got a near certain chance of trapping, an almost unimaginably choice victim. For one of the show girls, whether by ignorance or foolhardy daring, and perhaps tempted by the relatively mild, gem-begetting air, had strolled on the crusty snow away from the safety of the actors' tents, past Godshall on the precipice side, and from thence between two sky-thrusting corpses of snow-laden evergreens, out onto the snow-carpeted natural rock bridge that had been the start of the Old Road south to Gnampf Nar until some five man-lengths of its central section had fallen three score years ago.

A short step from the up-curving perilous brink she had paused and looked for a long while south through the wisps of mist that, in the distance, grew thin as pluckings of long-haired wool. Below her in the canyon's overhung slot, the snow-capped pines flooring Trollstep Canyon looked tiny as the white tents of an army of Ice Gnomes. Her gaze slowly traced Trollstep Canyon from its far eastern beginnings to where, narrowing, it passed directly beneath her and then, slowly widening, curved south, until the buttress opposite her, with its matching, jutting section of the onetime rock bridge, cut off the view south. Then her gaze went back to trace the New Road from where it began its descent beyond the actors' tents and clung to the far wall of the canyon until, after many a switchback and many a swing into great gully and out again—unlike the far swifter, straighter descent of the Old Road—it plunged into the midst of the flooring pines and went with them south.

From her constant yearning look, one might have thought the actress a silly homesick soubrette, already regretting this freezing northern tour and pining for some hot, fleabitten actors' alley beyond the Land of the Eight Cities and the Inner Sea—except for the quiet confidence of her movements, the proud set of her shoulders, and the perilous spot she had chosen for her peering. For this spot was not only physically dangerous, but also as near the Tent of the Snow Women as it was to Godshall, and in addition the spot was taboo because a chief and his children had plunged to their deaths when the central rock span had cracked away three score years ago, and because the wooden replacement had fallen under the weight of a brandy merchant's cart some two score years later. Brandy of the fieriest, a loss fearsome enough to justify the sternest of taboos, including one against ever rebuilding the bridge.

And as if even those tragedies were not sufficient to glut the jealous gods and make taboo absolute, only two years past the most skillful skier the Snow Clan had produced in decades, one Skif, drunk with snow brandy and an icy pride, had sought to jump the gap from the Cold Corner side. Towed to a fast start and thrusting furiously with his sticks, he had taken off like a gliding hawk, yet missed the opposite snowy verge by an arm's length, the prows of his skis had crashed into rock, and he himself smashed in the rocky depths of the canyon.

The bemused actress wore a long coat of auburn fox fur belted with a light, gold-washed brass chain. Icy crystals had formed in her high-piled, fine, dark-brown hair.

From the narrowness of her coat, her figure promised to be scrawny or at least thinly muscular enough to satisfy the Snow Women's notion of female players, but she was almost six feet tall, which was not at all as actresses should be and definitely an added affront to the tall Snow Women now approaching her from behind in a silent white rank.

An overhasty white fur boot sang against the glazed snow.

The actress spun around and without hesitation raced back the way she had come. Her first three steps broke the snow crust, losing her time, but then she learned the trick of running in a glide, feet grazing the crust.

She hitched her russet coat high. She was wearing black fur boots and bright scarlet stockings.

The Snow Women glided swiftly after her, pitching their hard-packed snowballs.

One struck her hard on the shoulder. She made the mistake of looking back.

By ill chance two snowballs took her in jaw and forehead, just beneath painted lip and on an arched black eyebrow.

She reeled then, turning fully back, and a snowball thrown almost with the force of a slinger's stone struck her in the midriff, doubling her up and driving the breath from her lungs in an open-mouthed *whoosh*.

She collapsed. The white women rushed forward, blue eyes a-glare.

A big, thinnish, black-mustached man in a drab, quilted jacket and a low black turban stopped watching from beside a becrystaled, rough-barking living pillar Godshall, and ran toward the fallen woman. His footsteps broke the crust, but his strong legs drove him powerfully on.

Then he slowed in amaze as he was passed almost as if he were at a standstill by a tall, white, slender figure glide-running so swiftly that it seemed for a moment it went on skis. For an instant the turbaned man thought it was another Snow Woman, but then he noted that it wore a short fur jerkin rather than a long fur robe—and so was presumably a Snow Man or Snow Youth, though the black-turbaned man had never seen a Snow Clan male dressed in white.

The strange, swift figure glide-ran with chin tucked down and eyes bent away from the Snow Women, as if fearing to meet their wrathful blue gaze. Then as he swiftly knelt by the felled actress, long reddish-blond hair spilled from his hood. From that and the figure's slenderness, the black-turbaned man knew an instant of fear that the intercomer was a very tall Snow Girl, eager to strike the first blow at close quarters.

But then he saw a jut of downy male chin in the reddish-blond hair and also a pair of massive silver bracelets of the sort one gained only by pirating. Next the youth picked up the actress and glide-ran away from the Snow Women, who now could see only their victim's scarlet-stockinged legs. A volley of snowballs struck the rescuer's back. He staggered a little, then sped determinedly on, still ducking his head.

The biggest of the Snow Women, one with the bearing of a queen and a haggard face still handsome, though the hair falling to either side of it was white, stopped running and shouted in a deep voice, "Come back, my son! You hear me, Fafhrd, come back now!"

The youth nodded his ducked head slightly, though he did not pause in his flight. Without turning his head, he called in a rather high voice, "I will come back, revered Mor, my mother . . . later on."

The other women took up the cry of "Come back now!" Some of them added such epithets as "Dissolute youth!" "Curse of your good mother Mor!" and "Chaser after whores!"

Mor silenced them with a curt, sidewise sweep of her hands, palms down. "We will wait here," she announced with authority.

The black-turbaned man paused a bit, then strolled after the vanished pair, keeping a weary eye on the Snow Women. They were supposed not to attack traders, but with barbarian females, as with males, one could never tell.

Fafhrd reached the actors' tents, which were pitched in a circle around a trampled stretch of snow at the altar end of Godshall. Farthest from the precipice was the tall, conical tent of the Master of the Show. Midway stretched the common actors' tent, somewhat fish-shaped, one-third for the girls, two-thirds for the men. Nearest Trollstep Canyon was a medium-size, hemicylindrical tent supported on half-hoops. Across its middle, an evergreen sycamore thrust a great heavy branch balanced by two lesser branches on the opposite side, all spangled with crystals. In his tent's semicircular front was a laced entry flap, which Fafhrd found difficult to open, since the long form in his arms was still limp.

A swag-bellied little old man came strutting toward him with something of the bounce of youth. This one wore ragged finery touched up with gilt. Even his long gray mustache and goatee glittered with specks of gold above and below his dirty-toothed mouth. His heavily pouched eyes were rheumy and red all around, but dark and darting at the center. Above them was a purple turban supporting in turn a gilt crown set with battered gems of rock crystal, poorly aping diamonds.

Behind him came a skinny, one-armed Mingol, a fat Easterner with a vast black beard that stank of burning, and two scrawny girls who, despite their yawning and the heavy blankets huddled around them, looked watchful and evasive as alley cats.

"What's this now?" the leader demanded, his alert eyes taking in every detail of Fafhrd and his burden. "Vlana slain? Raped and slain, eh? Know, murderous youth, that you'll pay high for your fun. You may not know who I am, but you'll learn. I'll have reparations from your chiefs, I will! Vast reparations! I have influence, I have. You'll lose those pirate's bracelets of yours and that silver chain peeping from under your collar. Your family'll be beggared, and all your relatives, too. As for what *they'll* do to *you*—"

"You are Essedinex, Master of the Show," Fafhrd broke

in dogmatically, his high tenor voice cutting like a trumpet through the other's hoarse, ranting baritone. "I am Fafhrd, son of Mor and of Nalgron the Legend-Breaker. Vlana the culture dancer is not raped or dead, but stunned with snowballs. This is her tent. Open it."

"We'll take care of her, barbarian," Essedinex asserted, though more quietly, appearing both surprised and somewhat intimidated by the youth's almost pedantic precision as to who was who, and what was what. "Hand her over. Then depart."

"I will lay her down," Fafhrd persisted. "Open the tent!"

Essedinex shrugged and motioned to the Mingol, who with a sardonic grin used his one hand and elbow to unlace and draw aside the entry flap. An odor of sandalwood and closetberry came out. Stooping, Fafhrd entered. Midway down the length of the tent he noted a pallet of furs and a low table with a silver mirror propped against some jars and squat bottles. At the far end was a rack of costumes.

Stepping around a brazier from which a thread of pale smoke wreathed, Fafhrd carefully knelt and most gently deposited his burden on the pallet. Next he felt Vlana's pulse at jaw hinge and wrist, rolled back a dark lid, and peered into each eye, delicately explored with his fingertips the sizable bumps that were forming on jaw and forehead. Then he tweaked the lobe of her left ear and, when she did not react, shook his head and, drawing open her russet robe, began to unbutton the red dress under it.

Essedinex, who with the others had been watching the proceedings in a puzzled fashion, cried out, "Well, of all— Cease, lascivious youth!"

"Silence," Fafhrd commanded, and continued unbuttoning.

The two blanketed girls giggled, then clapped hand to mouth, darting amused glances at Essedinex and the rest.

Drawing aside his long hair from his right ear, Fafhrd laid that side of his face on Vlana's chest between her breasts, small as half-pomegranates, their nipples rosy bronze in hue. He maintained a solemn expression. The girls giggled smotheredly again. Essedinex strangledly cleared his throat, preparing for large speech.

Fafhrd sat up and said, "Her spirit will shortly return. Her bruises should be dressed with snow bandages, renewed when they begin to melt. Now I require a cup of your best brandy."

"My best brandy!" Essedinex cried outragedly. "This goes too far. First you must have a help-yourself peep show, then strong drink! Presumptious youth, depart at once!"

"I am merely seeking—" Fafhrd began in clear and at last slightly dangerous tones.

His patient interrupted the dispute by opening her eyes, shaking her head, wincing, then determinedly sitting up—whereupon she grew pale and her gaze wavered. Fafhrd helped her lie down again and put pillows under her feet. Then he looked at her face. Her eyes were still open and she was looking back at him curiously.

He saw a face small and sunken-cheeked, no longer girlish-young, but with a compact catlike beauty despite its lumps. Her eyes, being large, brown-irised, and long-lashed, should have been melting, but were not. There was the look of the loner in them, and purpose, and a thoughtful weighing of what she saw.

She saw a handsome, fair-complexioned youth of about eighteen winters, wide-headed and long-jawed, as if he had not done growing. Fine red-gold hair cascaded down his cheeks. His eyes were green, cryptic, and as staring as a cat's. His lips were wide, but slightly compressed, as if they were a door that locked words in and opened only on the cryptic eyes' command.

One of the girls had poured a half-cup of brandy from a bottle on the low table. Fafhrd took it and lifted Vlana's head for her to drink it in sips. The other girl came with powder snow folded in woolen cloths. Kneeling on the far side of the pallet, she bound them against the bruises.

After inquiring Fafhrd's name and confirming that he had rescued her from the Snow Women, Vlana asked, "Why do you speak in such a high voice?"

"I study with a singing skald," he answered. "They use the voice and are the true skalds, not the roaring ones who use deep tones."

"What reward do you expect for rescuing me?" she asked boldly.

"None," Fafhrd replied.

From the two girls came further giggles, quickly cut off at Vlana's glance.

Fafhrd added, "It was my personal obligation to rescue you, since the leader of the Snow Women was my mother. I must respect my mother's wishes, but I must also prevent her from performing wrong actions."

"Oh. Why do you act like a priest or healer?" Vlana continued. "Is that one of your mother's wishes?" She had not bothered to cover her breasts, but Fafhrd was not looking at them now, only at the actress's lips and eyes.

"Healing is part of the singing skald's art," he answered. "As for my mother, I do my duty toward her, nor less, nor more."

"Vlana, it is not politic that you talk thus with this youth," Essedinex interposed, now in a nervous voice. "He must—"

"Shut up!" Vlana snapped. Then, back to Fafhrd, "Why do you wear white?"

"It is the proper garb for all Snow Folk. I do not follow the new custom of dark and dyed furs for males. My father always wore white."

"He is dead?"

"Yes. While climbing a tabooed mountain called White Fang."

"And your mother wishes you to wear white, as if you were your father returned?"

Fafhrd neither answered nor frowned at that shrewd question. Instead, he asked, "How many languages can you speak— besides this pidgin Lankhmarese?"

She smiled at last. "What a question! Why, I speak— though not too well—Mingol, Kvarchish, High and Low Lankhmarese, Quarmallian, Old Ghoulish, Desert-talk, and three Eastern tongues."

Fafhrd nodded. "That's good."

"Forever why?"

"Because it means you are very civilized," he answered.

"What's so great about that?" she demanded with a sour laugh.

"You should know; you're a culture dancer. In any case, I am interested in civilization."

"One comes," Essedinex hissed from the entry. "Vlana, the youth must—"

"He must not!"

"As it happens, I must indeed leave now," Fafhrd said, rising. "Keep up the snow bandages," he instructed Vlana. "Rest until sundown. Then more brandy, with hot soup."

"Why must you leave?" Vlana demanded, rising on an elbow.

"I made a promise to my mother," Fafhrd said without looking back.

"Your mother!"

Stooping at the entry, Fafhrd finally did stop to look back. "I owe my mother many duties," he said. "I owe you none, as yet."

"Vlana, he *must* leave. It's *the* one," Essedinex stage-whispered hoarsely. Meanwhile he was shoving at Fafhrd, but for all the youth's slenderness, he might as well have been trying to push a tree off of its roots.

"Are you afraid of him who comes?" Vlana was buttoning up her dress now.

Fafhrd looked at her thoughtfully. Then without replying in any way whatever to her question, he ducked through the entry and stood up, waiting the approach through the persistent mist of a man in whose face anger was gathering.

This man was tall as Fafhrd, half again as thick and wide, and about twice as old. He was dressed in brown sealskin and amethyst-studded silver except for the two massive gold bracelets on his wrists and the gold chain about his neck, marks of a pirate chief.

Fafhrd felt a touch of fear, not at the approaching man, but at the crystals which were now thicker on the tents than he recalled them being when he had carried Vlana in. The element over which Mor and her sister witches had most power was cold—whether in a man's soup or loins, or in his sword or climbing rope, making them shatter. He often wondered whether it was Mor's magic that had made his own heart so cold. Now the cold would close in on the dancer. He should warn her, except she was civilized and would laugh at him.

The big man came up.

"Honorable Hringorl," Fafhrd greeted softly.

For reply, the big man aimed a backhanded uppercut at Fafhrd with his near arm.

Fafhrd leaned sharply away, slithering under the blow, and then simply walked off the way he had first come.

Hringorl, breathing heavily, glared after him for a couple of heartbeats, then plunged into the hemicylindrical tent.

Hringorl was certainly the most powerful man in the Snow

Clan, Fafhrd reflected, though not one of its chiefs because of his bullying ways and defiances of custom. The Snow Women hated, but found it hard to get a hold on, him, since his mother was dead and he had never taken a wife, satisfying himself with concubines he brought back from his piratings.

From wherever he'd been inconspicuously standing, the black-turbaned and black-mustached man came up quietly to Fafhrd. "That was well done, my friend. And when you brought in the dancer."

Fafhrd said impassively, "You are Vellix the Venturer."

The other nodded. "Bringing brandy from Klelg Nar to this mart. Will you sample the best with me?"

Fafhrd said, "I am sorry, but I have an engagement with my mother."

"Another time, then," Vellix said easily.

"Fafhrd!"

It was Hringorl who called. His voice was no longer angry. Fafhrd turned. The big man stood by the tent, then came striding up when Fafhrd did not move. Meanwhile, Vellix faded back and away in a fashion easy as his speech.

"I'm sorry, Fafhrd," Hringorl said gruffly. "I did not know you had saved the dancer's life. You have done me a great service here." He unclasped from his wrist one of the heavy gold bracelets and held it out.

Fafhrd kept his hands at his sides. "No service whatever," he said. "I was only saving my mother from committing a wrong action."

"You've sailed under me," Hringorl suddenly roared, his face reddening, though he still grinned somewhat, or tried to. "So you'll take my gifts as well as my orders." He caught hold of Fafhrd's hand, pressed the weighty torus into it, closed Fafhrd's lax fingers on it, and stepped back.

Instantly Fafhrd knelt, saying swiftly, "I am sorry, but I may not take what I have not rightly won. And now I must keep an engagement with my mother." Then he swiftly rose, turned, and walked away. Behind him, on an unbroken crust of snow, the golden bracelet gleamed.

He heard Hringorl's snarl and choked-back curse, but did not look around to see whether or not Hringorl picked up his spurned gratuity, though he did find it a bit difficult not to weave in his stride or duck his head a trifle, in case Hringorl decided to throw the massive wristlet at his skull.

Shortly he came to the place where his mother was sitting among seven Snow Women, making eight in all. They stood up. He stopped a yard short. Ducking his head and looking to the side, he said, "Here I am, Mor."

"You took a long while," she said. "You took too long." Six heads around her nodded solemnly. Only Fafhrd, noted, in the blurred edge of his vision, that the seventh and slenderest Snow Woman was moving silently backward.

"But here I am," Fafhrd said.

"You disobeyed my command," Mor pronounced coldly. Her haggard and once beautiful face would have looked very unhappy, had it not been so proud and masterful.

"But now I am obeying it," Fafhrd countered. He noted that the seventh Snow Woman was now silently running, her great white cloak a-stream, between the home tents toward the high, white forest that was Cold Corner's boundary everywhere that Trollstep Canyon wasn't.

"Very well," Mor said. "And now you will obey me by following me to the steam tent for ritual purification."

"I am not defiled," Fafhrd announced. "Moreover, I purify myself after my own fashion, one also agreeable to the gods."

There were clucks of shocked disapproval from all Mor's coven. Fafhrd had spoken boldly, but his head was still bent, so that he did not see their faces and their entrapping eyes, but only their long-robed white forms, like a clump of great birches.

Mor said, "Look me in the eyes."

Fafhrd said, "I fulfill all the customary duties of a grown son, from food-winning to sword-guarding. But as far as I can ascertain, looking my mother in the eyes is not one of those duties."

"You father always obeyed me," Mor said ominously.

"Whenever he saw a tall mountain, he climbed her, obeying no one but himself," Fafhrd contradicted.

"Yes, and died doing so!" Mor cried, her masterfulness controlling grief and anger without hiding them.

Fafhrd said hardly, "Whence came the great cold that shattered his rope and pick on White Fang?"

Amid the gasps of her coven, Mor pronounced in her deepest voice, "A mother's curse, Fafhrd, on your disobedience and evil thinking!"

Fafhrd said with strange eagerness, "I dutifully accept your curse, Mother."

Mor said, "My curse is not on you, but on your evil imaginings."

"Nevertheless, I will forever treasure it," Fafhrd cut in. "And now, obeying myself, I must take leave of you, until the wrath devil has let you go."

And with that, head still bent down and away, he walked rapidly toward a point in the forest east of the home tents, but west of the great tongue of the forest that stretched south almost to Godshall. The angry hissings of Mor's coven followed him, but his mother did not cry out his name, or any word at all. Fafhrd would almost rather that she had.

Youth heals swiftly, on the skin side. By the time Fafhrd plunged into his beloved wood without jarring a single becrystaled twig, his senses were alert, his neck joint supple, and the outward surface of his inner being as cleared for new experience as the unbroken snow ahead. He took the easiest path, avoiding bediamonded thorn bushes to left and huge pine-screened juttings of pale granite to right.

He saw bird tracks, squirrel tracks, day-old bear tracks; snow birds snapped their black beaks at red snowberries; a furred snow snake hissed at him, and he would not have been startled by the emergence of a dragon with ice-crusted spines.

So he was in no wise amazed when a great high-branched pine opened its snow-plastered bark and showed him its dryad—a merry, blue-eyed, blond-haired girl's face, a dryad no more than seventeen years old. In fact, he had been expecting such an apparition ever since he had noted the seventh Snow Woman in flight.

Yet he pretended to be amazed for almost two heartbeats. Then he sprang forward crying, "Mara, my witch," and with his two arms separated her white-cloaked self from her camouflaging background, and kept them wrapped around her while they stood like one white column, hood to hood and lips to lips for at least twenty heartbeats of the most huddlingly delightful sort.

Then she found his right hand and drew it into her cloak and, through a placket, under her long coat, and pressed it against her crisply ringleted lower belly.

"Guess," she whispered, licking his ear.

"It's a part of a girl. I do believe it's a—" he began most

gayly, though his thoughts were already plunging wildly in a direly different direction.

"No, idiot, it's something that belongs to you," the wet whisper coached.

The dire direction became an iced chute leading toward certainty. Nevertheless he said bravely, "Well, I'd hoped you hadn't been trying out others, though that's your right. I must say I am vastly honored—"

"Silly beast! I meant it's something that belongs to *us*."

The dire direction was now a black icy tunnel, becoming a pit. Automatically and with an appropriately great heart thump, Fafhrd said, "Not—?"

"Yes! I'm certain, you monster. I've missed twice."

Better than ever in his life before, Fafhrd's lips performed their office of locking in words. When they opened at last, they and the tongue behind them were utterly under control of the great green eyes. There came forth in a joyous rush: "O gods! How wonderful! I am a father! How clever of you, Mara!"

"Very clever indeed," the girl admitted, "to have fashioned anything so delicate after your rude handling. But now I must pay you off for that ungracious remark about 'trying out others.' " Hitching up her skirt behind, she guided both his hands under her cloak to a knot of thongs at the base of her spine. (Snow Women wore fur hoods, fur boots, a high fur stocking on each leg gartered to a waist thong, and one or more fur coats and cloaks—it was a practical garb, not unlike the men's except for the longer coats.)

As he fingered the knot, from which three thongs led tightly off, Fafhrd said, "Truly, Mara dearest, I do not favor these chastity girdles. They are not a civilized device. Besides, they must interfere with the circulation of your blood."

"You and your fad for civilization! I'll love and belabor you out of it. Go on, untie the knot, making sure you and no other tied it."

Fafhrd complied and had to agree that it was his knot and no other man's. The task took some time and was a delightful one to Mara, judging from her soft squeals and moans, her gentle nips and bites. Fafhrd himself began to get interested. When the task was done, Fafhrd got the reward of all courteous liars: Mara loved him dearly because he had told her all the right lies and she showed it in her beguiling behavior, and his interest in her and his excitement became vast.

After certain handlings and other tokens of affection, they fell to the snow side by side, both mattressed and covered entirely by their white fur cloaks and hoods.

A passerby would have thought that a snow mound had come alive convulsively and was perhaps about to give birth to a snowman, elf, or demon.

After a while the snow mound grew utterly quiescent and the hypothetical passerby would have had to lean very close to catch the voices coming from inside it.

MARA: Guess what I'm thinking.

FAFHRD: That you're the Queen of Bliss. Aaah!

MARA: Aaaah back at you, and ooooh! And that you're the King of Beasts. No, silly, I'll tell you. I was thinking of how glad I am that you've had your southward adventurings before marriage. I'm sure you've raped or even made indecent love to dozens of southern women, which perhaps accounts for your wrongheadedness about civilization. But I don't mind a bit. I'll love you out of it.

FAFHRD: Mara, you have a brilliant mind, but just the same you greatly exaggerate that one pirate cruise I made under Hringorl, and especially the opportunities it afforded for amorous adventures. In the first place, all the inhabitants and especially all the young women of any shore town we sacked, ran away to the hills before we'd even landed. And if there were any women raped, I being youngest would have been at the bottom of the list of rapists and so hardly tempted. Truth to tell, the only interesting folk I met on that dreary voyage were two old men held for ransom, from whom I learned a smattering of Quarmallian and High Lankhmarese, and a scrawny youth apprenticed to a hedge wizard. He was deft with the dagger, that one, and had a legend-breaking mind, like mine and my father's.

MARA: Do not grieve. Life will become more exciting for you after we're married.

FAFHRD: That's where you're wrong, dearest Mara. Hold, let me explain! I know my mother. Once we're married, Mor will expect you to do all the cooking and tentwork. She'll treat you as seven-eighths slave and—perhaps—one-eighth my concubine.

MARA: Ha! You really will have to learn to rule your

mother, Fafhrd. Yet do not fret, dearest, even about that. It's clear you know nothing of the weapons a strong and untiring young wife has against an old mother-in-law. I'll put her in her place, even if I have to poison her—oh, not to kill, only to weaken sufficiently. Before three moons have waxed, she'll be trembling at my gaze and you'll feel yourself much more a man. I know that you being an only child and your wild father perishing young, she got an unnatural influence over you, but—

FAFHRD: I feel myself very much the man at this instant, you immoral and poisoning witchlet, you ice-tigress; and I intend to prove it on you without delay. Defend yourself! Ha, would you—!

Once more the snow mound convulsed, like a giant ice-bear dying of fits. The bear died to a music of sistrums and triangles, as there clashed together and shattered the flashing ice crystals which had grown in unnatural numbers and size on Mara's and Fafhrd's cloaks during their dialogue.

The short day raced toward night as if even the gods who govern the sun and stars were impatient to see the show.

Hringorl conferred with his three chief henchmen, Hor, Harrax, and Hrey. There was scowling and nodding, and Fafhrd's name was mentioned.

The youngest husband of the Snow Clan, a vain and thought-less cockerel, was ambushed and snowballed unconscious by a patrol of young Snow Wives who had seen him in brazen converse with a Mingol stage girl. Thereafter, a sure casualty for the two-day run of the show, he was tenderly but slowly nursed back toward life by his wife, who had been the most enthusiastic of the snowballers.

Mara, happy as a snow dove, dropped in on this household and helped. But as she watched the husband so helpless and the wife so tender, her smiles and dreamy grace vanished. She grew tense and, for an athletic girl, fidgety. Thrice she opened her lips to speak, then pursed them, and finally left without saying a word.

In the Women's Tent, Mor and her coven put a spell on Fafhrd to bring him home and another to chill his loins, then went on to discuss weightier measures against the whole universe of sons, husbands, and actresses.

The second enchantment had no effect on Fafhrd, probably

because he was taking a snow bath at the time—it being a well-known fact that magic has little effect on those who are already inflicting upon themselves the same results which the spell is trying to cause. After parting with Mara, he had stripped, plunged into a snowbank, then rubbed every surface, crack, and cranny of his body with the numbing powdery stuff. Thereafter he used thickly needled pine branches to dust himself off and beat his blood back into motion. Dressed, he felt the pull of the first enchantment, but opposed it and secretly made his way into the tent of two old Mingol traders, Zax and Effendrit, who had been his father's friends, and he snoozed amid a pile of pelts until evening. Neither of his mother's spells was able to follow him into what was, by trading custom, a tiny area of Mingol territory—though the Mingols' tent did begin to sag with an unnaturally large number of ice crystals, which the Mingol oldsters, wizened and nimble as monkeys, beat off janglingly with poles. The sound penetrated pleasantly into Fafhrd's dream without arousing him, which would have irked his mother had she known—she believed that both pleasure and rest were bad for men. His dream became one of Vlana dancing sinuously in a dress made of a net of fine silver wires, from the intersections of which hung myriads of tiny silver bells, a vision which would have irked Mor beyond endurance; fortunate indeed that she was not at that moment using her power of reading minds at a distance.

Vlana herself slumbered, while one of the Mingol girls, paid a half smerduk in advance by the injured actress, renewed the snow bandages as necessary and, when they looked dry, wet Vlana's lips with sweet wine, of which a few drops trickled between. Vlana's mind was a-storm with anticipations and plots, but whenever she waked, she stilled it with an Eastern circle charm that went something like "Creep, sleep; rouse, drowse; browse, soughs; slumber, umber; raw, claw; burnt, earn'd; cumber, number; left, death; cunt, won't; count, fount; mount, down't; leap, deep; creep, sleep," and so on back around the incestuous loop. She knew that a woman can get wrinkles in her mind as well as her skin. She also knew that only a spinster looks after a spinster. And finally she knew that a trouper, like a soldier, does well to sleep whenever possible.

Vellix the Venturer, idly slipping about, overheard some of

Hringorl's plottings, saw Fafhrd enter his tent of retreat, noted that Essedinex was drinking beyond his wont, and eavesdropped for a while on the Master of the Show.

In the girls' third of the actors' fish-shaped tent, Essedinex was arguing with the two Mingol girls, who were twins, and a barely nubile Ilthmarix, about the amount of grease they proposed to smear on their shaven bodies for tonight's performance.

"By the black bones, you'll beggar me," he wailingly expostulated. "And you'll look no more lascivious than lumps of lard."

"From what I know of Northerners, they like their women well larded, and why not outside as well as in?" the one Mingol girl demanded.

"What's more," her twin added sharply, "if you expect us to freeze off our toes and tits, to please an audience of smelly old bearskins, you've got your head on upside down."

"Don't worry, Seddy," the Ilthmarix said, patting his flushed cheek and its sparse white hairs, "I always give my best performance when I'm all gooey. We'll have them chasing us up the walls, where we'll pop from their grabs like so many slippery melon seeds."

"Chasing—?" Essedinex gripped the Ilthmarix by her slim shoulder. "You'll provoke no orgies tonight, do you hear me? Teasing pays. Orgies don't. The point is to—"

"We know just how far to tease, Daddy-Pooh," one of the Mingol girls put in.

"We know how to control them," her sister continued.

"And if we don't, Vlana always does," the Ilthmarix finished.

As the almost imperceptible shadows lengthened and the mist-wreathed air grew dark, the omnipresent crystals seemed to be growing even a little more swiftly. The palaver at the trading tents, which the thick snowy tongue of the forest shut off from the home tents, grew softer-voiced, then ceased. The unending low chant from the Women's Tent became more noticeable, and also higher-pitched. An evening breeze came from the north, making all the crystals tinkle. The chanting grew gruffer and the breeze and the tinkling ceased, as if on command. The mist came wreathing back from east and west, and the crystals were growing again. The women's chanting faded to a murmur. All of Cold Corner grew tautly and expectantly silent with the approach of night.

Day ran away over the ice-fanged western horizon as if she were afraid of the dark.

In the narrow space between the actors' tents and Godshall there was movement, a glimmer, a bright spark that sputtered for nine, ten, eleven heartbeats, then a flash, a flaring, and there rose up—slowly at first, then swifter and swifter—a comet wth a brushy tail of orange fire that dribbled sparks. High above the pines, almost on the edge of heaven—twenty-one, twenty-two, twenty-three—the comet's tail faded and it burst with a thunderclap into nine white stars.

It was the rocket signaling the first performance of the show.

Godshall on the inside was a tall, crazy long ship of chill blackness, inadequately lit and warmed by an arc of candles in the prow, which all the rest of the year was an altar, but now a stage. Its masts were eleven vast living pines thrusting up from the ship's bow, stern, and sides. Its sails—in sober fact, its walls—were stitched hides laced tautly to the masts. Instead of sky overhead, there were thickly interthrusting pine branches, white with drifting snow, beginning a good five man's heights above the deck.

The stern and waist of this weird ship, which moved only on the winds of imagination, were crowded with Snow Men in their darkly colorful furs and seated on stumps and thick blanket rolls. They were laughing with drink and growling out short talk and jokes at each other, but not very loudly. Religious awe and fear touched them on entering Godshall, or more properly, God's Ship, despite or more likely because of the profane use to which it was being put tonight.

There came a rhythmic drumming, sinister as the padding of a snow leopard and at first so soft that no man might say exactly when it began, except that one moment there was talk and movement in the audience and the next none at all, only so many pairs of hands gripping or lightly resting on knees, and so many pairs of eyes scanning the candlelit stage between two screens painted with black and gray whorls.

The drumming grew louder, quickened, complicated itself into weaving arabesques of tapped sound, and returned to the leopard's padding.

There loped onto the stage, precisely in time with the

drumbeats, a silver-furred, short-bodied, slender feline with long legs, long ears a-prick, long whiskers, and long, white fangs. It stood about a yard high at the shoulder and rump. The only human feature was a glossy mop of long, straight, black hair falling down the back of its neck and thence forward over its right shoulder.

It circled the stage thrice, ducking its head and sniffing as if on a scent and growling deep in its throat.

Then it noticed the audience and with a scream crouched back from them rampant, menacing them with the long, glittering claws which terminated its forelegs.

Two members of the audience were so taken in by the illusion that they had to be restrained by neighbors from pitching a knife or hurling a short-handled ax at what they were certain was a genuine and dangerous beast.

The beast scanned them, writhing its black lips back from its fangs and lesser teeth. As it swiftly swung its muzzle from side to side, inspecting them with its great brown eyes, its short-furred tail lashed back and forth in time.

Then it danced a leopardly dance of life, love, and death, sometimes on hind legs, but mostly on all fours. It scampered and investigated, it menaced and shrank, it attacked and fled, it caterwauled and writhed cat-lasciviously.

Despite the long black hair, it became no easier for the audience to think of it as a human female in a close-fitting suit of fur. For one thing, its forelegs were as long as its hindlegs and appeared to have an extra joint in them.

Something white squawked and came fluttering upward from behind one of the screens. With a swift leap and slash of foreleg, the great silvery cat struck and pounced on it.

Everyone in Godshall heard the scream of the snow pigeon and the crack of its neck.

Holding the dead bird to its fangs, the great cat, standing womanly tall now, gave the audience a long look, then walked without haste behind the nearest screen.

There came from the audience a sigh compounded of loathing and longing, of a wonder as to what would happen next, and of a wish to see what was going on now.

Fafhrd, however, did not sigh. For one thing, the slightest movement might have revealed his hiding place. For another, he could clearly see all that was going on behind both whorl-marked screens.

Being barred from the show by his youth, let alone by Mor's wishes and witcheries, he had half an hour before showtime mounted one of the trunk-pillars of Godshall on the precipice side when no one was looking. The strong lacings of the hide walls made it the easiest of climbs. Then he cautiously crawled out onto two of several stout pine branches growing inward close together over the hall, being very careful to disturb neither browning needles nor drifted snow, until he had found a good viewing hole, one opening toward the stage, but mostly hidden from the audience. Thereafter, it had been simply a matter of holding still enough so that no betraying needles or snow dropped down. Anyone looking up through the gloom and chancing to see parts of his white garb, would take it for snow, he hoped.

Now he watched the two Mingol girls rapidly pull off from Vlana's arms the tight fur sleeves together with the fur-covered, claw-tipped, rigid extra lengths in which they ended and which her hands had been gripping. Next they dragged from Vlana's legs *their* fur coverings, while she sat on a stool and, after drawing her fangs off her teeth, speedily unhooked her leopard mask and shoulder piece.

A moment later she slouched back on stage—a cave woman in a brief sarong of silvery fur and lazily gnawing at the end of a long, thick bone. She mimed a cave woman's day: fire- and baby-tending, brat-slapping, hide-chewing, and laborious sewing. Things got a bit more exciting with the return of her husband, an unseen presence made visible by her miming.

Her audience followed the story easily, grinning when she demanded what meat her husband had brought, showed dissatisfaction with his meager kill, and refused him an embrace. They guffawed when she tried to clobber him with her chewing bone and got knocked sprawling in return, her children cowering around her.

From that position she scuttled off stage behind another screen, which hid the actors' doorway (normally the Snow Priest's) and also concealed the one-armed Mingol, whose flickering five fingers did all the drum music on the instrument clutched between his feet. Vlana whipped off the rest of her fur, changed the slant of her eyes and eyebrows by four deft strokes of makeup, seemingly in one movement shouldered into a long gray gown with hood, and was back on stage in the persona of a Mingol woman of the Steppes.

After another brief session of miming, she squatted gracefully down at a low, jar-stocked table stage front and began carefully to make up her face and do her hair, the audience serving as her mirror. She dropped back hood and gown, revealing the briefer red silk garment her fur one had hidden. It was most fascinating to watch her apply the variously colored salves and powders and glittering dusts to her lips, cheeks, and eyes, and see her comb up her dark hair into a high structure kept in place by long, gem-headed pins.

Just then Fafhrd's composure was tested to the uttermost, when a large handful of snow was clapped to his eyes and held there.

He stayed perfectly still for three heartbeats. Then he captured a rather slender wrist and dragged it down a short distance, meantime gently shaking his head and blinking his eyes.

The trapped wrist twisted free and the clot of snow fell down the neck of the wolfskin coat of Hringorl's man Hor seated immediately below. Hor gave a strange low cry and started to glare upward, but fortunately at that moment Vlana pulled down her red silk sarong and began to anoint her nipples with a coral salve.

Fafhrd looked around and saw Mara grinning fiercely at him from where she lay outstretched on the two branches next his, her head level with his shoulder.

"If I'd been an ice gnome, you'd be dead!" she hissed at him. "Or if I'd set my four brothers to trap you, as I should have. Your ears *were* dead, your mind all in your eyes straining toward that skinny harlot. I've heard how you challenged Hringorl for her! And refused his gift of a gold bracelet!"

"I admit, dear, that you slithered up behind me most skillfully and silently," Fafhrd breathed at her softly, "while you seem to have eyes and ears for all things that transpire—and some that don't—at Cold Corner. But I must say, Mara—"

"Hah! Now you'll tell me I shouldn't be here, being a woman. Male prerogatives, intersexual sacrilege, and so forth. Well, neither should you be here."

Fafhrd gravely considered part of that. "No, I think all the women should be here. What they would learn would be much to their interest and advantage."

"To caper like a cat in heat? To slouch about like a silly

slave? Yes, I saw those acts too, while you were drooling dumb and deaf. You men will laugh at anything, especially when your stupid, gasping, red-faced lust's been aroused by a shameless bitch making a show of her scrawny nakedness!''

Mara's heated hissings were getting dangerously loud and might well have attracted the attention of Hor and others, but once again good fortune intervened, in that there was a ripple of drumming as Vlana streaked off the stage, and then there began a wild, somewhat thin but galloping music, the one-armed Mingol being joined by the little Ilthmarix playing a nose flute.

''I did not laugh, my dear,'' Fafhrd breathed somewhat loftily, ''nor did I drool or flush or speed my breath, as I am sure you noted. No, Mara, my sole purpose in being here is to learn more about civilization.''

She glared at him, grinned, then of a sudden smiled tenderly. ''You know, I honestly think you believe that, you incredible infant,'' she breathed back wonderingly. ''Granting that the decadence called civilization could possibly be of interest to anyone, and a capering whore able to carry its message, or rather absence of message.''

''I neither think nor believe, I *know* it,'' Fafhrd replied, ignoring Mara's other remarks. ''A whole world calls and have we eyes only for Cold Corner? Watch with me, Mara, and gain wisdom. The actress dances the cultures of all lands and ages. Now she is a woman of the Eight Cities.''

Perhaps Mara was in some small part persuaded. Or perhaps it was that Vlana's new costume covered her thoroughly—sleeved, green bodice, full, blue skirt, red stockings, and yellow shoes—and that the culture dancer was panting a trifle and showing the cords in her neck from the stamping and whirling dance she was doing. At any rate, the Snow Girl shrugged and smiled indulgently and whispered, ''Well, I must admit it all has a certain disgusting interest.''

''I knew you'd understand, dearest. You have twice the mind of any woman of our tribe, aye, or of any man,'' Fafhrd cooed, caressing her tenderly but somewhat absently as he peered at the stage.

In succession, always making lightning costume changes, Vlana became a houri of the Eastern Lands, a custom-hobbled Quarmallian queen, a languorous concubine of the King of Kings, and a haughty Lankhmar lady wearing a black toga.

This last was theatrical license—only the men of Lankhmar wear the toga, but the garment was Lankhmar's chiefest symbol across the world of Nehwon.

Meanwhile Mara did her best to share the eccentric whim of her husband-to-be. At first she was genuinely intrigued and made mental notes on details of Vlana's dress styles and tricks of behavior which she might herself adopt to advantage. But then she was gradually overwhelmed by a realization of the older woman's superiority in training, knowledge, and experience. Vlana's dancing and miming clearly couldn't be learned except with much coaching and drill. And how, and especially where, could a Snow Girl ever wear such clothes? Feelings of inferiority gave way to jealousy and that to hatred.

Civilization was nasty, Vlana ought to be whipped out of Cold Corner, and Fafhrd needed a woman to run his life and keep his mad imagination in check. Not his mother, of course—that awful and incestuous eater of her own son—but a glamorous and shrewd young wife. Herself.

She began to watch Fafhrd intently. He didn't look like an infatuated male, he looked cold as ice, but he was certainly utterly intent on the scene below. She reminded herself that a few men are adept at hiding their true feelings.

Vlana shed her toga and stood in a wide-meshed tunic of fine silver wires. At each crossing of the wires a tiny silver bell stood out. She shimmied and the bells tinkled, like a tree of tiny birds all chirruping together a hymn to her body. Now her slenderness seemed that of adolescence, while from between the strands of her sleekly cascading hair, her large eyes gleamed with mysterious hints and invitations.

Fafhrd's controlled breathing quickened. So, his dream in the Mingols' tent had been true! His attention, which had half been off to the lands and ages Vlana had danced, centered wholly on her and became desire.

This time his composure was put to an even sorer test, for without warning, Mara's hand clutched his crotch.

But he had little time in which to demonstrate his composure. She let go and crying, "Filthy beast! You *are* lusting!" struck him in the side, below the ribs.

He tried to catch her wrists, while staying on his branches. She kept trying to hit him. The pine boughs creaked and shed snow and needles.

In landing a clout on Fafhrd's ear, Mara's upper body overbalanced, though her feet kept hooked to branchlets.

Growling, "God freeze you, you bitch!" Fafhrd gripped his stoutest bough with one hand and lunged down with the other to catch Mara's arm just beneath the shoulder.

Those looking up from below—and by now there were some, despite the strong counterattraction of the stage—saw two struggling, white-clad torsos and fair-haired heads dipping out of the branchy roof, as if about to descend in swan dives. Then, still struggling, the figures withdrew upward.

An older Snow Man cried out, "Sacrilege!" A younger, "Peepers! Let's thrash 'em!" He might have been obeyed, for a quarter of the Snow Men were on their feet now, if it hadn't been that Essedinex was keeping a close eye on things through a peephole in one of the screens and that he was wise in the ways of handling unruly audiences. He shot a finger at the Mingol behind him, then sharply raised that hand, palm upward.

The music surged. Cymbals clashed. The two Mingol girls and the Ilthmarix bounded on stage stark naked and began to caper around Vlana. The fat Easterner clumped past them and set fire to his great black beard. Blue flames crawled up and flickered before his face and around his ears. He didn't put the fire out—with a wet towel he carried—until Essedinex hoarsely stage-whispered from his peephole, "That's enough. We've got 'em again." The length of the black beard had been halved. Actors make great sacrifices, which the yokels and even their co-mates rarely appreciate.

Fafhrd, dropping the last dozen feet, lighted in the high drift outside Godshall at the same instant Mara finished her downward climb. They faced each other calf-deep in crusted snow, across which the rising, slightly gibbous moon threw streaks of white glimmer and made shadow between them.

Fafhrd asked, "Mara, where did you hear that lie about me challenging Hringorl for the actress?"

"Faithless lecher!" she cried, punched him in the eye, and ran off toward the tent of the women, sobbing and crying strangely, "I *will* tell my brothers! You'll see!"

Fafhrd jumped up and down, smothering a howl of pain, sprinted after her three steps, stopped, clapped snow to his pain-stabbed eye, and as soon as it was only throbbing, began to think.

He looked around with the other eye, saw no one, made his way to a clump of snow-laden evergreens on the edge of the precipice, concealed himself among them, and continued to think.

His ears told him that the show was still going at a hot pace inside Godshall. There were laughs and cheers, sometimes drowning the wild drumming and fluting. His eyes—the hit one was working again—told him there was no one near him. They swiveled to the actors' tents at that end of Godshall which lay nearest the new road south, and at the stables beyond them, and at the traders' tents beyond the stables. Then they came back to the nearest tent: Vlana's hemicylindrical one. Crystals clothed it, twinkling in the moonlight, and a giant crystal flatworm seemed to be crawling across its middle just below the evergreen sycamore bough.

He slitheringly walked toward it across the bediamonded snow crust. The knot joining the lacings of its doorway was hidden in shadow and felt complex and foreign. He went to the back of the tent, loosened two pegs, went on belly through the crack like a snake, found himself among the hems of the skirts of Vlana's racked garments, took four steps, and lay down on the pallet. A little heat radiated from a banked brazier. After a while he reached to the table and poured himself a cup of brandy.

At last he heard voices. They grew louder. As the lacings of the door were being unknotted and loosened, he felt for his knife and also prepared to draw a large fur rug over himself.

Saying with laughter but also decision, "No, no, *no,*" Vlana swiftly stepped in backward over the slack lashings, held the door closed with one hand while she gave the lashings a tightening pull with the other, and glanced over her shoulder.

Her look of stark surprise was gone almost before Fafhrd marked it, to be replaced by a quick welcoming grin that wrinkled her nose comically. She turned away from him, carefully drew the lashings tight, and spent some time tying a knot on the inside. Then she came over and knelt beside him where he lay, her body erect from her knees. There was no grin now as she looked down at him, only a composed, enigmatic thoughtfulness, which he sought to match. She was wearing the hooded robe of her Mingol costume.

"So you changed your mind about a reward," she said

quietly but matter-of-factly. "How do you know that I too may not have changed mine since?"

Fafhrd shook his head, replying to her first statement. Then, after a pause, he said, "Nevertheless, I have discovered that I desire you."

Vlana said, "I saw you watching the show from . . . from the gallery. You almost stole it, you know—I mean the show. Who was the girl with you? Or was it a youth? I couldn't be quite sure."

Fafhrd did not answer her inquiries. Instead he said, "I also wish to ask you questions about your supremely skillful dancing and . . . and acting in loneliness."

"Miming." She supplied the word.

"Miming, yes. *And* I want to talk to you about civilization."

"That's right, this morning you asked me how many languages I knew," she said, looking straight across him at the wall of the tent. It was clear that she too was a thinker. She took the cup of brandy out of his hand, swallowed half of what was left, and returned it to him.

"Very well," she said, at last looking down at him, but with unchanged expression. "I will give you your desire, my dear boy. But now is not the time. First, I must rest and gather strength. Go away and return when the star Shadah sets. Wake me if I slumber."

"That's an hour before dawn," he said, looking up at her. "It will be a chilly wait for me in the snow."

"Don't do that," she said quickly. "I don't want you three-quarters frozen. Go where it's warm. To stay awake, think of me. Don't drink too much wine. Now go."

He got up and made to embrace her. She drew back a step, saying, "Later. Later—everything." He started toward the door. She shook her head, saying, "You might be seen. As you came."

Passing her again, his head brushed something hard. Between the hoops supporting the tent's middle, the supple hide of the tent bulged down, while the hoops themselves were bowed out and somewhat flattened bearing the weight. He cringed down for an instant, ready to grab Vlana and jump any way, then began methodically to punch and sweep at the bulges, always striking outward. There was a crashing and a loud tinkling as the massed crystals, which outside had reminded him of a giant flatworm—must be a giant snow serpent by now!—broke up and showered off.

Meanwhile he said, "The Snow Women do not love you. Nor is Mor, my mother, your friend."

"Do they think to frighten me with ice crystals?" Vlana demanded contemptuously. "Why, I know of Eastern fire sorceries compared to which their feeble magickings—"

"But you are in *their* territory now, at the mercy of *their* element, which is crueler and subtler than fire," Fafhrd interposed, brushing away the last of the bulgings, so that the hoops stood up again and the leather stretched almost flat between them. "Do not underrate their powers."

"Thank you for saving my tent from being crumpled. But now—and swiftly—go."

She spoke as if of trivial matters, but her large eyes were thoughtful.

Just before snaking under the back wall, Fafhrd looked over his shoulder. Vlana was gazing at the side wall again, holding the empty cup he had given her, but she caught his movement and, now smiling tenderly, put a kiss in her palm and blew it toward him.

Outside, the cold had grown bitter. Nevertheless, Fafhrd went to his clump of evergreens, drew his cloak closely around him, dropped its hood over his forehead, tightened the hood's drawstring, and sat himself facing Vlana's tent.

When the cold began to penetrate his furs, he thought of Vlana.

Suddenly he was crouching and had loosened his knife in its sheath.

A figure was approaching Vlana's tent, keeping to the shadows when it could. It appeared to be clad in black.

Fafhrd silently advanced.

Through the still air came the faint sound of fingernails scratching leather.

There was a flash of dim light as the doorway was opened.

It was bright enough to show the face of Vellix the Venturer. He stepped inside and there was the sound of lacings being drawn tight.

Fafhrd stopped ten paces from the tent and stood there for perhaps two dozen breaths. Then he softly walked past the tent, keeping the same distance.

There was a glow in the doorway of the high, conical tent

of Essedinex. From the stables beyond, a horse whickered twice.

Fafhrd crouched and peered through the low, glowing doorway a knife-cast away. He moved from side to side. He saw a table crowded with jugs and cups set against the sloping wall of the tent opposite the doorway.

To one side of the table sat Essedinex. To the other, Hringorl.

On the watch for Hor, Harrax, or Hrey, Fafhrd circled the tent. He approached it where the table and the two men were faintly silhouetted. Drawing aside his hood and hair, he set his ear against the leather.

"Three gold bars—that's my top," Hringorl was saying surlily. The leather made his voice hollow.

"Five," Essedinex answered, and there was the *slup* of wine mouthed and swallowed.

"Look here, old man," Hringorl countered, his voice at its most gruffly menacing, "I don't need you. I can snatch the girl and pay you nothing."

"Oh no, that won't do, Master Hringorl." Essedinex sounded merry. "For then the show would never return again to Cold Corner, and how would your tribesmen like that? Nor would there be any more girls brought you by me."

"What matter?" the other answered carelessly. The words were muffled by a gulp of wine, yet Fafhrd could hear the bluff in them. "I have my ship. I can cut your throat this instant and snatch the girl tonight."

"Then do so," Essedinex said brightly. "Only give me a moment for one more quaff."

"Very well, you old miser. Four gold bars."

"Five."

Hringorl cursed sulfurously. "Some night, you ancient pimp, you will provoke me too far. Besides, the girl is old."

"Aye, in the ways of pleasure. Did I tell you that she once became an acolyte of the Wizards of Azorkah, so that she might be trained by them to become a concubine of the King of Kings and their spy in the court at Horbori Xen? Aye, and eluded those dread necromancers most cleverly when she had gained the erotic knowledge she desired."

Hringorl laughed with a forced lightness. "Why should I pay even one silver bar for a girl who has been possessed by dozens? Every man's plaything."

"By hundreds," Essedinex corrected. "Skill is gained only by experience, as you know well. And the greater the experience, the greater the skill. Yet this girl is never a plaything. She is the instructress, the revelator, she plays with a man for his pleasure, she can make a man feel king of the universe and perchance—who knows?—even *be* that. What is impossible to a girl who knows the pleasure ways of the gods themselves? Aye, and of the arch-demons? And yet— you won't believe this, but it's true—she remains in her fashion forever virginal. For no man has ever mastered her."

"That will be seen to!" Hringorl's words were almost a laughing shout. There was the sound of wine gulped. Then his voice dropped. "Very well, five gold bars it is, you usurer. Delivery after tomorrow night's show. The gold paid against the girl."

"Three hours after the show, when the girl's drugged and all's quiet. No need to rouse the jealousy of your fellow tribesmen so soon."

"Make it two hours. Agreed? And now let's talk of next year. I'll want a black girl, a full-blooded Kleshite. And no five-gold-bar deal ever again. I'll not want a witchy wonder, only youth and great beauty."

Essedinex answered, "Believe me, you won't ever again desire another woman, once you've known and—I wish you luck—mastered Vlana. Oh, of course, I suppose—"

Fafhrd reeled back from the tent a half-dozen paces and there planted his feet firm and wide, feeling strangely dizzy, or was it drunk? He had early guessed they were almost certainly talking of Vlana, but hearing her name spoken made a much greater difference than he'd expected.

The two revelations, coming so close, filled him with a mixed feeling he'd never known before: an overmastering rage and also a desire to laugh hugely. He wanted a sword long enough to slash open the sky and tumble the dwellers in paradise from their beds. He wanted to find and fire off all the show's sky rockets into the tent of Essedinex. He wanted to topple Godshall with its pines and drag it across all the actors' tents. He wanted—

He turned around and swiftly made for the stable tent. The one groom was snoring on the straw beside an empty jug and near the light sleigh of Essedinex. Fafhrd noted with a fiendish grin that the horse he knew best happened to be one of

Hringorl's. He found a horse collar and a long coil of light, strong rope. Then making reassuring mumbles behind half-closed lips, he led out the chosen horse—a white mare—from the rest. The groom only snored louder.

He again noted the light sleigh. A risk-devil seized him and he unlaced the stiff, pitchy tarpaulin covering the storage space behind the two seats. Beneath it among other things was the show's supply of rockets. He selected three of the biggest—with their stout ash tails they were long as ski sticks—and then took time to relace the tarpaulin. He still felt the male desire for destruction, but now it was under a measure of control.

Outside, he put the collar on the mare and firmly knotted to it a roomy noose. Then, coiling the rest of the rope and gripping the rockets under his left elbow, he nimbly mounted the mare and walked it near the tent of Essedinex. The two dim silhouettes still confronted each other across the table.

He whirled the noose above his head and cast. It settled around the apex of the tent with hardly a sound, for he was quick to draw in the slack before it rattled against the tent's wall.

The noose tightened around the top of the tent's central mast. Containing his excitement, he walked the mare toward the forest across the moon-bright snow, paying out the rope. When there were only four coils of it left, he urged the mare into a lope. He crouched over the collar, holding it firm, his heels clamped to the mare's sides. The rope strained. There was a satisfying, muffled *crack* behind him. He shouted a triumphant laugh. The mare plunged on against the rope's irregular restraint. Looking back, he saw the tent dragging after them. He saw fire and heard yells of surprise and anger. Again he shouted his laughter.

At the edge of the forest he drew his knife and slashed the rope. Vaulting down, he buzzed approvingly in the mare's ear and gave her a slap on the flank that set her cantering toward the stable. He considered firing off the rockets toward the fallen tent, but decided it would be anticlimax. With them still clamped under his elbow, he walked into the edge of the woods. So hidden, he started home. He walked lightly to minimize footprints, found a branch of fringe pine and dragged it behind him, and when he could, he walked on rock.

His mountainous humor was gone and his rage too, replaced by black depression. He no longer hated Vellix or even Vlana, but civilization seemed a tawdry thing, unworthy of his interest. He was glad he had spilled Hringorl and Essedinex, but they were wood lice. He himself was a lonely ghost, doomed to roam the Cold Waste.

He thought of walking north through the woods until he found a new life or froze, of fetching and strapping on his skis and attempting to leap the tabooed gap that had been the death of Skif, of getting sword and challenging Hringorl's henchmen all at once, and of a hundred other doom-treadings.

The tents of the Snow Clan looked like pale mushrooms in the light of the crazily glaring moon. Some were cones topping a squat cylinder; others, bloated hemispheres, turnip shapes. Like mushrooms, they did not quite touch the ground at the edges. Their floors of packed branches, carpeted with hides and supported by heavier boughs, stood on overhung chunky posts, so that a tent's heat would not turn the frozen ground below it to a mush.

The huge, silvery trunk of a dead snow oak, ending in what looked like a giant's split fingernails, where an old lightning bolt had shattered it midway up, marked the site of Mor's and Fafhrd's tent—and also of his father's grave, which the tent overlay. Each year it was pitched just so.

There were lights in a few of the tents and in the great Tent of the Women lying beyond in the direction of Godshall, but Fafhrd could see no one abroad. With a dispirited grunt he headed for his home door; then, remembering the rockets, he veered toward the dead oak. It was smooth-surfaced, the bark long gone. The few remaining branches were likewise bare and broken off short, the lowest of them appearing well out of reach.

A few paces away he paused for another look around. Assured of secrecy, he raced toward the oak, and making a vertical leap more like a leopard's than a man's, he caught hold of the lowest branch with his free hand and whipped himself up onto it before his upward impetus was altogether spent.

Standing lightly on the dead branch with a finger touching the trunk, he made a final scan for peepers and late walkers, then with pressure of fingers and tease of fingernails, opened in the seemingly seamless gray wood a doorway tall as himself but scarcely half as wide. Feeling past skis and ski sticks, he found a long thin shape wrapped thrice around with lightly oiled sealskin. Undoing it, he uncovered a powerful-looking bow and a quiver of long arrows. He added the rockets to it, replaced the wrappings, then shut the queer door of his tree-safe and dropped to the snow below, which he brushed smooth.

Entering his home tent, he felt again like a ghost and made as little noise as one. The odors of home comforted him uncomfortably and against his will: smells of meat, cooking, old smoke, hides, sweat, and chamberpot, Mor's faint, sour-sweet stench. He crossed the springy floor, and fully clad, he stretched himself in his sleeping furs. He felt tired as death. The silence was profound. He couldn't hear Mor's breathing. He thought of his last sight of his father, blue and shut-eyed, his broken limbs straightened, his best sword naked at his side with his slate-colored fingers fitted around the hilt. He thought of Nalgron now in the earth under the tent, worm-gnawed to a skeleton, the sword black rust, the eyes open now—sockets staring upward through solid dirt. He remembered his last sight of his father alive: a tall wolfskin cloak striding away with Mor's warnings and threats spattering against it. Then the skeleton came back into his mind. It was a night for ghosts.

"Fafhrd?" Mor called softly from across the tent.

Fafhrd stiffened and held his breath. When he could no longer, he began to let it out and draw it in, open-mouthed, in noiseless drafts.

"Fafhrd?" The voice was a little louder, though still like a ghost cry. "I heard you come in. You're not asleep."

No use keeping silent. "You haven't slept either, Mother?"

"The old sleep little."

That wasn't true, he thought. Mor wasn't old, even by the Cold Waste's merciless measure. At the same time, it *was* the truth. Mor was as old as the tribe, the Waste itself, as old as death.

Mor said composedly—Fafhrd knew she had to be lying on her back, staring straight upward—"I am willing that you should take Mara to wife. Not pleased, but willing. There is need for a strong back here, so long as you daydream, shooting your thoughts like arrows loosed high and at random, and prank about and gad after actresses and such gilded dirt.

Besides, you have got Mara with child and her family does not altogether lack status."

"Mara spoke to you tonight?" Fafhrd asked. He tried to keep his voice dispassionate, but the words came strangledly.

"As any Snow Girl should. Except she ought to have told me earlier. And you earlier still. But you have inherited threefold your father's secretiveness, along with his urge to neglect his family and indulge himself in useless adventurings. Except that in you the sickness takes a more repulsive form. Cold mountaintops were his mistresses, while you are drawn to civilization, that putrid festering of the hot south, where there is no natural stern cold to punish the foolish and luxurious and to see that the decencies are kept. But you will discover that there is a witchy cold that can follow you anywhere in Nehwon. Ice once went down and covered all the hot lands, in punishment for an earlier cycle of lecherous evil. And wherever ice once went, witchery can send it again. You will come to believe that and shed your sickness, or else you will learn as your father learned."

Fafhrd tried to make the accusation of husband-murder that he had hinted at so easily that morning, but the words stuck, not in his throat, but in his very mind, which felt invaded. Mor had long ago made his heart cold. Now, up in his brain, she was creating among his privatest thoughts crystals which distorted everything and prevented him from using against her the weapons of duty coldly performed and joined by a cold reason which let him keep his integrity. He felt as if there were closing in on him forever the whole world of cold, in which the rigidity of ice and the rigidity of morals and the rigidity of thought were all one.

As if sensing her victory and permitting herself to joy in it a little, Mor said in the same dead, reflective tones, "Aye, your father now bitterly regrets Gran Hanack, White Fang, the Ice Queen, and all his other mountain paramours. They cannot help him now. They have forgotten him. He stares up endlessly from lidless sockets at the home he despised and now yearns for, so near, yet so impossibly far. His fingerbones scrabble feebly against the frozen earth, he tries futilely to twist under its weight . . ."

Fafhrd heard a faint scratching, perhaps of icy twigs against tent leather, but his hair rose. Yet he could move no other part of him, he discovered as he tried to lift himself. The black-

ness all around him was a vast weight. He wondered if Mor
had magicked him down under the ground beside his father.
Yet it was a greater weight than that of eight feet of frozen
earth that pressed on him. It was the weight of the entire Cold
Waste and its killingness, of the taboos and contempts and
shut-mindedness of the Snow Clan, of the pirate greed and
loutish lust of Hringorl, of even Mara's merry self-absorption
and bright, half-blind mind, and atop them all, Mor with ice
crystals forming on her fingertips as she wove them in a
binding spell.

And then he thought of Vlana.

It may not have been the thought of Vlana that did it. A
star may have chanced to crawl across the tent's tiny smoke
hole and shoot its tiny silver arrow into the pupil of one of his
eyes. It may have been that his held breath suddenly puffed
out and his lungs automatically sucked another breath in,
showing him that his muscles *could* move.

At any rate he shot up and dashed for the doorway. He
dared not stop for the lashings, because Mor's ice-jagged
fingers were clutching at him. Instead he ripped the brittle,
old leather with one downward sweep of his clawed right
hand and then *leapt* from the door, because Nalgron's skeletal
arms were straining toward him from the narrow black space
between the frozen ground and the tent's elevated floor.

And then he ran as he had never run before. He ran as if all
the ghosts of the Cold Waste were at his heels—and in some
fashion they were. He passed the last of the Snow Clan's
tents, all dark, and the faintly tinkling Tent of the Women,
and sprinted out onto the gentle slope, all silvered by the
moon, leading down to the upcurving lip of Trollstep Canyon.
He felt the urge to dash off that verge, challenging the air to
uphold him and bear him south or else hurl him to instant
oblivion—and for a moment there seemed nothing to choose
between those two fates.

Then he was running not so much away from the cold and
its crippling, supernatural horrors, as toward civilization, which
was once again a bright emblem in his brain, an answer to all
small-mindedness.

He slowed down a little and some sense came back into his
head, so that he peered for living late-walkers as well as for
demons and fetches.

He noted Shadah twinkling blue in the western treetops.

He was walking by the time he reached Godshall. He went between it and the canyon's rim, which no longer tugged him.

He noted that Essedinex's tent had been set up again and was once more lit. No new snow worm crawled across Vlana's tent. The snow sycamore bough above it glittered with crystals in the moonlight.

He entered without warning by the back door, silently drawing out the loosened pegs and then thrusting together under the wall and the hems of the racked costumes his head and right fist, the latter gripping his drawn knife.

Vlana lay asleep alone on her back on the pallet, a red, woolen, light blanket drawn up to her naked armpits. The lamp burned yellow and small, yet brightly enough to show all the interior and no one but her. The unbanked and newly stoked brazier radiated heat.

Fafhrd came all the way in, sheathed his knife, and stood looking down at the actress. Her arms seemed very slender, her hands long-fingered and a shade large. With her big eyes shut, her face seemed rather small at the center of its glory of outspread, dark-brown hair. Yet it looked both noble and knowing and its moist, long, generous lips, newly and carefully carmined, roused and tempted him. Her skin had a faint sheen of oil. He could smell its perfume.

For a moment Vlana's supine posture reminded him of both Mor and Nalgron, but this thought was instantly swept away by the brazier's fierce heat, like that of a small wrought-iron sun, by the rich textures and graceful instruments of civilization all around him, and by Vlana's beauty and couth grace, which seemed self-aware even in sleep. She was civilization's sigil.

He moved back toward the rack and began to strip off his clothes and neatly fold and pile them. Vlana did not wake, or at least her eyes did not open.

Getting back under the red blanket again some time later, after crawling out to relieve himself, Fafhrd said, "Now tell me about civilization and your part in it."

Vlana drank half of the wine Fafhrd had fetched her on his way back, then stretched luxuriously, her head resting on her intertwined hands.

"Well, to begin with, I'm not a princess, though I liked

being called one," she said lightly. "I must inform you that you have not got yourself even a lady, darlingest boy. As for civilization, it stinks."

"No," Fafhrd agreed, "I have got myself the skillfullest and most glamorous actress in all Nehwon. But why has civilization an ill odor for you?"

"I think I must disillusion you still further, beloved," Vlana said, somewhat absently rubbing her side against his. "Otherwise you might get silly notions about me and even devise silly plans."

"If you're talking about pretending to be a whore in order to gain erotic knowledge and other wisdoms—" Fafhrd began.

She glanced at him in considerable surprise and interrupted rather sharply, "I'm worse than a whore, by some standards. I'm a thief. Yes, Red Ringlets, a cutpurse and filchpocket, a roller of drunks, a burglar and alleybasher. I was born a farm girl, which I suppose makes me lower still to a hunter, who lives by the death of animals and keeps his hands out of the dirt and reaps no harvest except with the sword. When my parents' plot of land was confiscated by the law's trickery to make a tiny corner of one of the new, vast, slave-worked, Lankhmar-owned grain farms, and they in consequence starved to death, I determined to get my own back from the grain merchants. Lankhmar City would feed me, aye, feed me well!—and be paid only with lumps and perhaps a deep scratch or two. So to Lankhmar I went. Falling in there with a clever girl of the same turn of mind and some experience, I did well for two full rounds of moons and a few more. We worked only in black garb, and called ourselves to ourselves the Dark Duo.

"For a cover, we danced, chiefly in the twilight hours, to fill in the time before the big-name entertainers. A little later we began to mime too, taught by a famous actor fallen by wine on evil days, the darlingest and courtliest old trembler who ever begged for a drink at dawn or contrived to fondle a girl one-quarter his age at dusk. And so, as I say, I did quite well . . . until I fell afoul, as my parents had, of the law. No, not the Overlord's courts, dear boy, and his prisons and racks and head-and-hand-chopping blocks, though they are a shame crying to the stars. No, I ran afoul of a law older even than Lankhmer's and a court less merciful. In short, my friend's and my own cover was finally blown by the Thieves' Guild, a most ancient organization with locals in every city of the civilized world with a hidebound law against female membership and with a deep detestation of all freelance pilferers. Back on the farm I had heard of the guild and hoped in my innocence to become worthy to join it, but soon learned their byword, 'Sooner give a cobra a kiss, than a secret to a woman.' Incidentally, sweet scholar of civilization's arts, such women as the guild must use as lures and attention-shifters and such, they hire by the half-hour from the Whore's Guild.

"I was lucky. At the moment when I was supposed to be slowly strangling somewhere else, I was stumbling over Vilis' body, having looped swiftly home to get a key I'd forgot. I lit a lamp in our close-shuttered abode and saw the long agony in Vilis' face and the red silken cord buried deep in her neck. But what filled me with the hottest rage and coldest hate—besides a second measure of knee-melting fear—was that they had strangled old Hinerio too. Vilis and I were at least competitors and so perhaps fair game by civilization's malodorous standards, but he had never even suspected us of thievery. He had assumed merely that we had other lovers or else—and also—erotic clients.

"So I scuttled out of Lankhmar as swiftly as a spied crab, eyes behind me for pursuit, and in Ilthmar encountered Essedinex' troup, headed north for the off-season. By good fortune they needed a leading mime and my skill was sufficient to satisfy old Seddy.

"But at the same time, I swore an oath by the morning star to avenge the deaths of Vilis and Hinerio. And someday I shall! With proper plans and help and a new cover. More than one high potentate of the Thieves' Guild will learn how it feels to have his weasand narrowed a fingerclip's breadth at a time, aye, and worse things!

"But this is a hellish topic for a comfy morning, lover, and I raise it only to show you why you must not get deeply involved with a dirty and vicious one such as me."

Vlana turned her body then so that it leaned against Fafhrd's and she kissed him from the corner of the lip to the lobe of the ear, but when he would have returned these courtesies in full measure and more, she carried away his groping hands and, bracing herself on his arms, thereby confining them, pushed herself up and gazed at him with her enigma look, saying,

"Dearest boy, it is the gray of dawn and soon comes the pink and you must leave me at once, or at most after a last engagement. Go home, marry that lovely and nimble tree-girl—I'm sure now it was not a male youth—and live your proper, arrow-straight life far from the stinks and snares of civilization. The show packs up and leaves early, day after tomorrow, and I have my crooked destiny to tread. When your blood has cooled, you will feel only contempt for me. Nay, deny it not—I know men! Though there is a tiny chance that you, being you, will recall me with a little pleasure. In which case I advise one thing only: never hint of it to your wife!"

Fafhrd matched her enigma look and answered, "Princess, I've been a pirate, which is nothing but a water thief, who often raids folk poor as your parents. While barbarism can match civlization's every stench. Not one move in our frostbit lives but is strictured by a mad god's laws, which we call customs, and by black-handed irrationalities from which there is no escape. My own father was condemned to death by bone-breaking by a court I dare not name. His offense: climbing a mountain. And there are murders and thievings and pimpings and—Oh, there are tales I could tell you if—"

He broke off to lift his hands so that he was holding her half above him, grasping her gently below the armpits, rather than she propped on her arms. "Let me come south with you, Vlana," he said eagerly, "whether as member of your troupe or moving alone—though I *am* a singing skald, I can also sword dance, juggle four whirling daggers, and hit with one at ten paces a mark the size of my thumbnail. And when we get to Lankhmar City, perhaps disguised as two Northerners, for you are tall, I'll be your good right arm of vengeance. I can thieve by land, too, believe me, and stalk a victim through alleys, I should think, as sightlessly and silently as through forests. I can—"

Vlana, supported by his hands, laid a palm across his lips while her other hand wandered idly under the long hair at the back of his neck. "Darling," she said, "I doubt not that you are brave and loyal and skillful for a lad of eighteen. And you make love well enough for a youth—quite well enough to hold your white-furred girl and mayhap a few more wenches, if you choose. But—despite your ferocious words—forgive my frankness—I sense in you honesty, nobility even, a love of fair play, and a hatred of torture. While the lieutenant I seek for my revenge must be cruel and treacherous and fell as a serpent, while knowing at least as much as I of the fantastically twisty ways of the great cities and the ancient guilds. And, to be blunt, he must be old as I, which you miss by almost the fingers of two hands. So come kiss me, dear boy, and pleasure me once more and—"

Fafhrd suddenly sat up and lifted her a little and sat her down, so that she sat sideways on his thighs, he shifting his grasp to her shoulders.

"No," he said firmly. "I see nothing to be gained by subjecting you once more to my inexpert caresses. But—"

"I was afraid you would take it that way," she interrupted unhappily. "I did not mean—"

"But," he continued with cool authority, "I want to ask you one question. Have you already chosen your lieutenant?"

"I will not answer that," she replied, eyeing him as coolly and confidently.

"Is he—?" he began, and then pressed his lips together, catching the name "Vellix" before it was uttered.

She looked at him with undisguised curiosity as to what his next move would be. "Very well," he said at last, dropping his hands from her shoulders and propping himself with them. "You have tried, I think, to act in what you believe to be my best interests, so I will return like with like. What I have to reveal indicts barbarism and civilization equally." And he told her of Essedinex' and Hringorl's plan for her.

She laughed heartily when he was done, though he fancied she had turned a shade pale.

"I must be slipping," she commented. "So that was why my somewhat subtle mimings so easily pleased Seddy's rough and ready tastes, and why there was a place open for me in the troupe, and why he did not insist I whore for him after the show, as the other girls must." She looked at Fafhrd sharply. "Some pranksters overset Seddy's tent this midnight. Was it—?"

He nodded. "I was in a strange humor, last night, merry yet furious."

Honest, delighted laughter from her then, followed by another of the sharp looks. "So you did not go home when I sent you away after the show?"

"Not until afterward," he said. "No, I stayed and watched."

She looked at him in a tender, mocking, wondering way which asked quite plainly, "And what did you see?" But this time he found it very easy not to name Vellix.

"So you're a gentleman, too," she joked. "But why didn't you tell me about Hringorl's base scheme earlier? Did you think I'd become too frightened to be amorous?"

"A little of that," he admitted, "but it was chiefly that I did not decide until this moment to warn you. Truth to tell, I only came back to you tonight because I was frightened by ghosts, though later I found other good reasons. Indeed, just before I came to your tent, fear and loneliness—yes, and a certain jealousy too—had me minded to hurl myself into Trollstep Canyon, or else don skis and attempt the next-to-impossible leap which has teased my courage for years—"

She clutched his upper arm, digging in fingers. "Never do that," she said very seriously. "Hold on to life. Think only of yourself. The worse always changes for the better—or oblivion."

"Yes, so I was thinking when I would have let the air over the canyon decide my destiny. Would it cradle me or dash me down? But selfishness, of which I've aplenty, whatever you think—that and a certain leeriness of all miracles—quashed that whim. Also, I was earlier half-minded to trample your tent before pulling down the Show Master's. So there *is* some evil in me, you see. Aye, and a shut-mouthed deceitfulness."

She did not laugh, but studied his face most thoughtfully. Then for a time the enigma look came back into her eyes. For a moment Fafhrd thought he could peer past it, and he was troubled, for what he thought he glimpsed behind those large, brown-irised pupils was not a sibyl surveying the universe from a mountaintop, but a merchant with scales in which he weighed objects most carefully, at whiles noting down in a little book old debts and new bribes and alternate plans for gain.

But it was only one troubling glimpse, so his heart joyed when Vlana, whom his big hands still held tilted above him, smiled down into his eyes and said, "I will now answer your question, which I would and could not earlier. For I have only this instant decided that my lieutenant will be . . . *you.* Hug me on it!"

Fafhrd grappled her with eager warmth and a strength that made her squeal, but then just before his body had fired unendurably, she pushed up from him, saying breathlessly, "Wait, wait! We must first lay our plans."

"Afterward, my love. Afterward," he pleaded, straining her down.

"No!" she protested sharply. "Afterward loses too many battles to Too Late. If you are lieutenant, I am captain and give directions."

"Harkening in obedience," he said, giving way. "Only be swift."

"We must be well away from Cold Corner before kidnap time," she said. "Today I must gather my things together and provide us with sleigh, swift horses, and a store of food. Leave all that to me. You behave today exactly as is your wont, keeping well away from me, in case our enemies set spies on you, as both Seddy and Hringorl are most like to do—"

"Very well, very well," Fafhrd agreed hurriedly. "And now, my sweetest—"

"Hush and have patience! To cap your deception, climb into the roof of Godshall well before the show, just as you did last night. There just might be an attempt to kidnap me during the show—Hringorl or his men becoming overeager, or Hringorl seeking to cheat Seddy of his gold—and I'll feel safest with you on watch. Then when I exit after wearing the toga and the silver bells, come you down swiftly and meet me at the stable. We'll escape during the break between the first and second halves of the show, when one way or another all are too intent on what more's coming, to take note of us. You've got that? Join me at the halves break? Very well! And now, darlingest lieutenant, banish all discipline. Forget every atom of respect you owe your captain and—"

But now it was Fafhrd's turn to delay. Vlana's talk had allowed time for his own worries to rouse and he held her away from him, although she had knit her hands behind his neck and was straining to draw their two bodies together.

He said, "I will obey you in every particular. Only one warning more, which it's vital you heed. Think as little as you can today about our plans, even while performing actions vital to them. Keep them hid behind the scenery of your other thoughts. As I shall mine, you may be sure. For Mor, my mother, is a great reader of minds."

"Your mother! Truly she has overawed you inordinately,

darling, in a fashion which makes me itch to set you wholly
free—oh, do not hold me off! Why, you speak of her as if
she were the Queen of Witches."

"And so she is, make no mistake," Fafhrd assured her
dourly. "She is the great white spider, while the whole Cold
Waste, both above and below, is her web, on which we flies
must go tippy-toe, o'erstepping sticky stretches. You *will*
heed me?"

"Yes, yes, yes! And now—"

He brought her slowly down toward him, as a man might
put a wineskin to his mouth, tantalizing himself. Their skins
met. Their lips poised.

Fafhrd became aware of a profound silence above, around,
below, as if the very earth were holding her breath. It frightened him.

They kissed, drinking deeply of each other, and his fear
was drowned.

They parted for breath. Fafhrd reached out and pinched the
lamp's wick so that the flame fled and the tent was dark
except for the cold silver of dawn seeping in by cranny and
crack. His fingers stung. He wondered why he'd done it—
they'd loved by lamplight before. Again fear came.

He clasped Vlana tightly in the hug that banishes all fears.

And then of a sudden—he could not possibly have told
why—he was rolling over and over with her toward the back
of the tent. His hands gripping her shoulders, his legs clamped
hers together, he was hurling her sideways over him and then
himself over her in swiftest alteration.

There was a *crack* like thunder and the jolt of a giant's fist
hammered against the granite-frozen ground behind them,
where the middle of the tent became nothing high, while the
hoops above them leaned sharply that way, drawing the tent's
leather skin after.

They rolled into the racked garments spilling down. There
was a second monster *crack* followed by a crashing and
crunching like some supergiant beast snapping up a behemoth
and crunching it between its jaws. Earth quivered for a space.

Then all was silent after that great noise and ground-
shaking, except for the astonishment and fear buzzing in their
ears. They clutched each other like terrified children.

Fafhrd recovered himself first. "Dress!" he told Vlana,

and squirmed under the back of the tent and stood up naked in the biting cold under the pinkening sky.

The great bough of the snow sycamore, its crystals dashed off in a vast heap, lay athwart the middle of the tent, pressing it and the pallet beneath into the frozen earth.

The rest of the sycamore, robbed of its great balancing bough, had fallen entire in the opposite direction and lay mounded around with shaken-off crystals. Its black, hairy, broken-off roots were nakedly exposed.

All the crystals shone with a pale flesh-pink from the sun.

Nothing moved anywhere, not even a wisp of breakfast smoke. Sorcery had struck a great hammerstroke and none had noted it except the intended victims.

Fafhrd, beginning to shake, slithered under again. Vlana had obeyed his word and was dressing with an actress's swiftness. Fafhrd hurried into his own garments, piled so providentially at this end of the tent. He wondered if he had been under a god's directions in doing that and in snuffing out the lamp, which else by now would have had the crushed tent flaming.

His clothes felt colder than the icy air, but he knew that would change.

He crawled with Vlana outside once more. As they stood up, he faced her toward the fallen bough with the great crystal heap around it and said, "Now laugh at the witchy powers of my mother and her coven and all the Snow Women."

Vlana said doubtfully, "I see only a bough that was overweighted with ice."

Fafhrd said, "Compare the mass of crystals and snow that was shaken off that bough with those elsewhere. Remember: hide your thoughts!"

Vlana was silent.

A black figure was racing toward them from the traders' tents. It grew in size as it grotesquely bounded.

Vellix the Venturer was gasping as he stamped to a stop and seized Vlana's arms. Controlling his breathing, he said, "I dreamed a dream of you struck down and mashed. Then a thunderclap waked me."

Vlana answered. "You dreamed the beginning of the truth, but in a matter like this, almost is as good as not at all."

Vellix at last saw Fafhrd. Lines of jealous anger engraved his face and his hand went to the dagger at his belt.

"Hold!" Vlana commanded sharply. "I had indeed been mashed to a mummy, except that this youth's senses, which ought to have been utterly engrossed in something else, caught the first cues of the bough's fall, and he whipped me out of death's way in the very nick. Fafhrd's his name."

Vellix changed his hand's movement into part of a low bow, sweeping his other arm out wide. "I am much indebted to you, young man," he said warmly, and then after a pause, "for saving the life of a notable *artiste*."

By now other figures were in view, some hurrying toward them from the nearby actors' tents, others at the doors of the far-off Snow Tribes' tents and not moving at all.

Pressing her cheek to Fafhrd's, as if in formal gratitude, Vlana whispered rapidly, "Remember my plan for tonight and for all our future rapture. Do not depart a jot from it. Efface yourself."

Fafhrd managed, "Beware ice and snow. Act without thought."

To Vellix, Vlana said more distantly, though with courtesy and kindness, "Thank you, sir, for your concern for me, both in your dreams and your wakings."

From out a fur robe, whose collar topped his ears, Essedinex greeted with gruff humor, "It's been a hard night on tents." Vlana shrugged.

The women of the troupe gathered around her with anxious questions and she talked with them privately as they walked to the actors' tent and went in through the girls' door flap.

Vellix frowned after her and pulled at his black mustache.

The male actors stared and shook their heads at the beating the hemicylindrical tent had taken.

Vellix said to Fafhrd with warm friendliness, "I offered you brandy before and now I'd guess you need it. Also, since yestermorning I've had a great desire to talk with you."

"Your pardon, but once I sit I will not be able to stay awake for a word, were they wise as owls', nor for even a brandy swig," Fafhrd answered politely, hiding a great yawn which was only half-feigned. "But I thank you."

"It appears I am fated always to ask at the wrong time," Vellix commented with a shrug. "Perhaps at noon? Or midafternoon?" he added swiftly.

"The latter, if it please you," Fafhrd replied, and rapidly

walked off, taking great strides, toward the trading tents. Vellix did not seek to keep up with him.

Fafhrd felt more satisfied than he ever had in his life. The thought that tonight he would forever escape this stupid snow world and its man-chaining women almost made him nostalgic about Cold Corner. Thought-guard, he told himself. Feelings of eerie menace or else his hunger for sleep turned his surroundings spectral, like a childhood scene revisited.

He drained a white porcelain tankard of wine given him by his Mingol friends Zax and Effendrit, let them conduct him to a glossy pallet hidden by piles of other furs, and fell at once into a deep sleep.

After aeons of absolute, pillowy darkness, lights came softly on. Fafhrd sat beside Nalgron, his father, at a stout banquet table crowded with all savory foods smoking hot and all fortified wines in jugs of earthenware, stone, silver, crystal, and gold. There were other feasters lining the table, but Fafhrd could make nothing of them except their dark silhouettes and the sleepy sound of their unceasing talk too soft to be understood, like many streams of murmuring water, though with occasional bursts of low laughter, like small waves running up and returning down a gravelly beach. While the dull clash of knife and spoon against plate and each other was like the clank of the pebbles in that surf.

Nalgron was clad and cloaked in ice-bear furs of the whitest with pins and chains and wristlets and rings of purest silver, and there was silver also in his hair, which troubled Fafhrd. In his left hand he held a silver goblet, which at intervals he touched to his lips, but he kept his eating hand under his cloak.

Nalgron was discoursing wisely, tolerantly, almost tenderly of many matters. He directed his gaze here and there around the table, yet spoke so quietly that Fafhrd knew his conversation was directed at his son alone.

Fafhrd also knew he should be listening intently to every word and carefully stowing away each aphorism, for Nalgron was speaking of courage, of honor, of prudence, of thoughtfulness in giving and punctilio in keeping your word, of following your heart, of setting and unswervingly striving toward a high, romantic goal, of self-honesty in all these things but especially in recognizing your aversions and desires, of the need to close your ears to the fears and naggings of women, yet freely forgive them all their jealousies, attempted trammelings, and even extremest wickednesses, since those all sprang from their ungovernable love, for you or another, and of many a different matter most useful to know for a youth on manhood's verge.

But although he knew this much, Fafhrd heard his father only in snatches, for he was so troubled by the gauntness of Nalgron's cheek and by the leanness of the strong fingers lightly holding the silver goblet and by the silver in his hair, and a faint overlay of blue on his ruddy lips, although Nalgron was most sure and even sprightly in every movement, gesture, and word, that he was compelled to be forever searching the steaming platters and bowls around him for especially succulent portions to spoon or fork onto Nalgron's wide, silver plate to tempt his appetite.

Whenever he did this, Nalgron would look toward him with a smile and a courteous nod, and with love in his eyes, and then touch his goblet to his lips and return to his discoursings, but never would he uncover his eating hand.

As the banquet progressed, Nalgron began to speak of matters yet more important, but now Fafhrd heard hardly one of the precious words, so greatly agitated was he by his concern for his father's health. Now the thin skin seemed stretched to bursting on the jutting cheekbone, the bright eyes ever more sunken and dark-ringed, the blue veins more bulgingly a-crawl across the stout tendons of the hand lightly holding the silver goblet—and Fafhrd had begun to suspect that although Nalgron often let the wine touch his lips, he drank never a drop.

"Eat, Father," Fafhrd pleaded in a low voice taut with concern. "At least drink."

Again the look, the smile, the agreeable nod, the bright eyes warmer still with love, the brief tipping of goblet against unparted lips, the looking away, the tranquil, unattendable discourse resumed.

And now Fafhrd knew fear, for the lights were growing blue and he realized that none of the black, unfeatured fellow-feasters were or had all the while been lifting so much as hand, let alone cup rim, to mouth, though making an unceasing dull clatter with their cutlery. His concern for his father became an agony, and before he rightly knew what he was doing, he had brushed back his father's cloak and gripped his father's right arm at forearm and wrist and so shoved his eating hand toward his high-piled plate.

Then Nalgron was not nodding, but thrusting his head at Fafhrd, and not smiling, but grinning in such fashion as to show all his teeth of old ivory hue, while his eyes were cold, cold, cold.

The hand and arm that Fafhrd gripped felt like, looked like, *were* bare brown bone.

Of a sudden shaking violently in all his parts, but chiefly in his arms, Fafhrd recoiled swift as a serpent down the bench.

Then Fafhrd was not shaking, but being shaken by strong hands of flesh on his shoulders, and instead of the dark there was the faintly translucent hide of the Mingols' tent roof, and in place of his father's face the sallow-cheeked, black-mustached one, somber yet concerned, of Vellix the Venturer.

Fafhrd stared dazedly, then shook his shoulders and head to bring a quicker-tempoed life back into his body and throw off the gripping hands.

But Velix had already let go and seated himself on the next pile of furs.

"Your pardon, young warrior," he said gravely. "You appeared to be having a dream no man would care to continue."

His manner and the tone of his voice were like the nightmare-Nalgron's. Fafhrd pushed up on an elbow, yawned, and with a shuddery grimace shook himself again.

"You're chilled in body, mind, or both," Vellix said. "So we've good excuse for the brandy I promised."

He brought up from beside him two small silver mugs in one hand and in the other a brown jug of brandy which he now uncorked with that forefinger and thumb.

Fafhrd frowned inwardly at the dark tarnish on the mugs and at the thought of what might be crusted or dusted in their bottoms, or perhaps that of one only. With a troubled twinge, he reminded himself that this man was his rival for Vlana's affections.

"Hold," he said as Vellix prepared to pour. "A silver cup played a nasty role in my dream. Zax!" he called to the Mingol looking out the tent door. "A porcelain mug, if you please!"

"You take the dream as a warning against drinking from silver?" Vellix inquired softly with an ambiguous smile.

"No," Fafhrd answered, "but it instilled an antipathy into

my flesh, which still crawls." He wondered a little that the Mingols had so casually let in Vellix to sit beside him. Perhaps the three were old acquaintances from the trading camps. Or perhaps there'd been bribery.

Vellix chuckled and became freer of manner. "Also, I've fallen into filthy ways, living without a woman or servant. Effendrit! Make that two porcelain mugs, clean as newly debarked birch!"

It was indeed the other Mingol who had been standing by the door—Vellix knew them better than Fafhrd did. The Venturer immediately handed over one of the gleaming white mugs. He poured a little of the nose-tickling drink into his own porcelain mug, then a generous gush for Fafhrd, then more for himself—as if to demonstrate that Fafhrd's drink could not possibly be poisoned or drugged. And Fafhrd, who had been watching closely, could find no fault in the demonstration. They lightly clinked mugs, and when Vellix drank deeply, Fafhrd took a large though carefully slow sip. The stuff burned gently.

"It's my last jug," Vellix said cheerfully. "I've traded my whole stock for amber, snow gems, and other smalls—aye, and my tent and cart too, everything but my two horses and our gear and winter rations."

"I've heard your horses are the swiftest and hardiest on the Steppes," Fafhrd remarked.

"That's too large a claim. Here they rank well, no doubt."

"Here!" Fafhrd said contemptuously.

Vellix eyed him as Nalgron had in all but the last part of the dream. Then he said, "Fafhrd—I may call you that? Call me Vellix. May I make a suggestion? May I give you advice such as I might give son of mine?"

"Surely," Fafhrd answered, feeling not only uncomfortable now but wary.

"You're clearly restless and dissatisfied here. So is any sound young man, anywhere, at your age. The wide world calls you. You've an itching foot. Yet let me say this: it takes more than wit and prudence—aye, and wisdom, too—to cope with civilization and find any comfort. That requires low cunning, a smirching of yourself as civilization is smirched. You cannot climb to success there as you climb a mountain, no matter how icy and treacherous. The latter demands all your best. The former, much of your worst—a calculated self-evil you have yet to experience, and need not. I was born a renegade. My father was a man of the Eight Cities who rode with the Mingols. I wish now I had stuck to the Steppes myself, cruel as they are, nor harkened to the corrupting call of Lankhmar and the Eastern Lands.

"I know, I know, the folk here are narrow-visioned, custombound. But matched with the twisted minds of civilization, they're straight as pines. With your natural gifts you'll easily be a chief here—more, in sooth, a chief paramount, weld a dozen clans together, make the Northerners a power for nations to reckon with. Then, if you wish, you can challenge civilization. On your terms, not hers."

Fafhrd's thoughts and feelings were like choppy water, though he had outwardly become almost preternaturally calm. There was even a current of glee in him, that Vellix rated a youth's chances with Vlana so high that he would ply him with flattery as well as brandy.

But across all other currents, making the chop sharp and high, was the impression, hard to shake, that the Venturer was not altogether dissimulating, that he did feel like a father toward Fafhrd, that he was truly seeking to save him hurt, that what he said of civilization had an honest core. Of course that might be because Vellix felt so sure of Vlana that he could afford to be kind to a rival. Nevertheless . . .

Nevertheless, Fafhrd now once again felt more uncomfortable than anything else.

He drained his mug. "Your advice is worth thought, sir— Vellix, I mean. I'll ponder it."

Refusing another drink with a headshake and smile, he stood up and straightened his clothes.

"I had hoped for a longer chat," Vellix said, not rising.

"I've business to attend," Fafhrd answered. "My hearty thanks."

Vellix smiled thoughtfully as he departed.

The concourse of trodden snow winding among the trader's tents was rackety with noise and crowdedly a-bustle. While Fafhrd slept, the men of the Ice Tribe and fully half of the Frost Companions had come in and now many of these were gathered around two sunfires—so called for their bigness, heat, and the height of their leaping flames—quaffing steaming mead and laughing and scuffling together. To either side were oases of buying and bargaining, encroached on by the merrymakers or given careful berth according to the rank of those involved in the business doings. Old comrades spotted one another and shouted and sometimes drove through the press to embrace. Food and drink were spilled, challenges made and accepted, or more often laughed down. Skalds sang and roared.

The tumult irked Fafhrd, who wanted quiet in which to disentangle Vellix from Nelgron in his feelings, and banish his vague doubts of Vlana, and unsmirch civilization. He walked as a troubled dreamer, frowning yet unmindful of elbowings and other shoves.

Then all at once he was tinglingly alert, for he glimpsed angling toward him through the crowd Hor and Harrax, and he read the purpose in their eyes. Letting an eddy in the crush spin him around, he noted Hrey, one other of Hringorl's creatures, close behind him.

The purpose of the three was clear. Under guise of comradely scuffling, they would give him a vicious beating or worse.

In his moody concern with Vellix, he had forgotten his more certain enemy and rival, the brutally direct yet cunning Hringorl.

Then the three were upon him. In a frozen instant he noted that Hor bore a small bludgeon and that Harrax' fists were overly large, as if they gripped stone or metal to heavy their blows.

He lunged backward, as if he meant to dodge between that couple and Hrey, then as suddenly reversed course and with a shocking bellow raced toward the sunfire ahead. Heads turned at his yell and a startled few dodged from his way. But the Ice Tribesmen and Frost Companions had time to take in what was happening: a tall youth pursued by three huskies. This promised sport. They sprang to either side of the sunfire to block his passage past it. Fafhrd veered first to left, then to right. Jeering, they bunched more closely.

Holding his breath and throwing up an arm to guard his eyes, Fafhrd leapt straight through the flames. They lifted his fur cloak from his back and blew it high. He felt the stab of heat on hand and neck.

He came out with his furs a-smolder, blue flames running up his hair. There was more crowd ahead except for a swept, carpeted, and canopied space between two tents, where chiefs and priests sat intently around a low table where a merchant weighed gold dust in a pair of scales.

He heard bump and yell behind, someone cried, "Run, coward," another, "A fight, a fight," he saw Mara's face ahead, red and excited.

Then the future chief paramount of Northland—for so he happened at that instant to think of himself—half-sprang, half-dived aflame across the canopied table, unavoidably tumbling the merchant and two chiefs, banging aside the scales, and knocking the gold dust to the winds before he landed with a steaming zizzle in the great, soft snowbank beyond.

He swiftly rolled over twice to make sure all his fires were quenched, then scrambled to his feet and ran like a deer into the woods, followed by gusts of curses and gales of laughter.

Fifty big trees later he stopped abruptly in the snowy gloom and held his breath while he listened. Through the soft pounding of his blood, there came not the faintest sound of pursuit. Ruefully he combed with his fingers his stinking, diminished hair and sketchily brushed his now patchy, equally fire-stinking furs.

Then he waited for his breath to quiet and his awareness to expand. It was during this pause that he made a disconcerting discovery. For the first time in his life the forest, which had always been his retreat, his continent-spanning tent, his great private needle-roofed room, seemed hostile to him, as if the very trees and the cold-fleshed, warm-bowled mother-earth in which they were rooted knew of his apostasy, his spurning, jilting, and intended divorce of his native land.

It was not the unusual silence, nor the sinister and suspicious quality of the faint sounds he at last began to hear: scratch on bark of small claw, pitter of tiny paw steps, hoot of a distant owl anticipating night. Those were effects, or at most concomitants. It was something unnamable, intangible, yet profound, like the frown of a god. Or goddess.

He was greatly depressed. At the same time he had never known his heart feel as hard.

When at last he set out again, it was as silently as might be, and not with his unusual relaxed and wide-open awareness, but rather the naked-nerved sensitivity and bent-bow readiness of a scout in enemy territory.

And it was well for him that he did so, since otherwise he might not have dodged the nearly soundless fall of an icicle sharp, heavy, and long as a siege-catapult's missile, nor the down-clubbing of a huge snow-weighted dead branch that broke with a single thunderous crack, nor the venomous dart of a snow adder's head from its unaccustomed white coil in the open, nor the sidewise slash of the narrow, cruel claws of a snow leopard that seemed almost to materialize a-spring in the frigid air and that vanished as strangely when Fafhrd slipped aside from its first attack and faced it with dirk drawn. Nor might he have spotted in time the up-whipping, slipknotted snare, set against all custom in this home area of the forest and big enough to strangle not a hare but a bear.

He wondered where Mor was and what she might be muttering or chanting. Had his mistake been simply to dream of Nalgron? Despite yesterday's curse—and others before it—and last night's naked threats, he had never truly and wholly imagined his mother seeking to kill him. But now the hair on his neck was lifted in apprehension and horror, the watchful glare in his eyes was febrile and wild, while a little blood dripped unheeded from the cut in his cheek where the great icicle down-dropping had grazed it.

So intent had he become on spying dangers that it was with a little surprise that he found himself standing in the glade where he and Mara had embraced only yesterday, his feet on the short trail leading to the home tents. He relaxed a little then, sheathing his dirk and pressing a handful of snow to his bleeding cheek—but he relaxed only a little, with the result that he was aware of one coming to meet him before he consciously heard footsteps.

So silently and completely did he then melt into the snowy background that Mara was three paces away before she saw him.

"They hurt you," she exclaimed.

"No," he answered curtly, still intent on dangers in the forest.

"But the red snow on your cheek. There was a fight?"

"Only a nick got in the woods. I outran 'em."

Her look of concern faded. "First time I saw you run from a quarrel."

"I had no mind to take on three or more," he said flatly.

"Why do you look behind? They're trailing you?"

"No."

Her expression hardened. "The elders are outraged. The

younger men call you scareling. My brothers among them. I didn't know what to say.''

"Your brothers!" Fafhrd exclaimed. "Let the stinking Snow Clan call me what they will. I care not."

Mara planted her fists on her hips. "You've grown very free with your insults of late. I'll not have my family berated, do you hear? Nor myself insulted, now that I think of it." She was breathing hard. "Last night you went back to that shriveled old whore of a dancer. You were in her tent for hours."

"I was not!" Fafhrd denied, thinking, An hour and a half at most. The bickering was warming his blood and quelling his supernatural dread.

"You lie! The story's all around the camp. Any other girl would have set her brothers on you ere this."

Fafhrd came back to his schemy self almost with a jerk. On this eve of all eves he must not risk needless trouble—the chance of being crippled, it might even be, or dead.

Tactics, man, tactics, he told himself as he moved eagerly toward Mara, exclaiming in hurt, honeyed tones, "Mara my queen, how can you believe such of me, who love you more than—"

"Keep off me, liar and cheat!"

"And you carrying my son," he persisted, still trying to embrace her. "How does the bonny babe?"

"Spits at his father. Keep off me, I say."

"But I yearn to touch your ticklesome skin, than which there is no other balm for me this side of hell, oh, most beauteous made more beautiful by motherhood."

"Go to hell, then. And stop these sickening pretenses. Your acting wouldn't deceive a drunken she-scullion. Hamfatter!"

Stung to his blood, which instantly grew hot, Fafhrd retorted, "And what of your own lies? Yesterday you boasted of how you'd cow and control my mother. Instanter you went sniveling to tell her you were with child by me."

"Only after I knew you lusted after the actress. And was it anything but the complete truth? Oh, you twister!"

Fafhrd stood back and folded his arms. He pronounced, "Wife of mine must be true to me, must trust me, must ask me first before she acts, must comport herself like the mate of a chief-paramount-to-be. It appears to me that in all of these you fall short.''

"True to you? You're one to talk!" Her fair face grew unpleasantly red and strained with rage. "Chief paramount! Set your sights merely on being called a man by the Snow Clan, which they've not done yet. Hear me now, sneak and dissembler. You will instantly plead for my pardon on your knees and then come with me to ask my mother and aunts for my hand, or else—''

"I'd sooner kneel to a snake! Or wed a she-bear!" Fafhrd cried out, all thoughts of tactics vanished.

"I'll set my brothers on you," she screamed back. "Cowardly boor!"

Fafhrd lifted his fist, dropped it, set his hands to his head, and rocked it in a gesture of maniacal desperation, then suddenly ran past her toward the camp.

"I'll set the whole tribe on you! I'll tell it in the Tent of the Women. I'll tell your mother . . .'' Mara shrieked after him, her voice fading fast with the intervening boughs, snow, and distance.

Barely pausing to note that none was abroad among the Snow Clan's tents, either because they were still at the trading fair or inside preparing supper, Fafhrd bounded up his treasure tree and flipped open the door of his hidey-hole. Cursing the fingernail he broke doing so, he got out the sealskin-wrapped bow and arrows and rockets and added thereto his best pair of skis and ski sticks, a somewhat shorter package holding his father's second-best sword well-oiled, and a pouch of smaller gear. Dropping to the snow, he swiftly bound the longer items into a single pack, which he slung over shoulder.

After a moment of indecision, he hurtled inside Mor's tent, snatching from his pouch a small fire pot of bubblestone, and filled it with glowing embers from the hearth, sprinkled ashes over them, laced the pot tight shut, and returned it to his pouch.

Then turning in frantic haste toward the doorway, he stopped dead. Mor stood in it, a tall silhouette white-edged and shadow-faced.

"So you're deserting me and the Waste. Not to return. You think."

Fafhrd was speechless.

"Yet you will return. If you wish it to be a-crawl on four

feet, or blessedly on two, and not stretched lifeless on a litter of spears, weigh soon your duties and your birth.''

Fafhrd framed a bitter answer, but the very words were a gag in his gullet. He stalked toward Mor.

"Make way, Mother," he managed in a whisper.

She did not move.

His jaws clamped in a horrid grimace of tension, he shot forth his hands, gripped her under the armpits—his flesh crawling—and set her to one side. She seemed as stiff and cold as ice. She made no protest. He could not look her in the face.

Outside, he started at a brisk pace for Godshall, but there were men in his way—four hulking young blond ones flanked by a dozen others.

Mara had brought not only her brothers from the fair, but all her available kinsmen.

Yet now she appeared to have repented of her act, for she was dragging at her eldest brother's arm and talking earnestly to him, to judge by her expression and the movements of her lips.

Her eldest brother marched on as if she weren't there. And now as his gaze hit Fafhrd he gave a joyous shout, jerked from her grasp, and came on a-rush followed by the rest. All waved clubs or their scabbarded swords.

Mara's agonized, "Fly, my love!" was anticipated by Fafhrd by at least two heartbeats. He turned and raced for the woods, his long, stiff pack banging his back. When the path of his flight joined the trail of footprints he'd made running out of the woods, he took care to set a foot in each without slackening speed.

Behind him they cried, "Coward!" He ran faster.

When he reached the juttings of granite a short way inside the forest, he turned sharply to the right, and leaping from bare rock to rock, making not one additional print, he reached a low cliff of granite and mounted it with only two handgrabs, then darted on until the cliff's edge hid him from anyone below.

He heard the pursuit enter the woods, angry cries as in veering around trees they bumped each other, then a masterful voice crying for silence.

He carefully lobbed three stones so that they fell along his false trail well ahead of Mara's human hounds. The thud of the stones and the rustle of branches they made falling drew cries of "There he goes!" and another demand for silence.

Lifting a larger rock, he hurled it two-handed so that it struck solidly the trunk of a stout tree on the nearer side of the trail, jarring down great branchfuls of snow and ice. There were muffled cries of startlement, confusion, and rage from the showered and likely three-quarters-buried men. Fafhrd grinned, then his face sobered and his eyes grew dartingly watchful as he set off at a lope through the darkening woods.

But this time he felt no inimical presences and the living and the lifeless, whether rock or ghost, held off their assaults. Perhaps Mor, deeming him sufficiently harried by Mara's kinsmen, had ceased to energize her charms. Or perhaps— Fafhrd left off thinking and devoted all of himself to silent speeding. Vlana and civilization lay ahead. His mother and barbarism behind—but he endeavored not to think of her.

Night was near when Fafhrd left the woods. He had made the fullest possible circuit through them, coming out next to the drop into Trollstep Canyon. The strap of his long pack chafed his shoulder.

There were the lights and sounds of feasting among the traders' tents. Godshall and the actors' tents were dark. Still nearer, loomed the dark bulk of the stable tent.

He silently crossed the frosty, rutted gravel of the New Road leading south into the canyon.

Then he saw that the stable tent was not altogether dark. A ghostly glow moved inside it. He approached its door cautiously and saw the silhouette of Hor peering in. Still the soul of silence, he came up behind Hor and peered over his shoulder.

Vlana and Vellix were harnessing the latter's two horses to Essedinex' sleigh, from which Fafhrd had stolen the three rockets.

Hor tipped up his head and lifted a hand to his lips to make some sort of owl or wolf cry.

Fafhrd whipped out his knife and, as he was about to slash Hor's throat, reversed his intent and his knife too, and struck him senseless with a blow of the pommel against the side of his head. As Hor collapsed, Fafhrd hauled him to one side of the doorway.

Vlana and Vellix sprang into the sleigh, the latter touched

his horses with the reins, and they came thud-slithering out. Fafhrd gripped his knife fiercely . . . then sheathed it and shrank back into the shadows.

The sleigh went gliding off down the New Road. Fafhrd stared after it, standing tall, his arms as straight down his sides as those of a corpse laid out, but with his fingers and thumbs gripped into tightest fists.

He suddenly turned and fled toward Godshall.

There came an owl-hooting from behind the stable tent. Fafhrd skidded to a stop in the snow and turned around, his hands still fists.

Out of the dark, two forms, one trailing fire, raced toward Trollstep Canyon. The tall form was unmistakably Hringorl's. They stopped at the brink. Hringorl swung his torch in a great circle of flame. The light showed the face of Harrax beside him. Once, twice, thrice, as if in signal to someone far south down the canyon. Then they raced for the stable.

Fafhrd ran for Godshall. There was a harsh cry behind him. He stopped and turned again. Out of the stable galloped a big horse. Hringorl rode it. He dragged by rope a man on skis: Harrax. The pair careened down the New Road in a flaring upswirl of snow.

Fafhrd raced on until he was past Godshall and a quarter way up the slope leading to the Tent of the Women, He cast off his pack, opened it, drew his skis from it, and strapped them to his feet. Next he unwrapped his father's sword and belted it to his left side, balancing his pouch on right.

Then he faced Trollstep Canyon where the Old Road had gone. He took up two of his ski sticks, crouched, and dug them in. His face was a skull, the visage of one who casts dice with Death.

At that instant, beyond Godshall, the way he had come, there was a tiny yellow sputtering. He paused for it—counting heartbeats, he knew not why.

Nine, ten, eleven—there was a great flare of flame. The rocket rose, signaling tonight's show. Twenty-one, twenty-two, twenty-three—the tail flame faded and the nine shite stars burst out.

Fafhrd dropped his ski sticks, picked up one of the three rockets he'd stolen, and drew its fuse from its end, pulling just hard enough to break the cementing tar without breaking the fuse.

Holding the slender, finger-long tarry cylinder delicately between his teeth, he took his fire pot out of his pouch. The bubblestone was barely warm. He unlaced the top and brushed away the ashes below until he saw—and was stung by—a red glow.

He took the fuse from between his teeth and placed it so that one end leaned on the edge of the fire pot while the other end touched the red glow. There was a sputtering. Seven, eight, nine, ten, eleven, twelve—and the sputtering became a flaring jet, then was done.

Setting his fire pot on the snow, he took up the two remaining rockets and hugged their thick bodies under his arms and dug their tails into the snow, testing them against the ground. The tails were truly as stiff and strong as ski sticks.

He held the rockets propped parallel in one hand and blew hard on the glowing fire patch in his fire pot and brought it up toward the two fuses.

Mara ran out of the dark and said, "Darling, I'm so glad my kin didn't catch you!"

The glow of the fire pot showed the beauty of her face.

Staring at her across it, Fafhrd said, "I'm leaving Cold Corner. I'm leaving the Snow Tribe. I'm leaving you."

Mara said, "You can't."

Fafhrd set down the fire pot and the rockets.

Mara stretched out her hands.

Fafhrd took the silver bracelets off his wrists and put them in Mara's palms.

Mara clenched them and cried, "I don't ask for these. I don't ask for anything. You're the father of my child. You're mine!"

Fafhrd whipped the heavy silver chain off his neck, laid it across her wrists, and said, "Yes! You're mine forever, and I'm yours. Your son is mine. I'll never have another Snow Clan wife. We're married."

Meanwhile he had taken up the two rockets again and held their fuses to the fire pot. They sputtered simultaneously. He set them down, thonged shut the fire pot, and thrust it in his pouch. Three, four . . .

Mor looked over Mara's shoulder and said, "I witness your words, my son. Stop!"

Fafhrd grabbed up the rockets, each by its sputtering body, dug in the stick ends, and took off down the slope with a great shove. Six, seven . . .

Mara screamed, "Fafhrd! Husband!" as Mor shouted, "No son of mine!"

Fafhrd shoved again with the sputtering rockets. Cold air whipped his face. He barely felt it. The moonlit lip of the jump was close ahead. He felt its upcurve. Beyond it, darkness. Eight, nine . . .

He hugged the rockets fiercely to his sides, under his elbows, and was flying through darkness. Eleven, twelve . . .

The rockets did not fire. The moonlight showed the opposite wall of the canyon rushing toward him. His skis were directed at a point just beneath its top and that point was steadily falling. He tilted the rockets down and hugged them more fiercely still.

They fired. It was as if he were clinging to two great wrists that were dragging him up. His elbows and sides were warm. In the sudden glare the rock wall showed close, but now below. Sixteen, seventeen . . .

He touched down smoothly on the fair crust of snow covering the Old Road and hurled the rockets to either side. There was a double thunderclap and white stars were shooting around him. One smote and stung, then tortured his cheek as it died. There was time for the one great laughing thought, I depart in a burst of glory.

Then no time for large thoughts at all as he gave all his attention to skiing down the steep slope of the Old Road, now bright in the moonlight, now pitch-black as it curved, crags to his right, a precipice to his left. Crouching and keeping his skis locked side to side, he steered by swaying his hips. His face and his hands grew numb. Reality was the old Road hurled at him. Tiny bumps became great jolts. White rims came close. Black shoulders threatened.

Deep, deep down there were nevertheless thoughts. Even as he strained to keep all his attention on his skiing, they were there. *Idiot, you should have grabbed a pair of sticks with the rockets. But how would you have held them when casting aside the rockets? In your pack? Then they'd be doing you no good now. Will the fire pot in your pouch prove more worthwhile than sticks? You should have stayed with Mara. Such loveliness you'll never see again. But it's Vlana you want. Or is it? How, with Vellix? If you weren't so cold-hearted and good, you'd have killed Vellix in the stable, instead of speeding to— Did you truly intend killing yourself?*

What do you intend now? Can Mor's charms outspeed your skiing? Were the rocket wrists really Nalgron's, reaching from Hell? What's that ahead?

That was a hulking shoulder skidded around. He lay over on his right side as the white edge to his left narrowed. The edge held. Beyond it, on the opposite wall of the widening canyon, he saw a tiny streak of flame. Hringorl still had his torch as he galloped down the New Road dragging Harrax. Fafhrd lay over again to his right as the Old Road curved farther that way in a tightening turn. The sky reeled. Life demanded that he lay still farther over, breaking to a stop. But Death was still an equal player in this game. Ahead was the intersection where Old and New Road met. He must reach it as soon as Vellix and Vlana in their sleigh. Speed was the essence. Why? He was uncertain. New curves ahead.

By infinitesimal stages the slope grew less. Snow-freighted treetops thrust from the sinister depths—to the left—then shot up to either side. He was in a flat black tunnel. His progress became soundless as a ghost's. He coasted to a stop just at the tunnel's end. His numb fingers went up and feather-touched the bulge of the star-born blister on his cheek. Ice needles crackled very faintly inside the blister.

No other sound but the faint tinkle of the crystals growing all around in the still, damp air.

Five paces ahead of him, down a sudden slope, was a bulbous roll bush weighted with snow. Behind it crouched Hringorl's chief lieutenant, Hrey—no mistaking that pointed beard, though its red was gray in the moonlight. He held a strung bow in his left hand.

Beyond him, two dozen paces down slope, was the fork where New and Old Road met. The tunnel going south through the trees was blocked by a pair of roll bushes higher than a man's head. Vellix' and Vlana's sleigh was stopped short of the pile, its two horses great loomings. Moonlight struck silvery manes and silvery bushes. Vlana sat hunched in the sleigh, her head fur-hooded. Vellix had got down and was casting the roll bushes out of the way.

Torchlight came streaking down the New Road from Cold Corner. Vellix gave up his work and drew his sword. Vlana looked over her shoulder.

Hringorl galloped into the clearing with a laughing cry of triumph and threw his torch high in the air, reined his horse to a stop behind the sleigh. The skier he towed—Harrax—shot past him and halfway up the slope. There Harrax braked to a stop and stooped to unlace his skis. The torch came down and went out sizzling.

Hringorl dropped from his horse, a fighting ax ready in his right hand.

Vellix ran toward Hringorl. Clearly he understood that he must dispose of the giant pirate before Harrax got off his skis and he would be fighting two at once. Vlana's face was a small white mask in the moonlight as she half-lifted from her seat to stare after him. The hood fell back from her head.

Fafhrd could have helped Vellix, but he still hadn't made a move to unlash his skis. With a pang—or was it relief?—he remembered he'd left his bow and arrows behind. He told himself that he should help Vellix. Hadn't he skied down here at incalculable risk to save the Venturer and Vlana, or at least warn them of the ambush he had suspected ever since he'd seen Hringorl whirl his torch on the precipice's edge? And didn't Vellix look like Nalgron, now more than ever in his moment of bravery? But the phantom Death still stood at Fafhrd's side, inhibiting all action.

Besides, Fafhrd felt there was a spell on the clearing, making all acting inside it futile. As if a giant spider, white-furred, had already spun a web around it, shutting it off from the rest of the universe, making it a volume inscribed "This space belongs to the White Spider of Death." No matter that this giant spider spun not silk, but crystals—the result was the same.

Hringorl aimed a great ax swipe at Vellix. The Venturer evaded it and thrust his sword into Hringorl's forearm. With a howl of rage, Hringorl shifted his ax to his left hand, lunged forward, and struck again.

Taken by surprise, Vellix barely dodged back out of the way of the hissing curve of steel, bright in the moonlight. Yet he was nimbly on guard again, while Hringorl advanced more warily, ax head high and a little ahead of him, ready to make short chops.

Vlana stood up in the sleigh, steel flashing in her hand. She made as if to hurl it, then paused uncertainly.

Hrey rose from his bush, an arrow nocked to his bow.

Fafhrd could have killed him, by hurling his sword spearwise if in no other way. But the sense of Death beside him was still paralyzingly strong, and the sense of being in the White

Ice Spider's great womblike trap. Besides, what did he really feel toward Vellix, or even Nalgron?

The bowstring twanged. Vellix paused in his fencing, transfixed. The arrow had struck him in the back, to one side of his spine, and protruded from his chest, just below the breastbone.

With a chop of the ax, Hringorl knocked the sword from the dying man's grip as he started to fall. He gave another of his great, harsh laughs. He turned toward the sleigh.

Vlana screamed.

Before he quite realized it, Fafhrd had silently drawn his sword from its well-oiled sheath and, using it as a stick, pushed off down the white slope. His skis sang very faintly, though very high-pitched, against the snow crust.

Death no longer stood at his side. Death had stepped inside him. It was Death's feet that were lashed to the skis. It was Death who felt the White Spider's trap to be home.

Hrey turned, just in convenient time for Fafhrd's blade to open the side of his neck in a deep, slicing thrust that slit gullet as well as jugular. His sword came away almost before the gushing blood, black in the moonlight, had wet it, and certainly before Hrey had lifted his great hands in a futile effort to stop the great choking flow. It all happened very easily. His skis had thrust, Fafhrd told himself, not he. His skis, which had their own life, Death's life, and were carrying him on a most doomful journey.

Harrax, too, as if a very puppet of the gods, finished unlacing his skis and rose and turned just in time for Fafhrd's thrust, made upward from a crouch, to take him high in the guts, just as his arrow had taken Vellix, but in reverse direction.

The sword grated against Harrax' spine, but came out easily. Fafhrd sped downhill with hardly a check. Harrax stared wide-eyed after him. The great brute's mouth was wide open, too, but no sound came from it. Likely the thrust had sliced a lung and his heart as well, or else some of the great vessels springing from it.

And now Fafhrd's sword was pointed straight at the back of Hringorl, who was preparing to mount into the sleigh, and the skis were speeding the bloody blade faster and faster.

Vlana stared at Fafhrd over Hringorl's shoulder, as if she were looking at the approach of Death himself, and she screamed.

Hringorl swung around and instantly raised his ax to strike

Fafhrd's sword aside. His wide face had the alert, yet sleepy look of one who has stared at Death many times and is never surprised by the sudden appearance of the Killer of All.

Fafhrd braked and turned, so that, his rush slowing, he went past the back end of the sleigh. His sword strained all the while toward Hringorl without quite reaching him. It evaded the chop Hringorl made at it.

Then Fafhrd saw, just ahead, the sprawled body of Vellix. He made a right-angle turn, braking instantly, even thrusting his sword into the snow so that it struck sparks from the rock below, to keep from tumbling over the corpse.

He wrenched his body around then, as far as he could when his feet were still lashed to the skis, just in time to see Hringorl rushing down on him, out of the snow thrown up by the skis, and aiming his ax in a great blow at Fafhrd's neck.

Fafhrd parried the blow with his sword. Held at right angle to the sweep of the ax, the blade would have been shattered, but Fafhrd held his sword at just the proper angle for the ax to be deflected with a screech of steel and go whistling over his head.

Hringorl louted past him, unable to stop his rush.

Fafhrd again wrenched around his body, cursing the skis that now nailed his feet to the earth. His thrust was too late to reach Hringorl.

The thicker man turned and came rushing back, aiming another ax swipe. This time the only way Fafhrd could dodge it was by falling flat on the ground.

He glimpsed two streakings of moonlit steel. Then he used his sword to thrust himself to his feet, ready for another blow at Hringorl, or another dodge, if there were time.

The big man had dropped his ax and was clawing at his own face.

Lunging by making a clumsy sidewise step with his ski—no place this for style!—Fafhrd ran him through the heart.

Hringorl dropped his hands as his body pitched over backward. From his right eye socket protruded the silver pommel and black grip of a dagger. Fafhrd wrenched out his sword. Hringorl hit with a great soft thud and an outblow of snow around him, writhed violently twice, and was still.

Fafhrd poised his sword and his gaze darted around. He was ready for any other attack, by anyone at all.

But not one of the five bodies moved—the two at his feet, the two sprawled on the slope, nor Vlana's erect in the sleigh.

While with a little surprise he realized that the gasping he heard was his own breath. Otherwise the only sound was a faint, high tinkling, which for the present he ignored. Even Vellix' two horses hitched to the sleigh and Hringorl's big mount standing a short way up the Old Road, were unaccountably silent.

He leaned back against the sleigh, resting his left arm on the icy tarpaulin covering the rockets and other gear. His right hand still held his sword poised, a little negligently now, but ready.

He inspected the bodies once more, ending at Vlana's. Still none of them had moved. Each of the first four was surrounded by its blotches of blood-blackened snow, huge for Hrey, Harrax, and Hringorl, tiny for the arrow-slain Vellix.

He fixed his gaze on Vlana's staring, white-rimmed eyes. Controlling his breath, he said, "I owe you thanks for slaying Hringorl. Perhaps. I doubt I could have bested him, he on his feet, I on my back. But was your knife aimed at Hringorl, or at my back? And did I 'scape death simply by falling, while the knife passed over me to strike down another man?"

She answered not a word. Instead her hands flew up to press her cheeks and lips. She continued to stare, now over her fingers, at Fafhrd.

He continued, his voice growing still more casual, "You chose Vellix over me, after making me a promise. Why not Hringorl then over Vellix—and over me—when Hringorl seemed the likelier man to win? Why didn't you help Vellix with your knife, when he so bravely tackled Hringorl? Why did you scream when you saw me, spoiling my chance to kill Hringorl with one silent thrust?"

He emphasized each question by idly poking his sword in her direction. His breath was coming easily now, weariness departing from his body even as black depression filled his mind.

Vlana slowly took her hand from her lips and swallowed twice. Then she said, her voice harsh, but clear, and not very loud, "A woman must always keep all ways open, can you understand that? Only by being ready to league with any man, and discard one for another as fortune shifts the plan, can she begin to counter men's great advantage. I chose Vellix over you because his experience was greater and because—believe this or not, as you will—I did not think a partner of mine would have much chance for long life and I wanted you to live. I did not help Vellix here at the roadblock because I thought then that he and I were doomed. The roadblock and from it the knowledge that there must be ambushers around cowed me—though Vellix seemed not to think so, or to care. As for my screaming when I saw you, I did not recognize you. I thought you were Death himself.''

"Well, it appears I was," Fafhrd commented softly, looking around for a third time at the scattered corpses. He unlashed his skis. Then, after stamping his feet, he knelt by Hringorl and jerked the dagger from his eye and wiped it on the dead man's furs.

Vlana continued, "And I fear death even more than I detested Hringorl. Yes, I would eagerly flee with Hringorl, if it were away from death."

"This time Hringorl was headed in the wrong direction," Fafhrd commented, hefting the dagger. It balanced well for thrusting or throwing.

Vlana said, "Now of course I'm yours. Eagerly and happily—again believe it or not. If you'll have me. Perhaps you still think I tried to kill you."

Fafhrd turned toward her and tossed the dagger. "Catch," he said. She caught.

He laughed and said, "No, a showgirl who's also been a thief would be apt to be expert at knife-throwing. And I doubt that Hringorl was struck in his brains through his eye by accident. Are you still minded to have revenge on the Thieves' Guild?"

"I am," she answered.

Fafhrd said, "Women are horrible. I mean, quite as horrible as men. Oh, is there anyone in the wide world that has aught but ice water in his or her veins?"

And he laughed again, more loudly, as if knowing there could be no answer to that question. Then he wiped his sword on Hringorl's furs, thrust it in his scabbard, and without looking at Vlana strode past her and the silent horses to the pile of roll bushes and began to cast their remainder aside. They were frozen to each other and he had to tug and twist to get them loose, putting more effort into it, fighting the bushes more than he recalled Vellix having to do.

Vlana did not look at him even as he passed. She was gazing straight up the slope with its sinuous ski track leading to the black tunnel mouth of the Old Road. Her white gaze was not fixed on Harrax and Hrey, nor on the tunnel mouth. It went higher.

There was a faint tinkling that never stopped.

Then there was a crystal clatter and Fafhrd wrenched loose and hurled aside the last of the ice-weighted roll bushes.

He looked down the road leading south. To civilization, whatever that was worth now.

This road was a tunnel, too, between snow-shouldered pines.

And it was filled, the moonlight showed, with a web of crystals that seemed to go on forever, strands of ice stretching from twig to twig and bough to bough, depth beyond icy depth.

Fafhrd recalled his mother's words, "There is a witchy cold that can follow you anywhere in Nehwon. Wherever ice once went, witchery can send it again. Your father now bitterly regrets . . ."

He thought of a great white spider, spinning its frigid way around this clearing.

He saw Mor's face, beside Mara's, atop the precipice, the other side of the great leap.

He wondered what was being chanted now in the Tent of the Women, and if Mara were chanting too. Somehow he thought not.

Vlana cried out softly, "Women indeed are horrible. Look. Look. Look!"

At that instant, Hringorl's horse gave a great whinny. There was the pound of hooves as he fled up the Old Road.

An instant later, Vellix' horse reared and screamed.

Fafhrd smote the neck of the nearest horse with the outside of his arm. Then he looked toward the small, big-eyed, triangular white mask of Vlana's face and followed her gaze.

Growing up out of the slope that led to the Old Road were a half-dozen tenuous forms high as trees. They looked like hooded women. They became more and more solid as Fafhrd watched.

He crouched down in terror. This movement caught his pouch between his belly and his thigh. He felt a faint warmth.

He sprang up and dashed back the way he had come. He ripped the tarpaulin off the back of the sleigh. He grabbed the eight remaining rockets one by one and thrust the tail of each into the snow so that their heads pointed at the vast, thickening ice figures.

Then he reached in his pouch, took out his fire pot, unthonged its top, shook off its gray ashes, shook its red ashes to one side of the bowl, and rapidly touched them to the fuses of the rockets.

Their multiple spluttering in his ears, he sprang into the sleigh.

Vlana did not move as he brushed her. But she chinked. She seemed to have put on a translucent cloak of ice crystals that held her where she stood. Reflected moonlight shone stolidly from the crystals. He felt it would move only as the moon moved.

He grabbed the reins. They stung his fingers like frozen iron. He could not stir them. The ice web ahead had grown around the horses. They were part of it—great equine statues enclosed in a greater crystal. One stood on four legs, one reared on two. The walls of the ice womb were closing in. "There is a witchy cold that can follow you."

The first rocket roared, then the second. He felt their warmth. He heard the mighty tinkling as they struck their up-slope targets.

The reins moved, slapped the backs of the horses. There was a glassy smashing as they plunged forward. He ducked his head and, holding the reins in his left hand, swung up his right and dragged Vlana down into the seat. Her ice cloak jingled madly and vanished. Four, five . . .

There was a continuous jangling as horses and sleigh shot forward through the ice web. Crystals showered onto and glanced off his ducked head. The jangling grew fainter. Seven, eight . . .

All icy constraints fell away. Hooves pounded. A great north wind sprang up, ending the calm of day. Ahead the sky was faintly pink with dawn. Behind, it was faintly red with fire of pine needles ignited by the rockets. It seemed to Fafhrd that the north wind brought the roaring of flames.

He shouted, "Gnamph Nar, Mlurg Nar, great Kvarch Nar—we'll see them all! All the cities of the Forest Land! All the Land of the Eight Cities."

Beside him Vlana stirred warm under his embracing arm and took up his cry with "Sarheenmar, Ilthmar, Lankhmar! All the cities of the south! Quarmall! Horborixen! Slim-spired Tisilinilit! The Rising Land!"

It seemed to Fafhrd that mirages of all those unknown cities and places filled the brightening horizon. "Travel, love, adventure, the world!" he shouted, hugging Vlana to him with his right arm while his left slapped the horses with the reins.

He wondered why, although his imagination was roaringly aflame like the canyon behind him, his heart was still so cold.

INVISIBLE BOY

by Ray Bradbury

*More of a fantasist than a science-fiction writer, Ray
Bradbury (born in 1920) is one of the great stylists
of all time. A master of the short story, he has been
embraced by literary critics and the public alike.
The following story, filled with wistful humor, is an
example of his best work.*

She took the great iron spoon and the mummified frog and
gave it a bash and made dust of it, and talked to the dust
while she ground it in her stony fists quickly. Her beady gray
bird eyes flickered at the cabin. Each time she looked, a head
in the small thin window ducked as if she'd fired off a
shotgun.

"Charlie!" cried Old Lady. "You come outa there! I'm
fixing a lizard magic to unlock that rusty door! You come out
now and I won't make the earth shake or the trees go up in
fire or the sun set at high noon!"

The only sound was the warm mountain light on the high
turpentine trees, a tufted squirrel chittering around and around
on a green-furred log, the ants moving in a fine brown line at
Old Lady's bare, blue-veined feet.

"You been starving in there two days, darn you!" she
panted, chiming the spoon against a flat rock, causing the
plump gray miracle bag to swing at her waist. Sweating sour,
she rose and marched at the cabin, bearing the pulverized
flesh. "Come out, now!" She flicked a pinch of powder
inside the lock. "All right, I'll come get you!" she wheezed.

She spun the knob with one walnut-colored hand, first one
way, then the other. "O Lord," she intoned "fling this door
wide!"

When nothing flung, she added yet another philter and held her breath. Her long blue untidy skirt rustled as she peered into her bag of darkness to see if she had any scaly monsters there, any charm finer than the frog she'd killed months ago for such a crisis as this.

She heard Charlie breathing against the door. His folks had pranced off into some Ozark town early this week, leaving him, and he'd run almost six miles to Old Lady for company— she was by way of being an aunt or cousin or some such, and he didn't mind her fashions.

But then, two days ago, Old Lady, having gotten used to the boy around, decided to keep him for convenient company. She pricked her thin shoulder bone, drew out three blood pearls, spat wet over her right elbow, tromped on a crunch-cricket, and at the same instant clawed her left hand at Charlie, crying, "My son you are, you are my son, for all eternity!"

Charlie, bounding like a startled hare, had crashed off into the brush, heading for home.

But Old Lady, skittering quick as a gingham lizard, cornered him in a dead end, and Charlie holed up in this old hermit's cabin and wouldn't come out, no matter how she whammed door, window, or knothole with amber-colored fist or trounced her ritual fires, explaining to him that he was certainly her son *now*, all right.

"Charlie, you *there?*" she asked, cutting holes in the door planks with her bright little slippery eyes.

"I'm all of me here," he replied finally, very tired.

Maybe he would fall out on the ground any moment. She wrestled the knob hopefully. Perhaps a pinch too much frog powder had grated the lock wrong. She always overdid or underdid her miracles, she mused angrily, never doing them *exact*, Devil take it!

"Charlie, I only wants someone to night-prattle to, someone to warm hands with at the fire. Someone to fetch kindling for me mornings and fight off the spunks that come creeping of early fogs! I ain't got no fetchings on you for myself, son, just for your company." She smacked her lips. "Tell you what, Charles, you come out and I *teach* you things!"

"What things?" he suspicioned.

"Teach you how to buy cheap, sell high. Catch a snow

weasel, cut off its head, carry it warm in your hind pocket. There!''

"Aw," said Charlie.

She made haste. "Teach you to make yourself shotproof. So if anyone bangs at you with a gun, nothing happens."

When Charlie stayed silent, she gave him the secret in a high, fluttering whisper. "Dig and stitch mouse-ear roots on Friday during full moon, and wear 'em around your neck in a white silk.''

"You're *crazy*," Charlie said.

"Teach you how to stop blood or make animals stand frozen or make blind horses see, all them things I'll teach you! Teach you to cure a swelled-up cow and unbewitch a goat. Show you how to make yourself invisible!''

"Oh," said Charlie.

Old Lady's heart beat like a Salvation tambourine.

The knob turned from the other side.

"You," said Charlie, "are funning me."

"No, I'm not," exclaimed Old Lady. "Oh, Charlie, why, I'll make you like a window, see right through you. Why, child, you'll be surprised!''

"Real invisible?"

"Real invisible!"

"You won't fetch onto me if I walk out?"

"Won't touch a bristle of you, son."

"Well," he drawled reluctantly, "all right."

The door opened. Charlie stood in his bare feet, head down, chin against chest. "Make me invisible," he said.

"First we got to catch us a bat," said Old Lady. "Start lookin'!''

She gave him some jerky beef for his hunger and watched him climb a tree. He went high up and high up and it was nice seeing him there and it was nice having him here and all about after so many years alone with nothing to say good morning to but bird droppings and silvery snail tracks.

Pretty soon a bat with a broken wing fluttered down out of the tree. Old Lady snatched it up, beating warm and shrieking between its porcelain white teeth, and Charlie dropped down after it, hand upon clenched hand, yelling.

That night, with the moon nibbling at the spiced pine cones, Old Lady extracted a long silver needle from under her

wide blue dress. Gumming her excitement and secret anticipation, she sighted up the dead bat and held the cold needle
steady-steady.

She had long ago realized that her miracles, despite all
perspirations and salts and sulfurs, failed. But she had always
dreamed that one day the miracles might start functioning,
might spring up in crimson flowers and silver stars to prove
that God had forgiven her for her pink body and her pink
thoughts and her warm body and her warm thoughts as a
young miss. But so far God had made no sign and said no
word, but nobody knew this except Old Lady.

"Ready?" she asked Charlie, who crouched cross-kneed,
wrapping his pretty legs in long goose-pimpled arms, his
mouth open, making teeth. "Ready," he whispered, shivering.

"There!" She plunged the needle deep in the bat's right
eye. "So!"

"Oh!" screamed Charlie, wadding up his face.

"Now I wrap it in gingham, and here, put it in your
pocket, keep it there, bat and all. Go on!"

He pocketed the charm.

"Charlie!" she shrieked fearfully. "Charlie, where *are*
you? I can't *see* you, child!"

"Here!" He jumped so the light ran in red streaks up his
body. "I'm here, Old Lady!" He stared wildly at his arms,
legs, chest, and toes. "I'm here!"

Her eyes looked as if they were watching a thousand
fireflies crisscrossing each other in the wild night air.

"Charlie, oh, you went *fast!* Quick as a hummingbird! Oh,
Charlie, come *back* to me!"

"But I'm *here!*" he wailed.

"Where?"

"By the fire, the fire! And—and I can see myself. I'm not
invisible at all!"

Old Lady rocked on her lean flanks. " 'Course *you* can see
you! Every invisible person knows himself. Otherwise, how
could you eat, walk, or get around places? Charlie, touch me.
Touch me so I *know* you."

Uneasily he put out a hand.

She pretended to jerk, startled, at his touch. *"Ah!"*

"You mean to say you can't *find* me?" he asked. "Truly?"

"Not the least half rump of you!"

She found a tree to stare at, and stared at it with shining

eyes, careful not to glance at him. "Why, I sure *did* a trick *that* time!" She sighed with wonder. "Whooeee. Quickest invisible I *ever* made! Charlie. Charlie, how you *feel?*"

"Like creek water—all stirred."

"You'll settle."

Then after a pause she added, "Well, what you going to do now, Charlie, since you're invisible?"

All sorts of things shot through his brain, she could tell. Adventures stood up and danced like fire in his eyes, and his mouth, just hanging, told what it meant to be a boy who imagined himself like the mountain winds. In a cold dream he said, "I'll run across wheat fields, climb snow mountains, steal white chickens off'n farms. I'll kick pink pigs when they ain't looking. I'll pinch pretty girls' legs when they sleep, snap their garters in schoolrooms." Charlie looked at Old Lady, and from the shiny tips of her eyes she saw something wicked shape his face. "And other things I'll do, I'll do, I will," he said.

"Don't try nothing on me," warned Old Lady. "I'm brittle as spring ice and I don't take handling." Then: "What about your folks?"

"My folks?"

"You can't fetch yourself home looking like that. Scare the inside ribbons out of them. Your mother'd faint straight back like timber falling. Think they want you about the house to stumble over and your ma have to call you every three minutes, even though you're in the room next her elbow?"

Charlie had not considered it. He sort of simmered down and whispered out a little "Gosh," and felt of his long bones carefully.

"You'll be mighty lonesome. People looking through you like a water glass, people knocking you aside because they didn't reckon you to be underfoot. And women, Charlie, *women*—"

He swallowed. "What about women?"

"No woman will be giving you a second stare. And no woman wants to be kissed by a boy's mouth they can't even *find!*"

Charlie dug his bare toe in the soil contemplatively. He pouted. "Well, I'll stay invisible, anyway, for a spell. I'll have me some fun. I'll just be pretty careful, is all. I'll stay out from in front of wagons and horses and Pa. Pa shoots at the nariest sound." Charlie blinked. "Why, with me invisible, someday Pa might just up and fill me with buckshot, thinkin' I was a hill squirrel in the dooryard. Oh . . ."

Old Lady nodded at a tree. "That's likely."

"Well," he decided slowly, "I'll stay invisible for tonight, and tomorrow you can fix me back all whole again, Old Lady."

"Now if that ain't just like a critter, always wanting to be what he can't be," remarked Old Lady to a beetle on a log.

"What you mean?" said Charlie.

"Why," she explained, "it was real hard work, fixing you up. It'll take a little *time* for it to wear off. Like a coat of paint wears off, boy."

"You!" he cried. "You did this to me! Now you make me back, you make me seeable!"

"Hush," she said. "It'll wear off, a hand or a foot at a time."

"How'll it look, me around the hills with just one hand showing!"

"Like a five-winged bird hopping on the stones and bramble."

"Or a foot showing!"

"Like a small pink rabbit jumping thicket."

"Or my head floating!"

"Like a hairy balloon at the carnival!"

"How long before I'm *whole?*" he asked.

She deliberated that it might pretty well be an entire year.

He groaned. He began to sob and bite his lips and make fists. "You magicked me, you did this, you did this thing to me. Now I won't be able to run home!"

She winked. "But you *can* stay here, child, stay on with me real comfortlike, and I'll keep you fat and saucy."

He flung it out: "You did this on purpose! You mean old hag, you want to keep me here!"

He ran off through the shrugs on the instant.

"Charlie, come back!"

No answer but the patter of his feet on the soft dark turf and his wet choking cry which passed swiftly off and away.

She waited and then kindled herself a fire. "He'll be back," she whispered. And thinking inward on herself, she said, "And now I'll have me my company through spring and into late summer. Then, when I'm tired of him and want a silence, I'll send him home.''

Charlie returned noiselessly with the first gray of dawn, gliding over the rimed turf to where Old Lady sprawled like a bleached stick before the scattered ashes.

He sat on some creek pebbles and stared at her.

She didn't dare look at him or beyond. He had made no sound, so how could she know he was anywhere about? She couldn't.

He sat there, tear marks on his cheeks.

Pretending to be just waking—but she had found no sleep from one end of the night to the other—Old Lady stood up, grunting and yawning, and turned in a circle to the dawn.

''Charlie?''

Her eyes passed from pines to soil, to sky, to the far hills. She called out his name, over and over again, and she felt like staring plumb straight at him, but she stopped herself. ''Charlie? Oh, Charles!'' she called, and heard the echoes say the very same.

He sat, beginning to grin a bit, suddenly, knowing he was close to her, yet she must feel alone. Perhaps he felt the growing of a secret power, perhaps he felt secure from the world, certainly he was *pleased* with his invisibility.

She said aloud, ''Now, where *can* that boy be? If he only made a noise so I could tell just where he is, maybe I'd fry him a breakfast.''

She prepared the morning victuals, irritated at his continuous quiet. She sizzled bacon on a hickory stick. ''The smell of it will draw his nose,'' she muttered.

While her back was turned, he swiped all the frying bacon and devoured it tastily.

She whirled, crying out, ''Lord!''

She eyed the clearing suspiciously. ''Charlie, that *you?*''

Charlie wiped his mouth clean on his wrists.

She trotted about the clearing, making like she was trying to locate him. Finally, with a clever thought, acting blind, she headed straight for him, groping. ''Charlie, where *are* you?''

A lightning streak, he evaded her, bobbing, ducking.

It took all her willpower not to give chase, but you can't chase invisible boys, so she sat down, scowling, sputtering, and tried to fry more bacon. But every fresh strip she cut he would steal bubbling off the fire and run away far. Finally, cheeks burning, she cried, "I know where you are! Right *there!* I hear you run!" She pointed to one side of him, not too accurate. He ran again. "Now you're there!" she shouted. "There, and there!" pointing to all the places he was in the next five minutes. "I hear you press a grass blade, knock a flower, snap a twig. I got fine shell ears, delicate as roses. They can hear the stars moving!"

Silently he galloped off among the pines, his voice trailing back, "Can't hear me when I'm set on a rock. I'll just *set!*"

All day he sat on an observatory rock in the clear wind, motionless and sucking his tongue.

Old Lady gathered wood in the deep forest, feeling his eyes weaseling on her spine. She wanted to babble: "Oh, I see you, I see you! I was only fooling about invisible boys! You're right there!" But she swallowed her gall and gummed it tight.

The following morning he did the spiteful things. He began leaping from behind trees. He made toad-faces, frog-faces, spider-faces at her, clenching down his lips with his fingers, popping his raw eyes, pushing up his nostrils so you could peer in and see his brain thinking.

Once she dropped her kindling. She pretended it was a blue jay startled her.

He made a motion as if to strangle her.

She trembled a little.

He made another move as if to bang her shins and spit on her cheek.

These motions she bore without a lid flicker or a mouth twitch.

He stuck out his tongue, making strange bad noises. He wiggled his loose ears so she wanted to laugh, and finally she did laugh and explained it away quickly by saying, "Sat on a salamander! Whew, how it poked!"

By high noon the whole madness boiled to a terrible peak.

For it was at that exact hour that Charlie came racing down the valley stark boy-naked!

Old Lady nearly fell flat with shock!

"Charlie!" she almost cried.

Charlie raced naked up one side of a hill and naked down the other—naked as day, naked as the moon, raw as the sun and a newborn chick, his feet shimmering and rushing like the wings of a low-skimming hummingbird.

Old Lady's tongue locked in her mouth. What could she say? Charlie, go dress? For *shame? Stop* that? *Could* she? Oh, Charlie, Charlie, God! Could she say that now? *Well?*

Upon the big rock, she witnessed him dancing up and down, naked as the day of his birth, stomping bare feet, smacking his hands on his knees and sucking in and out his white stomach like blowing and deflating a circus balloon.

She shut her eyes tight and prayed.

After three hours of this she pleaded, "Charlie, Charlie, come here! I got something to *tell* you!"

Like a fallen leaf he came, dressed again, praise the Lord.

"Charlie," she said, looking at the pine trees, "I see your right toe. *There* it is."

"You do?" he said.

"Yes," she said very sadly. "There it is like a horny toad on the grass. And there, up there's your left ear hanging on the air like a pink butterfly."

Charlie danced. "I'm forming in, I'm forming in!"

Old Lady nodded. "Here comes your ankle!"

"Gimme *both* my feet!" ordered Charlie.

"You got 'em."

"How about my hands?"

"I see one crawling on your knee like a daddy longlegs."

"How about the other one?"

"It's crawling too."

"I got a body?"

"Shaping up fine."

"I'll need my head to go home, Old Lady."

To go home, she thought wearily. "No!" she said, stubborn and angry. "No, you ain't got no head. No head at all," she cried. She'd leave that to the very last. "No head, no head," she insisted.

"No head?" he wailed.

"Yes, oh, my God, yes, yes, you got your blamed head!" she snapped, giving up. "Now, fetch me back my bat with the needle in his eye!"

He flung it at her. "Haaaa-yoooo!" His yelling went all up the valley, and long after he had run toward home she heard his echoes, racing.

Then she plucked up her kindling with a great dry weari-

ness and started back toward her shack, sighing, talking. And
Charlie followed her all the way, *really* invisible now, so she
couldn't see him, just hear him, like a pine cone dropping or
a deep underground stream trickling, or a squirrel clambering
a bough; and over the fire at twilight she and Charlie sat, him
so invisible, and her feeding him bacon he wouldn't take, so
she ate it herself, and then she fixed some magic and fell
asleep with Charlie, made out of sticks and rags and pebbles,
but still warm and her very own son, slumbering and nice in
her shaking mother arms . . . and they talked about golden
things in drowsy voices until dawn made the fire slowly,
slowly wither out. . . .

THE HERO WHO RETURNED

by Gerald W. Page

*Born in Tennessee and residing in Georgia, Gerald
W. Page (born in 1939) is the author or editor of
many works of fantasy and horror. But he insists
that his major interest is really science fiction. His
emphasis on character is illustrated by the following
story of a knight's decision to rest a spell.*

There was a place where the river Amdemon broadened,
becoming not a lake but something like a lake, where there
was almost no discernible current, a place just far enough
across so that, with a little imagination you might stand on
one shore and ignore the other, pretending it did not exist,
imagining that you stood on the very edge of Land, staring
out at the rest of the world, which is water, brown-green and
cool, inviting and peaceful.

But there was another side, of course, and it was quite
close by the standards of lakes, if not rivers, and could be
plainly seen even on those mornings when the mists dispatched their doomed armadas against the invasion of the
sun's heat; and evenings when the fog rolled in from the
marshes to the south, you could see it too, a ghostly presence
across the shrouded water, another world firmly anchored to
the one of this shore. Here, where the river Amdemon broadened and its currents gentled, here Dunsan had built his ferry.

There was a sloping pier that dipped down into the water
and onto which, by means of a strong windlass, the ferryboat
could be hauled out of the river. The boat itself was a
platform of thick, square-hewn logs, lashed and pegged
together, secured to a long cable that ran from this side to the
other, where it joined another landing pier. By means of this

cable and a windlass on the boat itself, Dunsan could pull the boat across the Amdemon in either direction, whatever the current or whim of the river, and in most sorts of weather.

And also on this side of the river, Dunsan lived in a small house with his young wife, Maelwyd. It was a quiet life for the two of them, and at times that worried Dunsan. For while he was well enough suited to such a life, Maelwyd was young; and it seemed to him that a woman like Maelwyd was more than he had the right to expect of life. Hers was a slender, strong, and supple body, and a cheerful disposition; she was a capable and caring wife for a ferryman such as Dunsan. But there were times when he would catch her staring out across the river, except that he could tell she saw no water, and likely not the land. He knew not what were the images in her mind, then, what thoughts, what longings. The idea of her like that, especially knowing how she strove to keep such things hidden from him, hurt Dunsan sorely. There were needs in her, he realized, that he had no way of satisfying. To the north the river might broaden to make its fierce current tame itself and remain thus calmed until it narrowed again to the south, but there was no broadening Dunsan knew of which might calm the longing in Maelwyd's heart, save the broadening of time.

And there was another thing, too, that cast a grim shadow across Dunsan's thoughts: the cold thing men crossed this river to do.

Faulk was such a man. He came afoot and Dunsan knew by the very glint of sunlight on his polished helm as he appeared on the hill and stared down to the yard, that he was such a man. He carried a sword at his side and wore a round shield slung across his back. As he came down the hill, Faulk removed his helm and slung it to his shield, for the sun was hot that afternoon. His hair, of middle length, was brown, and his crisp short beard was trimmed to the barest suggestion of a point. When Faulk came into the yard, Dunsan discerned a hint of gray among the brown of that hair and beard, and he saw more, much more, in those smoldering volcanic eyes that peered from under thick, lowered brows.

Faulk stopped at a polite distance and said his name to Dunsan, who nodded and gave his own name back to the visitor, thinking as he did so, of all of them, all those fine, strong heroes who came to this place where the Amdemon broadened and grew calm. . . . Came to cross the river on Dunsan's ferryboat, to meet the thing that waited for them in that keep on the other side. . . .

But he hid his thoughts and muttered the same polite formalities he always muttered, inviting the man to stay the night and share meals with Dunsan and his wife. And Faulk, as all the fine heroes did, nodded and thanked him, giving the appearance of a man most impressed with the hospitality of another toward a stranger; save that he begged the coming indoors of it, explaining, "I'm a man not comfortable with walls, and less so with roofs above me. The comfort of your yard will do me tonight for a bed and this fine grass covers as good a table as any silken cloth."

To which Dunsan replied, "It's not likely you'll find anything silken in this house, although my good wife is a gentle woman to whom I would soon give all such things as she might ask, if it were in my power. But you are not the first guest here to have no love of walls, and you'll find no less hospitality for that."

And afterward, Faulk went down to look at the ferryboat, which was hoisted onto the sloping log pier, and the two men fell to discussing the price of the meals and the morrow's ride, for which Dunsan named a figure that Faulk found agreeable. That settled, the warrior rose his eyes from the ferry and, for the first time, gazed toward the far side of the river, where a row of trees could be seen like a horizon of green smoke just above the water, and where, beyond those trees, a vertical line of smoke, gray and possibly real, rose up.

For a moment, Dunsan watched Faulk's face, but he saw no change. So he said, "Even on the hottest day there's smoke from that place."

"Kershenlee's keep?"

"Aye. It rises every day, warm or wintry."

"A ghostly smoke," Faulk said. Then he looked at Dunsan and his thick brows rose. "Have you ever thought of going there to see the thing yourself?"

Dunsan laughed. "Have you ever thought of crossing the river with your own ferry?" And Faulk returned the laughter.

Dunsan went into the house, leaving Faulk to his own comfort. Maelwyd was staring out the small window. She had a pale face with large, shining blue eyes above high, flaring cheekbones. Her long, pale-red hair was tied back, her custom while working, and she stood on her toes to reach the window. Dunsan closed the door and she reached out to touch his hand, without looking back. Dunsan peered over her shoulder, through the window. Faulk was unloading gear in the shade of the apple tree midway between the house and the river.

"Look at him," she said, hush-voiced. "Look at how fine he is."

"A type we've seen often enough before," said Dunsan, turning away to wash the yard dirt from his hands in the crockery bowl on the stand by the window. "In truth, he seems less fine than most, with that plain suit of his, and the shield that has no emblem, and his plain sword. He even lacks a horse."

"And how," she asked, "do we know but what he rode a great beast that was but recently slain in combat. Not that it matters. There's still a quality to him, horse or not. And he's no prince's hireling, but a champion in earnest. A man whose shield has no blazonment serves no conscience but his own."

To which Dunsan tossed up both hands in defeat and said, "Your imagination will likely be my death, child-bride. Belike the man outside is too practical for these musings and would prefer the solid comforts of our kitchen to your speculations."

And Maelwyd smiled deeply at him, though it struck Dunsan that there was a peculiarity to her smile just then, that he did not understand. But he shoved that from his thoughts as Maelwyd began busying herself with the fixing of the meal.

That night the sky was cloudless. It seemed that every star there was crowded into the heavens to look down in Dunsan's yard to see who it was that guested there. And when Faulk had eaten and drank a measure of Dunsan's metheglin, he leaned himself against the apple tree's trunk, thanked the husband and wife for their hospitality, and then looked where the river was glistening with moon and starlight. After a moment of such looking, Faulk said, "It saddens me that I won't be able to spend more time on this bank of the river."

Maelwyd glanced over at him. "Yet if you came here on foot, then you must be anxious about that which calls you to the other shore."

Faulk delivered a sigh with his answer. "Oh, yes, I'm anxious enough. Though the way of it is heavy on me."

Maelwyd was seated on the grass, and Dunsan beside her, watching. He saw his wife lean forward, her eyes shining as much with eagerness as with moonlight. She said, "There must be hundreds of stories you could tell us."

"And be a poor guest to bore you with them," Faulk replied. "No. No, on a night like this it's best to count stars and taste the air."

"The stars are there almost every night," she said. "And the air is plentiful. But guests and their stories are rare, and not to be wasted when we have them. So tell us some of yours and let us be the judges of whether they bore us or not."

And there was no arguing with Maelwyd's words, and less with the look of her child-woman's face, and in her grown-woman's eyes, and Faulk surrendered, as he might never have surrendered to a troll or tyrant. And seated there, with his back against the tree, he began to speak in his slow, deep voice about things he had seen, had heard, had done in his life; about the two ogres of Allanfroth, and how they were slain with his sword; of his encounter with the witch Nrostin, whom he could not bring himself to slay because of the way she wept over the corpse of her lover, dead these four hundred years; of how he accompanied Ongeau in the campaign against the evil lords of Narosyde and Glester. He spoke, also, of heroes he had campaigned with; at the sound of his voice those legends seemed to spring to very life, there in the yard: Sebor the Monk; Clourmwendel, who single-handedly held the Ligl pass against an army for four days before he was slain; Quey-Jinair and Sreka and Blayshorn and Merthandor—true men, each of them, but who might have been gods for all that Maelwyd had ever seen of them.

And Dunsan, who had run the ferry since long before he married Maelwyd, had met none of them either, because none of them had yet sought their death across the river, as Faulk was now seeking his.

After a time Faulk came to an end of storytelling, and Dunsan and Maelwyd went inside their small house.

In the flickering light of a single candle, Dunsan watched Maelwyd comb her hair.

She sat in front of the mirror that was her most treasured possession and that had cost Dunsan the revenue of four passages across the river. But tonight her gaze seemed not merely to peer into her mirror but through it and beyond it, to another world, perhaps. Or possibly, only to just beyond the wall, where, in the yard, a strong, grim hero stretched himself out to sleep. Maelwyd's face, her softly lovely face, child and woman, lover and goddess, that infinite face of hers, fascinated Dunsan; but he could not read it. He could not fathom the thoughts that worked behind that face. But he could hear, in his mind, the seeming echo of Faulk's voice telling how he and Blayshorn had ridden down on a caravan of ghouls to rout them and free their captives; and how he had mistakenly engaged King Ongeau in a battle that had raged for most of a day before, exhausted, each discovered who it was he fought. Dunsan could not but believe that the same echo ran in the wistful canyons of Maelwyd's mind.

And after a time, her hair was combed and Maelwyd changed into her nightclothes, while her husband changed into his own. She bent low to blow out the candle, and on her face, in the last glow of that fitful light, Dunsan saw that same remote expression he had watched in the mirror. He spent the night in restive sleep.

He rose early, well before the light, and dressed hurriedly to hide the mass confusion of his thoughts. Maelwyd was still asleep, her soft fine hair an umbra for her delicate pale face, in the lucent darkness. For the space between heartbeats, he gazed absently at her face. Then he went from the room and out of the house and across to one of the small sheds that occupied a corner of the yard.

There were few animals to be tended. A goat, which gave them milk, a part of which they drank and another part of which Maelwyd made into cheese; and a few chickens, which provided them with eggs. The river provided an occasional catch of fish and the nearby forest provided game. Their vegetables came from a small garden, which they tended. The shed Dunsan went to, therefore, housed no animals, but was filled with other things: barrels and tools, wood stored for the needs of the winter, some pots, some chests. There were not many things, and what there was certainly represented no conceivable wealth, but the variety was notable. Dunsan rummaged in the largest chest and there, behind a leather harness for the plow horse he did not have, he found his sword.

Or what he called his sword. And indeed it was his by right of possession, for it had been handed him as a gift by his uncle, an old campaigner who had retired, with the loss of an eye at the battle of Heas. But whether Dunsan had ever earned such a thing as the right to carry any sword that had been a sword in battle, that was a question. Dunsan had worn the thing only once, the day it was given to him. It had been too large for his not-yet-grown body and he had let himself be talked into putting it away until such time as he grew into it. But by then, there were other things to worry with than swords. This one had not been used since his uncle had lost his eye.

Though the sword and scabbard were kept wrapped in good cloth, the scabbard was dingy and worn. Dunsan took the sword's time-dulled hilt and pulled the blade free, finding it reluctant to come at first. And when it did come, he saw that the metal of the blade was darkened, though it was not too pitted with rust, except where it joined the hilt. He held it to the light of his lantern. Somehow it did not seem the formidable thing it had seemed to be when he was younger. It was a common-looking blade. Its single edge was dull and bore two small nicks. He had worked iron in his youth, before becoming a ferryman, and he judged this metal to be rather cheap. He was sure it could not hold an edge through much use.

But why should it? What need did he have of a sword with or without an edge?

None, he told himself. But then why was he here, looking at the blade he had not unwrapped in all these years?

Because he was a fool, he told himself. And a fearful fool, at that.

Dunsan shoved the sword back into its scabbard, slamming the hilt in place with a loud, satisfying smack of the guard against the scabbard lip. Wrapping it back in its cloth, he put the sword back into the chest and closed the lid.

Outside, the sun was beginning to cast its light. Frugally, Dunsan blew the lantern out and glanced toward the apple tree. He saw the glint of sunlight off the edge of Faulk's shield, propped against the tree's trunk.

Faulk was arranging his meager gear. Dunsan watched him work, telling himself that his interest in Faulk was merely an excuse to enjoy the fresh morning air that was still tinted with dew. But he watched for a moment only, then went to tend to the feeding of the goat and chickens.

That done, he started for the house. Maelwyd stood in the doorway and Faulk was seated nearby on the ground.

She was so beautiful standing there, the Maelwyd he loved so dearly, Dunsan was almost robbed of breath. She was wearing her finest dress, which was the color of beryl, and cut simply, although on her it looked as good as any gown on any queen. A band of white ribbon held her hair back from her brow, but let it fall thick and full to her shoulders. The morning light, now full, spun gold in that hair of Maelwyd's, and cast diamond glints in her eyes. She glanced up briefly as Dunsan approached, but her eyes left him as they came and returned to watching their guest. Faulk held her attention fully.

Dunsan felt something inside him, a thing he had suspected, even feared, before, but had never felt until now. It made it hard to breathe.

Faulk looked up from his breakfast, at his approaching host, and said, "Your fine wife recalled my dislike of walls, Dunsan, and bade me eat my breakfast here."

"He's been telling me more of his adventures," said she.

Slowly, sadly, Faulk shook his head. "No, not adventures, lady. Mischance, perhaps. But not adventure."

"They have the sound of adventure to me," she persisted. "The life you've led, the places you've seen—Lemas, Coingcerlejon, Muysange, Nickling, Tylosk, Pevery . . . places such as I've never seen."

"Fine places," Faulk agreed, though there was a definite hint of reservation in his tone. "Or fine enough. But they aren't to my taste, though I've seen them. Walls. Too many walls. You have a better place here than any of those cities are. These trees are more splendid than all the banners of Lemas, or the frescoes of Tylosk. And this river—!"

"Amdemon is the same river that flows past Lemas," she reminded.

"Maybe so," he said, wiping gravy from his plate with a piece of bread. "But there it has a stronger current than here. It might be that the Amdemon is the gentlest of the Nine Rivers, but here and only here is it truly placid, and here and only here are the shores anything but rocky coasts and high cliffs. Here. . ."

He let his words trail off, as if he knew what he wanted to

say, but had concluded it did not need saying. Maelwyd's eyes stayed on him, and Dunsan's remained on her.

Dunsan moved to Maelwyd's side, and though her hand sought his, it seemed more a gesture of habit than affection: a reflex of their married state; a signal of time, not feeling. Again he felt the quivering gelid fear that made it hard to breathe. Maelwyd's eyes came up, at last, from their gazing at Faulk and looked out across the land to the water, across the water, which was already glittering silver veined with dull iron. Her forehead furrowed, the habit of one who views critically.

She tugged at Dunsan's hand.

They went inside. His place at the table was set, but not hers. She let go of his hand and hastened about the room, serving food into his dish. He asked, "And you?"

"I've eaten already," she said. "I knew you'd want me to, since it would be a courtesy for one of us to eat with our guest."

"Aye," said Dunsan, sitting to his breakfast and not looking at her.

As he started eating, she sat down across the table from him.

"Tell me," she said.

Startled, he looked up at her. "Tell you what?"

"Your life. Before I knew you. Before you were a ferryman."

He chewed a mouthful of food and swallowed it before answering. "I was always a ferryman."

"Stranger than a caul, to be born with a ferryboat!" she said, laughing.

"Don't mock me," he said evenly. "You already know my life."

"But as a youth," she pleaded.

"I was a farmer," he said. "And then I worked as a smith. But I found the river cooler than the forge. I've told all this to you."

"And that's your life?" There was frustration in her tone. "That's the whole of your life? You've never been anything else? You never wanted to be anything else? Not even a soldier?"

"There haven't been any wars since I was a child," he told her.

She looked at him as if something in his words bore a

significance he had not realized. She said, "You never were, but you wanted to be. Is that so?"

"A soldier? It's dull work. And a hard life for little pay and less freedom—to say nothing of the risk."

"All men dream about being soldiers at one time or another, don't they? Even you, I suspect, when you were a child. Haven't you ever owned a sword at some time or other?"

He chewed his food slowly. "What difference does that make?"

"You did own one!"

"It was my uncle's. He gave it to me when he grew unfit for it."

"Ah! And a good keen blade it was, I'll wager. Were strong runes inscribed in it? Had it drunk much blood? I wager it had a deep runnel for the blood—"

"The grooves they put in the lengths of swordblades aren't for that purpose," he said pedantically. "They're there to lighten the blade and give strength—"

"Then you know a bit about such matters?"

"I told you. I was an ironsmith."

"And this sword your uncle gave you. Was it the way I described?"

"It was an ordinary sword for an ordinary soldier. It was cheaply made, sturdy, and usable. There were no fancy carvings on it. It had a poor balance to it. The blade was plain and practical and took a nick every time it struck another sword, and sometimes when all it struck was bone. It was too heavy. I doubt it was any good to be anything more than a plain sword and to slaughter a pig for dinner, on occasion." He paused a moment, thinking back. "I gave some thought to it once. I could have fixed the balance. Could have hollowed the pommel and filled it with lead. It would still have been too . . . But no matter, I never did it."

"What became of it?"

"It's in a chest. Out in the shed."

"Then let me see it."

He moved uncomfortably in his chair. "There's nothing to see. It's old. It has a tarnished blade. It's been fifteen years since the thing was sharpened, Maelwyd. It ought to be sold. Or better, it ought to be melted down and the metal put to some practical use."

"My practical husband," she called him. And, though she

smiled, he felt himself shudder at her voice, not because it frightened him with the import of its tone, but because he could discover no import in it at all. He gave his head a slow shaking and pushed his chair back from the table. "I have a passenger needs taking across the river," he said.

Still smiling, she watched him as he stood. Then she rose and began clearing the table. Bleakly, Dunsan went outside. Faulk was waiting by the ferryboat, seated on a huge rock by the pier. Dunsan watched him a moment, then turned, and instead of going down to the river, went to the shed in the corner of the yard.

He found the sword, still wrapped, and lifted it from the chest. It seemed to him, even as he did it, a foolish thing, but he did it anyway, not knowing why. He left the shed and went down the slope to the ferryboat.

Faulk nodded at him. Dunsan returned the nod. Without a word, he stored the wrapped sword in a chest that was filled with rope, then he began inspecting the boat, as he always did before a crossing. Faulk watched him without a word, until he was finished. Then he said, "You're a cautious man."

"The boat's not in use as much as it should be."

"Not many cross here, I suppose?"

"One sort only," Dunsan said pointedly. "And there's never a return trip."

Faulk nodded and stared at the river.

Dunsan peered at Faulk, trying to see more in the warrior's face than could possibly be seen there. He asked, "Why?"

Faulk looked at him strangely.

"Why?" Dunsan asked again. "I—I want to know."

Faulk nodded in that slow, certain way he had, and gave a quick glance up the slope, toward the house. Then he looked across the river. Beyond the trees on the far shore, a plume of thin smoke trailed upward in the morning air.

And Faulk said, "If you mean my life, I can't tell you."

"I mean only Kershenlee," said Dunsan. "You aren't like the others who come to challenge that ghost. The others are young. They have things to prove, if not to the world, then to themselves. What have you to prove, and who must you prove it to?"

Faulk's eyes flashed, and for a moment Dunsan feared he had made him angry. But when he spoke, his voice was not angry. "Perhaps two months back, there was another who came this way. Can you remember him?"

"I remember all of them. You mean a youth, fine, strong, well-armed, in expensive armor? He was the last before you, and the first this year."

Faulk spoke then, in a strange voice. "A hero. Fine, stalwart hero."

"Most that I carry across the river are."

"This one. Have you seen him since?"

"I never see any of them but the once," said Dunsan.

And Faulk nodded, as if the fact were elemental. "But this one, Tarvern, was my son."

"Oh," said Dunsan.

He had been on the verge of begging Faulk not to go, but now he knew that was not possible. He asked, "Have you other sons?"

"None but Tarvern. Are we ready yet, ferryman?"

"We're ready," Dunsan said. Then, suddenly, he added, "Do you know how many there've been? One comes every few months. Almost every one of them is young, and all of them are strong and well-armed. And since this is the only place the river can be safely crossed, they come to me and pay me a few coins, and I take them across. And I never see them again."

"So?"

"What makes you think you aren't going to your death?"

"The others were young," Faulk said. "None of them had faced as many foes as I have, none survived as many battles. Are we ready to cross?"

Dunsan gave a gesture of hopelessness. "We are. But—"

"The day won't get any younger," Faulk said, and didn't look at him.

It was not until they were almost to the middle of the river that either spoke again. Dunsan turned to Faulk and said, "At least you don't have to go alone."

"And who would go with me?" Faulk asked. "You? You're no fighting man."

"I'd be better than nothing."

"No, you wouldn't. I'd have to watch out for you constantly. I'd have to tell you what to do. Kershenlee is no ordinary foe. If you made a wrong move, it would be the end of both of us, likely."

"Then go back. Find others who are fighting men to go with you. It doesn't make sense to do this thing alone."

"Sense. That word means nothing in this world. Where's the sense in you asking to come with me?"

Dunsan knew no answer to that one.

Faulk went on with a certain melancholy. "She's young, but she's not stupid. It's you she loves, Dunsan. You could make yourself a grave mistake if you aren't careful."

"She was once in love with me, I know that. I'm not so sure now."

"Then look into her face."

"She's never known anyone but me. For years I've been virtually the only person she's seen, me and the ones who buy passage to cross the river. I saw her face when you came, Faulk."

"I'm an older man than you are," Faulk reminded.

"But you're no ferryman or farmer. That sword you carry cuts away the years, in her eyes, as easily as it cuts butter. Can a life like mine compare to one so romantic as your own?"

"Romance. Can you show me how to spend it? Or eat it, or wear it?"

"You can barely do those things with a ferryman's income," Dunsan said. "Maelwyd is young. She longs to see more of the world, to do things she's only heard about, before the years rob her of the opportunity."

Faulk made a scoffing noise.

"I'm fearful of losing her," Dunsan heard himself say weakly.

Faulk stood at the rail, staring out over the brown river. "She'd not be the happier knowing you could die in combat the way my son died."

"She might," Dunsan said quickly. He was shamed by the words as soon as he spoke them. "I—I didn't mean that. Of course, she wouldn't—"

He cut off his words and the only sound was the lapping of the water against the wood of the boat. Faulk said, "We're almost to the shore now."

So Dunsan busied himself with the landing. But when they were on the ground again, he turned to Faulk and said, "Tell me about this Kershenlee."

Faulk was adjusting his shield across his back once more. "You're his nearest neighbor."

"I've never met him. Or anyone who has."

"He was once a great hero," Faulk said. "He fought in wars and duels before either of us was born."

"I know that. This curse—"

"He slew a wizard, but not quickly enough to prevent a curse from being laid on him. He was betrayed, later, and slain, when you and I were still at our mothers' knees. He haunts what was once his own keep, and many a fine young man has died fighting his ghost."

"You'd think there would be fewer fighting men come to fight a ghost, and more priests. Or maybe minor wizards."

"You might think that. Have you carried any on your boat?"

"A few. And as armed as the plain soldiers."

"And did they return, Dunsan? Any of them?"

"None."

"Then it is as likely a soldier's job as a priest's, isn't it?" And with those words, Faulk smiled, and turned, and vanished into the forest.

"I'll wait here for you," Dunsan shouted after him, as he always shouted. He always waited—for a while. He owed them that.

Besides, what more could he do?

The morning gave way to noon, and noon to afternoon, and the waiting Dunsan went, every once in a while, to the forest's edge, to peer in among the trees and patchwork shadows, but there came no sign of any returning hero. And Dunsan fretted, and thought to himself, and worried over Faulk. The afternoon was not old at all by the time Dunsan told himself that Faulk would not be coming back.

But still he stared into the forest, while telling himself that a thinking man would go back across the river to his own landing, to his own, small house, back to Maelwyd. And after a time he stopped arguing with himself. He got to his feet and went to the boat and rummaged among the coils of rope and found the sword he had put there. Leaving it still wrapped in its cloth, he made a sling for it and hung it across his back as he had seen Faulk do with his shield. And with no idea why, and no idea what he would do when the time came that something had to be done, he followed the trail Faulk had made into the woods.

He walked slowly, listening. He found a deer path and

judged that Faulk had followed it, and he did likewise. He heard only those normal forest sounds, such as the wind makes, and birds, and even time. The deer path led to a small brook at the edge of the woods. Beyond, the ground sloped up, as his own yard sloped up from the river. He could see a portion of a fallen wall on the crest of the slope.

And there was a cold, slow chill along Dunsan's spine, too, but he ignored the thing and made himself go up the hill to the wall.

It was old. It was crudely made of rounded, imperfectly matched stones. The remarkable thing wasn't that it had fallen in places, but that it stood at all, in others. It was overgrown with vines and weeds and moss, so that there were places where you had to peer closely to see stone.

Past the wall, the ground leveled off, almost to a plateau, grassed over like a king's courtyard, but not tended with sheep, though Dunsan could not say how that meadow might really be tended. Again, the slow coldness on his spine. Again, it was ignored. He climbed over a fallen scatter of rocks, then stopped abruptly as something caught his eye.

Bones, scattered like the rocks, off to Dunsan's left, in no particular part of the field. They were plucked clean, bleached by the sun. Dunsan found bits of metal near them, all that survived of the trappings that had covered the flesh that had covered the bones.

It was as if the bones were tended and cared for, loved in their condition, while there was no concern for weapons or armor here. The skull had been cleft by a great sword. Broken and rusted, such a sword lay close by.

Dunsan walked over the placid meadow to its far side where the ground dipped down toward a road. Before starting down, he looked toward the plume of smoke that rose beyond the remaining stand of trees. And for the first time in his life, he could see the keep as well.

It was nothing more than a tower, and a rude one at that. Hardly a fortress worthy of the duels that must have been fought there. Hardly the keep of a great prince or warrior. No hero's keep.

But it was a good place for a ghost.

The road was narrow. Unlike the meadow, it gave no indication of ever having been kept in repair. It had holes where brackish water had pooled, and it was corrugated with random scars. Weeds, dry and sere, choked and almost hid the shallow, indifferent ditches that were dug on either side of the road. The trees by the road were gnarled and bent, and there were grotesquely shaped rocks, many of them taller than Dunsan himself. These rocks, and the trees, did not crowd the road by any means, and Dunsan could see the sky over his head. But his feeling, on that road, was the feeling of being in a close, dark place: a room without space to lie or sit, with barely enough height to stand in. Dunsan felt a growing anxiety and a wavering determination; but now, more than ever, it seemed to him that going back would be wrong. Then, at last, he reached the keep and it was too late to turn back.

Kershenlee's tower was a broken finger of gray dead stone that pushed against the sky. Ivy, no longer living, hung from the walls of the keep, almost to its broken upper regions. It was not tall now, and had not been when it was complete; a man with a good, strong arm would never have had much trouble throwing a rock into its upper parapet. What remained of a moat circled the keep, a sunken place for scraps of trees and various unwanted and doubtlessly unsavory plants and weeds. A shattered bridge lay with one end on the near bank, most of its timbers within.

But Dunsan ignored the bridge for now and looked, instead, at the yard that surrounded the keep. It was littered with bones and bits of bright metal. Perhaps as many as a score of men had come here to decorate this yard with their trappings and their remains, which were scattered about like a child's discarded playthings. Dunsan thought about Faulk. There had not been time for Faulk's bones to shed their skin—that is, by any normal means. But were normal means at work here? Dunsan tried not to think about it. He could not see Faulk from where he stood, but he did see one skeleton, obviously more recent than the others. It had been a tall, strong man, not old, and the armor that fell against the unfleshed bones was the armor he remembered as worn by the last young man to be ferried across the Amdemon to this shore: Faulk's son, Tarvern. His head had been dashed to pieces with an ax, much like the one he had come armed with. Dunsan shuddered and turned away from the bones of Faulk's fine young son, and went to the ancient, rotting bridge, and heard a sound.

It might have been a moan. Ghosts? He looked around. Bleak as the sky and countryside were, it was still broad daylight. Did ghosts moan in daylight? Then the sound came again, and Dunsan knew it was no ghost, but a living man. He moved to the edge of the moat and looked, and there, among the debris of the wrecked bridge, Dunsan saw Faulk. Faulk's eyes were shut, and though he moaned again, Dunsan could not tell if he was conscious.

Even without the evidence that it had fallen while Faulk was on it, Dunsan would not have trusted that bridge. He went to the moat's edge and found it steep. He drove his knife into the hard ground and held it by the hilt as he lowered himself into the waterless ditch.

When Dunsan reached his side, Faulk's eyes were open, watching. The ferryman bent beside the fighting man. He touched Faulk's right leg, and though his touch was light, Faulk shouted, "Damn that!" and slammed his open hand against the ground. "Broken leg," Dunsan said unnecessarily. Faulk looked away and uttered a disgusted curse. Dunsan quickly checked for other broken bones or injuries, finding none.

Faulk's helmet had fallen away. There was a large bruise on the right side of his forehead. Dunsan asked, "Is there any pain, except the leg and the head?"

"A broken leg," Faulk said, as if cursing himself. "Like some blasted, snot-nosed son-of-a-farmer!"

"Do you feel anything except the leg and the head?"

"I feel a damnable fool!" Faulk said. Then, "Ah! No. No pain, none but what you named, plague the devil that set my foot to that bridge!" He gave Dunsan a hard look. "Can you set it?"

"I can set it. I'm not sure I can find anything to splint it with, though."

"There's wood enough here to rebuild that ferryboat of yours."

"But you'd not get me on it, if you did," Dunsan said. "There's no wood here stout enough to use."

He took the bundle he had slung across his back and set it on the ground, still wrapped in its covering. He found two rocks, suitable to his purpose. He took the cloth from the sword and held the blade so Faulk could see it. "An heirloom," Dunsan said. "I've never used it before," he added, putting a finger to the tarnished metal. "It's of little use for its original purpose, but it might serve us here."

He propped the blade on one of the rocks, bracing the hilt on the ground with his foot. He took the other rock and brought it down hard on the sword. The blade broke with a sharp ring, loud in the dry, afternoon air. Dunsan picked up the length of broken metal. Faulk's eyes were intent upon him.

"One won't be enough," he told Faulk.

Faulk could not disguise his self-disgust as he answered, "Go ahead, go ahead," and tried to draw his sword from its scabbard, but could not. Dunsan drew it for him.

Afterward, Dunsan wrapped the blades in cloth so they would not cut into the bindings or into Faulk's leg. Then he set them down and moved to set the injured man's leg. Hesitating, he looked in Faulk's face.

"You don't have to warn me it'll hurt," Faulk said. "Just get it done with."

So Dunsan nodded—and set the leg. Faulk kept his cry to a stark intake of breath. His haggard face went pale, but he did not pass out. Dunsan quickly tied the splints in place.

Faulk talked while Dunsan worked. "Did you see Tarvern?"

Dunsan, barely attentive to the words, nodded.

Faulk lay back, staring up at the sky. "Tarvern . . . There's so many out there. I didn't realize how many there would be. Did you ferry all of them?"

"No. Some of them were already on this side of the river. Hold still."

"Their wounds. There's something strange about them, about the variety of the weapons with which they've been slain, if nothing else. It almost seems—"

"How important can that be now? Hold still."

"Oh, it's important. I don't know what makes it so, yet, but it's important. . . ."

"There. How does it feel?"

Faulk pushed himself into a sitting position and looked down at his splinted leg. "It feels well enough for a broken leg on an unarmed man," he said.

"That couldn't very well be helped," Dunsan said, standing up. He glanced toward the bank he had climbed down. Scowling, he said, "I can't get you back up that way, not without help, or at least a rope. And I don't think it would be wise to leave you here while I went back to the ferryboat to get some rope.''

"The inside bank isn't so steep," Faulk said.

"I could get you up it, I suppose," Dunsan said, looking. "But how'd I get you across the moat? The bridge is down.''

"There's another bridge, around the back. Those inside the keep wouldn't want a quick escape cut off, if they should need one, after all. But it's raised. We'll have to—''

"It's as old a bridge as this one, and likely as rotten.''

"It's been raised, and not as exposed to the elements. But we don't have any choice, do we?''

Dunsan was looking at the keep, stark and gray above them. "And us not armed," he said.

Faulk said, "Help me to my feet.''

They retrieved Faulk's shield and made their way to the inner side of the moat, close to where the fallen bridge had joined that side. Here, the moat was no more than waist-deep. Dunsan climbed out, then helped Faulk. It was a difficult chore, and a time-consuming one, but at last Faulk lay on level ground. As Dunsan sat by the moat's edge, reclaiming his breath, Faulk stared with interest at the great doorway of the keep.

Dunsan watched his face for a moment. "Even weaponless you hope to meet the thing that slew your son, don't you?''

Faulk's only answer was a grunt. Using his shield, Faulk worked himself to a standing position and moved toward the tower.

Dunsan came beside Faulk and let the soldier's arm slip across his shoulders. He took the shield from Faulk. "This thing's the wrong shape for a crutch," he said.

"The shield's the best tool a soldier has," Faulk said. "It protects as well as most armor, is lighter and more mobile. It makes a serviceable table for eating, or writing, or the reading of maps. It can be a weapon. I've killed as many men with the rim of a shield to the throat as I've killed with an ax. And if the need arises, it can be a serviceable crutch.''

"And how do you kill a ghost with a shield?" Dunsan asked.

"If there's nothing more at hand, then I'll at least make the effort," Faulk said with steadfast grimness.

The tower door was shattered, the doorway a hole of gaping blackness in the stone, a cave in gray mountains.

Dunsan, supporting Faulk, moved to the opening and stopped, peering in. The air that came from inside seemed colder, as if the darkness chilled it.

"You want to wait out here while I lower the bridge?" Dunsan said.

"No," Faulk said. But not all the starkness in his face was the result of his injury.

"Your hatred of being inside walls," Dunsan said. "It would be better if—"

"No!" Faulk shouted. Dunsan gave up the argument. They moved toward the doorway.

Inside, all was dusk, limned bleakly in shadows. Dunsan had the irrational suspicion that even in the blackness of night, it would be like this, in these ruins: luminous gray, a murky sea of clouded air through which solid objects were perceived as reefs, or rearing islands, of black.

They found a block of stone for Faulk to sit on. It was close enough to the wall that he could rest his back if he wanted to. Dunsan brushed away the cobwebs, and stirred the dust a bit, and helped Faulk to get as comfortable as he could. Then he looked around.

He saw thin sunlight through cracks around the doorway on the far side of the room. He went to the door and managed to force it open.

The bridge, just beyond the doorway, was raised. Dunsan found the mechanism that lowered it, but time and rust had done their work on it. "I'll have to find something to pry it with," he said.

"Over there," Faulk said. "Is that an ax?"

His eyes were better than Dunsan's, but a moment's peering into the lucent dusk, and Dunsan spotted the haft of what might be an ax, jutting up out of the rubble. Carefully, he moved toward it.

Faulk leaned back against the wall. "You know, those wounds," he said slowly. "Has it occurred to you that not only have the men here fallen from such a variety of wounds, but that the wounds were delivered by a ghost?"

"No ordinary ghost," Dunsan said.

"No, no ordinary one," Faulk agreed. "But still a ghost. What did your wife ask? How does a ghostly weapon kill a solid man?"

Dunsan reached the mound of rubble from which the haft

of the ax protruded. He worked it loose carefully and found that it was a good, heavy ax with a large, sharp head. It was almost unmarked by the years. He held it up for Faulk to see.

"This should break the pins that hold the chains to the windlass," he said. "And if the bridge still doesn't fall, the ax looks sturdy enough to help it along, right?"

"It looks too sturdy," Faulk managed to say. "Dunsan—"

"Probably belonged to one of them out there," Dunsan said, making his way back to the mechanism. He gave it a good hard look, decided where best to aim his blows, and started in.

They were strong, stout chains, but the pins that held the wheel had been skimped on and had suffered the rigors of time as well. First one, then another, they broke. The chains rattled and fell slack. Dunsan sat aside the ax and tugged one of the chains until it slipped free. He barely let go of it in time. It unwrapped from the wheel like a whip and one side of the raised bridge creaked and dipped down. Then the other.

The bridge fell outward from the doorway, a felled tree. Dunsan watched. He saw the far end of it strike the far bank of the moat. So fast it had fallen that one of the chains came free of the pulley and fell after the bridge like a paper streamer. The bridge shook and jounced and rocked, but it did not shatter, did not break, or even crack. A cloud of dust rose up and Dunsan watched it settle before turning to Faulk.

"The thing's sturdy," he said. "We'll be across it in—"

He heard a sound, then, on the stairs.

His head jerked up and around and his grip tightened on the ax. "We may still have need of this," he said in a dry voice.

The stairs coiled around the inside wall of the tower, leading up into the night-thick shadow. It came to Dunsan that while it might be daylight outside, such things mattered little here, if they mattered at all. This ruin held its own capsuled night as a fearful man might cling to a woman he was unsure of. In here a ghost could walk at any hour. Another sound came downward from the tower, something descending. Dunsan lifted the ax in his hands.

Faulk tried to stand and cried out in pain and sank heavily back on the stone. Dunsan moved to face the stairs.

"No," Faulk said, and Dunsan was scared enough to think he meant his pain. "No, don't. No—"

Something appeared on the stairs, something that was darker than the surrounding gloom. It moved down slowly.

Dunsan swallowed and took a step into the center of the room, toward the foot of the stairs, to meet whatever it was that was coming.

Then he could see it. Or enough of it. Looming, shadowy, man-shaped. Part of the blackness that was the coming thing gleamed like polished armor. Where eyes should be, there was terrible, indefinable softness that seemed somehow inconsolable. Kershenlee reached the bottom of the stairs and halted, facing Dunsan.

The ghost held a sword, a great broad one that wasn't black like the rest of the ghost, but bright like steel just handed over by the swordmaker. It stood with a stillness that was beyond any living thing, and Dunsan sensed that those terrible soft shadows of eyes were upon him and it increased his fear and his desire to run, but in that moment he was neither foolish enough to run, nor had he the wisdom. He heard Faulk stir behind him but didn't dare look back.

Softly, desperately, Faulk called his name. "Don't fight it—"

Just as desperately, Dunsan answered, "I've no choice now."

"No!" Faulk fairly shouted. "It's a ghost, no more solid than a vapor. Don't you see? The place is in ruins, rusted and corroded, yet you find an ax in here that looks as new as if it were just made—"

Then the ghost moved.

It came toward Dunsan and its movement had the fluid grace of a practiced swordsman's. Its weapon rose in a glittering arc among the dismal gloomy shadows of the keep, and then it stopped, poised in its fighter's stance and stood there, just stood there.

Faulk said, "The wounds on the dead out there . . . *All were delivered with the weapons they carried*—"

Dunsan had started to spring. Kershenlee stood as if waiting, the sword held high, body unprotected, vulnerable. Dunsan checked himself. Fear washed over him, but there was more uncertainty than fear. They battled with each other; they battled with him.

"Don't strike," Faulk called in his straining voice. "Don't—"

The words echoed from the stone walls and the echoes snapped like whips around Dunsan's feet. He hesitated.

The ax dipped in his hand.

He saw the glistening trail of the sword in its swift sudden arc in the shadow-laden air, and he realized it was swinging toward his unprotected neck. His reflexes brought the ax up for protection, but he knew he was too late. He closed his eyes as tightly as he could and took two quick awkward steps back.

And stood there, waiting. Waiting.

How Faulk, injured Faulk, made it across that littered floor to Dunsan's side, the ferryman never knew. But Faulk was there, his hand on Dunsan's shoulder. Faulk was talking to him, crooning the words softly, reassuringly. "It's done. The thing is over. You've won."

Dunsan opened his eyes.

Kershenlee's long body lay sprawled across the broken floor. The corpse was no longer shadowy and the once-gleaming armor was dull and tarnished, the enamel chipped and scarred, and the fabric of his clothing faded and grimy. The corpse had been beheaded. Dunsan took one look at the head—the gleaming white skull—that lay a short distance away, and knew his ax had had nothing to do with its removal.

It had been the sword.

And it was obvious that it had been the sword. The way it lay, it couldn't have been anything else.

"A suitable weapon for a ghost," Faulk said almost dully. "No weapon of a living man could work against a shade, but no ghostly weapon could work against a solid man, either."

"But how?" Dunsan heard himself ask.

Faulk gave his head a slow shake from side to side. "The magic of a curse could do it, I suppose. A curse could govern that a man's own weapon might turn against him, and conversely that if the ghost used its weapon first—"

"Faulk," Dunsan said, "that doesn't matter, not now. I'm alive, we're alive, that's what matters—"

So it was two heroes who returned to the ferryboat, and one who wondered, as he crossed the broad brown-green water of the Amdemon, what he might tell his wife. But he did not speak his concern aloud. It was dusk now, and the exertion of the long walk back to the ferry from the keep had

worked a toll on Faulk, who sat in the boat half-delirious with
the other side, Maelwyd was on the landing, waiting. She
helped Dunsan get the unconscious soldier out of the boat.

"Dislike of walls or not," said Dunsan, "he'll be best off
inside."

"No need," said Maelwyd, and shook her small head.
"Up by the apple tree. While you were gone I prepared a
shelter where he'll be comfortable enough."

In the twilight, Dunsan had missed it, a fine lean-to near
the tree, built to keep the rain and the worst of the wind from
Faulk while his bones knitted. Dunsan gaped and Maelwyd
said his name to snap him back to what needed to be done,
and he bent to the chore of supporting the weakened Faulk.
Together they got the hero to the shelter and then Maelwyd
fed him and cleansed his face and Dunsan watched and mar-
veled at this small, wondrous creature his life centered on.
And he thought of what he had done, of the foolish risk of it,
and felt ashamed, and felt fear also, as he had felt before, but
somehow new as well. Afterward, Faulk slept. Maelwyd
walked toward the house and would have gone inside except
that Dunsan placed his hands on her shoulders from behind
and asked her, "How did you know he would be back?"

"It was a guess about him," she said. "And I guessed also
he would be injured. But there was no guess about you—"

"Maelwyd," he said softly, but she would not be interrupted.

"It was in your eyes, Dunsan, that you would go with him,
that you wouldn't let him go alone. I don't know why, but I
knew you had made up your mind, whether you knew it
yourself or not, and I knew that I couldn't stop you, no
matter how hard I tried."

She turned toward him and in the starlight he saw the glint
of tears on her pale face. "It was you I didn't have to guess
about, Dunsan, it was you I knew would return, you I knew
wouldn't leave me alone. Knew—or wished."

Then there were no more words. Dunsan took his wife in
his arms and held her close a long, long time.

TOADS OF GRIMMERDALE

by Andre Norton

*One of the best-selling science-fiction writers, Andre
Norton (Alice Mary Norton; born in 1912) has shifted
increasingly into fantasy during the last twenty years.
Though noted mainly for juvenile novels, the following story—which may be the best of her shorter
works—is a tough look at adult problems.*

1

The drifts of ice-crusted snow were growing both taller and
wider. Hertha stopped to catch her breath, ramming the butt
of the hunting spear she had been using as a staff into the drift
before her, the smooth shaft breaking through the crust with
difficulty. She frowned at the broken hole without seeing it.

There was a long dagger at her belt, the short-hafted spear
in her mittened hand. And under her cloak she hugged to her
the all-too-small bundle which she had brought with her out
of Horla's Hold. The other burden which she carried lay
within her, and she forced herself to face squarely the fate it
had brought upon her.

Now her lips firmed into a line, her chin went up. Suddenly she spat with a hiss of breath. Shame—why should she
feel shame? Had Kuno expected her to whine and wail,
perhaps crawl before him so he could "forgive" her, prove
thus to his followers his greatness of spirit?

She showed her teeth as might a cornered vixen and aimed
a harder blow at the drift. There was no reason for her to feel
shame, the burden in her was not of wanton seeking. Such
things happened in times of war. She guessed that when
matters worked so, Kuno had not been backward himself in
taking a woman of the enemy.

140

It remained that her noble brother had sent her forth from Horla's Hold because she had not allowed his kitchen hags to brew some foul potion to perhaps poison her, as well as what she bore. Had she so died he could have piously crossed hands at the Thunderer's altar and spoken of Fate's will. And it would have ended neatly. In fact, she might believe that perhaps that had been the intention.

For a moment Hertha was startled at the grim march of her thoughts. Kuno—Kuno was her *brother!* Two years ago she could not have thought so of him or any man! Before the war nearer the Hold. But that was long before she set out for Landendale. Before she knew the world as it was and not as she had believed it.

Hertha was glad she had been able to learn her lesson quickly. The thin-skinned maid she had once been could not have fronted Kuno, could not have taken this road—

She felt the warmth of anger, a sullen, glowing anger, heating as if she carried a small brazier of coals under her cloak's edge. So she went on, setting her rough boots firmly to crunch across the drift edge. Nor did she turn to look back down at that stone-walled keep which had sheltered those of her blood for five generations. The sun was well westward, she must not linger on the trail. Few paths were broken now, times in number she must halt and use the spear to sound out the footing. But it was easy to keep in eye her landmarks of Mulma's Needle and the Wyvern's Wing.

Hertha was sure Kuno expected her to return to accept his conditions. She smiled wryly. Kuno was so very certain of everything. And since he had beaten off the attack of a straggling band of the enemy trying to fight their way to the dubious safety of the coast, he had been insufferable.

The dales were free in truth. But for Kuno to act as if the victories hard won there were his alone! It had required all the might of High Hallack, together with strange allies from the Waste, to break the invaders, to hunt and harry them to the sea from which they had come. And that had taken a score of years to do.

Trewsdale had escaped, not because of any virtue, but by chance. But because fire and sword had not riven there was no reason to cry upon unbroken walls like gamecocks. Kuno had harried men already three-quarters beaten.

She reached the divide, to plod steadily on. The wind had

been at work here, and her path was free of snow. It was very old, that road, one of the reminders to be found all across the dale land that her own people were latecomers. Who had cut these ways for their own treading?

The well-weathered carvings at the foot of the Wyvern's Wing could be seen easily now. So eroded they were by time that none could trace their meaning. But men—or intelligent beings—had shaped them to a purpose. And that task must have been long in the doing. Hertha reached out her mittened fingers to mark one of the now vague curves. She did not believe they had any virtue in themselves, though the fieldworkers did. But they marked well her road.

Downslope again from this point, and now the wind's lash did not cut at her. Though again snow drifted. Two tens of days yet to the feast of Year Turn. This was the last of the Year of the Hornet, next lay the Year of the Unicorn, which was a more fortunate sign.

With the increase of snow Hertha once more found the footing dangerous. The bits of broken crust worked in over the tops of her boots, even though she had drawn tight their top straps, melted clammily against her foot sacks. She plodded on as the track entered a fringe of scrub trees.

Evergreens, the foliage was dark in the dwindling light. But they arose to roof over a road, keep off the drifts. And she came to a stream where ice had bridged from one stony bank to the other. There she turned east to gain Gunnora's shrine.

About its walls was a tangle of winter-killed garden. It was a low building, and an archway faced her. No gate or door barred that and she walked boldly in.

Once inside the outer wall, she could see windows—round, like the eyes of some great feline regarding her sleepily— flanking a door by which hung a heavy bellpull of wrought metal in the form of Gunnora's symbol of a ripened grain stalk entwined with a fruit-laden branch.

Hertha leaned her spear against the wall that her hand might be free for a summons pull. What answered was not any peal of bell, rather an odd, muted sound, as if someone called in words she did not understand. That, too, she accepted, though she had not been this way before and had only a few whispered words to send her here.

The leaves of the door parted. Though no one stood there

to give her house greeting, Hertha took that for an invitation to enter. She moved into gentle warmth, a fragrance of herbs and flowers. As if she had, in that single step, passed from the sere death of midwinter into the life of spring.

With the warmth and fragrance came a lightening of heart, so that the taut lines in her face smoothed a little and her aching shoulders and back lost some of the stiffening tension.

What light there was came from two lamps set on columns, one right, one left. She was in a narrow entry, its walls painted with such colors as to make her believe that she had truly entered a garden. Before her those ranks of flowers rippled, and she realized that there hung a curtain, fashioned to repeat the wall design. Since there still came no greeting, she put out her hand to the folds of that curtain.

But before she could finger it, the length looped aside of itself and she came into a large room. Inside was a table with a chair drawn up to it. The table was set with dishes, some covered as if they held viands which were to be kept warm, and a goblet of crystal filled with a green liquid.

"Eat—drink—" a voice sighed through the chamber.

Startled, Hertha looked about the room over her shoulder. No one— And now that hunger of which she had hardly been aware awoke full force. She dropped the spear to the floor, laid her bundle beside it, let her cloak fall over both, and sat down in the chair.

Though she could see no one, she spoke:

"To the giver of the feast, fair thanks. For the welcome of the gate, gratitude. To the ruler of this house, fair fortune and bright sun on the morrow—" The formal words rang a little hollow here. Hertha smiled at a sudden thought.

This was Gunnora's shrine. Would the Great Lady need the well-wishing of any mortal? Yet it seemed fitting that she make the guest speech.

There was no answer, though she hoped for one. At last, a little hesitantly, she sampled the food spread before her, and found it such fare as might be on the feast table of a dale lord. The green drink was refreshing, yet warming, with a subtle taste of herbs. She held it in her mouth, trying to guess which gave it that flavor.

When she had finished, she found that the last and largest covered basin held warm water, on the surface of which floated petals of flowers. Flowers in the dead of winter! And beside it was a towel, so she washed her hands and leaned back in the chair, wondering what came next in Gunnora's hall.

The silence in the room seemed to grow the greater. Hertha stirred. Surely there were priestesses at the shrine? Someone had prepared that meal, offered it to her with those two words. She had come here for a purpose, and the need for action roused in her again.

"Great Lady." Hertha arose. Since she could see no one, she would speak to the empty room. There was a door at the other end of the chamber, but it was closed.

"Great Lady," she began again. She had never been deeply religious, though she kept Light Day, made the harvest sacrifices, listened respectfully to the Mouth of Astron at Morn Service. When she had been a little maid, her foster mother had given her Gunnora's apple as a pendant to wear. But according to custom that had been laid on the house altar when she came to marriageable age. Of Gunnora's mysteries she knew only what she had heard repeated woman to woman when they sat apart from the men. For Gunnora was only for womankind, and when one was carrying ripening seed within one, then she listened—

For the second time her words echoed. Now that feeling of impatience changed to something else—awe, perhaps, or fear? Yet Gunnora did not hold by the petty rules of men. It did not matter when you sought her if you be lawful wife or not.

As her distrust grew the second door swung silently open— another invitation. Leaving her cloak, bundle, spear where they lay, Hertha went on. Here the smell of flowers and herbs was stronger. Lazy curls of scented smoke arose from two braziers standing at the head and foot of a couch, set as an altar at the foot of a pillar carved with the ripened grain and fruited branch.

"Rest—" the sighing voice bade. And Hertha, the need for sleep suddenly as great as her hunger had been, moved to that waiting bed, stretched out her wearied and aching body. The curls of smoke thickened, spread over her as a coverlet. She closed her eyes.

She was in a place of half-light in which she sensed others coming and going, busied about tasks. But she felt alone, lost. Then one moved to her and she saw a face she knew, though a barrier of years had half-dimmed it in her mind.

"Elfreda!" Hertha believed she had not called that name aloud, only thought it. But her foster mother smiled, holding out her arms in the old, old welcome.

"Little dove, little love—" The old words were as soothing as healing salve laid on an angry wound.

Tears came as Hertha had not allowed them to come before. She wept out sore hurt and was comforted. Then that shade who was Elfreda drew her on, past all those about their work, into a place of light, in which there was Another. And that one Hertha could not look upon directly. But she heard a question asked, and to it she made truthful answer.

"No"—she pressed her hands to her body—"what I carry I do not want to lose."

And that brightness which was the Other grew. But there was another question, and again Hertha answered:

"I hold two desires—that this child be mine alone, taking of no other heritage from the manner of its begetting and him who forced me so. And, second, I wish to bring to account the one who will not stand as its father."

There was a long moment before the reply came. Then a spear of light shot from the center core of the radiance, traced a symbol before Hertha. Though she had no training in the Mysteries yet, this was plain for her reading.

Her first prayer would be answered. The coming child would be only of her, taking naught from her ravisher. And the destiny for it was auspicious. But, though she waited, there was no second answer. The great One—was gone! But Elfreda was still with her, and Hertha turned to her quickly:

"What of my need for justice?"

"Vengeance is not of the Lady." Elfreda shook her veiled head. "She is life, not death. Since you have chosen to give life, she will aid you in that. For the rest—you must walk another road. But—do not take it, my love, for out of darkness comes even greater dark."

Then Hertha lost Elfreda also and there was nothing, only the memory of what happened in that place. So she fell into deeper slumber where no dreams walked.

She awoke, how much later she never knew. But she was renewed in mind and body, feeling as if some leechcraft had been at work during her rest, banishing all ills. There was no more smoke rising from the braziers, the scent of flowers was faint.

When she arose from the couch, she knelt before the pillar, bowing her head, giving thanks. Yet still in her worked her second desire, in nowise lessened by Elfreda's warning.

In the outer room there was again food and drink waiting. And she ate and drank before she went forth from Gunnora's house. There was no kin far or near she might take refuge with. Kuno had made loud her shame when he sent her forth. She had a few bits of jewelry, none of worth, sewn into her girdle, some pieces of trade money. Beyond that she had only a housewife's skills, and those not of the common sort, rather the distilling of herbs, the making of ointments, the fine sewing of a lady's teaching. She could read, write, sing a stave—none of these arts conducive to the earning of one's bread.

Yet her spirit refused to be darkened by hard facts. From her waking that sense of things about to come right held. And she thought it best that she limit the future to one day ahead at a time.

In the direction she now faced lay two holdings. Nordendale was the first. It was small and perhaps in a state of disorder. The lord of the dale and his heir had both fallen at the battle of Ruther's Pass, two years gone. Who kept order there now, if there was any who ruled, she did not know. Beyond that lay Grimmerdale.

Grimmerdale! Hertha set down the goblet from which she had drained the last drop. Grimmerdale—

Just as the shrine of Gunnora was among the heights near the ancient road, so did Grimmerdale have a place of mystery. But no kind and welcoming one, if rumor spoke true. Not of her race at all, but one as old as the ridge road. In fact, perhaps that road had first been cut to run there.

Hertha tried to recall all she had heard of Grimmerdale. Somewhere in the heights there was the Circle of the Toads. Men had gone there, asked for certain things. By ill report they had received all they asked for. What had Elfreda warned—that Gunnora did not grant death, that one must follow another path to find that. Grimmerdale might be the answer.

She looked about her, almost in challenge, half-expecting to feel condemnation in the air of the room. But there was nothing.

"For the feast, my thanks," she spoke the guesting words,

"for the roof, my blessing, for the future all good, as I take my road again."

She fastened the throat latch of her cloak, drew the hood over her head. Then with bundle in one hand and spear in the other, she went out into the light of day, her face to the ridges behind which lay Grimmerdale.

On the final slope above Nordendale she paused in the afternoon to study the small settlement below. It was inhabited, there was a curl of smoke from more than one chimney, the marks of sleds, footprints in the snow. But the tower keep showed no such signs of life.

How far ahead still lay Grimmerdale she did not know, and night came early in the winter. One of those cottages below was larger than the rest. Nordendale had once been a regular halt for herdsmen with wool from mountain sheep on their way to the market at Komm High. That market was of the past, but the inn might still abide, at least be willing to give her shelter.

She was breathing hard when she trudged into the slush of the road below. But she had been right, over the door of the largest cottage hung a wind-battered board, its painted device long weathered away but still proclaiming this an inn. She made for that, passing a couple of men on the way. They stared at her as if she were a fire-drake or wyvern. Strangers must be few in Nordendale.

The smell of food, sour village ale, and too many people too long in an unaired space was like a smothering fog as she came into the common room. At one end was a wide hearth, large enough to take a good-sized log, and fire burned there, giving off a goodly heat.

A trestle table with flanking benches, and a smaller table stacked with tankards and settles by the hearth were the only furnishings. As Hertha entered, a wench in a stained smock and kirtle and two men on a hearth settle, turned and started with the same astonishment she had seen without.

She pushed back her hood and looked back at them with that belief in herself which was her heritage.

"Good fortune to this house."

For a moment they made no answer at all, seemingly too taken back at seeing a stranger to speak. Then the maidservant came forward, wiping her hands on her already well-besplattered apron.

"Good fortune"—her eyes were busy taking in the fine material of Hertha's cloak, her air of ease—"lady. How may we serve you?"

"With food, a bed—if such you have."

"Food—food we have, but it be plain, coarse feeding, lady," the girl stammered. "Let me but call mistress—"

She ran to an inner door, bolting through it as if Hertha was minded to pursue her.

But she rather laid aside her spear and bundle, threw back the edges of her cloak, and went to stand before the hearth, pulling with her teeth at mitten fastenings, to bare her chilled hands. The men hunched away along the settle, mum-mouthed and still staring.

Hertha had thought her clothing plain. She wore one of the divided riding skirts, cut shorter for the scrambling up and down of hills, and it was now shabby and much worn, yet very serviceable. There was an embroidered edge on her jerkin, but no wider than some farm daughter might have. And her hair was tight-braided, with no band of ribbon or silver to hold it so. Yet she might be clad in some festival finery the way they looked upon her. And she stood as impassive as she could under their stares.

A woman wearing the close coif of a matron, a loose shawl about her bent shoulders, a kirtle but little cleaner than the maid's, looped up about her wide hips and thick thighs, bustled in.

"Welcome, my lady. Thrice welcome! Up you, Henkin, Sim, let the lady to the fire!" The men pushed away in a hurry at the ordering. "Malka says you would bide the night. This roof is honored."

"I give thanks."

"Your man—outside? We have stabling—"

Hertha shook her head. "I journey alone and on foot." At the look on the woman's face she added, "In these days we take what fortune offers, we do not always please ourselves."

"Alas, lady, that is true speaking if such ever came to ear! Sit you down!" She jerked off her shawl and used it to dust along the settle.

Later, in a bed spread with coverings fire-warmed, in a room which manifestly had been shut up for some time, Hertha lay in what comfort such a place could offer and mused over what she had learned from her hostess.

As she had heard, Nordendale had fallen on dreary times. Along with their lord and his heir, most of their able-bodied men had been slain. Those who survived and drifted back lacked leadership and had done little to restore what had been a prosperous village. There were very few travelers along the road, she had been the first since winter closed in. Things were supposed to be somewhat better in the east and south, and her tale of going to kinsmen there had seemed plausible to those below.

Better still, she had news of Grimmerdale. There was another inn there, a larger place, with more patronage, which the mistress here spoke of wistfully. An east-west road, now seeing much travel with levies going home, ran there. But the innkeeper had a wife who could not keep serving maids, being of jealous nature.

Of the Toads she dared not ask, and no one had volunteered such information, save that the mistress here had warned against the taking farther of the Old Road, saying it was better to keep to the highway. Though she admitted that was also dangerous and it was well to be ready to take to the brush at the sighting of some travelers.

As yet Hertha had no more than the faint stirrings of a plan. But she was content to wait before she shaped it more firmly.

2

The inn room was long but low, the crossbeams of its ceiling not far above the crown of a tall man's head. Smoking oil lamps hung on chains from those beams. But the light they gave was both murky and limited. Only at the far corner, where a carven screen afforded some privacy, were there tallow candles set on a table. And the odor of their burning added to the general smell of the room.

The room was crowded enough to loosen the thin-lipped mouth of Uletka Rory, whose small eyes darted hither and yon, missing no detail of service or lack of service as her two laboring slaves limped and scuttled between benches and stools. She herself waited upon the candlelit table, a mark of favor. She knew high blood when she saw it.

Not that in this case she was altogether right, in spite of her years of dealing with travelers. One of the men there, yes, was the younger son of a dale lord. But his family holding had long since vanished in the red tide of war, and no one was left in Corriedale to name him master. One had been Master of Archers for another lord, promoted hurriedly after three better men had been killed. And the third, well, he was not one who talked, and neither of his present companions knew his past.

Of the three he was the middle in age. Though that, too, could not be easily guessed, since he was one of those lean, spare-framed men who once they begin to sprout beard hair can be any age from youth to middle years. Not that he went bearded now—his chin and jaw were as smooth as if he had scraped them within the hour, displaying along the jawline the steam of a scar that drew a little at one corner of his lip.

He wore his hair cropped closer than most also, perhaps because of the heavy helm now planted on the table at his right hand. That was battered enough to have served through the war. And the crest it had once mounted was splintered down to a meaningless knob, though the protective bowl was unbreached.

His mail shirt, under a scuffed and warn tabbard, was whole. And the plain hilted sword in his belt sheath, the war bow now resting against the wall at his back were the well-kept tools of a professional. But if he was a mercenary he had not been successful lately. He wore none of those fine buckles or studs which could be easily snapped off to pay for food or lodging. Only when he put out his hand to take up his tankard did the candelight glint on something which was not dull steel or leather. For the bowguard on his wrist was true treasure, a wide band of cunningly wrought gold set with small colored stones, though the pattern of that design was so complicated that to make anything of it required close study.

He sat now sober-faced, as if he were deep in thought, his eyes half-veiled by heavy lids. But he was in truth listening, not so much to the half-drunken mumblings of his companions, but to words arising here and there in the common room.

Most of those gathered there were either workers on the land come in to nurse an earthen mug of home-brewed barley beer and exchange grumbles with their fellows, or else drifting men-at-arms seeking employment now that their lords were dead or so ruined that they had to release the men of their levies. The war was over, these were the victors. But the land they returned to was barren, largely devastated, and it would take much time and energy to win back prosperity for High Hallack.

What the invaders from overseas had not early raped, looted for shiploads sent back to their own lands, they had destroyed in a frenzy when the tide of war began to wash them away. He had been with the war bands in the smoking port, sent to mop up desperate enemies who had fallen back too late to find that their companions had taken off in the last ships, leaving them to be ground between the men of the dales and the sullen sea itself.

The smoke of the port had risen from piles of supplies set burning, oil poured over them and torches set to the spoilage. The stench of it had been near enough to kill a man. Having stripped the country bare—and this being the midwinter—the enemy had made a last defiant gesture with that great fire. It would be a long cold line of days before the coming of summer, and even then men would go pinched of belly until harvest time—harvest if, that is, they could find enough grain to plant, if enough sheep still roamed the upper dales and enough cattle, wild now, found forage in the edges of the Waste to make a beginning of new flocks and herds.

Many dales had been swept clean of people. The men were dead in battle; the women were fled inland, if they were lucky, or slaving for the invaders overseas—or dead also. Perhaps those were the luckiest of all. Yes, there had been a great shaking and leveling, sorting and spilling.

He had put down the tankard. Now his other hand went to that bowguard, turning it about, though he did not look down at it, but rather stared at the screen and listened.

In such a time a man with boldness, and a plan, could begin a new life. That was what had brought him inland, kept him from taking service with Fritigen of Summersdale. Who would be Master of Archers when he could be more, much more?

The invaders had not reached this Grimmerdale, but there were other lands beyond with darker luck. He was going to find one of those—one where there was no lord left to sound the war horn. If there was a lady trying to hold a heritage, well, that might even fit well with his ambitions. Now his tongue showed for an instant on his lower lip, flicking across as if he savored in anticipation some dish which pleased him.

He did not altogether believe in the override of good or ill fortune. In his calculations a man mostly made his own luck by knowing what he wanted and bending all his actions toward that end. But he had a feeling that this was the time when he must move if he were ever to bring to truth the dream which had lain in him since early boyhood.

He, Trystan out of nowhere, was going to end Lord Trystan of some not inconsiderable stretch of land—with a keep for his home and a dale under his rule. And the time to move was here and now.

"Fill!" His near companion, young Urre, pounded his tankard on the tabletop so that one of the candles shook, spattering hot grease. He bellowed an oath and threw his empty pot beyond the screen to clatter across the flagstones.

The lame potboy stooped to pick it up, casting a frightened look at Urre and a second at his scowling mistress, who was already on her way with a tray of freshly filled tankards. Trystan pushed back from the table. They were following a path he had seen too many nights. Urre would drink himself sodden, sick not only with the rank stuff they called drink back here in the hills, but also with his life, wherein he could only bewail what he had lost, taking no thought of what might be gained.

Onsway would listen attentively to his mumbling, willing to play liegeman as long as Urre's money lasted, or he could use his kin ties to win them food and lodging at some keep. When Urre made a final sot of himself, Onsway would no longer wallow in the sty beside him. While he, Trystan, thought it time now to cut the thread which had brought them this far in uneasy company. Neither had anything to give, and he knew now that traveling longer with them he would not do.

But he was not minded to quit this inn soon. Its position on the highway was such that a man could pick up a wealth of information by just sitting and listening. Also, here he had already picked out two likely prospects for his own purposes. The money pouch at his belt was flat enough, he could not afford to spin a coin before the dazzled eyes of an archer or pike man and offer employment.

However, there were men like himself to be found, rootless men who wanted roots in better circumstances than they had known, men who could see the advantage of service under a rising man with opportunities for rising themselves in his wake. One did not need a large war band to overawe masterless peasants; half a dozen well-armed and experienced fighting men at his back, a dale without a lord—and he would be in!

Excitement awoke in him as it did every time his plan reached that place in his thoughts. But he had learned long since to keep a tight rein on his emotions. He was a controlled man, abstemious to a degree astounding among his fellows, though he did what he could to conceal that difference. He could loot, he could whore, he could kill—and he had, but always calculatingly.

"I'm for bed"—he arose and reached for his bow—"the road this day was long—"

Urre might not have heard him at all, his attention was fixed on the tray of tankards. Onsway nodded absently; he was watching Urre, as he always did. But the mistress was alert to the hint of more profit.

"Bed, good master? Three coins—and a fire on the hearth, too."

"Good enough." He nodded, and she screeched for the potboy, who came at a limping waddle, wiping his grimed hands on the black rags of an apron knotted about him.

While the inn gave the impression of space below, on the second floor it was much more cramped. At least the room into which Trystan tramped was no more than a narrow slit of space with a single window covered by a shutter heavily barred. There was a litter of dried rushes on the floor and a rough bed frame, on which a pile of bedding lay as if tossed. The hearth fire promised did not exist. But a legged brazier with some glowing coals gave off a little heat, and a stool beside a warp-sided chest did service as a table. The potboy set the candle down on that and was ready to scuttle away when Trystan, who had gone to the window, hailed him.

"What manner of siege have you had here, boy? This shutter has been so long barred it is rusted tight."

The boy cringed back against the edge of the door, his slack mouth hanging open. He was an ugly lout, and looked half-witted into the bargain, Trystan thought. But surely there was something more than just stupidity in his face when he looked to the window—there was surely fear also.

"Thhheee tooods—" His speech was thick. He had lifted his hands breast-high, was clasping them so tightly together that his knuckles stood out as bony knobs.

Trystan had heard the enemy called many things, but never toads, nor had he believed they had raided into Grimmerdale.

"Toads?" He made a question of the word.

The boy turned his head away so that he looked neither to the window nor at Trystan. It was very evident he planned escape. The man crossed the narrow room with effortless and noiseless strides, caught him by the shoulder.

"What manner of toads?" He shook the boy slightly.

"Toodss—thhheee toods—" The boy seemed to think Trystan should know of what he spoke. "They—that sit 'mong the Standing Stones—that what do men evil." His voice, while thick, no longer sputtered so. "All men know the Toods o' Grimmerdale!" Then, with a twist which showed he had long experience in escaping, he broke from Trystan's hold and was gone. The man did not pursue him.

Rather, he stood frowning in the light of the single candle. Toads—and Grimmerdale—together they had a faintly familiar sound. Now he set memory to work. Toads and Grimmerdale—what did he know of either?

The dale was of importance, more so now than in the days before the war when men favored a more southern route to the port. That highway had fallen almost at once into invader hands, and they had kept it forted and patrolled. The answer had been this secondary road, which heretofore had been used mainly by shepherds and herdsmen. Three different trails from upcountry united at the western mouth of Grimmerdale.

However: had he not once heard of yet a fourth way, one which ran the ridges yet was mainly shunned, a very old way, antedating the coming of his own people? Now—he nodded as memory supplied answers. The Toads of Grimmerdale! One of the many stories about the remnants of those other people, or things, which had already mostly faded from this land, so that the coming of man did not dislodge them, for the land had been largely deserted before the first settlement ship arrived.

Still there were places in plenty where certain powers and presences were felt to this day, where things could be invoked—by men who were crazed enough to summon them. Had the lords of High Hallack not been driven at the last to make such a bargain with the unknown when they signed solemn treaty with the Were Riders? All men knew that it had been the aid of those strange outlanders which had broken the invaders at the last.

Some of the presences were beneficial, others neutral, still others dangerous. Perhaps not actively so in these days. Men were not hunted, harried, or attacked by them. But they had their own places, and the man who was rash enough to trespass there did so at risk.

Among such were the Standing Stones of the Toads of Grimmerdale. The story went that they would answer appeals, but that the manner of answer sometimes did not please the petitioner. For years now men had avoided their place.

But why a shuttered window? If, as according to legend, the toads (people were not sure now if there really *were* toads) did not roam from their portion of the dale, had they once? Making it necessary to bolt and bar against them? And why a second-story window in this dusty room?

Moved by a curiosity he did not wholly understand, Trystan drew his belt knife, pried at the fastenings. They were deeply bitten with rust, and he was sure that the window had not been opened night or day for years. At last the fastenings yielded to his efforts; he was now stubborn about it, somehow even a little angry.

Even though he was at last able to withdraw the bar, he had a second struggle with the warped wood, finally using sword point to lever it. The shutters grated open, the chill of the night entered, making him aware at once of how very odorous and sour was the fog within.

Trystan looked out upon snow and a straggle of dark trees, with the upslope of the dale wall beyond. There were no other buildings set between the inn and that rise. And the thick vegetation showing dark above the sweep of white on the ground suggested that the land was uncultivated. The trees there were not tall, it was mainly brush alone, and he did not like it.

His war-trained instincts saw there a menace. Any enemy could creep in its cover to within a spear-cast of the inn. Yet perhaps those of Grimmerdale did not have such fears, and so saw no reason to grub out and burn there.

The slope began gradually and shortly the tangled growth thinned out, as if someone had there taken the precautions Trystan thought right. Above was smooth snow, very white and unbroken in the moonlight. Then came outcrops of rock. But after he had studied those with an eye taught to take quick inventory of a countryside, he was sure they were no natural formations but had been set with a purpose.

They did not form a connected wall. There were wide spaces between as if they had served as posts for some stringing of fence. Yet for that they were extra thick.

And the first row led to a series of five such lines, though in successive rows the stones were placed closer and closer together. Trystan was aware of two things. One, bright as the moon was, it did not, he was sure, account for all the light among the stones. There was a radiance which seemed to rise either from them or the ground about them. Second, no snow lay on the land from the point where the lines of rock pillar began. And above the stones there was a misting, as if something there bewildered or hindered clear sight.

Trystan blinked, rubbed his hands across his eyes, looked again. The clouding was more pronounced when he did so. As if whatever lay there increased the longer he watched it.

That this was not of human Grimmerdale he was certain. It had all the signs of being one of those strange places where old powers lingered. And that this was the refuge or strong-hold of the "toads" he was now sure. That the shutter had been bolted against the weird sight he could also understand, and he rammed and pounded the warped wood back into place, though he could not reset the bar he had levered out.

Slowly he put aside mail and outer clothing, laying it across the chest. He spread out the bedding over the hide webbing. Surprisingly the rough sheets, the two woven covers were clean. They even (now that he had drawn lungfuls of fresh air to awaken his sense of smell) were fragrant with some kind of herb.

Trystan stretched out, pulled the covers about his ears, drowsy and content, willing himself to sleep.

He awoke to a clatter at the door. At first he frowned up at the cobwebbed rafters above. What had he dreamed? Deep in his mind there was a troubled feeling, a sense that a message of some importance had been lost. He shook his head against such fancies and padded to the door, opened it for the entrance of the elder serving man, a dour-faced, skeleton-thin fellow who was more cleanly of person than the potboy. He carried a covered kettle, which he put down on the chest before he spoke.

"Water for washing, master. There be grain mush, pig cheek, and ale below."

"Well enough." Trystan slid the lid off the pot. Steam curled up. He had not expected this small luxury, and he took its arrival as an omen of fortune for the day.

Below, the long room was empty. The lame boy was washing off tabletops, splashing water on the floor in great scummy dollops. His mistress stood, hands on her hips, her elbows outspread like crooked wings, her sharp chin with its two haired warts outthrust like a spear to threaten the woman before her, well cloaked against the outside winter, but with her hood thrown back to expose her face.

That face was thin, with sharp features lacking any claim to comeliness, since the stretched skin was mottled with unsightly brown patches. But her cloak, Trystan saw, was good wool, certainly not that of a peasant wench. She carried a bundle in one hand, and in the other was a short-hafted hunting spear, its butt scarred as if it had served her more as a journey staff than a weapon.

"Well enough, wench. But here you work for the food in your mouth, the clothing on your back." The mistress shot a single glance at Trystan before she centered her attention once more on the girl.

Girl, Trystan thought she was. Though, by the Favor of Likerwolf, certainly her face was not that of a dewy maid, being rather enough to turn a man's thoughts more quickly to other things when he looked upon her.

"Put your gear on the shelf yonder." The mistress gestured. "Then come to work, if you speak the truth on wanting that."

She did not watch to see her orders obeyed, but came to the table where Trystan had seated himself.

"Grain mush, master. And slicing of pig jowl—ale fresh drawn—"

He nodded, sitting much as he had the night before, fingering the finely wrought guard about his wrist, his eyes half-closed as if he were still wearied, or else turned his thoughts on things not about him.

The mistress stumped away. But he was not aware she had returned until someone slid a tray onto the table. It was the girl, her shrouding of cloak gone, so that the tight bodice of the pleated skirt could be seen. And he was right; she did not wear peasant clothes; that was a skirt divided for riding, though it had now been shortened enough to show boots, scuffed and worn, straw protruding from their tops. Her figure was thin, yet shapely enough to make a man wonder at the fate which wedded such to that horror of a face. She did not need her spear for protection; all she need do was show her face to any would-be ravisher and she would be as safe as the statue of Gunnora the farmers carried through their fields at first sowing.

"Your food, master." She was deft, far more so than the mistress, as she slid the platter of crisp browned mush and thin-sliced pink meat onto the board.

"Thanks given." Trystan found himself making civil answer as he might in some keep were one of the damsels there noticing him in courtesy.

He reached for the tankard and at that moment saw her head sway, her eyes wide open rested on his hand. And he thought, with a start of surprise, that her interest was no slight one. But when he looked again, she was moving away, her eyes downcast like those of any proper serving wench.

"There will be more, master?" she asked in a colorless voice. But her voice also betrayed her. No girl save one hold bred would have such an accent.

There had been many upsets in the dales. What was it to him if some keep woman had been flung out of her soft nest to tramp the roads, serve in an inn for bread and a roof? With her face she could not hope to catch a man to fend for her—unless he be struck blind before their meeting.

"No," he told her.

She walked away with the light and soundless step of a forest hunter, the grace of one who sat at high tables by right of blood.

Well, he, too, would sit at a high table come next year's end. Of that he was as certain as if it had been laid upon him by some Power Master as an unbreakable geas. But it would be because of his own two hands, the cunning of his mind, and as such his rise would be worth more than blood right. She had come down, he would go up. Seeing her made him just more confident of the need for moving on with his plan.

3

The road along the ridges was even harder footing after Nordendale, Hertha discovered. There were gaps where landslides had cut away sections, making the going very slow. However, she kept on, certain this was the only way to approach what she sought.

As she climbed and slid, edged with caution, even in places had to leap recklessly with her spear as a vaulting pole, she considered what might lie ahead. In seeking Gunnora she had kept to the beliefs of her people. But if she continued to the shrine of the Toads, she turned her back on what safety she knew.

Around her neck was hung a small bag of grain and dried herbs, Gunnora's talisman for home and hearth. Another such was sewn into the breast of her undersmock. And in the straw which lined each boot were other leaves with their protection for the wayfarer. Before she had set out on this journey, she had marshaled all she knew of protective charms.

But whether such held against alien powers, she could not tell. To each race its own magic. The old ones were not men, and their beliefs and customs must have been far different. That being so, did she now tempt great evil?

Always when she reached that point she remembered. And memory was as sharp as any spur on a rider's heel. She had been going to the abbey in Lethendale, Kuno having suggested it. Perhaps that was the way he had turned from her, feeling guilt in the matter.

Going to Lethendale, she must ever remember how it was, every dark part of it. For if she did not hold that in mind, then she would lose the bolster of anger for her courage. A small party because Kuno was sure there was naught to fear from the fleeing invaders. But after all, it was not the invaders she had to fear.

There had come a rain of arrows out of nowhere. She could hear yet the bubbling cry of young Jannesk as he fell from the saddle with one through his throat. They had not even seen the attackers, and all the men had been shot down in only moments. She had urged her mount on, only to have him entangle hooves in a trip rope. After that she could remember only flying over his head—

Until she awoke in the dark, her hands hands tied, looking

out into a clearing where a fire burned between rocks. Men
sat about the fire tearing at chunks of half-roasted meat.
Those had been the invaders. And she had lain cold, knowing
well what they meant for her when they had satisfied one
appetite and were ready—

They had come to her at last. Even with tied hands she had
fought. So they had laughed and cuffed her among them,
tearing at her garments and handling her shamefully, though
they did not have time for the last insult and degradation
of all. No, that was left for some—some *man* of her own
people!

Thinking on it now made rage rise to warm her, even
though the sun had withdrawn from this slope and there was a
chill rising wind.

For the ambushers had been attacked in turn, fell under
spear and arrow out of the dark. Half-conscious she had been
left lying until a harsh weight on her, hard, bruising hands
brought her back to terror and pain.

She had never seen his face, but she had seen (and it was
branded on her memory for all time) the bow guard encircling
the wrist tightened as a bar across her throat to choke her
unconscious. And when she had once more stirred, she was
alone.

Someone had thrown a cloak over her nakedness. There
was a horse nearby. There was for the rest only dead men
under a falling snow. She never understood why they had not
killed her and been done with it. Perhaps in that little her
attacker had been overridden by his companions. But at the
time she had been sorely tempted to lie where she was and let
the cold put an end to her. Only the return of that temper
which was her heritage roused her. Somewhere living was the
man who should have been her savior and instead had rift
from her what was to be given only as a free gift. To bring
him down, for that she would live.

Later, when she found she carried new life, yes, she had
been tempted again—to do as they urged, rid herself of that.
But in the end she could not. For though part of the child was
of evil, yet a part was hers. Then she recalled Gunnora and
the magic which could aid. So she had withstood Kuno's
urging, even his brutal anger.

She held to two things with all the stubborn strength she
could muster—that she would bear this child, which must be

hers only, and that she would have justice on the man who would never in truth be its father. The first part of her desire Gunnora had given. Now she went for answer to the second.

At last night came and she found a place among the rocks where she could creep in, the stone walls giving refuge from the wind, a carpet of dried leaves to blanket her. She must have slept, for when she roused she was not sure where she was. Then she was aware of the influence which must have brought her awake. There was an uneasiness of the very air about her, tension as if she stood on the verge of some great event.

With the spear as her staff, Hertha came farther into the open. The moon showed her unmarked snow ahead, made dark pits of her own tracks leading here. With it for a light she started on.

A wan radiance, having no light of fire, shown in the distance. It came from no torch either, she was sure. But it might well mark what she sought.

Here the Old Road was unbroken though narrow. She prodded the snow ahead, lest there be some hidden crevice. But she hurried as if to some important meeting.

Tall shapes arose, stones set on end in rows. In the outer lines there were wide spaces between, but the stones of the inner rows were placed closer and closer together. She followed a road cut straight between these pillars.

On the crest of each rested a small cone of light, as if these were not rocks but giant candles to light her way. And that light was cold instead of warm, blue instead of the orange-red of true flame. Also here the moonlight was gone, so that even though there was no roof she could see, yet it was shut away.

Three stone rows she passed, then four more, each with the stones closer together, so that the seventh brought them touching to form a wall. The road dwindled to a path which led through a gate in the wall.

Hertha knew that even had she wanted to retreat, now she could not. It was as if her feet were held to the path and it moved, bearing her with it.

So she came into a hexagonal space within the wall. There was a low curbing of stone to fence off the centermost portion and in each angle blazed a flame at ground level. But she could go no farther, just as she could not draw away.

Within the walled area were five blocks of green stone. These glistened in the weird light as if they were carved of polished gems. Their tops had been squared off to give seating for those who awaited her.

What she had expected, Hertha was not sure. But what she saw was so alien to all she knew that she did not even feel fear, but rather wonder that such could exist in a world where men also walked. Now she could understand why these bore the name of toads, for that was the closest mankind could come in descriptive comparison.

Whether they went on two limbs or four she could not be sure the way they hunched upon their blocks. But they were no toads in spite of their resemblance. Their bodies were bloated of paunch, the four limbs seemingly too slender beside that heaviness. Their heads sat upon narrow shoulders with no division of neck. And those heads were massive, with large golden eyes high on their hairless skulls, noses which were slits only, and wide mouths stretching above only a vestige of chin.

"Welcome, seeker—"

The words rang in her head, not her ears. Nor could she tell which of the creatures had addressed her.

Now that Hertha had reached her goal, she found no words, she was too bemused by the sight of those she had sought. Yet it seemed that she did not have to explain, for the mind speech continued:

"You have come seeking our aid. What would you, daughter of men—lose that which weighs your body?"

At that Hertha found her tongue to speak.

"Not so. Though the seed in me was planted not by lawful custom but in pain and torment of mind and body, yet will I retain it. I shall bear a child who shall be mine alone, as Gunnora has answered my prayers."

"Then what seek you here?"

"Justice! Justice upon him who took me by force and in shame!"

"Why think you, daughter of men, that you and your matters mean aught to us, who were great in this land before your feeble kind came and who will continue to abide even after man is again gone? What have we to do with you?"

"I do not know. Only I have listened to old tales, and I have come."

She had an odd sensation then: if one could sense laughter in one's mind, she was feeling it. They were amused, and knowing that, she lost some of her assurance.

Again a surge of amusement, and then a feeling as if they had withdrawn, conferred among themselves. Hertha would have fled, but she could not. And she was afraid as she had not been since she faced horror on the road to Lethendale.

"Upon whom ask you justice, daughter of men? What is his name, where lies he this night?"

She answered with the truth. "I know neither. I have not even seen his face. Yet"—she forgot her fear, knew only that which goaded her on—"I have that which shall make him known to me. And I may find him here in Grimmerdale, since men in many now pass along this road, the war being ended."

Again that withdrawal. Then another question.

"Do you not know that services such as ours do not come without payment? What have you to offer us in return, daughter of men?"

Hertha was startled, she had never really thought past making her plea here. That she had been so stupid amazed her. Of course there would be payment! Instinctively she dropped her bundle, clasped her hands in guard over where the child lay.

Amusement once more.

"Nay, daughter of men. From Gunnora you have claimed that life, nor do we want it. But justice can serve us too. We shall give you the key to that which you wish, and the end shall be ours. To this do you agree?"

"I do." Though she did not quite understand.

"Look—you there!" One of the beings raised a forefoot and pointed over her shoulder. Hertha turned her head. There was a small glowing spot on the surface of the stone pillar. She put out her hand and at her touch a bit of stone loosened, so she held a small pebble.

"Take that, daughter of men. When you find him you seek, see it lies in his bed at the coming of night. Then your justice will fall upon him—here! And you will not forget, nor think again and change your mind, we shall set a reminder where you shall see it each time you look into your mirror."

Again the being pointed, this time at Hertha. From the forelimb curled a thin line of vapor. That gathered to form a ball which flew at her. Though she flinched and tried to duck, it broke against her face with a tingling feeling which lasted only for a second.

"You shall wear that until he comes hither, daughter of men. So will you remember your bargain."

What happened then she was not sure, it was all confused. When she was clearheaded again, dawn was breaking, and she clawed her way out of the leaf-carpeted crevice. Was it all a dream? No, her fingers were tight about something, cramped and in pain from that hold. She looked down at a pebble of green-gray stone. So in truth she had met the Toads of Grimmerdale.

Grimmerdale itself lay spread before her, easy to see in the gathering light. The lord's castle was on the farther slope, the village and inn by the highway. And it was the inn she must reach.

Early as it was, there were signs of life about the place. A man went to the stable without noticing her as she entered the courtyard. She advanced to the half-open door, determined to strike some bargain for work with the mistress, no matter how difficult the woman was reputed to be.

The great room was empty when she entered. But moments later a woman with a forbidding face stumped in. Hertha went directly to her. The woman stared at her and then grinned maliciously.

"You've no face to make trouble, wench, one can be certain of that," she said when Hertha asked for work. "And it is true that an extra pair of hands is wanted. Not that we have a purse so fat we can toss away silver—"

As she spoke, a man came down the steep inner stair, crossed to sit at a table half-screened from the rest. It was almost as if his arrival turned the scales in Hertha's favor. For she was told to put aside her bundle and get to work. So it was she who took the food tray to where he sat.

He was tall, taller than Kuno, with well-set, wide shoulders. And there was a sword by his side, plain-hilted, in a worn scabbard. His features were sharp, his face thin, as if he might have gone on short rations too often in the past. Black hair peaked on his forehead and she could not guess his age, though she thought he might be young.

But it was when she put down her tray and he reached out for an eating knife that it seemed the world stopped for an instant. She saw the bowguard on his wrist. And her whole existence narrowed to that metal band. Some primitive instinct of safety closed about her, she was sure she had not betrayed herself.

As she turned from the table, she wondered if this was by the power of the Toads, if they had brought her prey to her hand so. What had they bade her—to see that the pebble was in his bed. But this was early morn and he had just risen, what if he meant not to stay another night but would push on? How could she then carry out their orders? Unless she followed after him, somehow crept upon him at nightfall.

At any rate he seemed in no hurry to be up and off, if that was his purpose. Finally, with relief, she heard him bargain with the mistress for a second night's stay. She found an excuse to go above, carrying fresh bedding for a second room to be made ready. And as she went down the narrow hall, she wondered how best she could discover which room was his.

So intent was she upon this problem that she was not aware of someone behind her until an ungentle hand fell on her shoulder and she was jerked about.

"Now here's a new one—" The voice was brash and young. Hertha looked at a man with something of the unformed boy still in his face. His thick yellow hair was uncombed, his jaw beard-stubbled, his eyes red-rimmed.

As he saw her clearly, he made a grimace of distaste, shoved her from him with force, so she lost her balance and fell to the floor.

"Leave kiss a toad!" He spat, but the trail of spittle never struck her. Instead, hands fell on him, slammed him against the other wall. While the man of the bowguard surveyed him steadily.

"What's to do?" The younger man struggled. "Take your hands off me, fellow!"

"Fellow, is it?" observed the other. "I am no liegeman of yours, Urre. Nor are you in Roxdale now. As for the wench, she's not to blame for her face. Perhaps she should thank whatever Powers she lights a candle to that she had it. With such as you ready to lift every skirt they meet."

"Toad! She is a toad-face—" Urre worked his mouth as if he wished to spit again, then something in the other's eyes must have warned him. "Hands off me!" He twisted and the other stepped back. With an oath Urre lurched away, heading unsteadily for the stair.

Hertha got to her feet, stooped to gather up the draggle of covers she had dropped.

"Has he hurt you?"

She shook her head dumbly. It had all been so sudden, and that *he*—this one—had lifted hand in her defense dazed her. She moved away as fast as she could, but before she reached the end of the passage, she looked back. He was going through a door a pace away from where the one called Urre had stopped her. So—she had learned his room. But "toad-face"? That wet ball which had struck her last night—what had it done to her?

Hertha used her fingers to trace any alteration in her features. But to her touch she was as she had always been. A mirror— she must find a mirror! Not that the inn was likely to house such a luxury.

In the end she found one in the kitchen, in a tray which she had been set to polishing. Though her reflection was cloudy, there was no mistaking the ugly brown patches on her skin. Would they be so forever, a brand set by her trafficking with dark powers, or would they vanish with the task done? Something she had remembered from that strange voiceless conversation made her hope the latter was true.

If so, the quicker she moved to the end, the better. But she did not soon get another chance to slip aloft. The man's name was Trystan. The lame potboy had taken an interest in him and was full of information. Trystan had been a Marshal and a Master of Archers—he was now out of employment, moving inland probably to seek a new lord. But perhaps he was thinking of raising a war band on his own; he had talked already with other veterans staying here. He did not drink much, though those others with him—Urre, who was son to a dale lord, and his liegeman—ordered enough to sink a ship.

Crumbs, yes, but she listened eagerly for them, determined to learn all she could of this Trystan she must enmesh in her web. She watched him, too, given occasion when she might do so without note. It gave her a queer feeling to look this way upon the man who had used her so and did not guess now she was so near.

Oddly enough, had it not been for the evidence of the bowguard she would have picked him last of those she saw beneath this roof. Urre, yes, and two or three others, willing to make free with her until they saw her face clearly. But when she had reason to pass by this Trystan, he showed her small courtesies, as if her lack of comeliness meant nothing. He presented a puzzle which was disturbing.

But that did not change her plan. So, at last, when she managed close to dusk to slip up the stairway quickly, she sped down the hall to his room. There was a huddle of coverings on the bed. She could not straighten them, but she thrust the pebble deep into the bag pillow and hurried back to the common room, where men were gathering. There she obeyed a stream of orders, fetching and carrying tankards of drink, platters of food.

The fatigue of her long day of unaccustomed labor was beginning to tell. And there were those among the patrons who used cruel humor to enliven the evening. She had to be keen-witted and clear-eyed to avoid a foot slyly thrust forth to trip her, a sudden grab at her arm to dump a filled platter or tray of tankards. Twice she suffered defeat and was paid by a ringing buffet from the mistress's hand for the wasting of food.

But at length she was freed from their persecution by the mistress (not out of any feeling for her, but as a matter of saving spillage and spoilage) and set to the cleaning of plates in a noisome hole where the stench of old food and greasy slops turned her stomach and made her so ill she was afraid she could not last. Somehow she held out until finally the mistress sourly shoved her to one of the fireside settles and told her that was the best bed she could hope for. Hertha curled up, so tired she ached, while the rest of the inn people dragged off to their holes and corners—chambers were for guests alone.

The fire had been banked for the night, but the hearth was warm. Now that she had the great room to herself, though her body was tired, her mind was alert, and she rested as best she could while she waited. If all went well, surely the stone would act this night, and she determined to witness the action. Beyond that she had not planned.

Hertha waited for what seemed a long time, shifting now and then on her hard bed. Near to hand were both her cloak and the spear staff; her boots, new filled with fresh straw, were on her feet.

She was aware of a shadow at the head of the stairs, or steps. She watched and listened. Yes, she had been right—this was the man Trystan, and he was walking toward the door. Whirling her cloak about her, Hertha rose to follow.

4

She clung to the shadow of the inn wall for fear he might look behind. But he strode on with the sure step of a man on some mission of such importance his present surroundings had little meaning, rounding the back of the inn, tramping upslope.

Though a moon hung overhead, there was also a veiling of cloud. Hertha dropped farther and farther behind, for the brambles of the scrub caught at her cloak, the snow weighted her skirt, and the fatigue of her long day's labor was heavy on her. Yet she felt that she must be near to Trystan when he reached his goal. Was it that she must witness the justice of the Toads? She was not sure anymore, concentrating all her effort on the going.

Now she could see the stones stark above. They bore no candles on their crests this night, were only grim blots of darkness. Toward them Trystan headed in as straight a line as the growth would allow.

He reached the first line of stones; not once had he looked around. Long since Hertha abandoned caution. He was almost out of sight! She gathered up her skirts, panting heavily as she plunged and skidded to where he had disappeared.

Yes, now she could see him, though he was well ahead. But when he reached that final row, the one forming a real wall, he would have to move along it to the entrance of the Old Road. While she, already knowing the way, might gain a few precious moments by seeking the road now. And she did that, coming to better footing with her breath whistling through her lips in gasps.

She had no spear to lean on and she nursed a sharp pain in her side. But she set her teeth and wavered on between those rows of stones, seeing the gate ahead and in it a dark figure. Trystan was still a little before.

There came a glow of light, the cold flames were back on pillar top. In its blue radiance her hands looked diseased and foul when she put them out to steady herself as she went.

Trystan was just within the gate of the hexagon. He had

not moved, but rather stared straight ahead at whatever awaited
him. His sword was belted at his side, the curve of his bow
was a pointing finger behind his shoulder. He had come fully
armed, yet he made no move to draw weapon now.

Hertha stumbled on. That struggle upslope had taken much
of her strength. Yet in her was the knowledge that she must
be there. Before her now, just beyond her touching even if
she reached forth her arm, was Trystan. His head was
uncovered, the loose hood of his surcoat lay back on his
shoulders. His arms dangled loosely at his sides. Hertha's
gaze followed to the object of his staring concentration.

There were the green blocks. But no toad forms humped
upon them. Rather lights played there, weaving in and out in
a flickering dance of shades of blue—from a wan blight
which might have emanated from some decaying bit on a forest
floor, to a brilliant sapphire.

Hertha felt the pull of those weaving patterns until she
forced herself (literally forced her heavy hands to cover her
eyes) not to look upon the play of color. When she did so,
there was a sensation of release. But it was plain her companion was fast caught.

Cupping her hands to shut out all she could of the lights,
she watched Trystan. He made no move to step across the
low curbing and approach the blocks. He might have been
turned into stone himself, rapt in a spell which had made of
him ageless rock. He did not blink an eye, nor could she even
detect the rise and fall of his chest in breathing.

Was this their judgment, then: the making of a man into a
motionless statue? Somehow Hertha was sure that whatever
use the Toads intended to make of the man they had entrapped through her aid, it was more than this. Down inside
her something stirred. Angrily she fought against that awaken-
ing of an unbidden thought, or was it merely emotion? She
drew memory to her, lashed herself with all shameful, degrad-
ing detail. This had he done to her and this and this! By his
act she was homeless, landless, a nothing, wearing even a
toad face. Whatever came now to him, he richly deserved it.
She would wait and watch, and then she would go hence, and
in time, as Gunnora had promised, she would bear a son or
daughter who had none of this father—none!

Still watching him, her hands veiling against the play of
the ensorcelling light, Hertha saw his lax fingers move, clench

into a fist. And then she witnessed the great effort of that gesture, and she knew that he was in battle, silent though he stood, that he fought with all his strength against what held him fast.

That part of her which had stirred and awakened grew stronger. She battled it. He deserved nothing but what would come to him here, he deserved nothing from her but the justice she had asked from the Toads.

His fist arose, so slowly that it might have been chained to some great weight. When Hertha looked from it to his face, she saw the agony the movement was causing him. She set her shoulders to the rock wall—had she but a rope she would have bound herself there, that no weakness might betray her plan.

Strange light before him and something else, formless as yet, but with a cold menace greater than any fear of battle heat. For this terror was rooted not in any ordinary danger, but grew from a horror belonging by rights far back in the beginnings of his race. How he had come here, whether this be a dream or no, Trystan was not sure. And he had no time to waste on confused memory.

What energy he possessed must be used to front that which was keeping him captive. It strove to fill him with its own life, and that he would not allow, not while he could summon will to withstand it.

Somehow he thought that if he broke the hold upon his body, he could also shatter its would-be mastery of his mind and will. Could he act against its desires, he might regain control. So he set full concentration on his hand—his fingers. It was as if his flesh were nerveless, numb— But he formed a fist. Then he brought up his arm, so slowly that had he allowed himself to waver he might have despaired. But he knew that he must not relax the intense drive of will centered in that simple move. Weapons—what good would his bow, his sword be against what dwelt here? He sensed dimly that this menace could well laugh at weapons forged and carried by those of his kind.

Weapons—sword—steel—there was something hovering just at the fringe of memory. Then for an instant he saw a small, sharp mind picture. Steel! That man from the Waste-side dale who had set his sword as a barrier at the head of his sleeping roll, plunged his dagger point deep in the soil at his feet the night they had left him on the edge of the very ancient ruins with their mounts. Between cold iron a man lay safe, he said. Some scoffed at his superstition, others had nodded agreement. Iron—cold iron—which certain old Powers feared.

He had a sword at his belt now, a long dagger at his hip—iron—talisman? But the struggle of possession of his fist, his arm was so hard he feared he would never have a chance to put the old belief to the proof.

What did they want of him, those who abode here? For he was aware that there was more than one will bent on him. Why had they brought him? Trystan shied away from questions. He must concentrate on his hand—his arm!

With agonizing slowness he brought his hand to his belt, forced his fingers to touch the hilt of his sword.

That was no lord's proud weapons with a silvered, jeweled hilt, but a serviceable blade nicked and scratched by long use. So that the hilt itself was metal, wound with thick wire to make a good grip which would not turn in a sweating hand. His fingertips touched that and—his hand was free!

He tightened hold instantly, drew the blade with a practiced sweep, and held it up between him and that riot of blending and weaving blue lights. Relief came, but it was only minor, he knew after a moment or two of swelling hope. What coiled here could not be so easily defeated. Always that other will weighted and plucked at his hand. The sword blade swung back and forth, he was unable to hold it steady. Soon he might not be able to continue to hold it at all!

Trystan tried to retreat even a single step. But his feet were as if set in a bog, entrapped against any move. He had only his failing hand and the sword, growing heavier every second. Now he was not holding it erect, as if on guard, but doubled back as if aimed at his own body!

Out of the blue lights arose a tendril of wan phosphorescent stuff which looped into the air and held there, its tip pointed in his direction. Another weaved up to join it, swell its substance. A third came, a fourth was growing—

The tip, which had been narrow as a finger, was now thickening. From that smaller tips rounded and swelled into being. Suddenly Trystan was looking at a thing of active evil, a grotesque copy of a human hand, four fingers, a thumb too long and thin.

When it was fully formed, it began to lower toward him.

Trystan with all his strength brought up the sword, held its point as steady as he could against that reaching hand.

Again he knew a fleeting triumph. For at the threat of the sword, the hand's advance was stayed. Then it moved right, left, as if to strike at a foeman's point past his guard. But he was able by some miracle of last reserves to counter each attack.

Hertha watched the strange duel wide-eyed. The face of her enemy was wet, great trickles of sweat ran from his forehead to drip from his chin. His mouth was a tight snarl, lips flattened against his teeth. Yet he held that sword and the emanation of the Toads could not pass it.

"You!"

The word rang in her head with a cold arrogance which hurt.

"Take from him the sword!"

An order she must obey if she was to witness her triumph. Her triumph? Hertha crouched against the rock watching that weird battle—sword point swinging with such painful slowness, but ever just reaching the right point in time so that the blue hand did not close. The man was moving so slowly, why could the Toads not beat him by a swift dart past his guard? Unless their formation of the hand, their use of it was as great an effort for them as his defense seemed to be for him.

"The sword!" That demand in her mind hurt.

Hertha did not stir. "I cannot!" Did she cry that aloud, whisper it, or only think it? She was not sure. Nor why she could not carry through to the end that which had brought her here—that, she did not understand either.

Dark—and her hands were bound. There were men struggling. One went down with an arrow through him. Then cries of triumph. Someone came to her through shadows. She could see only mail—a sword—

Then she was pinned down by a heavy hand. She heard laughter, evil laughter which scorched her, though her body shivered as the last of her clothing was ripped away. Once more—

NO! She would not remember it all! She would not! They could not make her—but they did. Then she was back in the here and now. And she saw Trystan fighting his stumbling, hopeless battle, knew him again for what he was.

"The sword—take from him the sword!"

Hertha lurched to her feet. The sword—she must get the sword. Then he, too, would learn what it meant to be helpless and shamed and—and what? Dead? Did the Toads intend to kill him?

"Will you kill him?" she asked them. She had never foreseen the reckoning to be like this.

"The sword!"

They did not answer, merely spurred her to their will. Death? No, she was certain they did not mean his death, at least not death such as her kind knew it. And—but—

"The sword!"

In her mind that order was a painful lash, meant to send her unthinking to their service. But it acted otherwise, alerting her to a new sense of peril. She had evoked that which had no common meeting with her kind. Now she realized she had loosed that which not even the most powerful man or women she knew might meddle with. Trystan could deserve the worst she was able to pull upon him. But that must be the worst by men's standards—not this!

Her left hand went to the bag of Gunnora's herbs where it rested between her swelling breasts. Her right groped on the ground, closed about a stone. Since she touched the herb bag, that voice was no longer a pain in her head. It faded like a far-off calling. She readied the stone—

Trystan watched that swinging hand. His sword arm ached up into his shoulder. He was sure every moment he would lose control. Hertha bent, tore at the lacing of her bodice so that the herb bag swung free. Fiercely she rubbed it back and forth on the stone. What so pitiful an effort might do—

She threw it through the murky air, struck against that blue hand. It changed direction, made a dart past him. Knowing that this might be his one chance, Trystan brought down the sword with all the force he could muster on the tentacle which supported the hand.

The blade passed through as if what he saw had no substance, had been woven of his own fears. There was a burst of pallid light. Then the lumpish hand, and that which supported it, were gone.

In the same moment he discovered he could move, and staggered back. And a hand fell upon his arm, jerking him in the same direction. He flailed out wildly at what could only

be an enemy's hold, broke it. There was a cry and he turned
his head.

A dark huddle lay at the foot of the stone door frame.
Trystan advanced the sword point, ready, as strength flowed
once more into him, to meet this new attack. The bundle
moved, a white hand clutched at the pillar, pulled.

His bemused mind cleared. This was a woman! Not only
that, but what had passed him through the air had not been
flung at him, but at the hand. She had been a friend and not
an enemy in that moment.

But now from behind he heard a new sound, like the hiss
of a disturbed serpent. Or there might be more than one snake
voicing hate. He gained the side of the woman, with the rock
at his back, looked once more at the center space.

That tentacle which had vanished at the sword stroke might
be gone, but there were others rising. And this time the
tentacles did not unite to form hands, but rather each produced something like unto a serpent head. And they arose in
such numbers that no one man could stand to front them
all—though he must try.

Once more he felt a light weight upon his shoulder, he
glanced to the side. The woman was standing, one hand tight
to her breast, the other resting on his upper arm now. Her
hood overshadowed her face so he could not see it. But he
could hear the murmur of her voice even through the hissing
of the pseudo-serpents. Though he could not understand the
words, there was a rhythmic flow as if she chanted a battle
song for his encouragement.

One of the serpent lengths swung at them, he used the
sword. At its touch the thing vanished. But one out of a
dozen, what was that? Again his arm grew heavy, he found
movement difficult.

Trystan tried to shake off the woman's hold, not daring to
take a hand from his sword to repel her.

"Loose me!" he demanded, twisting his body.

She did not obey, nor answer. He heard only that murmur
of sound. There was a pleading note in it, a frantic pleading,
he could feel her urgency, as if she begged of someone aid
for them both.

Then from where her fingers dug into his shoulder muscles
there spread downward along his arm, across his back and
chest a warmth, a loosing—not of her hold, but of the bonds

laid on him here. And within the center space the snake heads darted with greater vigor. Now and then two met in midair, and when they did, they instantly united, becoming larger.

These darted forth, striking at the two by the gate, while Trystan cut and parried. And they moved with greater speed, so he was hard put to keep them off. They showed no poison fangs, nor did they even seem to have teeth within their open jaws. Yet he sensed that if those mouths closed upon him or the woman, they would be utterly done.

He half-turned to beat off one which had come at him from an angle. His foot slipped and he went to one knee, the sword half out of his grasp. As he grabbed it tighter, he heard a cry. Still crouched, he slewed around.

The serpent head at which he had struck had only been a ruse. For his lunge at it had carried him away from the woman. Two other heads had captured her. To his horror he saw that one had fastened across her head, engulfing most of it on contact. The other had snapped its length of body about her waist. Gagged by the one on her head, she was quiet, nor did she struggle as the pallid lengths pulled her back to the snakes' lair. Two more reached out to fasten upon her, no longer heeding Trystan, intent on their capture.

He cried out hoarsely, was on his feet again striking savagely at those dragging her. Then he was startled by a voice which seemed to speak within his head.

"Draw back, son of men, lest we remember our broken bargain. This is no longer your affair."

"Loose her!" Trystan cut at the tentacle about her waist. It burst into light, but another was already taking its place.

"She delivered you to us, would you save her?"

"Loose her!" He did not stop to weigh the right or wrong of what had been said, he only knew that he would not see the woman drawn to that which waited—that he could not do and remain a man. He thrust again.

The serpent coils were moving faster, drawing back into the hexagon. Trystan could not even be sure she still lived, not with that dreadful thing upon her head. She hung limp, not fighting.

"She is ours! Go you—lest we take more for feasting."

Trystan wasted no breath in argument; he leapt to the left, mounting the curb of the hexagon. There he slashed into the coils which pulled at the woman. His arms were weak, he could hardly raise the sword, even two-handed, and bring it down. Yet still he fought stubbornly to cut her free. And little by little he thought that he was winning.

Now he noted that as the coils tightened about her they did not touch her hand where it still rested clasping something between her breasts. So he strove the more to cut the coils below, severing the last as her head and shoulders were pulled over the edge of the curb.

Then it seemed that, tug though they would, the tentacles could not drag her wholly in. As they fought to do so, Trystan had his last small grant of time. He now hewed those which imprisoned her head and shoulders. Others were rising for new holds. But, as she so lay, to do their will they must reach across her breast to take hold, and that they apparently could not do.

Wearily he raised the blade and brought it down again, each time sure he could not do so again. But at last there was a moment when she was free of them all. He flung out his left hand, clasped hers where it lay between her breasts, heaved her back and away.

There was a sharp hissing from the serpent things. They writhed and twisted. But more and more they sank to the ground, rolled there feebly. He got the woman on his shoulder, tottered back, still facing the enemy, readied as best he could be for another attack.

5

It would seem that the enemy was spent, at least the snakes did not strike outward again. Watching them warily, Trystan retreated, dared to stop and rest with the woman. He leaned above her to touch her cheek. To his fingers the flesh was cold, faintly clammy. Dead? Had the air been choked from her?

He burrowed beneath the edges of her hood, sought the pulse in her throat. He could find none, so he tried to lay his hand directly above her heart. In doing so he had to break her grip on what lay between her breasts. When he touched a small bag there was a throbbing, a warmth spread up in his hand, and he jerked hastily away before he realized this was not a danger but a source of energy and life.

Her heart still beat. Best get her well away while those

things in the hexagon were quiescent. For he feared their defeat was only momentary.

Trystan dared to sheath his sword, leaving both arms free to carry the woman. For all the bulk of her cloak and clothing she was slender, less than the weight he expected.

Now his retreat was that of a coastal sea crab, keeping part attention on the stewpot of blue light at his back, part on the footing ahead. And he drew a full breath again only when he had put two rings of the standing stones between him and the evil they guarded.

Nor was he unaware that there was still something dragging on him, trying to force him to face about. That he battled with will and his sense of self-preservation, his teeth set, a grimace of effort stiffening mouth and jaw.

One by one he pushed past the standing stones. As he went, the way grew darker, the weird light fading. And he was beginning to fear that he could no longer trust his own sight. Twice he found himself off the road, making a detour around a pillar which seemed to sprout before him—and thereby heading back the way he had come.

Thus he fought both the compulsion to return and the tricks of vision, learning to fasten his attention on some point only a few steps ahead and wait until he had passed that before he set another goal.

He came at last, the woman resting over his shoulder, into the clean night, the last of the stones behind him. Now he was weak, so weary that he might have made a twenty-four-hour march and fought a brisk skirmish at the end of it. He slipped to his knees, lowered his burden to the surface of the Old Road where, in the open, the wind had scoured the snow away.

There was no moon, the cloud cover was heavy. The woman was now only a dark bulk. Trystan squatted on his heels, his hands dangling loose between his knees, and tried to think coherently.

Of how he had come up here he had no memory at all. He had gone to bed in the normal manner at the inn, first waking to danger when he faced the crawling light in the hexagon. That he had also there fought a danger of the old time he had no doubt at all. But what had drawn him there?

He remembered forcing open the inn window to look upslope. Had that simple curiosity of his been the trigger for this adventure? But that the people of the inn could live unconcerned so close to such a peril—he could hardly believe that. Or because they had lived here so long, were the descendants of men rooted in Grimmerdale, had they developed an immunity to dark forces?

But what had the thing or things in the hexagon said? That she who lay here had delivered him to them. If so—why? Trystan hunched forward on his knees, twitched aside the edge of the hood, stooping very close to look at her. But it was hard to distinguish more than just the general outline of her features in this limited light.

Suddenly her body arched away from him. She screamed with such terror as startled him, and pushed against the road under her, her whole attitude one of such agony of fear as held him motionless. Somehow she got to her feet. She had only screamed that once; now he saw her arms move under the hindering folds of her cloak. The moon broke in a thin sliver from under the curtain of the cloud, glinted on what she held in her hand.

Steel swung in an arc for him. Trystan grappled with her before that blade bit into his flesh. She was like a wild thing, twisting, thrusting, kicking, even biting as she fought him. At length he handled her as harshly as he would a man, striking his fist against the side of her chin so her body went limply once more to the road.

There was nothing to do but take her back to the inn. Had her experience in that nest of standing stones affected her brain, turning all about her into enemies? Resigned, he ripped a strip from the hem of her cloak, tied her hands together. Then he got her up so she lay on his back, breathing shallowly, inert. So carrying her, he slipped and slid, pushed with difficulty through the scrub to the valley below and the inn.

What the hour might be he did not know, but there was a night lantern burning above the door, which swung open at his push. He staggered over to the fireplace, dropped his burden by the hearth, and reached for wood to build up the blaze, wanting nothing now so much as to be warm again.

Hertha's head hurt. The pain seemed to be in the side of her face. She opened her eyes. There was a dim light, but not that wan blue. No, this was flame glow. Someone hunched at the hearth setting wood lengths with expert skill to rebuild the fire. Already there was warmth her body welcomed. She tried to sit up. Only to discover that her wrists were clumsily bound together. Then she tensed, chilled by fear, watching intently him who nursed the fire.

His head was turned from her, she could not see his face, but she had no doubts that it was Trystan. And her last memory—him looming above her, hands outstretched— To take her again as he had that other time! Revulsion sickened her so that she swallowed hurriedly lest she spew openly on the floor. Cautiously she looked around. This was the large room of the inn, he must have carried her back. That he might take his pleasure in a better place than the icy cold of the Old Road? But if he tried that she could scream, fight— surely someone would come—

He looked to her now, watching her so intently that she felt he read easily every one of her confused thoughts.

"I shall kill you," she said distinctly.

"As you tried to do?" He asked that not as if it greatly mattered, but as if he merely wondered.

"Next time I shall not turn aside!"

He laughed. And with that laughter for an instant he seemed another man, one younger, less hardened by time and deeds. "You did not turn aside this time, mistress, I had a hand in the matter." Then that half-smile which had come with the laughter faded, and he regarded her with narrowed eyes, his mouth tight set lip to lip.

Hertha refused to allow him to daunt her and glared back. Then he said:

"Or are you speaking of something else, mistress? Something which happened before you drew steel on me? Was that—that *thing* right? Did I march to its lair by your doing?"

Somehow she must have given away the truth by some fraction of change he read in her face. He leaned forward and gripped her by the shoulders, dragging her closer to him in spite of her struggles, holding her so they were squarely eye to eye.

"Why? By the Sword Hand of Karther the Fair, why? What did I ever do to you, girl, to make you want to push me into that maw? Or would any man have sufficed to feed those pets? Are they your pets or your masters? Above all, how comes humankind to deal with *them?* And if you so deal, why did you break their spell to aid me? Why, and why, and why!"

He shook her, first gently, and then, with each question,

more harshly, so that her head bobbed on her shoulders and she was weak in his hands. Then he seemed to realize that she could not answer him, so he held her tight as if he must read the truth in her eyes as well as hear it from her lips.

"I have no kinsman willing to call you to a sword reckoning," she told him wearily. "Therefore, I must deal as best I can. I sought those who might have justice—"

"Justice! Then I was not just a random choice for some purpose of theirs! Yet I swear by the Nine Words of Min, I have never looked upon your face before. Did I in some battle slay close kin—father, brother, lover? But how may that be? Those I fought were the invaders. They had no women save those they rift from the dales. And would any daleswoman extract vengeance for one who was her master-by-force? Or is it that, girl? Did they take you and then you found a lord to your liking among them, forgetting your own blood?"

If she could have, she would have spat full in his face for that insult. And he must have read her anger quickly.

"So that is not it. Then, why? I am no ruffler who goes about picking quarrels with comrades. Nor have I ever taken any woman who came not to me willingly—"

"No?" She found speech at last, in a hot rush of words. "So you take no woman unwillingly, brave hero? What of three months since on the road to Lethendale? Is it such a usual course of action with you that it can be so lightly put out of mind?"

Angry and fearful though she was, she could see in his expression genuine surprise.

"Lethendale?" he repeated. "Three months since? Girl, I have never been that far north. As to three months ago—I was Marshal of Forces for Lord Ingrim before he fell at the siege of the port."

He spoke so earnestly that she could almost have believed him, had not that bowguard on his wrist proved him false.

"You lie! Yes, you may not know my face. It was in darkness you took me, having overrun the invaders who had taken me captive. My brother's men were all slain. For me they had other plans. But when aid came, then still I was for the taking—as you proved, Marshal!" She made of that a name to be hissed.

"I tell you, I was at the port!" He had released her and she backed against the settle, leaving a good space between them.

"You would swear before a Truth Stone it was me? You know my face, then?"

"I would swear, yes. As for your face—I do not need that. It was in the dark you had your will of me. But there is one proof I carry ever in my mind since that time."

He raised his hand, rubbing fingers along the old scar on his chin, the fire gleamed on the bowguard. That did not match the plainness of his clothing, how could anyone forget seeing it?

"That proof being?"

"You wear it on your wrist, in plain sight. Just as I saw it then, ravisher—your bowguard!"

He held his wrist out, studying the band. "Bowguard! So that is your proof, that made you somehow send me to the Toads." He was half-smiling again, but this time cruelly and with no amusement. "You did send me there, did you not?" He reached forward and, before she could dodge, pulled the hood fully from her head, stared at her.

"What have you done with the toad-face girl? Was that some trick of paint, or some magicking you laid on yourself? Much you must have wanted me to so despoil your own seeming to carry through your plan."

She raised her bound hands, touched her cheeks with cold fingers. This time there was no mirror, but if he said the loathsome spotting was gone, then it must be so.

"They did it," she said, only half-comprehending. She had pictured this meeting many times, imagined him saying this or that. He must be very hardened in such matters to hold to this pose of half-amused interest.

"They? You mean the Toads? But now tell me why, having so neatly put me in their power, you were willing to risk your life in my behalf? That I cannot understand. For it seems to me that to traffic with such as abide up that hill is a fearsome thing and one which only the desperate would do. Such desperation is not lightly turned aside—so, why did you save me, girl?"

She answered with the truth. "I do not know. Perhaps because the hurt being mine, the payment should also be mine—that, a little, I think. But even more—" She paused so long he prodded her.

"But even more, girl?"

"I could not in the end leave even such a man as you to *them!*"

"Very well, that I can accept. Hate and fear and despair can drive us all to bargains we repent of later. You made one and then found you were too human to carry it through. Then later on the road you chose to try with honest steel and your own hand—"

"You—you would have taken me—again!" Hertha forced out the words. But the heat in her cheeks came not from the fire but from the old shame eating her.

"So that's what you thought? Perhaps, given the memories you carry, it was natural enough." Trystan nodded. "But now it is your turn to listen to me, girl. Item first: I have never been to Lethendale, three months ago, three years ago—never! Second: this which you have come to judge me on"—he held the wrist closer, using the fingers of his other hand to tap upon it—"I did not have three months ago. When the invaders were close pent in the port during the last siege, we had many levies from the outlands come to join us. They had mopped up such raiding bands as had been caught out of there when we moved in to besiege.

"A siege is mainly a time of idleness, and idle men amuse themselves in various ways. We had only to see that the enemy did not break out along the shores while we waited for the coasting ships from Handlesburg and Vennesport to arrive to harry them from the sea. There were many games of chance played during that waiting. And, though I am supposed by most to be a cautious man, little given to such amusements, I was willing to risk a throw now and then.

"This I so won. He who staked it was like Urre, son to some dead lord, with naught but ruins and a lost home to return to if and when the war ended. Two days later he was killed in one of the sorties the invaders now and then made. He had begged me to hold this so that when luck ran again in his way he might buy it back, for it was one of the treasures of his family. In the fighting I discovered it was not only decorative but useful. Since he could not redeem it, being dead, I kept it—to my disfavor, it would seem. As for the boy, I do not even know his name—for they called him by some nickname. He was befuddled with drink half the time, being one of the walking dead—"

" 'Walking dead'?" His story carried conviction, not only his words but his tone, and the straight way he told it.

"That is what I call them. High Hallack has them in

many—some are youngsters, such as Urre, the owner of this.'' Again he smoothed the guard. ''Others are old enough to be their fathers. The dales have been swept with fire and sword. Those which were not invaded have been bled of their men, of their crops—to feed both armies. This is a land which can now go two ways. It can sink into nothingness from exhaustion, or there can rise new leaders to restore and with will and courage build again.''

It seemed to Hertha that he no longer spoke to her, but rather voiced his own thoughts. As for her, there was a kind of emptiness within, as if something she carried had been rift from her. That thought sent her bound hands protectively to her belly.

The child within her—who had been its father? One of the lost ones, some boy who had had all taken from him and so became a dead man with no hope in the future, one without any curb upon his appetites. Doubtless he had lived for the day only, taken ruthlessly all offered during that short day. Thinking so, she again sensed that queer light feeling. She had not lost the child, this child which Gunnora promised would be hers alone. What she had lost was the driving need for justice which had brought her to Grimmerdale—to traffic with the Toads.

Hertha shuddered, cold to her bones in spite of her cloak and the fire. What had she done in her blindness, her hate and horror? Almost she had delivered an innocent man to that she dared not now think upon. What had saved her from that at the very last, made her throw that stone rubbed with Gunnora's talisman? Some part of her that refused to allow such a foul crime?

And what could she ever say to this man who had now turned his head from her, was looking into the flames as if therein he could read message runes? She half-raised her bound hands; he looked again with a real smile, from which she shrank as she might from a blow, remembering how it might have been with him at this moment.

''There is no need for you to go bound. Or do you still thirst for my blood?'' He caught her hands, pulled at the cloth tying them.

''No,'' Hertha answered in a low voice. ''I believe you. He whom I sought is now dead.''

''Do you regret that death came not at your hand?''

She stared down at her fingers resting again against her middle, wondering dully what would become of her now. Would she remain a tavern wench, should she crawl back to Kuno? No! At that her head went up again, pride returned.

"I asked, are you sorry you did not take your knife to my gamester?"

"No."

"But still there are dark thoughts troubling you—"

"Those are none of your concern." She would have risen, but he put out a hand to hold her where she was.

"There is an old custom. If a man draw a maid from dire danger, he has certain rights—"

For a moment she did not understand; when she did, her bruised pride strengthened her to meet his eyes.

"You speak of maids—I am not such."

His indrawn breath made a small sound, but one loud in the silence between them. "So that was the why! You are no farm or tavern wench, are you? So you could not accept what he had done to you. But have you no kinsman to trade for your honor?"

She laughed raggedly. "Marshal, my kinsman had but one wish: that I submit to ancient practices among women so that he would not be shamed before his kind. Having done so, I would have been allowed to dwell by sufferance in my own home, being reminded not more than perhaps thrice daily of his great goodness."

"And this you would not do. But with your great hate against him who fathered what you carry—"

"No!" Her hands went to that talisman of Gunnora's. "I have been to the shrine of Gunnora. She has promised me my desire—the child I bear will be mine wholly, taking nothing from *him!*"

"And did she also send you to the Toads?"

Hertha shook her head. "Gunnora guards life. I knew of the Toads from old tales. I went to them in my blindness and they gave me that which I placed in your bed to draw you to them. Also they changed my face in some manner. But—that is no longer so?"

"No. Had I not known your cloak, I should not have known you. But this thing in my bed— Stay you here and wait. But promise me this, should I return as one under orders, bar the door in my face and keep me here at all costs!"

"I promise."

He went with the light-footed tread of one who had learned to walk softly in strange places because life might well depend upon it. Now that she was alone, her mind returned to the matter of what could come to her with the morn. Who would give her refuge—save perhaps the Wise Women of Lethendale. It might be that this Marshal would escort her there. Though what did he owe her except such danger as she did not want to think on. But although her thoughts twisted and turned, she saw no answer except Lethendale. Perhaps Kuno would someday— No! She would have no plan leading in that path!

Trystan was back, holding two sticks such as were used to kindle brazier flames. Gripped between their ends was the pebble she had brought from the Toads' hold. As he reached the fire, he hurled that bit of rock into the heart of the blaze.

He might have poured oil upon the flames so fierce was the answer as the pebble fell among the logs. Both shrank back.

"That trap is now set at naught," he observed. "I would not have any other fall into it."

She stiffened, guessing what he thought of her for the setting of that same trap.

"To say I am sorry is only mouthing words, but—"

"To one with such a burden, lady, I return that I understand. When one is driven by a lash, one takes any way to free oneself. And in the end you did not suffer that I be taken."

"Having first thrust you well into the trap! Also—you should have let them take me then as they wished. It would only have been fitting."

"Have done!" He brought his fist down on the seat of the settle beside which he knelt. "Let us make an end to what is past. It is gone. To cling to this wrong or that, keep it festering in mind and heart, is to cripple one. Now, lady"—she detected a new formality in his voice—"where do you go, if not to your brother's house? It is not in your mind to return there, I gather."

She fumbled with the talisman. "In that you are right. There is but one place left—the Wise Women of Lethendale. I can beg shelter from them." She wondered if he would offer the escort she had no right to ask, but his next question surprised her.

"Lady, when you came hither, you came by the Old Road over ridge, did you not?"

"That is so. To me it seemed less dangerous than the open highway. It has, by legend, those who sometimes use it, but I deemed those less dangerous than my own kind."

"If you came from that direction, you must have passed through Nordendale. What manner of holding is it?"

She had no idea why he wished such knowledge, but she told him what she had seen of that leaderless dale, the handful of people there deep sunk in a lethargy in which they clung to the ruins of what had once been thriving life. He listened eagerly to what she told him.

"You have a seeing eye, lady, and have marked more than most given such a short time to observe. Now listen to me, for this may be a matter of concern for both of us in the future. It is in my mind that Nordendale needs a lord, one to give the people heart, rebuild what man and time have wasted. I have come north seeking a chance to be not just my own man, but to have a holding. I am not like Urre, who was born to a hall and drinks and wenches now to forget what ill tricks fortune plays.

"Who my father was"—he shrugged—"I never heard my mother say. That he was of no common blood, that I knew, though in later years she drudged in a merchant's house before the coming of the invaders for bread to our mouths and clothing for our backs. When I was yet a boy, I knew that the only way I might rise was through this." He touched the hilt of his sword. "The merchant guild welcomed no nameless man, but for a sword and a bow there is always a ready market. So I set about learning the skills of war as thoroughly as any man might. Then came the invasion and I went from lord to lord, becoming at last Marshal of Forces. Yet always before me hung the thought that in such a time of upheaval, with the old families being killed out, this was my chance.

"Now there are masterless men in plenty, too restless after years of killing to settle back behind any plow. Some will turn outlaw readily, but with a half-dozen of such at my back, I can take a dale which lies vacant of rule, such as this Nordendale. The people there need a leader, I am depriving none of lawful inheritance, but will keep the peace and defend it against outlaws—for there will be many such now. There are men here, passing through Grimmerdale, willing to be hired for such a purpose. Enough so I can pick and choose at will.''

He paused and she read in his face that this indeed was the great moving wish of his life. When he did not continue, she asked a question:

"I can see how a determined man can do this thing. But how will it concern me in any way?"

He looked to her straightly. She did not understand the full meaning of what she saw in his eyes.

"I think we are greatly alike, lady. So much so that we could walk the same road, to profit of both. No, I do not ask an answer now. Tomorrow"—he got to his feet, stretching—"no, today, I shall speak to those men I have marked. If they are willing to take liege oath to me, we shall ride to Lethendale, where you may shelter as you wish for a space. It is not far—"

"By horse," she answered in relief, "perhaps two days west."

"Good enough. Then, having left you there, I shall go to Nordendale—and straightaway that shall cease to be masterless. Give me, say, threescore days, and I shall come riding again to Lethendale. Then you shall give me your answer as to whether our roads join or no."

"You forget"—her hands pressed upon her belly—"I am no maid, nor widow, and yet I carry—"

"Have you not Gunnora's promise upon the subject? The child will be wholly yours. One welcome holds for you both."

She studied his face, determined to make sure if he meant that. What she read there—she caught her breath, her hands rising to her breast, pressing hard upon the talisman.

"Come as you promise to Lethendale," she said in a low voice. "You shall be welcome and have your answer in good seeming."

A LITERARY DEATH

by Martin Harry Greenberg

Contrary to popular rumor, Martin Harry Greenberg (born in 1940) is not a house name for the entire faculty of the University of Wisconsin at Green Bay. But 170 books in eleven years is an amazing accomplishment, and Isaac and I are extremely proud of his success. His story below is about the curse every young writer must face.

Dear Isaac:

Things have settled down here sufficiently for me to try to answer your questions about the tragic death of Eddie Advent. As you know (perhaps too well) Eddie was a writer of ambition—he had a firmer grip on where he wanted to go and how he was going to get there than any sf writer I have ever met (and he would hate me if he could see me categorizing him in any way), and it may have been ambition which finally killed him.

Anyway, here are the "facts" as best I can reconstruct them: Eddie had worked for years on what he thought was his masterpiece—a 900-page manuscript with the working title of *The Political Geography of the Promised World,* and like almost all his work, it was difficult to classify—perhaps "science fantasy" would be the closest, but it doesn't matter now. I read the manuscript and liked it—it *was* the best thing he had ever done (will ever do), but I had serious reservations about who, if anyone, would publish it, given present commercial realities. I suggested a university press, but Eddie flatly refused my offer of contacts in those places—he wanted a major publisher, one who would give it maximum exposure and support. Well, the first big houses he tried all said

188

no, several after holding it for quite a while. It was at this point that he approached old Doc Greenston at W & W. Now W & W is a medium-to-small New York house, with a distinguished past but with its best days definitely behind it.

But Doc really liked the manuscript, fought it through a very skeptical editorial board, and made Eddie a decent offer (I know, because Eddie told me about it). After much thought and discussion—he talked about this with at least seven authors and two agents—he told Doc he would take their offer subject to a few minor changes. I thought that everything was set, and so did everybody who knew about the project. It was at this point that the trouble began—Peter Dean of Solomon and Solomon (who had just been promoted from senior editor in charge of who know's what to editor-in-chief of their trade books division) told Eddie that his new position made it possible for him to take the book at four times the advance that Doc had offered and with a guaranteed ad budget of $45,000 to boot. But Eddie had already verbally accepted Doc's offer. Well, this didn't stop Eddie—he told me that he had worked too long and too hard to let his word stand in the way of his destiny (or words to that effect), and he said he was going to tell Doc the same thing. Doc (rest his soul) always believed that the only important thing in life was honor (how he lasted so long in publishing must remain one of the Great Mysteries of the Western World), and he was mad as hell at Eddie.

Now things become grim—Doc saw Eddie at the SFWA Party in New York, and in front of several witnesses (including yours truly) put a curse on him, telling him that he "would die a literary death" by 2:00 P.M., November 20, some two weeks away at the time. Eddie laughed in his face and no more words were spoken between them (as far as I know).

Now, I spoke with Eddie (remember that we were working on that big anthology during this period) at least six times after that night, so I have a pretty good idea of what he was thinking. You may or may not know that Eddie was a great admirer of Cornell Woolrich, and of course was familiar with that great and sadly neglected author's *Night Has a Thousand Eyes*, in which a man is told by a mystic (as I recall the story—I'm actually afraid to go back and read it again) that he will "die by the jaws of a lion." The guy carefully avoids zoos, cats, and anything feline until just before his death by the jaws of the lion that sits in front of the New York Public Library at Forty-second and Fifth. I mention this because Eddie did—as time went by, he got more and more nervous, even desperate. He told me on the phone that he found himself avoiding bookstores, libraries, publishers, other writers, etc. (remember, the curse said he would die a *literary* death). This finally became an obsession by the time of my last two conversations with him (especially after poor Doc had committed suicide). I told him that the right thing to do was to honor his word to Doc, but he steadfastly refused—ole devil ambition, I guess, or maybe he just thought it was too late for the curse to be removed, now that Doc was dead.

As best as I can piece things together (and I talked with everyone, including the state police—you should see my phone bill for November), Eddie's concern turned into panic a few days before November 20 (you might recall that week because it was the week of the first big snowstorm in the Northeast), and he holed up in his apartment (he had apparently *given away* his typewriter and all his books by this time). On the morning of the twentieth, another tenant in his building saw him getting into his car—he had told me that he felt totally vulnerable in New York, the center of this country's literary world. Eddie had decided to flee the city on that fateful day. I don't know his exact route, but he was obviously (since that is where they found the body and car) heading out on the Garden State Parkway, making his way slowly (since the traffic was heavy and the melting snow made driving hazardous), and for all I know, watching out for bookmobiles! The last details are somewhat fuzzy, but his car apparently skidded on the melting snow, went into a spin and off the road just before 2:00 P.M. (the clock in the car was smashed and read 1:58). He died instantly of a broken neck, and with his car half buried—in a pile of slush.

All best wishes,
Marty the Other

SATAN AND SAM SHAY

by Robert Arthur

Robert Arthur (1909–1969) was a radio and TV producer, a knowledgeable editor, and a skillful writer of mysteries, fantasy, and science fiction. Proficient with both horror and comedy, many of his works, like the one below, are acknowledged classics.

I am told that sin has somewhat declined since Satan met Sam Shay. I cannot vouch for this, but they say that production has definitely fallen off since that evening when Sam Shay won three wagers from the Devil. And this is the tale of it.

Sam Shay, you'll understand, was a bold rascal with Irish blood in his veins, though Yankee-born and -bred. Six feet he stood, with wide shoulders and a grin and dark hair with a touch of curl to it. Looking at his hands and his brawn, you'd hardly have guessed he'd never done an honest day's labor in his life. But it was true. For Sam was a gambling man, and since he was a boy, matching coppers or playing odd and even with his fellows, every penny passing through his fingers had been the fruit of wagering. And he was now approaching his thirtieth year.

Do not think to his discredit, however, that Sam Shay was a flint-hearted professional betting only on things that were sure or at odds much tipped in his favor. He bet not mathematically but by intuition, and the betting was as important as the winning. Were you to have given him the money, he would not have taken it; there would have been no savor to it. He must win it by his wits to enjoy it, and he could find fun in losing a good wager too.

So it was a sad thing to Sam that the girl of his heart, Shannon Malloy, should be dead set against gambling. But

191

the late Malloy had squandered all his earnings in just such divertissements as Sam Shay enjoyed, and the Widow Malloy had brought her daughter up most strictly to abjure men who loved the sound of rolling dice, the riffle of the cards, or the quickening of the pulse that comes as the horses turn into the homestretch and stream for the finish line.

In the early days of their acquaintance Shannon Malloy, who was small, with dark eyes that held a glow in their depths, had overlooked Sam's failing, feeling that Sam would mend his ways for love of her. And indeed Sam promised. But he could no more live without betting than he could without eating—less, for he could go a day without food undistressed, but in twenty years no sun had set without his making a wager of some kind, however small, just to keep his hand in.

Frequently, therefore, Sam Shay found himself in disgrace, while Shannon, more in sorrow than in anger, pleaded with him. And each time Sam once again promised to reform, knowing in his heart that once again he would fail. Inevitably, then, there came the time when Shannon, putting aside the veils that love cast upon her vision, saw with sad clarity that Sam Shay was Sam Shay, and naught would alter him. She loved him, but her convictions were as adamant. So she gave him back the ring she had accepted from him when his resolves had been less tarnished.

"I'm sorry, Sam," she had said, this very evening, and her words rang knell-like in Sam's ears now as he strode homeward through the soft evening dusk that lay across the park. "I'm sorry," and her voice had broken. "But today I heard your name spoken. By some men. And they were saying you are a born gambler who could make three bets with Satan and win them all. And if that is true, I can't marry you. Not feeling as I do. Not until you change."

And Sam, knowing that only some force far stronger than himself could turn him from his wagering, took the ring and went with only one backward glance. That glance showed him Shannon Malloy weeping but resolute, and he was as proud of her resolution as disconsolate that she should feel so strongly about his little weakness.

The ring was in his pocket and his fingers touched it sadly as he walked. It was a circlet cold to the touch, a metal zero that summed the total of his chances for having Shannon

Malloy to wife. The twilight lay upon the park, and it was queerly hushed, as if something was impending. But, lost in his thoughts, he strode along taking no notice.

It was as he came abreast an ancient oak that the shadow of the tree, athwart the sidewalk, with great unexpectedness solidified into a pillar of blackness church-steeple-high, which condensed swiftly into a smallish individual with flowing white locks and a benign countenance.

The individual who had so unconventionally placed himself in Sam's path was clad in garments of sober cut, an old-fashioned cape slung over his shoulders, and a soft dark hat upon his white hair. He smiled with innocent engagingness at Samuel Shay and spoke in a voice both mild and friendly.

"Good evening, Sam," he said as one might to an acquaintance not seen in a great while. "I'll bet you don't know who I am."

But Sam Shay, his right hand gripping the stout thorn stick he liked to carry about with him, was not to be trapped. He had seen the shadow of an oak tree change into a man, and this, to say the least, was unusual.

"Why," he proclaimed boldly, "I have a hundred dollars in my pocket, and I'll lay it against one that you are Satan."

Satan—for Sam's intuition had not failed him—let an expression of displeasure cross the benign countenance he had assumed for this visit. For he, too, had heard the report Shannon Malloy had quoted to Sam—that he could make three bets with Satan and win them all. And, his curiosity aroused, the Devil had come to test Sam's prowess, for he was fond of gambling, though a bad loser.

But the expression was gone in an instant and the gentle smile resumed its place. The old gentleman reached beneath his cloak and brought out a wallet which bulged pleasingly, although it was of a leather whose appearance Sam did not care for.

"That may be, Sam," Satan replied genially. "And if I am, I owe you a dollar. But I have another hundred here says you can't prove it."

And he waited, well pleased, for this was a wager that had stumped many eminent philosophers in centuries past. But Sam Shay was a man of action, not of words.

"Taken," he agreed at once, and raised his thorn stick above his head. "I'll just bash you a time or two over the pate. If you're an honest citizen I'll take your wallet, and if you're Satan I'll win the wager. For you could not let a mortal man trounce you so and still look yourself in the eye—an accomplishment quite individually yours. So—''

And Sam brought the stick down in a whistling blow.

A sulfurous sheet of flame cracked out from the heart of the oak tree, and the thorn stick was riven into a thousand splinters that hissed away through the air. A strong pain shot up Sam's arm, a tingling, numbing sensation that extended to the shoulder. But, rubbing his wrist, he was well satisfied.

Not so Satan. In his anger the little old gentleman had shot upward until he loomed twelve feet high now and looked far more terrifying than benign.

"You win, Sam Shay," Satan told him sourly. "But there's a third bet yet to come." Which Sam knew to be true, for on any such occasion as this when the Devil showed himself to a mortal, the unhappy man must win three wagers from him to go free. "And this time we'll increase the stakes. Your soul against the contents of this wallet that you can't win from me again."

Sam did not hesitate. For he must wager, whether he would or not.

"Taken," he answered. "But I must name the bet, since you named the others, and it is my turn now."

Satan it was who hesitated, but right and logic were with Sam, so he nodded.

"Name it, then," he directed, and his voice was like grumbling thunder beyond the sky line.

"Why, as to that," Sam told him with an impudent grin, "I'm betting you do not intend for me to win this wager."

Hardly were the words out of his mouth before Satan, in uncontrolled rage, had shot up to a tremendous height, his black cloak flowing from him like night itself draping over the city. For Sam had caught him neatly. If he responded that he did intend for Sam to win, then Sam perforce must go free. And if he responded that he had not so intended, then Sam won anyway.

Glaring down from his great height, Satan directed an awful gaze upon Sam Shay.

"This is an ill night's work you have done!" he cried in a voice that shook with rage, so that the skyscrapers near by trembled a bit, and the next day's papers carried an item concerning a small earthquake. "Hear me well, Sam Shay! From this moment onward, never shall you win another wager! All the forces of hell will be marshaled to prevent you."

Then, while Sam still gaped upward in dismay, the great figure faded from sight. A vast blast of hot air fanned past Sam, singeing the leaves of the nearest trees. He heard a distant clanging sound, as of a metal gate closing. After that all was quiet as it had been before.

Sam Shay stood in thought for several minutes and then realized he still was fingering the ring Shannon Malloy had returned to him. He laughed in something of relief.

"Glory!" he said aloud. "I've been standing here dreaming, while my mind wandered. If I'm to have nightmares, I'd best have them in bed."

And he hurried homeward, stopping by the way only long enough to buy the next day's racing form.

By morning Sam had half-forgotten his queer bemusement of the evening before. But that Shannon had dismissed him and returned his ring he remembered all too well. The bit of gold seemed heavy in his pocket as the weight that lay on his heart, so that he set about choosing his wagers for the day's racing with a gloomy mind.

It was perhaps this gloom that made it harder than was customary for him to make a choice. Usually his intuition made quick decision. But today he labored long and was only half-satisfied when he had finished marking down his picks.

Then, having breakfasted, with Shannon Malloy's face coming betwixt him and his coffee, he rode out to the track. Today he desired action, crowds, noise, excitement to take his mind off Shannon's rejection of him. So that the pushing throngs about the mutuel windows, the crowd murmur that rose to a shrill ululation as the horses burst from the barrier, the heart-tightening sensation as they turned into the home-stretch, all fitted well into his mood.

And he was feeling better when, his tickets tucked inside his pocket, he stood with the rest and watched the leaders in the first swing around the turn. He was well pleased to note his choice to the fore by half a dozen lengths, when some-thing happened. Perhaps the nag put its hoof into a pocket in the track. Perhaps it broke stride or merely tired. At all events, it faltered, slowed as though the Devil himself had it by the tail—now why had that precise comparison flashed across his mind then? Sam Shay wondered—and was beaten to the finish by a neck.

Sam tore up his tickets and scattered them to the breeze. He was not distressed. There were six races yet to come, and his pockets were well filled with money.

But when in the second his pick threw its jockey rounding the three-quarter pole and in the lead, and when in the third a saddle girth broke just as the jockey was lifting his mount for a winning surge, Sam Shay began to whistle a bit beneath his breath.

It was queer. It was decidedly queer, and he did not like it in the least. And when in the fourth, just as it was in the clear, his choice swerved and cut across the nag behind it, thus being disqualified, Sam's whistle grew more tuneless. He sniffed and sniffed again. Yes, it was there—the faintest whiff of sulfur somewhere about. In a most meditative mood Sam purchased a single two-dollar ticket for the fifth.

The ticket, as he had been unhappily convinced would be the case, proved a poor investment, his horse throwing a shoe at the far turn and pulling up last, limping badly.

Sam's whistle dropped until it was quite inaudible. He made his way toward the paddock and stood close as they led the winded horses out. As his choice passed, he sniffed strongly. And this time there was the slightest touch of brimstone mixed with the smell of sulfur.

Walking with a slow pace that did not in any way reflect the churning of his thoughts, Sam Shay returned to the grandstand and in the minutes before the next race was run reflected fast and furiously. Already his pockets, so thickly lined but an hour before, were well-nigh empty. And apprehension was beginning to sit, a tiny cloud, on Sam's brow.

This time he bought no ticket. But he sought out an individual with whom he had had dealings and stood beside him as the race was run. The ponies were streaming around the three-quarter pole and into the stretch, with forty lengths and half-a-dozen horses separating the first nag from the last, when Sam spoke suddenly.

"Ten dollars," he said to his acquaintance, "to a dime that Seven doesn't win."

The bookie gave him an odd glance. For Seven was the

trailer, forty lengths behind and losing distance steadily. Any moral eye could see she couldn't win, and it came to him Sam might be daft.

"Twenty dollars!" said Samuel Shay. "To a five-cent piece!"

They were odds not to be resisted, and the bookie nodded.

"Taken!" he agreed, and the words were scarce out of his mouth before Seven put on a burst of speed. She seemed to rise into the air with the very rapidity of her motion. Her legs churned. And she whisked forward so fast her astonished jockey was but an ace from being blown out of the saddle by the very rush of air. Closing the gap in a manner quite unbelievable, she came up to the leaders and, with a scant yard to the finish, shot ahead to win.

The crowd was too dazed even to roar. The judges gathered at once in frowning conference. But nothing amiss with Seven's equipment could be found—no electric batteries or other illegal contrivances—so at last her number was posted.

Sam Shay paid over the twenty dollars, while his acquaintance goggled at him. He would have asked questions, but Sam was in no mood for conversation. He moved away and sought a seat. There he pondered.

There could no longer be any doubt. His dream of the evening before had been no dream. It was Satan himself he had met face to face in the park, and Satan was having his vengeance for being bested. Sam could not call to mind the name of any other man in history who had outwitted the Devil without ruing it, and it was plain he was not to be the exception.

Wagering was Sam's life and livelihood, as Satan had well known. And if Sam was never to win another bet— He swallowed hard at the thought. Not only would he have lost Shannon Malloy for naught, but he would even be forced to the indignity of earning his living by the strength of his hands, he who had lived by his wits so pleasantly for so long.

It was a sobering reflection. But for the moment no helpful scheme would come. Just before the warning bell for the last race of the day, however, Sam rose with alacrity. He counted his money. Aside from carfare back to town, he had just fourteen dollars upon him. Seven two-dollar tickets—and in the last there was a field of seven!

Sam chuckled and bought seven tickets to win, one on each

of the entries. Then, feeling somewhat set up, he found a position of vantage. "Now," he said beneath his breath, "let's see the Devil himself keep you from having a winning ticket this time, Samuel Shay!" And complacently he watched his seven horses get off to a good start.

The race proceeded normally toward the half, and then to the three-quarters, with nothing untoward come about. Sam chuckled some more, for if he cashed a ticket on this race, then Satan had been bested again, and his curse on Sam's wagering broken.

But the chuckle came too soon. As the seven turned into the stretch, into a sky that had been cerulean blue leaped a storm cloud purple and black. From the cloud a bolt of lightning sped downward, in a blinding flash, to strike among the branches of an ancient elm which stood beside the grand-stand near the finish line. A horrid thunderclap deafened the throng. The elm tottered. Then it toppled and fell across the track, so that the seven jockeys were just able to pull up their mounts in time to avoid plunging into it.

And as sudden as it had come, the storm cloud was gone.

But obviously there could be no winner of the last race. The perplexed and shaken stewards hurriedly declared it no race and announced that all bets would be refunded. Sam received his money back—but that was not winning. And with the bills thrust into his coat he gloomily returned to his lodgings to devote more thought to this matter. For it was plain the Devil had meant what he had said—Sam would never win another wager. And with all the myriad hosts of Hell arrayed against him, Sam did not see what he could do about it.

But the Shays were never a quitter stock. Though Beelzebub and all his myrmidons opposed him, Sam was of no mind to turn to honest labor without giving the Devil a run for his money. So in the days that followed, Sam, with dogged resolution, did not cease his efforts to make a wager he could win. And his endeavors were a source of some concern in Hell.

It was on an afternoon two weeks perhaps after the fateful meeting between Satan and Sam Shay that the Devil recalled the matter to his mind and pressed a button summoning his chief lieutenant to make report. Whisking from his private laboratory, where he was engaged in a delicate experiment leading toward the creation of a brand-new and improved form of sin, his head assistant covered seven million miles in no time at all and deposited himself in Satan's presence, still scorching from the speed at which he had come.

The Devil, seated behind a desk of basalt, frowned upon him.

"I wish," he stated, "to know if my orders concerning the mortal y-clept Sam Shay have been carried out."

"To the letter, Infernal Highness," his lieutenant replied with a slight air of reserve.

"He has not won a wager since I pronounced my curse upon him?"

"Not of the most inconsequential kind."

"He is thoroughly miserable?"

"Completely so."

"He is in such despair he might even commit suicide, and so place himself in our hands?"

The other was silent. Satan's voice took on sharpness.

"He is *not* in despair?"

"He is in a very low frame of mind indeed," his chief assistant replied with reluctance. "But there is no notion of suicide in his mind. He is defiant. And troublesome in the extreme, I must add."

"Troublesome?" The three-billion-bulb chandelier overhead rattled. "How can a mere mortal be troublesome to the hosts of Hell? Kindly explain yourself."

The tips of his lieutenant's batwings quivered with inward nervousness, and absently he plucked a loose scale from his chest. But summoning his resolution, he answered.

"He is a persistent mortal, this Sam Shay," he replied humbly. "Although your infernal curse has been passed upon him, he refuses to be convinced he cannot evade it. He is constantly scheming to get around the fiat by means of trickery and verbal quibbling. And I have had to assign a good many of my best and most resourceful workers to keep a twenty-four-hour watch on Sam Shay to see he does not succeed. Let me explain.

"Last week, having already tried some hundreds of wagers of various kinds, he offered to bet an acquaintance it would not rain before noon. The wager was the merest quibble of a bet, for it then lacked but ten seconds of the hour, the sun was shining in a cloudless sky, and, in addition, the Weather Bureau had actually predicted storm.

"Sam Shay, however, got his gamble accepted by promising to spend double his winnings, if he won, on strong drink for his companion. A completely specious wager if ever one was made. Nevertheless, had it not rained before the hour of noon, technically he would have been the winner of a bet, and so the letter of your hellish curse would have been violated.

"So, upon the notice of merest seconds, I had to call two hundred and eighty workers away from urgent duty in Proselytizing, to borrow on an instant's notice another hundred from Punishment, to take a score of my best laboratory technicians off Research, and rush them all to the spot. Between them they managed to divert a storm that was raging over Ohio and scheduled to cause a flood estimated to produce for us a job of a hundred and eighty souls, whisking it to cover New England within the time limit.

"But the affair caused widespread comment, threw us off schedule, and has disrupted my entire force, due to the necessity of keeping a large emergency squad upon twenty-four-hour duty in constant readiness for any other such calls. And there have been dozens of them. Simply dozens!"

A drop of sweat rolled down the unhappy demon's brow, dissolving in steam.

"That's only a sample," he said earnestly. "This Sam Shay has scores of such tricks up his sleeves. Only yesterday he was attempting to win a wager at the race track, and his efforts kept us busy the entire afternoon. In the fifth race he made such a complicated series of bets as to the relative positions in which the various horses would finish that my most trusted aide completely lost track of them. He had to call on me personally at the last moment, and since one of the wagers was that the race itself wouldn't be finished, the only solution I could hit upon in time was to have all the horses finish in a dead heat, save for the one Sam Shay had bet upon to win.

"This one, in order to confound the fellow, I was forced to remove entirely from the race and set down in Australia, so that none of Shay's various stipulations concerning it could come true. But the talk caused by a seven-horse dead heat, together with the complete disappearance of one of the beasts and its jockey, caused a considerable stir.

"Taken in conjunction with the storm I had to arrange, and a number of similiar matters, it has started a religious revival. People are flocking into the churches, undoing some of our best work. So, Your Infernal Highness, if only we could overlook one or two of Sam Shay's more difficult wagers, it would make things much easier to—"

The crash of Satan's hooves upon the adamantine tiling cut him short.

"Never! I have put my curse upon this Shay! It must be carried out to the letter. Tend to it!"

"Yes, Prince of Evil," his head assistant squeaked and, being a prudent demon, hurled himself away and across the seven million miles of space to his labatory so swiftly that he struck with such force at the other end he was lame for a month. And never again did he dare mention the matter.

But of all this Sam Shay had no inkling. He was immersed in his own problems. Having failed in every wager he had made, however difficult to lose, he was in a depressed state of mind.

His resources were coming to an end. There were but a few dollars left in his pockets and none in his bank account. Shannon Malloy refused to see him. He had not won a wager since the night he had met the Devil, and he was so low in his mind that several times he had caught himself glancing through the "Help Wanted" sections of the papers.

Upon this particular day he was so sunk in despair that it was the middle of the afternoon, and he had not once tried the Devil's mettle to see if this time he could slip a winning wager past the demonic forces on watchful guard all about him. It was a day cut and tailored to his mood. The sky was lowering gray, and rain whipped down out of the north as if each drop had personal anger against the earth upon which it struck. And Sam Shay sat in his room, staring out at the storm, as close to despair as it had ever been his misfortune to come.

At last he bestirred himself; it was not in the blood of a Shay to sit thus, forever wrapped in gray gloom. He found his hat and ulster and with heavy step made his way out and down the street to a cozy bar and grill where perhaps a cheery companion might lighten his mood.

Ensconced in a corner where a fireplace glowed he found Tim Malloy, who was by way of being Shannon's brother, a round, merry little man who was the merrier because a mug of dark stood upon the table before him. Tim Malloy greeted him with words of cheer, and Sam sat himself down, answering as nearly in kind as he might. He ordered himself a mug of dark, too, and made inquiry concerning Shannon.

"Why, as to that," Tim Malloy said, draining off half his mug, "sometimes of a night I hear her crying, behind her locked door. And"—he drained off the rest of his dark—"she never did that before she gave you back your ring, Sam."

"Have another," Sam invited, feeling suddenly somewhat heartened. "Then mayhap she might take back the ring if I asked her, you think?" he asked, hope in his tone.

Tim Malloy accepted the dark, but after dipping into it, shook his head, a mustache of foam on his lip.

"Never while you're a betting man, Sam, and that'll be forever," he said, "Unless some wondrous force stronger than she is makes her do it. Not though she's unhappy the rest of her life from sending you away."

Sam sighed.

"Would it make any difference if she knew I lost all the wagers I make now?" he asked.

"Not so much as a pinpoint of difference," Tim Malloy answered. "Not so much as a pinpoint. To change the subject, how long will it keep raining, would you say?"

"All day, I suppose," Sam said, in a gloom again. "And all night, too, I've no doubt. Though I could stop it raining in five minutes if I'd a mind to."

"Could you so?" Tim Malloy said, interested. "Let's see how it goes, Sam. Just for curiosity's sake."

Sam Shay shrugged.

"Bet me a dollar it'll stop raining within five minutes," he said. "And I'll bet the same it'll not. But since it'll be costing me a dollar to show, you must promise to spend it back again treating me."

"Fair's fair," Tim Malloy answered prompt. "And I promise. Then, Sam, I bet you a dollar it'll stop raining inside five minutes."

Lackadaisically Sam accepted, and they laid their wagers out upon the table. And sure enough, within the five minutes the storm clouds overhead abruptly whisked away. The blue sky appeared; the sun shone, and it was as if the storm had never been.

"Now that's a curious thing, Sam," Tim Malloy said, eyes wide, as he ordered up more dark. "And if you could do that any time you wished, your fortune would be made."

"Oh, I can do it." Sam sighed, disinterested. "Fair to storm and storm to fair; I need but wager on it to make it come the opposite of my bet. For that matter, any event I make a gamble on will come out the opposite, be it what it may. It's a curse laid upon me, Tim."

"Is it now?" said Tim Malloy, and his eyes grew wider. "And by whom would the curse be laid, Sam Shay?"

Sam leaned forward and whispered in his ear, and Tim Malloy's eyes bade fair to start from their sockets.

"Draw in a deep breath," Sam said, nodding. "Sniff hard, Tim. You'll see."

Tim Malloy sniffed long and deep, and awe crept upon his features.

"Sulfur!" he whispered. "Sulfur and brimstone!"

Sam but nodded and went on drinking his dark. Tim Malloy, though, stretched out a hand and put it upon his arm.

"Sam," he said, voice hoarse, "you have never heard that there's people willing to pay good money to insure the weather'll be as they want it upon a certain day? Have you never heard of insuring against storms, Sam, and against accidents, sickness, twins, and such misfortunes? And insuring isn't really betting. It's but a business—a legitimate, money-making business."

Sam stopped drinking his dark. He put his mug upon the table with a bang, and upon his face there came a look.

"So it is," he said, struck by the sudden thought. "So it is!"

"Sam," Tim Malloy said, emotion in his tone, "let us take but a single example. This Sunday coming the Loyal Sons of St. Patrick parade. Suppose, then, the Loyal Sons said to you, 'Sam, we want to insure it does not storm this Sunday coming. Here's twenty dollars insurance money against rain. If it storms, now, you must pay us five hundred, but if it's fair, you keep the twenty.'

"And then suppose, Sam, you came to me and, 'Tim,' you'd say, 'I want to make a bet. And the bet is one dollar against another dollar that this Sunday coming it will rain.' Whereupon I'd say to you, 'Sam, I accept the wager. One dollar that it does not rain this Sunday coming.'

"And as you are doomed to lose your gamble, it does not rain; you keep the twenty dollars paid you by the Loyal Sons, and your profit, Sam, your fair profit on a straightforward business deal which no one could call gambling, would be—"

"Nineteen dollars!" Sam said, much moved. "Nineteen dollars profit, Tim, and no wager involved. And you say there are many people wanting such insurance?"

"Thousands of them," said Tim Malloy. "Thousands upon thousands of them. And there's no reason why you shouldn't insure them against anything they wish—seeing as you're backed, one might say, by all the resources of a tremendous big firm."

Sam Shay stood up, and in his eyes there was a light.

"Tim," he said in a voice that rang, "here is twenty dollars. Rent me an office and have a sign painted saying 'Samuel Shay, Insurance.' The biggest sign that can be managed. And here, Tim, is a dollar. That dollar I bet you Shannon will not say 'yes' to me a moment hence when I call upon her. Do you take the wager?"

"I take it, Sam," agreed Tim Malloy, but already Sam was striding out and in scarce a minute was standing in the Malloy living room, large and masterful, while Shannon, who had tried to hold the door shut against him, stared at him with blazing eyes.

"Sam Shay," she cried hotly, "I won't see you!"

"You cannot help seeing me," Sam replied with tenderness, "for I am standing here before you."

"Then I won't look at you!" cried Shannon, and shut her eyes.

"In that case you must take the consequences," said Sam and, stepping forward, kissed her so that Shannon's eyes flew open again.

"Sam Shay," she exclaimed, "I—"

"I'll bet a dollar," Sam interrupted her, "you're going to say you hate me."

It was indeed what Shannon had been about to say, but now some perverse demon seemed to seize her tongue.

"I'm not!" she denied. "I was going to say I love you."

And, having said it, she stared at Sam as if she could not believe her ears.

"Then, Shannon darling," Sam Shay asked, "will you take back my ring and marry me? And I'll bet another dollar you're going to say no."

And "no" it was that Shannon tried to say. But once again it was as if a contrary devil had her tongue.

"Indeed I'm not," she declared, to her own consternation. "For I say yes, and I will."

With which Sam swept her into his arms and kissed her again, so soundly she had no more time to wonder at the way her tongue had twisted. Indeed, she was forced to believe it was some strange power in Sam himself that had drawn the words from her. And on this point Sam wisely refrained from ever correcting her.

Thus they were married, and at this moment Sam Shay's insurance business is prospering beyond belief. Money is flowing in from all sides, and being a prudent man, Sam has arranged his affairs in excellent order. He has wagered with Tim Malloy, his junior partner, that he and Shannon will not live in good health to be ninety-nine each, while Tim has wagered they will. Sam has likewise bet that he and Shannon will be desperately unhappy, Tim gambling to the contrary. Finally Sam has gambled that they will not have ten fine, strapping children, six boys and four girls, and Tim has placed his money that they will.

So sin continues to decline as Sam's business grows, and Sam himself sleeps soundly of nights. And if there is sometimes the faintest smell of brimstone and sulfur about the house, as though from much coming and going of harassed demons, no one in the household minds it, not even Dion, youngest of the ten young Shays.

LOT NO. 249

by Sir Arthur Conan Doyle

Sir Arthur Conan Doyle (1859–1930) created the world's most famous detective, Sherlock Holmes. But he also wrote many fine works of fantasy and science fiction, including the following tale, which just may have been the unofficial inspiration for the first mummy movie.

Of the dealings of Edward Bellingham with William Monkhouse Lee, and of the cause of the great terror of Abercrombie Smith, it may be that no absolute and final judgment will ever be delivered. It is true that we have the full and clear narrative of Smith himself, and such corroboration as he could look for from Thomas Styles the servant, from the Reverend Plumptree Peterson, Fellow of Old's, and from such other people as chanced to gain some passing glance at this or that incident in a singular chain of events. Yet, in the main, the story must rest upon Smith alone, and the most will think that it is more likely that one brain, however outwardly sane, has some subtle warp in its texture, some strange flaw in its workings, than that the path of Nature has been overstepped in open day in so famed a center of learning and light as the University of Oxford. Yet when we think how narrow and how devious this path of Nature is, how dimly we can trace it, for all our lamps of science, and how from the darkness which girds it around great and terrible possibilities loom ever shadowly upward, it is a bold and confident man who will put a limit to the strange bypaths into which the human spirit may wander.

In a certain wing of what we will call Old College in Oxford there is a corner turret of an exceeding great age. The heavy arch which spans the open door has bent downward in the center under the weight of its years, and the gray, lichen-blotched blocks of stone are bound and knitted together with withes and strands of ivy, as though the old mother had set herself to brace them up against wind and weather. From the door a stone stair curves upward spirally, passing two landings, and terminating in a third one, its steps all shapeless and hollowed by the tread of so many generations of the seekers after knowledge. Life has flowed like water down this winding stair, and, waterlike, has left these smooth-worn grooves behind it. From the long-gowned, pedantic scholars of Plantagenet days down to the young bloods of a later age, how full and strong had been that tide of a young English life. And what was left now of all those hopes, those strivings, those fiery energies, save here and there in some old-world churchyard a few scratches upon a stone, and perchance a handful of dust in a moldering coffin? Yet here were the silent stair and the gray, old wall, with bend and saltire and many another heraldic device still to be read upon its surface, like grotesque shadows thrown back from the days that had passed.

In the month of May, in the year 1884, three young men occupied the sets of rooms which opened onto the separate landings of the old stair. Each set consisted simply of a sitting room and of a bedroom, while the two corresponding rooms upon the ground floor were used, the one as a coal cellar, and the other as the living room of the servant, or scout, Thomas Styles, whose duty it was to wait upon the three men above him. To right and to left was a line of lecture rooms and of offices, so that the dwellers in the old turret enjoyed a certain seclusion, which made the chambers popular among the more studious undergraduates. Such were the three who occupied them now—Abercrombie Smith above, Edward Bellingham beneath him, and William Monkhouse Lee upon the lowest story.

It was ten o'clock on a bright, spring night, and Abercrombie Smith lay back in his armchair, his feet upon the fender, and his briar-root pipe between his lips. In a similar chair, and equally at his ease, there lounged on the other side of the fireplace his old school friend Jephro Hastie. Both men were in flannels, for they had spent their evening upon the river, but apart from their dress no one could look at their hard-cut, alert faces without seeing that they were open-air men—men whose minds and tastes turned naturally to all that was manly and robust. Hastie, indeed, was stroke of his college boat, and Smith was an even better oar, but a coming examination had already cast its shadow over him and held him to his work, save for the few hours a week which health demanded. A litter of medical books upon the table, with scattered bones, models, and anatomical plates, pointed to the extent as well as the nature of his studies, while a couple of single sticks and a set of boxing gloves above the mantelpiece hinted at the means by which, with Hastie's help, he might take his exercise in its most compressed and least-distant form. They knew each other very well—so well that they could sit now in that soothing silence which is the very highest development of companionship.

"Have some whiskey," said Abercrombie Smith at last between two cloudbursts. "Scotch in the jug and Irish in the bottle."

"No, thanks. I'm in for the sculls. I don't liquor when I'm training. How about you?"

"I'm reading hard. I think it best to leave it alone."

Hastie nodded, and they relapsed into a contented silence.

"By the way, Smith," asked Hastie presently, "have you made the acquaintance of either of the fellows on your stair yet?"

"Just a nod when we pass. Nothing more."

"Hum! I should be inclined to let it stand at that. I know something of them both. Not much, but as much as I want. I don't think I should take them to my bosom if I were you. Not that there's much amiss with Monkhouse Lee."

"Meaning the thin one?"

"Precisely. He is a gentlemanly little fellow. I don't think there is any vice in him. But then you can't know him without knowing Bellingham."

"Meaning the fat one?"

"Yes, the fat one. And he's a man whom I, for one, would rather not know."

Abercrombie Smith raised his eyebrows and glanced across at his companion.

"What's up, then?" he asked. "Drink? Cards? Cad? You used not to be censorious."

"Ah! You evidently don't know the man, or you wouldn't

ask. There's something damnable about him—something reptilian. My gorge always rises at him. I should put him down as a man with secret vices—an evil liver. He's no fool, though. They say that he is one of the best men in his line that they have ever had in the college.''

"Medicine or classics?"

"Eastern languages. He's a demon at them. Chillingworth met him somewhere above the second cataract last long, and he told me that he just prattled to the Arabs as if he had been born and nursed and weaned among them. He talked Coptic to the Copts, and Hebrew to the Jews, and Arabic to the Bedouins, and they were all ready to kiss the hem of his frock coat. There are some old hermit Johnnies up in those parts who sit on rocks and scowl and spit at the casual stranger. Well, when they saw this chap Bellingham, before he had said five words they just lay down on their bellies and wriggled. Chillingworth said that he never saw anything like it. Bellingham seemed to take it as his right, too, and strutted about among them and talked down to them like a Dutch uncle. Pretty good for an undergrad of Olds, wasn't it?''

"Why do you say you can't know Lee without knowing Bellingham?"

"Because Bellingham is engaged to his sister Eveline. Such a bright little girl, Smith! I know the whole family well. It's disgusting to see that brute with her. A toad and a dove, that's what they always remind me of.''

Abercrombie Smith grinned and knocked his ashes out against the side of the grate.

"You show every card in your hand, old chap," said he. "What a prejudiced, green-eyed, evil-thinking old man it is! You have really nothing against the fellow except that.''

"Well, I've known her ever since she was as long as that cherry-wood pipe, and I don't like to see her taking risks. And it is a risk. He looks beastly. And he has a beastly temper, a venomous temper. You remember his row with Long Norton?''

"No; you always forget that I am a freshman.''

"Ah, it was last winter. Of course. Well, you know the towpath along by the river. There were several fellows going along it, Bellingham in front, when they came on an old market woman coming the other way. It had been raining— you know what those fields are like when it has rained—and the path ran between the river and a great puddle that was nearly as broad. Well, what does this swine do but keep the path and push the old girl into the mud, where she and her marketings came to terrible grief. It was a blackguard thing to do, and Long Norton, who is as gentle a fellow as ever stepped, told him what he thought of it. One word led to another, and it ended in Norton laying his stick across the fellow's shoulders. There was the deuce of a fuss about it, and it's a treat to see the way in which Bellingham looks at Norton when they meet now. By Jove, Smith, it's nearly eleven o'clock!''

"No hurry. Light your pipe again."

"Not I. I'm supposed to be in training. Here I've been sitting gossiping when I ought to have been safely tucked up. I'll borrow your skull, if you can share it. Williams has had mine for a month. I'll take the little bones of your ear, too, if you are sure you won't need them. Thanks very much. Never mind a bag, I can carry them very well under my arm. Good night, my son, and take my tip as to your neighbor."

When Hastie, bearing his anatomical plunder, had clattered off down the winding stair, Abercrombie Smith hurled his pipe into the wastepaper basket, and drawing his chair nearer to the lamp, plunged into a formidable, green-covered volume, adorned with great, colored maps of that strange, internal kingdom of which we are the hapless and helpless monarchs. Though a freshman at Oxford, the student was not so in medicine, for he had worked for four years at Glasgow and at Berlin, and this coming examination would place him finally as a member of his profession. With his firm mouth, broad forehead, and clear-cut, somewhat hard-featured face, he was a man who, if he had no brilliant talent, was yet so dogged, so patient, and so strong that he might in the end overtop a more showy genius. A man who can hold his own among Scotchmen and North Germans is not a man to be easily set back. Smith had left a name at Glasgow and at Berlin, and he was bent now upon doing as much at Oxford, if hard work and devotion could accomplish it.

He had sat reading for about an hour, and the hands of the noisy carriage clock upon the side table were rapidly closing together upon the twelve, when a sudden sound fell upon the student's ear—a sharp, rather shrill sound, like the hissing intake of a man's breath who gasps under some strong emotion.

Smith laid down his book and slanted his ear to listen. There was no one on either side or above him, so that the interruption came certainly from the neighbor beneath—the same neighbor of whom Hastie had given so unsavory an account. Smith knew him only as a flabby, pale-faced man of silent and studious habits, a man whose lamp threw a golden bar from the old turret even after he had extinguished his own. This community in lateness had formed a certain silent bond between them. It was soothing to Smith when the hours stole on toward dawning to feel that there was another so close who set as small a value upon his sleep as he did. Even now, as his thoughts turned toward him, Smith's feelings were kindly. Hastie was a good fellow, but he was rough, strong-fibered, with no imagination or sympathy. He could not tolerate departures from what he looked upon as the model type of manliness. If a man could not be measured by a public-school standard, then he was beyond the pale with Hastie. Like so many who are themselves robust, he was apt to confuse the constitution with the character, to ascribe to want of principle what was really a want of circulation. Smith, with his stronger mind, knew his friend's habit, and made allowance for it now as his thoughts turned toward the man beneath him.

There was no return of the singular sound, and Smith was about to turn to his work once more, when suddenly there broke out in the silence of the night a hoarse cry, a positive scream—the call of a man who is moved and shaken beyond all control. Smith sprang out of his chair and dropped his book. He was a man of fairly firm fiber, but there was something in this sudden, uncontrollable shriek of horror which chilled his blood and pringled in his skin. Coming in such a place and at such an hour, it brought a thousand fantastic possibilities into his head. Should he rush down, or was it better to wait? He had all the national hatred of making a scene, and he knew so little of his neighbor that he would not lightly intrude upon his affairs. For a moment he stood in doubt and even as he balanced the matter there was a quick rattle of footsteps upon the stairs, and young Monkhouse Lee, half-dressed and as white as ashes, burst into his room.

"Come down!" he gasped. "Bellingham's ill."

Abercombie Smith followed him closely downstairs into the sitting room which was beneath his own, and intent as he was upon the matter in hand, he could not but take an amazed glance around him as he crossed the threshold. It was such a chamber as he had never seen before—a museum rather than a study. Walls and ceiling were thickly covered with a thousand strange relics from Egypt and the East. Tall, angular figures bearing burdens or weapons stalked in an uncouth frieze around the apartments. Above were bull-headed, stork-headed, cat-headed, owl-headed statues, with viper-crowned, almond-eyed monarchs, and strange, beetlelike deities cut out of the blue Egyptian lapis lazuli. Horus and Isis and Osiris peeped down from every niche and shelf, while across the ceiling a true son of Old Nile, a great, hanging-jawed crocodile, was slung in a double noose.

In the center of this singular chamber was a large, square table, littered with papers, bottles, and the dried leaves of some graceful, palmlike plant. These varied objects had all been heaped together in order to make room for a mummy case, which had been conveyed from the wall, as was evident from the gap there, and laid across the front of the table. The mummy itself, a horrid, black, withered thing, like a charred head on a gnarled bush, was lying half out of the case, with its clawlike hand and bony forearm resting upon the table. Propped up against the sarcophagus was an old, yellow scroll of papyrus, and in front of it, in a wooden armchair, sat the owner of the room, his head thrown back, his widely opened eyes directed in a horrified stare to the crocodile above him, and his blue, thick lips puffing loudly with every expiration.

"My God! He's dying!" cried Monkhouse Lee distractedly.

He was a slim, handsome young fellow, olive-skinned and dark-eyed, of a Spanish rather than of an English type, with a Celtic intensity of manner which contrasted with the Saxon phlegm of Abercrombie Smith.

"Only a faint, I think," said the medical student. "Just give me a hand with him. You take his feet. Now onto the sofa. Can you kick all those little wooden devils off? What a litter it is! Now he will be all right if we undo his collar and give him some water. What has he been up to at all?"

"I don't know. I heard him cry out. I ran up. I know him pretty well, you know. It is very good of you to come down."

"His heart is going like a pair of castanets," said Smith, laying his hand on the breast of the unconscious man. "He seems to me to be frightened all to pieces. Chuck the water over him! What a face he has got on him!''

It was indeed a strange and most repellent face, for color and outline were equally unnatural. It was white, not with the ordinary pallor of fear, but with an absolutely bloodless white, like the underside of a sole. He was very fat, but gave the impression of having at some time been considerably fatter, for his skin hung loosely in creases and folds, and was shot with a meshwork of wrinkles. Short, stubbly brown hair bristled up from his scalp, with a pair of thick, wrinkled ears protruding at the sides. His light-gray eyes were still open, the pupils dilated and the balls projecting in a fixed and horrid stare. It seemed to Smith as he looked down upon him that he had never seen Nature's danger signals flying so plainly upon a man's countenance, and his thoughts turned more seriously to the warning which Hastie had given him an hour before.

"What the deuce can have frightened him so?" he asked.

"It's the mummy."

"The mummy? How, then?"

"I don't know. It's beastly and morbid. I wish he would drop it. It's the second fright he has given me. It was the same last winter. I found him just like this, with that horrid thing in front of him."

"What does he want with the mummy, then?"

"Oh, he's a crank, you know. It's his hobby. He knows more about these things than any man in England. But I wish he wouldn't! Ah, he's beginning to come to."

A faint tinge of color had begun to steal back into Bellingham's ghastly cheeks, and his eyelids shivered like a sail after a calm. He clasped and unclasped his hands, drew a long, thin breath between his teeth, and suddenly jerking up his head, threw a glance of recognition around him. As his eyes fell upon the mummy, he sprang off the sofa, seized the roll of papyrus, thrust it into a drawer, turned the key, and then staggered back onto the sofa.

"What's up?" he asked. "What do you chaps want?"

"You've been shrieking out and making no end of a fuss," said Monkhouse Lee. "If our neighbor here from above hadn't come down, I'm sure I don't know what I should have done with you."

"Ah, it's Abercrombie Smith," said Bellingham, glancing

up at him. "How very good of you to come in! What a fool I am! Oh, my God, what a fool I am!"

He sank his head onto his hands and burst into peal after peal of hysterical laughter.

"Look here! Drop it!" cried Smith, shaking him roughly by the shoulder.

"Your nerves are all in a jangle. You must drop these little midnight games with mummies, or you'll be going off your chump. You're all on wires now."

"I wonder," said Bellingham, "whether you would be as cool as I am if you had seen—"

"What, then?"

"Oh, nothing. I meant that I wonder if you could sit up at night with a mummy without trying your nerves. I have no doubt that you are quite right. I daresay that I have been taking it out of myself too much lately. But I am all right now. Please don't go, though. Just wait for a few minutes until I am quite myself."

"The room is very close," remarked Lee, throwing open the window and letting in the cool night air.

"It's balsamic resin," said Bellingham. He lifted up one of the dried palmate leaves from the table and frizzled it over the chimney of the lamp. It broke away into heavy smoke wreaths, and a pungent, biting odor filled the chamber. "It's the sacred plant—the plant of the priests," he remarked. "Do you know anything of Eastern languages, Smith?"

"Nothing at all. Not a word."

The answer seemed to lift a weight from the Egyptologist's mind.

"By the way," he continued, "how long was it from the time that you ran down until I came to my senses?"

"Not long. Some four or five minutes."

"I thought it could not be very long," said he, drawing a long breath. "But what a strange thing unconsciousness is! There is no measurement to it. I could not tell from my own sensations if it were seconds or weeks. Now that gentleman on the table was packed up in the days of the eleventh dynasty, some forty centuries ago, and yet if he could find his tongue, he would tell us that this lapse of time has been but a closing of the eyes and a reopening of them. He is a singularly fine mummy, Smith."

Smith stepped over to the table and looked down with a

professional eye at the black and twisted form in front of him. The features, though horribly discolored, were perfect, and two little nutlike eyes still lurked in the depths of the black, hollow sockets. The blotched skin was drawn tightly from bone to bone, and a tangled wrap of black, coarse hair fell over the ears. Two thin teeth, like those of a rat, overlay the shriveled lower lip. In its crouching position, with bent joints and craned head, there was a suggestion of energy about the horrid thing which made Smith's gorge rise. The gaunt ribs, with their parchmentlike covering, were exposed, and the sunken, leaden-hued abdomen, with the long slit where the embalmer had left his mark; but the lower limbs were wrapped around with coarse yellow bandages. A number of little clovelike pieces of myrrh and of cassia were sprinkled over the body and lay scattered on the inside of the case.

"I don't know his name," said Bellingham, passing his hand over the shriveled head. "You see the outer sarcophagus with the inscriptions is missing. Lot 249 is all the title he has now. You see it printed on his case. That was his number in the auction at which I picked him up."

"He has been a very pretty sort of fellow in his day," remarked Abercrombie Smith.

"He has been a giant. His mummy is six feet seven in length, and that would be a giant over there, for they were never a very robust race. Feel these great, knotted bones, too. He would be a nasty fellow to tackle."

"Perhaps these very hands helped to build the stones into the pyramids," suggested Monkhouse Lee, looking down with disgust in his eyes at the crooked, unclean talons.

"No fear. This fellow has been pickled in natron and looked after in the most approved style. They did not serve hodsmen in that fashion. Salt or bitumen was enough for them. It has been calculated that this sort of thing cost about seven hundred and thirty pounds in our money. Our friend was a noble at the least. What do you make of that small inscription near his feet, Smith?"

"I told you that I know no Eastern tongue."

"Ah, so you did. It is the name of the embalmer, I take it. A very conscientious worker he must have been. I wonder how many modern works will survive four thousand years?"

He kept on speaking lightly and rapidly, but it was evident to Abercrombie Smith that he was still palpitating with fear.

His hands shook, his lower lip trembled, and look where he would, his eye always came sliding around to his gruesome companion. Through all his fear, however, there was a suspicion of triumph in his tone and manner. His eyes shone, and his footstep, as he paced the room, was brisk and jaunty. He gave the impression of a man who has gone through an ordeal, the marks of which he still bears upon him, but which has helped him to his end.

"You're not going yet?" he cried as Smith rose from the sofa.

At the prospect of solitude, his fears seemed to crowd back upon him, and he stretched out a hand to detain him.

"Yes, I must go. I have my work to do. You are all right now. I think that with your nervous system you should take up some less morbid study."

"Oh, I am not nervous as a rule; and I have unwrapped mummies before."

"You fainted last time," observed Monkhouse Lee.

"Ah, yes, so I did. Well, I must have a nerve tonic or a course of electricity. You are not going, Lee?"

"I'll do whatever you wish, Ned."

"Then I'll come down with you and have a shakedown on your sofa. Good night, Smith. I am so sorry to have disturbed you with my foolishness."

They shook hands, and as the medical student stumbled up the spiral and irregular stair, he heard a key turn in a door, and the steps of his two new acquaintances as they descended to the lower floor.

In this strange way began the acquaintance between Edward Bellingham and Abercrombie Smith, an acquaintance which the latter, at least, had no desire to push further. Bellingham, however, appeared to have taken a fancy to his rough-spoken neighbor, and made his advances in such a way that he could hardly be repulsed without absolute brutality. Twice he called to thank Smith for his assistance, and many times afterward he looked in with books, papers, and such other civilities as two bachelor neighbors can offer each other. He was, as Smith soon found, a man of wide reading, with catholic tastes and an extraordinary memory. His manner, too, was so pleasing and suave that one came, after a time, to overlook his repellent appearance. For a jaded and wearied man he was no unpleasant companion, and Smith found himself, after a time, looking forward to his visits, and even returning them.

Clever as he undoubtedly was, however, the medical student seemed to detect a dash of insanity in the man. He broke out at times into a high, inflated style of talk which was in contrast with the simplicity of his life.

"It is a wonderful thing," he cried, "to feel that one can command powers of good and of evil—a ministering angel or a demon of vengeance." And again, of Monkhouse Lee, he said, "Lee is a good fellow, an honest fellow, but he is without strength or ambition. He would not make a fit partner for a man with a great enterprise. He would not make a fit partner for me."

At such hints and innuendos stolid Smith, puffing solemnly at his pipe, would simply raise his eyebrows and shake his head, with little interjections of medical wisdom as to earlier hours and fresher air.

One habit Bellingham had developed of late which Smith knew to be a frequent herald of a weakening mind. He appeared to be forever talking to himself. At late hours of the night, when there could be no visitor with him, Smith could still hear his voice beneath him in a low, muffled monologue, sunk almost to a whisper, and yet very audible in the silence. This solitary babbling annoyed and distracted the student, so that he spoke more than once to his neighbor about it. Bellingham, however, flushed up at the charge and denied curtly that he had uttered a sound; indeed, he showed more annoyance over the matter than the occasion seemed to demand.

Had Abercrombie Smith had any doubt as to his own ears he had not to go far to find corroboration. Tom Styles, the little wrinkled manservant who had attended to the wants of the lodgers in the turret for a longer time than any man's memory could carry him, was sorely put to it over the same matter.

"If you please, sir," said he as he tidied down the top chamber one morning, "do you think Mr. Bellingham is all right, sir?"

"All right, Styles?"

"Yes, sir. Right in his head, sir."

"Why should he not be, then?"

"Well, I don't know, sir. His habits has changed of late.

He's not the same man he used to be, though I make free to say that he was never quite one of my gentlemen, like Mr. Hastie or yourself, sir. He's took to talkin' to himself something awful. I wonder it don't disturb you. I don't know what to make of him, sir."

"I don't know what business it is of yours, Styles."

"Well, I takes an interest, Mr. Smith. It may be forward of me, but I can't help it. I feel sometimes as if I was mother and father to my young gentlemen. It all falls on me when things go wrong and the relations come. But Mr. Bellingham, sir. I want to know what it is that walks about his room sometimes when he's out and when the door's locked on the outside."

"Eh? You're talking nonsense, Styles."

"Maybe so, sir, but I heard it more'n once with my own ears."

"Rubbish, Styles."

"Very good, sir. You'll ring the bell if you want me."

Abercrombie Smith gave little heed to the gossip of the old manservant, but a small incident occurred a few days later which left an unpleasant effect upon his mind and brought the words of Styles forcibly to his memory.

Bellingham had come up to see him late one night, and was entertaining him with an interesting account of the rock tombs of Beni Hassan in Upper Egypt, when Smith, whose hearing was remarkably acute, distinctly heard the sound of a door opening on the landing below.

"There's some fellow gone in or out of your room," he remarked.

Bellingham sprang up and stood helpless for a moment, with the expression of a man who is half-incredulous and half-afraid.

"I surely locked it. I am almost positive that I locked it," he stammered. "No one could have opened it."

"Why, I hear someone coming up the steps now."

Bellingham rushed out through the door, slammed it loudly behind him, and hurried down the stairs. About halfway down Smith heard him stop and thought he caught the sound of whispering. A moment later the door beneath him shut, a key creaked in a lock, and Bellingham, with beads of moisture upon his pale face, ascended the stairs once more and reentered the room.

"It's all right," he said, throwing himself down in a chair. "It was that fool of a dog. He had pushed the door open. I don't know how I came to forget to lock it."

"I didn't know you kept a dog," said Smith, looking very thoughtfully at the disturbed face of his companion.

"Yes, I haven't had him long. I must get rid of him. He's a great nuisance."

"He must be, if you find it so hard to shut him up. I should have thought that shutting the door would have been enough, without locking it."

"I want to prevent old Styles' from letting him out. He's of some value, you know, and it would be awkward to lose him."

"I am a bit of a dog-fancier myself," said Smith, still gazing hard at his companion from the corner of his eyes. "Perhaps you'll let me have a look at it."

"Certainly. But I am afraid it cannot be tonight; I have an appointment. Is that clock right? Then I am a quarter of an hour late already. You'll excuse me, I am sure."

He picked up his cap and hurried from the room. In spite of his appointment, Smith heard him reenter his own chamber and lock his door upon the inside.

This interview left a disagreeable impression upon the medical student's mind. Bellingham had lied to him, and lied so clumsily that it looked as if he had desperate reasons for concealing the truth. Smith knew that his neighbor had no dog. He knew, also, that the step which he had heard upon the stairs was not the step of an animal. But if it were not, then what could it be? There was old Styles' statement about the something which used to pace the room at times when the owner was absent. Could it be a woman? Smith rather inclined to the view. If so, it would mean disgrace and expulsion to Bellingham if it were discovered by the authorities, so that his anxiety and falsehoods might be accounted for. And yet it was inconceivable that an undergraduate could keep a woman in his rooms without being instantly detected. Be the explanation what it might, there was something ugly about it, and Smith determined, as he turned to his books, to discourage all further attempts at intimacy on the part of his soft-spoken and ill-favored neighbor.

But his work was destined to interruption that night. He had hardly caught up the broken threads when a firm, heavy footfall came three steps at a time from below, and Hastie, in blazer and flannels, burst into the room.

"Still at it!" said he, plumping down into his wonted armchair. "What a chap you are to stew! I believe an earthquake might come and knock Oxford into a cocked hat, and you would sit perfectly placid with your books among the ruins. However, I won't bore you long. Three whiffs of baccy, and I am off."

"What's the news, then?" asked Smith, cramming a plug of bird's-eye into his briar with his forefinger.

"Nothing very much. Wilson made seventy for the freshmen against the eleven. They say that they will play him instead of Buddicomb, for Buddicomb is clean off color. He used to be able to bowl a little, but it's nothing but half-volleys and long hops now."

"Medium right," suggested Smith, with the intense gravity which comes upon a varsity man when he speaks of athletics.

"Including to fast, with a work from leg. Comes with the arm about three inches or so. He used to be nasty on a wet wicket. Oh, by the way, have you heard about Long Norton?"

"What's that?"

"He's been attacked."

"Attacked?"

"Yes, just as he was turning out of the High Street, and within a hundred yards of the gate of Old's."

"But who—"

"Ah, that's the rub! If you said 'what,' you would be more grammatical. Norton swears that it was not human, and, indeed, from the scratches on his throat, I should be inclined to agree with him."

"What, then? Have we come down to spooks?"

Abercrombie Smith puffed his scientific contempt.

"Well, no; I don't think that is quite the idea, either. I am inclined to think that if any showman has lost a great ape lately, and the brute is in these parts, a jury would find a true bill against it. Norton passes that way every night, you know, about the same hour. There's a tree that hangs low over the path—the big elm from Rainy's garden. Norton thinks the thing dropped on him out of the tree. Anyhow, he was nearly strangled by two arms, which, he says, were as strong and as thin as steel bands. He saw nothing; only those beastly arms that tightened and tightened on him. He yelled his head nearly off, and a couple of chaps came running, and the thing went over the wall like a cat. He never got a fair sight of it the whole time. It gave Norton a shake-up, I can tell you. I tell him it has been as good as a change at the seaside for him.''

"A garroter, most likely," said Smith.

"Very possibly. Norton says not, but we don't mind what he says. The garroter had long nails and was pretty smart at swinging himself over walls. By the way, your beautiful neighbor would be pleased if he heard about it. He had a grudge against Norton, and he's not a man, from what I know of him, to forget his little debts. But hallo, old chap, what have you got in your noddle?''

"Nothing," Smith answered curtly.

He had started in his chair, and the look had flashed over his face which comes upon a man who is struck suddenly by some unpleasant idea.

''You looked as if something I had said had taken you on the raw. By the way, you have made the acquaintance of Master B. since I looked in last, have you not? Young Monkhouse Lee told me something to that effect.''

"Yes; I know him slightly. He has been up here once or twice.''

"Well, you're big enough and ugly enough to take care of yourself. He's not what I should call exactly a healthy sort of Johnny, though, no doubt, he's very clever and all that. But you'll soon find out for yourself. Lee is all right; he's a very decent little fellow. Well, so long, old chap! I row Mullins for the vice-chancelor's pot on Wednesday week, so mind you come down, in case I don't see you before.''

Bovine Smith laid down his pipe and turned stolidly to his books once more. But with all the will in the world, he found it very hard to keep his mind upon his work. It would slip away to brood upon the man beneath him, and upon the little mystery which hung around his chambers. Then his thoughts turned to this singular attack of which Hastie had spoken, and to the grudge which Bellingham was said to owe the object of it. The two ideas would persist in rising together in his mind, as though there were some close and intimate connection between them. And yet the suspicion was so dim and vague that it could not be put down in words.

"Confound the chap!" cried Smith as he shied his book on pathology across the room. "He has spoiled my night's reading, and that's reason enough, if there were no other, why I should steer clear of him in the future."

For ten days the medical student confined himself so closely to his studies that he neither saw nor heard anything of either of the men beneath him. At the hours when Bellingham had been accustomed to visit him, he took care to sport his oak, and though he more than once heard a knocking at his outer door, he resolutely refused to answer it. One afternoon, however, he was descending the stairs when, just as he was passing it, Bellingham's door flew open, and young Monkhouse Lee came out with his eyes sparkling and a dark flush of anger upon his olive cheeks. Close at his heels followed Bellingham, his fat, unhealthy face all quivering with malignant passion.

"You fool!" he hissed. "You'll be sorry."

"Very likely," cried the other. "Mind what I say. It's off! I won't hear of it!"

"You have promised, anyhow."

"Oh, I'll keep that! I won't speak. But I'd rather little Eva was in her grave. Once for all, it's off. She'll do what I say. We don't want to see you again."

So much Smith could not avoid hearing, but he hurried on, for he had no wish to be involved in their dispute. There had been a serious breach between them, that was clear enough, and Lee was going to cause the engagement with his sister to be broken off. Smith thought of Hastie's comparison of the toad and the dove, and was glad to think that the matter was at an end. Bellingham's face when he was in a passion was not pleasant to look upon. He was not a man to whom an innocent girl could be trusted for life. As he walked, Smith wondered languidly what could have caused the quarrel, and what the promise might be which Bellingham had been so anxious that Monkhouse Lee should keep.

It was the day of the sculling match between Hastie and Mullins, and a stream of men were making their way down to the banks of the Isis. A May sun was shining brightly, and the yellow path was barred with the black shadows of the tall elm trees. On either side the gray colleges lay back from the road, the hoary old mothers of minds looking out from their high, mullioned windows at the tide of young life which swept so merrily past them. Black-clad tutors, prim officials, pale, reading men, brown-faced, straw-hatted young athletes in white sweaters or many-colored blazers, all were hurrying toward the blue, winding river which curves through the Oxford meadows.

Abercrombie Smith, with the intuition of an old oarsman, chose his position at the point where he knew that the struggle, if there were a struggle, would come. Far-off he heard the hum which announced the start, the gathering roar of the approach, the thunder of running feet, and the shouts of the men in the boats beneath him. A spray of half-clad, deep-breathing runners shot past him, and craning over their shoulders, he saw Hastie pulling a steady thirty-six, while his opponent, with a jerky forty, was a good boat's length behind him. Smith gave a cheer for his friend, and pulling out his watch, was starting off again for his chambers, when he felt a touch upon his shoulder and found that young Monkhouse Lee was beside him.

"I saw you there," he said, in a timid, deprecating way. "I wanted to speak to you, if you could spare me a half-hour. This cottage is mine. I share it with Harrington of King's. Come in and have a cup of tea."

"I must be back presently," said Smith. "I am hard on the grind at present. But I'll come in for a few minutes with pleasure. I wouldn't have come out only Hastie is a friend of mine."

"So he is of mine. Hasn't he a beautiful style? Mullins wasn't in it. But come into the cottage. It's a little den of a place, but it is pleasant to work in during the summer months."

It was a small, square white building, with green doors and shutters, and a rustic trelliswork porch, standing back some fifty yards from the river's bank. Inside, the main room was roughly fitted up as a study—deal table, unpainted shelves with books, and a few cheap oleographs upon the wall. A kettle sang upon a spirit stove, and there were tea things upon a tray on the table.

"Try that chair and have a cigarette," said Lee. "Let me pour you out a cup of tea. It's so good of you to come in, for I know that your time is a good deal taken up. I wanted to say to you that, if I were you, I should change my rooms at once."

"Eh?"

Smith sat staring with a lighted match in one hand and his unlit cigarette in the other.

"Yes; it must seem very extraordinary, and the worst of it is that I cannot give my reasons, for I am under a solemn promise—a very solemn promise. But I may go so far as to say that I don't think Bellingham is a very safe man to live near. I intend to camp out here as much as I can for a time."

"Not safe! What do you mean?"

"Ah, that's what I mustn't say. But do take my advice and move your rooms. We had a grand row today. You must have heard us, for you came down the stairs."

"I saw that you had fallen out."

"He's a horrible chap, Smith. That is the only word for him. I have had doubts about him ever since that night when he fainted—you remember, when you came down. I taxed him today, and he told me things that made my hair rise, and wanted me to stand in with him. I'm not straitlaced, but I am a clergyman's son, you know, and I think there are some things which are quite beyond the pale. I only thank God that I found him out before it was too late, for he was to have married into my family."

"This is all very fine, Lee," said Abercrombie Smith curtly. "But either you are saying a great deal too much or a great deal too little."

"I give you a warning."

"If there is a real reason for warning, no promise can bind you. If I see a rascal about to blow a place up with dynamite, no pledge will stand in my way of preventing him."

"Ah, but I cannot prevent him, and I can do nothing but warn you."

"Without saying what you warn me against."

"Against Bellingham."

"But that is childish. Why should I fear him, or any man?"

"I can't tell you. I can only entreat you to change your rooms. You are in danger where you are. I don't even say that Bellingham would wish to injure you. But it might happen, for he is a dangerous neighbor just now."

"Perhaps I know more than you think," said Smith, looking keenly at the young man's boyish, earnest face. "Suppose I tell you that someone else shares Bellingham's rooms."

Monkhouse Lee sprang from his chair in uncontrollable excitement.

"You know, then?" he gasped.

"A woman."

Lee dropped back again with a groan.

"My lips are sealed," he said. "I must not speak."

"Well, anyhow," said Smith, rising, "it is not likely that I should allow myself to be frightened out of rooms which suit me very nicely. It would be a little too feeble for me to move out all my goods and chattels because you say that Bellingham might in some unexplained way do me an injury. I think that I'll just take my chance, and stay where I am, and as I see that it's nearly five o'clock, I must ask you to excuse me."

He bade the young student adieu in a few curt words and made his way homeward through the sweet spring evening, feeling half-ruffled, half-amused, as any other strong, unimaginative man might who has been menaced by a vague and shadowy danger.

There was one little indulgence which Abercrombie Smith always allowed himself, however closely his work might press upon him. Twice a week, on the Tuesday and the Friday, it was his invariable custom to walk over to Farlingford, the residence of Doctor Plumptree Peterson, situated about a mile and a half out of Oxford. Peterson had been a close friend of Smith's elder brother, Francis, and as he was a bachelor, fairly well-to-do, with a good cellar and a better library, his house was a pleasant goal for a man who was in need of a brisk walk. Twice a week, then, the medical student would swing out there along the dark country roads and spend a pleasant hour in Peterson's comfortable study, discussing, over a glass of old port, the gossip of the varsity or the latest developments of medicine or of surgery.

On the day which followed his interview with Monkhouse Lee, Smith shut up his books at a quarter-past eight, the hour when he usually started for his friend's house. As he was leaving his room, however, his eyes chanced to fall upon one of the books which Bellingham had lent him, and his conscience pricked him for not having returned it. However repellent the man might be, he should not be treated with discourtesy. Taking the book, he walked downstairs and knocked at his neighbor's door. There was no answer, but on turning the handle, he found that it was unlocked. Pleased at the thought of avoiding an interview, he stepped inside and placed the book with his card upon the table.

The lamp was turned half down, but Smith could see the details of the room plainly enough. It was all much as he had seen it before—the frieze, the animal-headed gods, the hanging crocodile, and the table littered over with papers and dried leaves. The mummy case stood upright against the wall, but the mummy itself was missing. There was no sign of any second occupant of the room, and he felt as he withdrew that he had probably done Bellingham an injustice. Had he a guilty secret to preserve, he would hardly leave his door open so that all the world might enter.

The spiral stair was as black as pitch, and Smith was slowly making his way down its irregular steps, when he was suddenly conscious that something had passed him in the darkness. There was a faint sound, a whiff of air, a light brushing past his elbow, but so slight that he could scarcely be certain of it. He stopped and listened, but the wind was rustling among the ivy outside, and he could hear nothing else.

"Is that you, Styles?" he shouted.

There was no answer, and all was still behind him. It must have been a sudden gust of air, for there were crannies and cracks in the old turret. And yet he could almost have sworn that he heard a footfall by his very side. He had emerged into the quadrangle, still turning the matter over in his head, when a man came running swiftly across the smooth-cropped lawn.

"Is that you, Smith?"

"Hullo, Hastie!"

"For God's sake come at once! Young Lee is drowned! Here's Harrington of King's with the news. The doctor is out. You'll do, but come along at once. There may be life in him."

"Have you brandy?"

"No."

"I'll bring some. There's a flask on my table."

Smith bounded up the stairs, taking three at a time, seized the flask, and was rushing down with it, when, as he passed Bellingham's room, his eyes fell upon something which left him gasping and staring upon the landing.

The door, which he had closed behind him, was now open,

and right in front of him, with the lamplight shining upon it, was the mummy case. Three minutes ago it had been empty. He could swear to that. Now it framed the lank body of its horrible occupant, who stood, grim and stark, with his black, shriveled face toward the door. The form was lifeless and inert, but it seemed to Smith as he gazed that there still lingered a lurid spark of vitality, some faint sign of consciousness in the little eyes which lurked in the depths of the hollow sockets. So astounded and shaken was he that he had forgotten his errand, and was still staring at the lean, sunken figure when the voice of his friend below recalled him to himself.

"Come on, Smith!" he shouted. "It's life and death, you know. Hurry up! Now, then," he added, as the medical student reappeared, "let us do a sprint. It is well under a mile, and we should do it in five minutes. A human life is better worth running for than a pot."

Neck and neck they dashed through the darkness, and did not pull up until, panting and spent, they had reached the little cottage by the river. Young Lee, limp and dripping like a broken water plant, was stretched upon the sofa, the green scum of the river upon his black hair and a fringe of white foam upon his leaden-hued lips. Beside him knelt his fellow-student, Harrington, endeavoring to chafe some warmth back into his rigid limbs.

"I think there's life in him," said Smith with his hand to the lad's side. "Put your watch glass to his lips. Yes, there's dimming on it. You take one arm, Hastie. Now work it as I do, and we'll soon pull him around."

For ten minutes they worked in silence, inflating and depressing the chest of the unconscious man. At the end of that time a shiver ran through his body, his lips trembled, and he opened his eyes. The three students burst out into an irrepressible cheer.

"Wake up, old chap. You've frightened us quite enough."

"Have some brandy. Take a sip from the flask."

"He's all right now," said his companion Harrington. "Heavens, what a fright I got! I was reading here, and he had gone out for a stroll as far as the river, when I heard a scream and a splash. Out I ran, and by the time I could find him and fish him out, all life seemed to have gone. Then Simpson couldn't get a doctor, for he has a game leg, and I had to run, and I don't know what I'd have done without you fellows. That's right, old chap. Sit up."

Monkhouse Lee had raised himself on his hands and looked wildly about him.

"What's up?" he asked. "I've been in the water. Ah, yes; I remember."

A look of fear came into his eyes, and he sank his face into his hands.

"How did you fall in?"

"I didn't fall in."

"How, then?"

"I was thrown in. I was standing by the bank, and something from behind picked me up like a feather and hurled me in. I heard nothing and I saw nothing. But I know what it was, for all that."

"And so do I," whispered Smith.

Lee looked up with a quick glance of surprise.

"You've learned, then?" he said. "You remember the advice I gave you?"

"Yes, and I begin to think that I shall take it."

"I don't know what the deuce you fellows are talking about," said Hastie, "but I think, if I were you, Harrington, I should get Lee to bed at once. It will be time enough to discuss the why and the wherefore when he is a little stronger. I think, Smith, you and I can leave him alone now. I am walking back to college; if you are coming in that direction, we can have a chat."

But it was little chat that they had upon their homeward path. Smith's mind was too full of the incidents of the evening, the absence of the mummy from his neighbor's rooms, the step that passed him on the stair, the reappearance— the extraordinary, inexplicable reappearance of the grisly thing—and then this attack upon Lee, corresponding so closely to the previous outrage upon another man against whom Bellingham bore a grudge. All this settled in his thoughts, together with the many little incidents which had previously turned him against his neighbor, and the singular circumstances under which he was first called in to him. What had been a dim suspicion, a vague, fantastic conjecture, had suddenly taken form, and stood out in his mind as a grim fact, a thing not to be denied. And yet, how monstrous it was! how unheard of! how entirely beyond all bounds of human experience. An impartial judge, or even the friend who walked by his side, would simply tell him that his eyes had deceived him, that the mummy had been there all the time, that young Lee had tumbled into the river as any other man tumbles into a river, and the blue pill was the best thing for a disordered liver. He felt that he would have said as much if the positions had been reversed. And yet he could swear that Bellingham was a murderer at heart, and that he wielded a weapon such as no man had ever used in all the grim history of crime.

Hastie had branched off to his rooms with a few crisp and emphatic comments upon his friend's unsociability, and Abercrombie Smith crossed the quadrangle to his corner turret with a strong feeling of repulsion for his chambers and their associations. He would take Lee's advice and move his quarters as soon as possible, for how could a man study when his ear was ever straining for every murmur or footstep in the room below? He observed, as he crossed over the lawn, that the light was still shining in Bellingham's window, and as he passed up the staircase, the door opened and the man himself looked out at him. With his fat, evil face he was like some bloated spider fresh from the weaving of his poisonous web.

"Good evening," said he. "Won't you come in?"

"No," cried Smith fiercely.

"No? You are as busy as ever? I wanted to ask you about Lee. I was sorry to hear that there was a rumor that something was amiss with him."

His features were grave, but there was the gleam of a hidden laugh in his eyes as he spoke. Smith saw it, and he could have knocked him down for it.

"You'll be sorrier still to hear that Monkhouse Lee is doing very well, and is out of all danger," he answered. "Your hellish tricks have not come off this time. Oh, you needn't try to brazen it out. I know all about it."

Bellingham took a step back from the angry student and half-closed the door as if to protect himself.

"You are mad," he said. "What do you mean? Do you assert that I had anything to do with Lee's accident?"

"Yes," thundered Smith. "You and that bag of bones behind you; you worked it between you. I tell you what it is, Master B., they have given up burning folk like you, but we still keep a hangman, and, by George, if any man in this college meets his death while you are here, I'll have you up, and if you don't swing for it, it won't be my fault. You'll find that your filthy Egyptian tricks won't answer in England.''

''You're a raving lunatic,'' said Bellingham.

''All right. You just remember what I say, for you'll find that I'll be better than my word.''

The door slammed, and Smith went fuming up to his chamber, where he locked the door upon the inside and spent half the night in smoking his old briar and brooding over the strange events of the evening.

Next morning Abercrombie Smith heard nothing of his neighbor, but Harrington called upon him in the afternoon to say that Lee was almost himself again. All day Smith stuck fast to his work, but in the evening he determined to pay the visit to his friend Doctor Peterson upon which he had started the night before. A good walk and a friendly chat would be welcome to his jangled nerves.

Bellingham's door was shut as he passed, but glancing back when he was some distance from the turret, he saw his neighbor's head at the window outlined against the lamplight, his face pressed apparently against the glass as he gazed out into the darkness. It was a blessing to be away from all contact with him, if but for a few hours, and Smith stepped out briskly and breathed the soft spring air into his lungs. The half-moon lay in the west between two Gothic pinnacles and threw upon the silvered street a dark tracery from the stonework above. There was a brisk breeze, and light, fleecy clouds drifted swiftly across the sky. Old's was on the very border of the town, and in five minutes Smith found himself beyond the houses and between the hedges of a May-scented, Oxfordshire lane.

It was a lonely and little-frequented road which led to his friend's house. Early as it was, Smith did not meet a single soul upon his way. He walked briskly along until he came to the avenue gate, which opened into the long, gravel drive leading up to Farlingford. In front of him he could see the cozy red light of the windows glimmering through the foliage. He stood with his hand upon the iron latch of the swinging gate, and he glanced back at the road along which he had come. Something was coming swiftly down it.

It moved in the shadow of the hedge, silently and furtively, a dark, crouching figure, dimly visible against the black background. Even as he gazed back at it, it had lessened its distance by twenty paces and was fast closing upon him. Out of the darkness he had a glimpse of a scraggy neck and of two eyes that will ever haunt him in his dreams. He turned, and with a cry of terror he ran for his life up the avenue. There were the red lights, the signals of safety, almost within a stone's throw of him. He was a famous runner, but never had he run as he ran that night.

The heavy gate had swung into place behind him but he heard it dash open again before his pursuer. As he rushed madly and wildly through the night, he could hear a swift, dry patter behind him, and could see, as he threw back a glance, that this horror was bounding like a tiger at his heels, with blazing eyes and one stringy arm outthrown. Thank God, the door was ajar. He could see the thin bar of light which shot from the lamp in the hall. Nearer yet sounded the clatter from behind. He heard a hoarse gurgling at his very shoulder. With a shriek he flung himself against the door, slammed and bolted it behind him, and sank half-fainting onto the hall chair.

"My goodness, Smith, what's the matter?" asked Peterson, appearing at the door of his study.

"Give me some brandy."

Peterson disappeared and came rushing out again with a glass and a decanter.

"You need it," he said as his visitor drank off what he poured out for him. "Why, man, you are as white as a cheese."

Smith laid down his glass, rose up, and took a deep breath.

"I am my own man again now," said he. "I was never so unmanned before. But, with your leave, Peterson, I will sleep here tonight, for I don't think I could face that road again except by daylight. It's weak, I know, but I can't help it."

Peterson looked at his visitor with a very questioning eye.

"Of course you shall sleep here if you wish. I'll tell Mrs. Burney to make up the spare bed. Where are you off to now?"

"Come up with me to the window that overlooks the door. I want you to see what I have seen."

They went up to the window of the upper hall, whence they could look down upon the approach to the house. The drive and the fields on either side lay quiet and still, bathed in the peaceful moonlight.

"Well, really, Smith," remarked Peterson, "it is well that I know you to be an abstemious man. What in the world can have frightened you?"

"I'll tell you presently. But where can it have gone? Ah, now, look, look! See the curve of the road just beyond your gate."

"Yes, I see; you needn't pinch my arm off. I saw someone pass. I should say a man, rather thin, apparently, and tall, very tall. But what of him? And what of yourself? You are still shaking like an aspen leaf."

"I have been within handgrip of the devil, that's all. But come down to your study and I shall tell you the whole story."

He did so. Under the cheery lamplight with a glass of wine on the table beside him, and the portly form and florid face of his friend in front, he narrated, in their order, all the events, great and small, which had formed so singular a chain, from the night on which he had found Bellingham fainting in front of the mummy case until this horrid experience of an hour ago.

"There now," he said as he concluded, "that's the whole black business. It is monstrous and incredible, but it is true."

Doctor Plumptree Peterson sat for some time in silence with a very puzzled expression upon his face.

"I never heard of such a thing in my life, never!" he said at last. "You have told me the facts. Now tell me your inferences."

"You can draw your own."

"But I should like to hear yours. You have thought over the matter, and I have not."

"Well, it must be a little vague in detail, but the main points seem to me to be clear enough. This fellow Bellingham, in his Eastern studies, has got hold of some infernal secret by which a mummy—or possibly only this particular mummy—can be temporarily brought to life. He was trying this disgusting business on the night when he fainted. No doubt the sight of the creature moving had shaken his nerve, even though he had expected it. You remember that almost the first words he said were to call out upon himself as a fool. Well, he got more hardened afterward and carried the matter through without fainting. The vitality which he could put into it was evidently only a passing thing, for I have seen it continually in its case as dead as this table. He has some elaborate process, I fancy, by which he brings the thing to pass. Having done it, he naturally bethought him that he might use the creature as an agent. It has intelligence and it has strength. For some purpose he took Lee into his confidence; but Lee, like a decent Christian, would have nothing to do with such a business. Then they had a row, and Lee vowed that he would tell his sister of Bellingham's true character. Bellingham's game was to prevent him, and he nearly managed it, by setting this creature of his on his track. He had already tried its powers upon another man—Norton—toward whom he had a grudge. It is the merest chance that he has not two murders upon his soul. Then, when I taxed him with the matter, he had the strongest reasons for wishing to get me out of the way before I could convey my knowledge to anyone else. He got his chance when I went out, for he knew my habits and where I was bound for. I have had a narrow shave, Peterson, and it is mere luck you didn't find me on your doorstep in the morning. I'm not a nervous man as a rule, and I never thought to have the fear of death put upon me as it was tonight.''

''My dear boy, you take the matter too seriously,'' said his companion. ''Your nerves are out of order with your work, and you make too much of it. How could such a thing as this stride about the streets of Oxford, even at night, without being seen?''

''It has been seen. There is quite a scare in the town about an escaped ape, as they imagine the creature to be. It is the talk of the place.''

''Well, it's a striking chain of events. And yet, my dear fellow, you must allow that each incident in itself is capable of a more natural explanation.''

''What! even my adventure of tonight?''

''Certainly. You come out with your nerves all unstrung and your head full of this theory of yours. Some gaunt, half-famished tramp steals after you and, seeing you run, is emboldened to pursue you. Your fears and imagination do the rest.''

''It won't do, Peterson, it won't do.''

''And again, in the instance of your finding the mummy

case empty, and then a few moments later with an occupant, you know that it was lamplight, that the lamp was half turned down, and that you had no special reason to look hard at the case. It is quite possible that you may have overlooked the creature in the first instance."

"No, no; it is out of the question."

"And then Lee may have fallen into the river, and Norton been garroted. It is certainly a formidable indictment that you have against Bellingham, but if you were to place it before a police magistrate, he would simply laugh in your face."

"I know he would. That is why I mean to take the matter into my own hands."

"Eh?"

"Yes, I feel that a public duty rests upon me, and besides, I must do it for my own safety, unless I choose to allow myself to be hunted by this beast out of the college, and that would be a little too feeble. I have quite made up my mind what I shall do. And first of all, may I use your paper and pens for an hour?"

"Most certainly. You will find all that you want upon that side table."

Abercrombie Smith sat down before a sheet of foolscap, and for an hour, and then for a second hour his pen traveled swiftly over it. Page after page was finished and tossed aside while his friend leaned back in his armchair, looking across at him with patient curiosity. At last, with an exclamation of satisfaction, Smith sprang to his feet, gathered his papers up into order, and laid the last one upon Peterson's desk.

"Kindly sign this as a witness," he said.

"A witness? Of what?"

"Of my signature and of the date. The date is the most important. Why, Peterson, my life might hang upon it."

"My dear Smith, you are talking wildly. Let me beg you to go to bed."

"On·the contrary, I never spoke so deliberately in my life. And I will promise to go to bed the moment you have signed it."

"But what is it?"

"It is a statement of all that I have been telling you tonight. I wish you to witness it."

"Certainly," said Peterson, signing his name under that of his companion. "There you are! But what is the idea?"

"You will kindly retain it and produce it in case I am arrested."

"Arrested? For what?"

"For murder. It is quite on the cards. I wish to be ready for every event. There is only one course open to me, and I am determined to take it."

"For heaven's sake, don't do anything rash!"

"Believe me, it would be far more rash to adopt any other course. I hope that we won't need to bother you, but it will ease my mind to know that you have this statement of my motives. And now I am ready to take your advice and to go to roost, for I want to be at my best in the morning."

Abercrombie Smith was not an entirely pleasant man to have as an enemy. Slow and easy-tempered, he was formidable when driven to action. He brought to every purpose in life the same deliberate resoluteness which had distinguished him as a scientific student. He had laid his studies aside for a day, but he intended that the day should not be wasted. Not a word did he say to his host as to his plans, but by nine o'clock he was well on his way to Oxford.

In the High Street he stopped at Clifford's, the gunmaker's, and bought a heavy revolver, with a box of central-fire cartridges. Six of them he slipped into the chambers and, half-cocking the weapon, placed it in the pocket of his coat. He then made his way to Hastie's rooms, where the big oarsman was lounging over his breakfast, with the *Sporting Times* propped up against the coffeepot.

"Hullo! What's up?" he asked. "Have some coffee?"

"No, thank you. I want you to come with me, Hastie, and do what I ask you."

"Certainly, my boy."

"And bring a heavy stick with you."

"Hullo!" Hastie stared. "Here's a hunting crop that would fell an ox."

"One other thing. You have a box of amputating knives. Give me the longest of them."

"There you are. You seem to be fairly on the war trail. Anything else?"

"No, that will do." Smith placed the knife inside his coat and led the way to the quadrangle. "We are neither of us chickens, Hastie," said he. "I think I can do this job alone,

but I take you as a precaution. I am going to have a little talk
with Bellingham. If I have only him to deal with, I won't, of
course, need you. If I shout, however, up you come, and lam
out with your whip as hard as you can lick. Do you
understand?''

"All right. I'll come if I hear you bellow.''

"Stay here, then. I may be a little time, but don't budge
until I come down.''

"I'm a fixture.''

Smith ascended the stairs, opened Bellingham's door, and
stepped in. Bellingham was seated behind his table, writing.
Beside him, among his litter of strange possessions, towered
the mummy case, with its sale number 249 still stuck upon its
front, and its hideous occupant stiff and stark within it. Smith
looked very deliberately around him, closed the door, and
then, stepping across to the fireplace, struck a match and set
the fire alight. Bellingham sat staring, with amazement and
rage upon his bloated face.

"Well, really now, you make yourself at home," he gasped.

Smith sat himself deliberately down, placing his watch
upon the table, drew out his pistol, cocked it, and laid it in
his lap. Then he took the long amputating knife from his
bosom and threw it down in front of Bellingham.

"Now, then," said he, "just get to work and cut up that
mummy."

"Oh, is that it?" said Bellingham with a sneer.

"Yes, that is it. They tell me that the law can't touch you.
But I have a law that will set matters straight. If in five
minutes you have not set to work, I swear by the God who
made me that I will put a bullet through your brain!''

"You would murder me?''

Bellingham had half-risen, and his face was the color of
putty.

"Yes.''

"And for what?''

"To stop your mischief. One minute has gone.''

"But what have I done?''

"I know and you know.''

"This is mere bullying.''

"Two minutes are gone.''

"But you must give reasons. You are a madman—a dangerous madman. Why should I destroy my own property? It is a valuable mummy.''

"You must cut it up and you must burn it."

"I will do no such thing."

"Four minutes are gone."

Smith took up the pistol and he looked toward Bellingham with an inexorable face. As the second hand stole around, he raised his hand, and the finger twitched upon the trigger.

"There, there! I'll do it!" screamed Bellingham.

In frantic haste he caught the knife and hacked at the figure of the mummy, ever glancing around to see the eye and the weapon of his terrible visitor bent upon him. The creature crackled and snapped under every stab of the keen blade. A thick yellow dust rose up from it. Spices and dried essences rained down upon the floor. Suddenly, with a rending crack, its backbone snapped asunder, and it fell, a brown heap of sprawling limbs, upon the floor.

"Now into the fire!" said Smith.

The flames leaped and roared as the dried and tinderlike debris was piled upon it. The little room was like the stoke-hole of a steamer and the sweat ran down the faces of the two men; but still the one stooped and worked, while the other sat watching him with a set face. A thick, fat smoke oozed out from the fire, and a heavy smell of burned resin and singed hair filled the air. In a quarter of an hour a few charred and brittle sticks were all that was left of Lot No. 249.

"Perhaps that will satisfy you," snarled Bellingham, with hate and fear in his little gray eyes as he glanced back at his tormentor.

"No, I must make a clean sweep of all your materials. We must have no more devil's tricks. In with all these leaves! They may have something to do with it."

"And what now?" asked Bellingham when the leaves also had been added to the blaze.

"Now the roll of papyrus which you had on the table that night. It is in that drawer, I think."

"No, no," shouted Bellingham. "Don't burn that. Why, man, you don't know what you do. It is unique; it contains wisdom which is nowhere else to be found."

"Out with it!"

"But look here, Smith, you can't really mean it. I'll share

the knowledge with you. I'll teach you all that is in it. Or, stay, let me only copy it before you burn it!''

Smith stepped forward and turned the key in the drawer. Taking out the yellow, curled roll of paper, he threw it into the fire and pressed it down with his heel. Bellingham screamed and grabbed at it, but Smith pushed him back and stood over it until it was reduced to a formless gray ash.

''Now, Master B.,'' said he, ''I think I have pretty well drawn your teeth. You'll hear from me again, if you return to your old tricks. And now good morning, for I must go back to my studies.''

And such is the narrative of Abercrombie Smith as to the singular events which occurred in Old College, Oxford, in the spring of '84. As Bellingham left the university immediately afterward, and was last heard of in the Sudan, there is no one who can contradict his statement. But the wisdom of men is small, and the ways of Nature are strange, and who shall put a bound to the dark things which may be found by those who seek for them?

THE WITCH IS DEAD

by Edward D. Hoch

Though noted primarily as a mystery writer, the extremely prolific Edward D. Hoch (born in 1930) has also produced many works of science fiction and fantasy. In fact, his first published story was about Simon Ark, the 2,000-year-old detective, who specializes in cases of the occult, such as the following case of witchcraft.

Her real name was Helen Marie Carrio, but for more years than anyone could remember she'd been known simply as Mother Fortune. She was a large, plump woman, somewhere near seventy years old, though she might easily have passed for a hundred.

As her name might have implied, Mother Fortune made her meager living by predicting the future, by peering into a mammoth crystal ball and telling you just what you wanted to hear about yourself. It was a dying profession—especially in Westchester County in the second decade of the Atomic Age—but there were still many to whom her word was almost sacred.

There were others, however, who had widely different views on the subject of Mother Fortune. There were some, in fact, who even accused her of being a modern-day witch.

And perhaps she was.

In any event, Mother Fortune died as all good witches must—in a burst of flames that would have brought cries of envy from the judges of centuries agone.

It was perhaps one of the paradoxes of life, though, that Mother Fortune's death was to prove even more fantastic than had her life. . . .

It was the first week in October, and the twelfth day of an early fall heat wave that had amazed both forecasters and suburbanites by sending the temperatures into the high eighties. I had taken the 5:12 train from New York, as I usually did on nights when things weren't too busy at the office.

Actually, I suppose I noticed the man in the seat ahead of me right from the very start, but it wasn't until he left the train with me at Hudsonville that I actually caught a glimpse of his face. It had been a long time since I'd seen him, but that heavyset, wrinkled, yet somehow handsome face was one you didn't forget easily.

I caught up with him in front of the tiny building that served to link Hudsonville with the New Haven Railroad, and asked him, "You're Simon Ark, aren't you?"

The smile came at once to his tight lips. "Of course. It has been many years. . . ."

It had been many years. I'd first met Simon Ark in a little western mining town years before, when I was still a newspaper reporter. I hadn't seen him since, but since he was probably the most unusual man I'd ever know, I wasn't likely to forget him.

I led him to a coffee shop across the street, and over two steaming cups of black coffee I told him of my life during recent years. "I'm with Neptune Books now," I said, "one of these paperbound book publishers. Been there about three years now. It's a lot better than chasing politicians and police cars for a living. I married Shelly Constance, you know."

"I'd heard," Simon Ark said. "It's quite good to see you again after all these years."

"You certainly don't look any older, Simon. What have you been doing with yourself?"

Simon Ark smiled again. "The usual things. I've been traveling mostly. To England, and other places."

"I hope things weren't as bad as in Gidaz."

"Sometimes they were worse," he replied, and the smile was no longer on his lips. "There is evil everywhere these days, and it is most difficult to separate the man-made evil from the more ancient type. . . ."

I'd formed many theories about Simon Ark since our brief encounter several years back, but I could see that I was still a long way from knowing the truth about him. He'd told me once that he was searching, searching for the ultimate evil, searching for the devil himself. And there were times when the look of his face seemed to tell me that he'd been searching a long, long time.

I lit a cigarette and sipped my coffee. "Well, what on earth are you doing up in Westchester, anyway? The most evil things up here are the commuters' trains and this current heat wave."

He frowned slightly at that. "You perhaps have not heard then about the kind of remarkable events at the Hudsonville College for Women, or about the woman who calls herself Mother Fortune."

"I guess I haven't. Maybe I don't want to, if they're the kind of thing to bring *you* to Hudsonville."

"I hope that I am in time to prevent anything really serious," he said, "but it is hard to say just yet."

"What is it that's happening, anyway?"

"Of course there hasn't been any public announcement of it as yet—and there probably won't be—but it seems that this woman named Mother Fortune fancies herself as something of a modern-day witch. In any event, she has cast a spell of some kind over the girl students of Hudsonville College."

I had to laugh at that. The whole idea of a witch invading a modern girls' college was too much for me. "You're not serious, certainly?"

"I fear that I am," he told me. "Three of the girls are apparently near death, and some forty others have become ill."

"Then there must be some other explanation," I was quick to insist. "Things like that just don't happen anymore, at least not around Hudsonville."

"Stranger things than that have happened in this world," Simon Ark replied. "I'm going out to the school now. You may accompany me if you wish. . . ."

Hudsonville College for Women was like no other institute of higher learning anywhere in the east. Sixty years of traditions, plus millions of dollars from a few lucky endowments, had made it possible to recreate in Westchester some of the great wonders of ancient Rome.

At the very entrance to the campus was a line of pillars suggesting the remains of Apollo's temple at Pompeii, and even the students' chapel was an exact duplicate, in miniature, of the Church of San Francesco at Assisi. The main road through the campus was called, appropriately enough, the Appian Way. And the huge assembly hall, which could never be filled by Hudsonville's moderate enrollment, was of course patterned on the Roman Forum. There was even a small bridge over a creek that bore a remarkable resemblance to Venice's Rialto Bridge.

The whole thing was like taking a tour of all of Italy in a little over an hour, but whether it actually contributed to the task of turning out modern, cultured young ladies prepared for business and marriage was something I didn't know. I suppose it did, however, attract a certain number of students whose mothers would otherwise have sent them up to Vassar or over to Bryn Mawr; and it had the distinction of getting regular picture stories in all the leading magazines by the simple method of staging annual pageants based on some forgotten lore of ancient Rome.

It was apparently Simon Ark's first glimpse of the unusual campus, for he spent some minutes strolling around aimlessly before we finally headed for the administration building, which oddly enough was the only one that failed to carry out the old Roman motif. Instead, it was an ancient limestone structure that apparently dated from the college's founding back in the mid-nineties, and had somehow survived the Romanizing of the remainder of the college.

I'd called Shelly to tell her I'd be late for supper, though I didn't really expect the trip to Hudsonville College to last too long. And I was still quite dubious about the whole thing when we were met at the door by a tall, scholarly-looking gentleman with a Roman nose that fitted in well with the rest of the campus.

"May I help you?" he asked quietly, and though his voice was polite, I noticed that he was carefully blocking the doorway and barring our way.

"Possibly. I am Simon Ark, and this is a friend of mine. I heard that you have had some trouble here, and I thought I might be able to offer some assistance. . . ."

"We already have a doctor . . ." the tall man began.

"I'm not a doctor."

"If you're a newspaper reporter or anything like that, I can tell you right now we've nothing to say."

Simon Ark grunted. "I'm not a reporter, either, but before I say any more, could you tell us who you are?"

"Sorry," the man said, smiling slightly. "Name's Hugh Westwood. I'm professor of ancient history here. Now, if you could tell me your business. . . ."

"We . . . happened to hear about your troubles here, Professor Westwood. I personally specialize in the investigation of such phenomena, and I thought I might be of some little assistance."

Westwood gazed at Simon Ark with searching eyes. "I don't know how you found out about it, but if you mean you've had experience in dealing with witches, you're certainly the man we want to see."

"Well . . ." Simon Ark hesitated a moment, "I have had some small experience with witches. . . ."

That was all Westwood needed to hear. He led them down a long hall to his office and motioned to two chairs. In a few moments he rejoined them with an older, white-haired man and a middle-aged woman.

"This is our president, Dr. Lampton, and the Dean of Women, Miss Bagly. You said your name was . . . Simon Ark?"

He nodded and introduced me as his assistant. I was amazed at how quickly he seemed to be accepted by these three frightened people. Perhaps it was their fear, coupled with Ark's compelling manner, that made them forget their aversion to publicity.

"It's this woman . . . this . . . this Mother Fortune," Miss Bagly began. "She's some kind of a witch, and she's put a spell over our girls. We . . . we don't know which way to turn, Mr. Ark; we really don't. If we reported something like this to the police, it would get into all the papers and our school would be ruined."

Simon Ark frowned, and I knew a question was coming. "But I understand that at least a few of these girls are extremely ill. You mean to say they aren't even receiving medical attention?"

"Oh, heavens," Miss Bagly exclaimed, "Dr. Lampton here is a real M.D., you know. He's been looking after them."

"That's correct," the doctor said. "I haven't had any

private practice in a good many years, ever since I became president of Hudsonville, but I still know enough to give those girls proper attention.''

"Then just what's wrong with them, Doctor?" Simon Ark asked.

"Well . . . by medical standards it's very difficult to say. They just seem . . . well, weak, without energy. Several girls have fainted, and one or two are in a mild coma of some sort.''

"I imagine you've thought of narcotics.''

"Certainly. There's no possibility of anything like that— not at Hudsonville!''

Simon Ark sighed. "I understand there have been letters . . .''

I knew better than to wonder how he knew about the letters, because Simon Ark had ways of finding out such things. Dr. Lampton nodded and pulled them from his pocket. They looked like he'd been carrying them and studying them for weeks.

There were three of them in all, dated about a week apart and starting three weeks previous, around the first day of the fall term. The writing was crude, intentionally crude, I thought. All three letters were identical in their wording: "To the president of Hudsonville College: Your cruel act of fifty years ago is at last avenged. I have cursed your school and every student in it. Before another moon has come your school will be a campus of the dead.'' The notes were signed "Mother Fortune.''

Simon Ark studied them carefully. "This Mother Fortune is a local gypsy-fortune-teller, I understand. Do you have any idea just why she should be putting a curse on the college?''

Professor Westwood, who'd remained silent for some time, joined in the conversation then. "Unfortunately, yes. That reference to fifty years ago sent us looking back through the school's old records, but we found it. The woman who calls herself Mother Fortune was once a student here. . . .''

This news made it a little easier for me to understand their reluctance to call in the police. It was bad enough to have an exclusive girls' college hexed by a witch, but when it turns out the witch was once a student at the school, that's even worse publicity.

"Her name was Helen Marie Carrio at that time,'' Westwood

continued. "We found from the records that she was expelled just two weeks before she was to have graduated."

"For what reason?" Simon Ark asked.

Dr. Lampton interrupted to answer. "You have to remember that this was fifty years ago, Mr. Ark. Many things were different then."

"Why was she expelled?" Ark repeated.

"For smoking cigarettes," Lampton replied weakly. "You must realize that at the time such a thing was unknown among young girls, and at a school like Hudsonville it would have been a most serious offense."

We were silent for a moment while we thought about it. Was it possible that such a girl, grown old fifty years later, should still remember this childhood tragedy? Was it possible that the old woman now known as Mother Fortune somehow had the power to strike down these young girls?

"Have you contacted Mother Fortune about these threats?" Simon Ark asked.

"I went to see her personally," Dr. Lampton said. "Two weeks ago. She admitted sending the notes and said she'd keep on sending them. She's a very odd woman indeed—half-insane, possibly—yet with a manner about her that almost makes you believe she is some sort of . . . witch." The last word was spoken very quietly, as if the president was afraid someone outside the room might be listening.

Simon Ark frowned once again. "There have been witches in this world, and quite possibly Mother Fortune is one, but it is too early to say for certain. Right now I'd like to see some of these girls who have suffered this odd sickness. Oh, and I'd like a list of their names if possible."

Professor Westwood nodded and pulled a pad of yellow lined paper from his desk. The top sheet was covered with the usual unintelligible notes of a history professor, phrases like *"tunica molesta,"* and "Plato—IX—Jowett." Westwood tore off the top sheet and began copying names from a typed list on his desk.

There were some forty-odd names on the list, ranging from Abbot, Mary, to Yeagen, Bernice. Some had grim-looking stars after them, and I figured correctly that these were the more serious cases. Simon Ark carefully folded the yellow list and we followed the three others out of Westwood's office.

They led us across the mildly rolling hills of the campus, past the ancient Roman columns, to a squat, three-story structure. "This is Venice Hall, the principal girls' dorm," Miss Bagly informed us. "All of our dorms are named after Italian cities."

We followed her in, amid a few questioning stares from casually dressed girls relaxing after supper. I gathered that the sick girls were simply being kept in their own rooms.

The first room we visited was a cheerful-looking one on the second floor. There were two girls in it, both of them in bed. One was sitting up and reading a thick historical novel, but the other was asleep.

Simon Ark examined them both with care, but except for a somewhat tired-out expression, there was nothing unusual about them. "When did you first begin to feel ill?" Ark inquired.

The girl sat up further in bed, revealing a fantastic pair of plaid pajamas. "Gosh, I don't know. About a week ago, I guess."

"Did you receive any burns or unusual injuries around that time?"

"No, nothing."

"Do you smoke?"

"Sometimes. Not too much."

"Have you had a cigarette recently?"

"Not in over a month; not since I was back home."

I could see that Simon Ark was mildly disappointed at this. He apparently had thought that the perfect weapon of Mother Fortune's revenge would be poisoned cigarettes of some kind. But such was not the case.

The other girl had awakened now, and I could see that she was in much worse shape. I think it gave us all an odd feeling, looking at those girls, realizing that they might be the innocent victims of a terror that couldn't happen, but was.

Later, when we left the room and the building, Simon Ark appeared deep in thought. Once he turned to Professor Westwood and asked, "Have any teachers shown signs of this . . . sickness?"

"No, just the students."

"And what symptoms have the more serious cases shown?"

"Oh . . . vomiting . . . partial paralysis of various muscles . . ."

Simon Ark frowned. "Has anyone taken a blood test of the sick girls?"

"A blood test? Why, no, I hardly think so. That would involve calling in the authorities. . . ."

"Perhaps you could do it in your own lab. At least I suggest that a blood test of some sort be made as soon as possible."

We left them shortly after that, and Simon Ark and I made our way across the now darkened campus to the street. Even with night upon us, the heat was still there, making us forget the fact that it was already early autumn.

"What do you think about it, Simon?" I asked after we had walked some distance.

Simon Ark gazed off into the night, and I thought for a moment he hadn't heard my question. But then gradually he turned to me. "I think that we should pay a visit to Mother Fortune. . . ."

We found her, later that night, in a little street in a little city not too far from Hudsonville College. It was just another city in the southern part of the county called Westchester. And the street, usually, was just another street.

But tonight it was different. Tonight it blazed with light, light from a thousand colored bulbs that spelled out a score of gay designs against the evening sky. From every direction lighted streets shot out from the large old church at their center, the church of St. Francis of Assisi.

"It's a celebration for the saint's feast day," I explained to Simon. "These old Italian churches go big for things like that. The thing is sort of one huge block party that lasts for three or four nights. You certainly don't expect to find Mother Fortune here, do you?"

"I never expect to find evil anywhere," Simon Ark replied, "and yet it is all around us. This poor church, I fear, is no exception."

We walked on, beneath the colored lights and past the booths and trucks and wagons, selling everything from religious statues to hot pizza. Presently we saw a short, fat priest moving among the crowd.

Simon Ark moved quickly through the crowd and caught the priest's arm. "Pardon, Father, but I seek information regarding a woman known as Mother Fortune. I believe she is near here.''

The little priest's face turned dark with rage. "Sir, if you seek her out, I hope it is to force her to move away from my church and my people. She came two days ago with her trailer and her crystal ball and her fortune-telling. My people— many of them—are simple superstitious Italians, not long in this country.''

Simon Ark frowned. "But don't you have any control over who takes part in your celebration?''

"Ah, no.'' The priest shrugged. "They even come here and sell meat to my people on Fridays. But there are regulations about trailers in Westchester County, as you know, and perhaps the police will force Mother Fortune to leave.''

As we'd talked, he had led us to the very end of the lighted area, and there, parked against the curb like some giant sleeping beetle, was a long house trailer with the name of Mother Fortune on its side.

The priest left us, fading into the bright lights at our backs, leaving us alone with the woman who was perhaps a witch. The trailer was a large silver one, and in addition to Mother Fortune's name I noticed the single word "Erebus" near the front of the vehicle, like the name on the prow of a ship.

"What kind of a bus is that?'' I asked Simon.

He smiled slightly. "Erebus was one of the names for hell used by the poet Milton. A fitting name for the home of a witch.''

There was no one down at that end of the street at all, and I imagined correctly that the little priest's campaign against Mother Fortune was meeting with much success. Simon Ark pressed a tiny button by the trailer door and we waited for it to open.

When it finally did, the woman who greeted us was a surprise. I didn't know just what I expected, and certainly Mother Fortune was no beauty, but neither was she the typical concept of a medieval witch. She was simply a very old white-haired woman who acted as if she might be a little drunk and probably was.

"What you want?'' she managed to mumble.

"My name is Simon Ark; I'd like to talk to you.''

"Want your fortune told?''

"Possibly.''

"Come in, then."

We entered the gleaming silver trailer and found ourselves in another world. I'd expected something unusual, but I hadn't been prepared for the ancient beaded drapes, the musty Oriental furnishings, and huge glowing crystal ball that filled the center of the trailer's main room.

The crystal ball, apparently lit by a bulb in its base, was a good three feet in diameter, and the way it gave off illumination reminded me of those big revolving glass globes they used to have in dance halls twenty years ago.

Simon Ark settled himself in one of the big overstuffed chairs with curling dragons for arms and said, "I want to talk about the trouble at Hudsonville College."

The words were hardly out of his mouth when the old woman was on her feet, shouting in a harsh voice that was almost a scream. "They've been here themselves. I already told them it would do no good. It's too late to stop me now. Too late, you hear? Too late! They can have me arrested if they want, but it will do no good. Before many moons have passed, the first of the girls will be dead! After that, the rest will die quickly. They'll regret the day they expelled Mother Fortune from their school!"

From the cigarette burns on the sleeve of her robe, it was obvious that she still had the habit that had led to her disgrace those many years before. In a way I felt sorry for this old woman whose aging brain had turned back fifty years for revenge.

"Helen," Simon Ark began, but the woman showed no emotion at the use of her real name. "Helen, you've got to stop all this foolishness. You're not a witch and you haven't put a curse on those girls."

"Haven't I?" She laughed shrilly. "Haven't I? Look at this!"

She opened a drawer and pulled out a thin book with heavily padded covers that I recognized as the yearbook of Hudsonville College. Several long black hatpins had been driven through the covers and the pages.

The sight of it was so incredulous that I would have laughed had I not remembered those girls I'd seen back at the college. Something had made them sick, and perhaps this was it. I'd learned a long time ago, at my first meeting with

Simon Ark, that there are things in this world beyond our powers of explanation.

She placed the book on a table and gazed into the huge crystal ball. "Back in the Middle Ages it was believed that tobacco was invented by the devil, and that only the devil's priests used it," she said. "When they threw me out of Hudsonville, I began to believe it."

I turned my face from her as she talked, unable to look at the lines of tragedy I saw there. What had happened during fifty years of heartbreak to turn this onetime college girl into a vengeful witch? That was something I never found out, and something that is perhaps better left unknown.

At length she fell silent, and I could see that Simon Ark would learn nothing more from her. "Get out of here now," she said with finality. "I have to change my robe and get ready for the evening business." She gestured toward the wall, where a glistening gold and purple garment decorated with blazing suns and half-moons hung from a hook.

Of course there would be no more customers for her fortunes this late at night, but she didn't seem to realize it. In her vague way, night and day had apparently merged into one.

We left her then and walked back through the lighted streets to the church of St. Francis of Assisi. And when I looked at Simon Ark's face in the light of the multicolored bulbs, I knew that neither one of us was certain whether we had just left a modern-day servant of Satan or simply a confused old woman. . . .

The following morning dawned hot and bright, with the sun beating down upon leaves and grass that waited in vain for the cool slumber of autumn. It was Saturday, and I spent the morning working around the house. Shelly was an avid listener to my account of the previous night's adventures, but by noon I had all but forgotten Simon Ark and Mother Fortune.

It was just after the church bells had sounded the midday hour in the distance that Shelly called to me. "Someone wants you on the telephone."

I dropped the garden hose I'd been using and went into the house. The voice on the phone was familiar at once, but it took me a moment to identify Simon Ark on the other end.

"The witch is dead," he said simply. "Would you like to meet me at the trailer?"

"I'll be right over."

With a shouted few words to Shelly, I jumped into my car and headed south toward the parish of St. Francis of Assisi. In those first few minutes I didn't even try to think of the meaning of Simon Ark's words. I only knew that something had happened, something strange and unknown.

To the west dark clouds were forming on the horizon, and the shiver that went down my spine told me the barometer was falling fast. The October heat wave was on its last legs.

In the distance I thought I heard the rumble of thunder. . . .

The street by the church, which last night had been a brightly lighted invitation to fun and merriment, was now dark with the threat of approaching rain. It was blocked off completely by nearly a dozen police and private cars, and additional policemen were busy keeping back the crowd of curious neighbors. Some seemed almost indignant that they should be kept from seeing this bit of drama that had been played out on their street. Others simply stood silently, aware that they were in the presence of death.

Simon Ark stood in the door of the trailer, and he signaled to the police to let me through. I had long ago stopped wondering about his strange power over people, and now it seemed only natural that he was already in the confidence of the police.

"Prepare yourself," he told me at the door, "it's not a pleasant sight."

And it wasn't.

It reminded me of a time, a lifetime ago, when we'd had to blast a Japanese machine-gun nest on a lonely Pacific isle. We'd used flamethrowers, and the bodies of the dead Japs came back to my memory now as I stared at the thing that had been Mother Fortune.

She lay on top of her giant crystal ball, with her arms hanging down limply almost to the floor. Her clothes had been burnt off her completely, and the withered flesh was black and scorched. Her hair, and much of the skin on her face, had been burnt away, but there was no doubt in my mind that it really was the body of the woman we'd talked to last night.

"What happened?" I asked finally.

Simon Ark continued gazing at the body as he answered. "The police came to tell her she'd have to move the trailer. They looked through the window and saw her like this." He paused a moment before continuing. "The trailer was locked. They had to force the door to get in."

"What started the fire?"

"The police don't know. Even the priest doesn't know. They think it might have been something . . . unnatural."

For the first time I realized that the trailer itself was virtually unmarked by the fire; the blaze apparently had been centered on the body of the woman.

"Do you think somebody killed her, burned her because she was a witch, like they did in Salem?"

"Nobody burned her to death because she was alone in a locked trailer at the time," Simon Ark replied. "And at Salem they hanged the witches—they hanged nineteen and pressed one to death. I know."

And when he said it, I knew that he really did know. He knew because he'd been there and seen it, just as I could tell that he'd seen something like this horror before, somewhere in the dark forgotten past of history.

The police were busy removing the body, and examining the crystal ball for some sign of the fire's origin. But of course they found nothing.

As he left the trailer I saw the priest from St. Francis of Assisi Church making the sign of the cross over the body, and I wondered how this man could bless the corpse of a woman who'd opposed him so just a few hours earlier, when she still lived. I was even more astonished when I saw Simon Ark take an odd-looking cross from his pocket and raise it for a second over the body.

As he walked away he mumbled something in a tongue I didn't understand. He'd told me once it was Coptic, and I suspected it was a prayer, a very old prayer from the dawn of civilization.

And then the rain began to fall, in great wet drops that brought wisps of steam from the dry hot pavement. Simon Ark followed me to my car, and we sat in the rain watching the morgue wagon pull slowly away with the body of Mother Fortune. . . .

*   *   *

"Did you ever hear of Charles Fort?" Simon Ark asked me some time later as we sipped a glass of wine in an almost deserted oak-lined cocktail lounge. "He was a writer of some twenty-five years back who collected odd and unexplained news reports. His writings contain several references to deaths by mysterious burns."

I'd heard of Fort, of course, but I wasn't familiar with his writings. Simon Ark counted them off on his fingers as he mentioned the odd deaths. "There was one in Blyth, England, about fifty years ago. An old woman in a locked house, burned to death on a sofa. And in Ayer, Massachusetts, in 1890—a woman burned to death in the woods. In London, Southampton, Liverpool—always women, always old women. Fort reports only one case of an old man burning to death mysteriously. You want more cases, closer to home? St. Louis in 1889, North Carolina, San Diego. . . . A similar case in Rochester, New York, was blamed on lightning. . . ."

As if on cue, a streak of lightning cut through the afternoon sky, followed almost at once by a crash of thunder. "Any chance that lightning could have killed Mother Fortune?" I asked.

"Hardly. The storm just started, and in any event a bolt of lightning would certainly not go unnoticed by the neighbors."

I sipped my wine and glanced behind the bar, where the Notre Dame football team had just faded from the TV set, to be replaced by a dark-haired girl singing "That Old Black Magic." The song seemed appropriate to the occasion.

"Then what killed her?" I asked. "Do you know?"

"I've known since before she died," Simon Ark replied unhappily. "It was one of the most difficult decisions I ever had to make, to let her die like that. But it was the only chance to save those college girls."

"You mean the spell will be lifted now that the witch is dead?"

"Not exactly, but it'll force a very clever killer into the open."

"Then Mother Fortune was murdered, and by natural means!"

"She was murdered, but who is to say that any method of murder is natural? They are all weapons of the devil, in one way or another. Always remember that—every murder, every crime, is supernatural, in the sense that it was inspired by Satan.''

The bartender switched off the television set, and we were alone with the constantly irregular crashes of thunder from the outside world.

''Did Satan kill her, then?'' I asked, and I knew that Simon Ark would not consider the question a foolish one. ''The way all those other people were burned to death?''

''Only indirectly. Perhaps the real killer is a man who's been dead for nearly two thousand years. Because in a way, you see, Mother Fortune was killed by the ancient Roman emperor, Lucius—better known as Nero. . . .''

Simon Ark would say no more on the subject of the old fortune-teller's mysterious death. He seemed to dismiss the subject from his mind and turned instead to questioning me about the activities of Hudsonville College.

''Do they have any summer courses at all?'' he wanted to know.

''No, it's closed up completely all summer. Most of these exclusive girls' colleges are. Why do you want to know that?''

''Just filling in bits of the picture. Now I must make an important telephone call to Washington. To the Atomic Energy Commission. Perhaps then we can return to the college.''

He talked on the telephone for some time, and when he came out of the booth, he seemed pleased. We left the bar and drove through the gentle rain toward the campus of Hudsonville College.

It was almost dark by the time we arrived, and already the remains of the heat wave had given way to an autumn dampness that chilled our bones. We went first to Miss Bagly's quarters, where Simon Ark inquired as to the girls' condition.

''It's not good, Mr. Ark,'' she told him. ''Nearly all the girls in the college are sick in one way or another now. For some it's probably all in the mind, but I'm really worried about a few of them. I do wish Dr. Lampton would allow us to call in outside help.''

''That has all been taken care of, Miss Bagly,'' he told her. ''There will be doctors here within a few hours. But first I must discover the cause of the evil that lurks within your walls.''

"I heard that the witch . . . Mother Fortune . . . was dead. Will that help the girls?"

"In a way it will, Miss Bagly. But I fear we'll be unable to completely save the good name of your school." She started to say something else, but he held up his hand to silence her. "Are you certain, Miss Bagly, that none of your faculty has been affected by this sickness?"

"Oh, yes, Mr. Ark. Just the girls have been stricken. Except, of course, for our swimming instructor, who's not really a . . ."

But she never had a chance to finish her sentence. Simon Ark was already out of the room and hurrying down the steps. I ran after him, and I heard him mumble, "Of course! The swimming pool. Of course . . ."

And we ran through the night, toward the shadowy building that resembled the old Roman baths. Inside, all was darkness, and even the glistening waters of the pool itself were black. We were alone, and Simon Ark drew me into the deeper shadows.

We waited, for what I did not know, and as we waited, Simon Ark talked, in a voice so low it hardly reached my ears.

"Suppose," he began, "suppose you were an agent of a foreign power, or even of some private enterprise. Suppose you stole a quantity of radioactive mineral—cobalt or something similar—to use for your own illegal purposes. Suppose you found it necessary to hide it, safely, for a period of several weeks. Where . . . where could you safely hide a supply of illegal radioactive mineral for several weeks? Where would it be far enough away from people so as not to harm anyone with its dangerous rays?"

And I answered him. "In the middle of a college campus closed for the summer vacation. With no one but an occasional watchman to be exposed briefly to its rays."

The darkness was very dark then, and the evil of the unknown hung heavy around us. "Exactly," Simon Ark continued. "And when the school reopened for the fall before you could get rid of the deadly metal, then what would you do? What would you do to explain the radioactivity that would begin to strike down the girls?"

"You mean . . .?"

"I mean that this building is full of low, but dangerous,

amounts of radioactivity. That's what's wrong with those girls, and any doctor who'd been active in recent years would probably have recognized the symptoms. Unfortunately, Dr. Lampton did not, and his pride kept him from calling in assistance. I knew it almost from the beginning, which is why I suggested the blood tests. But I didn't know until tonight just where the source of the dangerous rays was. It had to be some place that the girls used, but not the teachers. I never thought of the swimming pool until now.''

"Then the witch business was all a blind!" I said. "The person who hid the uranium or cobalt found out about Mother Fortune's past life and used it as an excuse for the radioactive sickness.''

"Correct. A clever but devilish plot. Of course he couldn't depend on the assistance of a crazed old woman forever, so he had to arrange for her death when he feared she might talk.''

"But whom . . . ?''

The question was answered for me by a sudden movement on the far side of the black pool. We were no longer alone in the building.

Simon Ark stepped out of the shadows and shouted across the width of the pool. "All right, Professor Westwood. We know all about your murderous activities. . . .''

Professor Hugh Westwood looked at them from across the pool, and he might have been a demon conjured up by Satan himself. Even in the darkness I could feel the evil that seemed now to radiate from him, just as another evil radiated from a rock hidden somewhere in this building.

"It's too late to escape, Professor Westwood. I've already talked to Washington, and they confirmed the theft of the radioactive minerals from a testing lab in New York two months ago. There are doctors and FBI agents on their way here right now. Of course your friends have already been arrested, which is why they never came for the rocks. Where is it, Professor? In the pool itself? In the drain pipe, possibly?''

But Westwood let out a cry of rage, and a tongue of fire seemed to leap from his fingers into the pool. Instantly a wall of flame shot up between Westwood and ourselves. I had just a second to realize that the water in the swimming pool was somehow on fire, and then everything was a nightmare. . . .

* * *

Of course we found out later that, in anticipation of danger, Westwood had poured oil on the waters of the pool and then thrown a match into it, but in that instant with the flames all around me, it seemed as though the very gates of hell had opened to receive us.

I'll never forget those final seconds, as Simon Ark and Professor Westwood stalked each other around the blazing pool, with the flames leaping high and beating at the skylight until at last the glass burst and showered down upon us.

This was hell, and here at last was Simon Ark, stalking a modern-day version of the devil himself, while the flames waited to consume them both. And then, finally, in a sudden clash of good and evil, their two bodies met and locked in deadly combat, and toppled together into the waiting flames. . . .

The fire died as quickly as it had started, leaving only the steaming water beneath. The oil fire had burnt itself out just in time, for I doubt if even a man such as Simon Ark could have survived another minute in the heated water under those flames. As it was, we were too late to save Professor Westwood. He was already dead when we pulled him from the water. . . .

Later, much later, after the doctors and the police and the FBI, after the finding of the thin tube of radioactive cobalt in the swimming pool drain, after everybody had talked and listened and asked . . .

"But how did he kill the woman, Simon? How did he kill Mother Fortune?"

He looked at me with eyes that seemed tired, and he replied, "Remember yesterday in his office, when he tore a sheet from his pad. Remember a Latin phrase that was written on that sheet? It said '*tunica molesta,*' and that told me the answer even before the crime was committed. *Tunica molesta* was a name given to one of Nero's particularly horrible devices for killing early Christians. It was a tunic or mantle embroidered with the finest gold. Early Christians and criminals were brought into public arenas dressed in these garments, which were made of a highly combustible cloth that burst into flames when touched with the slightest spark."

I remember the robe that had been hanging in Mother Fortune's trailer. "You mean Westwood made one of these things and gave it to her?"

"Exactly. He no doubt told her it was a reward for her part in the scheme, though I doubt if she ever realized the true nature of his plot to cover up the cache of radioactive cobalt. She was just a confused old woman who jumped at an opportunity of revenging herself upon the school that had once expelled her."

"But you said this garment needed a spark or something to ignite it. How did he get into the trailer to set the robe on fire?"

"He didn't. Once he'd given it to her, he didn't have to worry about the outcome. Remember those cigarette burns we noticed on the sleeves of her old robe? He knew that sooner or later she would smoke a cigarette while wearing the *tunica molesta*. And he knew that in her clumsy manner, she'd let a single deadly spark fall onto her robe. . . ."

"And you knew this all the time?"

"I suspected it. As a murder method it isn't as strange as you might think, considering the fact that the killer was a professor of ancient history at a school that specialized in the early Roman Empire. The term *'tunica molesta'* came easily to his mind, and his only mistake was in jotting it down on his pad one day. I knew, though, that once Mother Fortune was dead he'd have to get rid of the cobalt, or the whole idea of the hex would be exploded as a fake, and Dr. Lampton would start looking for some medical reason for the girls' illness."

"It still seems so fantastic," I said.

"Life itself is fantastic, and death even more so. There are men in this world far more evil and far more clever than Professor Westwood, and as long as these men live, the fantastic will be commonplace. . . ."

He left me then, walking out through the night as suddenly as he'd come, but this time I was sure I'd not heard the last of Simon Ark. . . .

I KNOW WHAT YOU NEED

by Stephen King

The most successful horror writer of all time, Stephen King (born in 1947) has had most of his novels, such as CARRIE and CUJO, turned into successful Hollywood films. A native of Maine, he sets the following story at his old alma mater, the University of Maine at Orono.

"I know what you need."

Elizabeth looked up from her sociology text, startled, and saw a rather nondescript young man in a green fatigue jacket. For a moment she thought he looked familiar, as if she had known him before; the feeling was close to déjà vu. Then it was gone. He was about her height, skinny, and . . . twitchy. That was the word. He wasn't moving, but he seemed to be twitching inside his skin, just out of sight. His hair was black and unkempt. He wore thick horn-rimmed glasses that magnified his dark-brown eyes, and the lenses looked dirty. No, she was quite sure she had never seen him before.

"You know," she said, "I doubt that."

"You need a strawberry double-dip cone. Right?"

She blinked at him, frankly startled. Somewhere in the back of her mind she *had* been thinking about breaking for an ice cream. She was studying for finals in one of the third-floor carrels of the Student Union, and there was still a woefully long way to go.

"Right?" he persisted, and smiled. It transformed his face from something overintense and nearly ugly into something else that was oddly appealing. The word "cute" occurred to her, and that wasn't a good word to afflict a boy with, but this one was when he smiled. She smiled back before she

259

could roadblock it behind her lips. This she didn't need, to have to waste time brushing off some weirdo who had decided to pick the worst time of the year to try to make an impression. She still had sixteen chapters of *Introduction to Sociology* to wade through.

"No thanks," she said.

"Come on, if you hit them any harder you'll give yourself a headache. You've been at it two hours without a break."

"How would you know that?"

"I've been watching you," he said promptly, but this time his gamin grin was lost on her. She already had a headache.

"Well, you can stop," she said, more sharply than she had intended. "I don't like people staring at me."

"I'm sorry." She felt a little sorry for him, the way she sometimes felt sorry for stray dogs. He seemed to float in the green fatigue jacket and . . . yes, he had on mismatched socks. One black, one brown. She felt herself getting ready to smile again and held it back.

"I've got these finals," she said gently.

"Sure," he said. "Okay."

She looked after him for a moment pensively. Then she lowered her gaze to her book, but an afterimage of the encounter remained: *strawberry double-dip.*

When she got back to the dorm, it was 11:15 P.M. and Alice was stretched out on her bed, listening to Neil Diamond and reading *The Story of O.*

"I didn't know they assigned that in Eh-Seventeen," Elizabeth said.

Alice sat up. "Broadening my horizons, darling. Spreading my intellectual wings. Raising my . . . Liz?"

"Hmmm?"

"Did you hear what I said?"

"No, sorry, I—"

"You look like somebody conked you one, kid."

"I met a guy tonight. Sort of a funny guy, at that."

"Oh? He must be something if he can separate the great Rogan from her beloved texts."

"His name is Edward Jackson Hamner. Junior, no less. Short. Skinny. Looks like he washed his hair last around Washington's birthday. Oh, and mismatched socks. One black, one brown."

"I thought you were more the fraternity type."

"It's nothing like that, Alice. I was studying at the Union on the third floor—the Think Tank—and he invited me down to the Grinder for an ice-cream cone. I told him no and he sort of slunk off. But once he started me thinking about ice cream, I couldn't stop. I'd just decided to give up and take a break and there he was, holding a big, drippy strawberry double-dip in each hand."

"I tremble to hear the denouement."

Elizabeth snorted. "Well, I couldn't really say no. So he sat down, and it turns out he had sociology with Professor Branner last year."

"Will wonders never cease, lawd a mercy. Goshen to Christmas—"

"Listen, this is really amazing. You know the way I've been sweating that course?"

"Yes. You talk about it in your sleep, practically."

"I've got a seventy-eight average. I've got to have an eighty to keep my scholarship, and that means I need at least an eighty-four on the final. Well, this Ed Hamner says Branner uses almost the same final every year. And Ed's eidetic."

"You mean he's got a whatzit . . . photographic memory?"

"Yes. Look at this." She opened her sociology book and took out three sheets of notebook paper covered with writing.

Alice took them. "This looks like multiple-choice stuff."

"It is. Ed says it's Branner's last year's final *word for word.*"

Alice said flatly, "I don't believe it."

"But it covers all the material!"

"Still don't believe it." She handed the sheets back. "Just because this spook—"

"He isn't a spook. Don't call him that."

"Okay. This little *guy* hasn't got you bamboozled into just memorizing this and not studying at all, has he?"

"Of course not," she said uneasily.

"And even if this is like the exam, do you think it's exactly ethical?"

Anger surprised her and ran away with her tongue before she could hold it. "That's great for you, sure. Dean's List every semester and your folks paying your way. You aren't . . . Hey, I'm sorry. There was no call for that."

Alice shrugged and opened *O* again, her face carefully

neutral. "No, you're right. Not my business. But why don't you study the book, too . . . just to be safe?"

"Of course I will."

But mostly she studied the exam notes provided by Edward Jackson Hamner, Jr.

When she came out of the lecture hall after the exam, he was sitting in the lobby, floating in his green army fatigue coat. He smiled tentatively at her and stood up. "How'd it go?"

Impulsively, she kissed his cheek. She could not remember such a blessed feeling of relief. "I think I aced it."

"Really? That's great. Like a burger?"

"Love one," she said absently. Her mind was still on the exam. It was the one Ed had given her, almost word for word, and she had sailed through.

Over hamburgers, she asked him how his own finals were going.

"Don't have any. I'm in Honors, and you don't take them unless you want to. I was doing okay, so I didn't."

"Then why are you still here?"

"I had to see how you did, didn't I?"

"Ed, you didn't. That's sweet, but—" The naked look in his eyes troubled her. She had seen it before. She was a pretty girl.

"Yes," he said softly. "Yes, I did."

"Ed, I'm grateful. I think you saved my scholarship. I really do. But I have a boyfriend, you know."

"Serious?" he asked, with a poor attempt to speak lightly.

"Very," she said, matching his tone. "Almost engaged."

"Does he know he's lucky? Does he know how lucky?"

"I'm lucky, too," she said, thinking of Tony Lombard.

"Beth," he said suddenly.

"What?" she asked, startled.

"Nobody calls you that, do they?"

"Why . . . no. No, they don't."

"Not even this guy?"

"No—" Tony called her Liz. Sometimes Lizzie, which was even worse.

He leaned forward. "But Beth is what you like best, isn't it?"

She laughed to cover her confusion. "Whatever in the world—"

"Never mind." He grinned his gamin grin. "I'll call you Beth. That's better. Now eat your hamburger."

Then her junior year was over, and she was saying good-bye to Alice. They were a little stiff together, and Elizabeth was sorry. She supposed it was her own fault; she *had* crowed a little loudly about her sociology final when grades were posted. She had scored a ninety-seven—highest in the division.

Well, she told herself as she waited at the airport for her flight to be called, it wasn't any more unethical than the cramming she had been resigned to in that third-floor carrel. Cramming wasn't real studying at all; just rote memorization that faded away to nothing as soon as the exam was over.

She fingered the envelope that poked out of her purse. Notice of her scholarship-loan package for her senior year— two thousand dollars. She and Tony would be working together in Boothbay, Maine, this summer, and the money she would earn there would put her over the top. And thanks to Ed Hamner, it was going to be a beautiful summer. Clear sailing all the way.

But it was the most miserable summer of her life.

June was rainy, the gas shortage depressed the tourist trade, and her tips at the Boothbay Inn were mediocre. Even worse, Tony was pressing her on the subject of marriage. He could get a job on or near campus, he said, and with her Student Aid grant, she could get her degree in style. She was surprised to find that the idea scared rather than pleased her.

Something was *wrong*.

She didn't know what, but something was missing, out of whack, out of kilter. One night late in July she frightened herself by going on a hysterical crying jag in her apartment. The only good thing about it was that her roommate, a mousy little girl named Sandra Ackerman, was out on a date.

The nightmare came in early August. She was lying in the bottom of an open grave, unable to move. Rain fell from a white sky onto her upturned face. Then Tony was standing over her, wearing his yellow high-impact construction helmet.

"Marry me, Liz," he said, looking down at her expressionlessly. "Marry me or else."

She tried to speak, to agree; she would do anything if only he would take her out of this dreadful muddy hole. But she was paralyzed.

"All right," he said. "It's or-else, then."

He went away. She struggled to break out of her paralysis and couldn't.

Then she heard the bulldozer.

A moment later she saw it, a high yellow monster, pushing a mound of wet earth in front of the blade. Tony's merciless face looked down from the open cab.

He was going to bury her alive.

Trapped in her motionless, voiceless body, she could only watch in dumb horror. Trickles of dirt began to run down the sides of the hole—

A familiar voice cried, "Go! Leave her now! *Go!*"

Tony stumbled down from the bulldozer and ran.

Huge relief swept her. She would have cried had she been able. And her savior appeared, standing at the foot of the open grave like a sexton. It was Ed Hamner, floating in his green fatigue jacket, his hair awry, his horn-rims slipped down to the small bulge at the end of his nose. He held his hand out to her.

"Get up," he said gently. "I know what you need. Get up, Beth."

And she could get up. She sobbed with relief. She tried to thank him; her words spilled out on top of each other. And Ed only smiled gently and nodded. She took his hand and looked down to see her footing. And when she looked up again, she was holding the paw of a huge, slavering timber wolf with red hurricane-lantern eyes and thick, spiked teeth open to bite.

She woke up sitting bolt upright in bed, her nightgown drenched with sweat. Her body was shaking uncontrollably. And even after a warm shower and a glass of milk, she could not reconcile herself to the dark. She slept with the light on.

A week later Tony was dead.

She opened the door in her robe, expecting to see Tony, but it was Danny Kilmer, one of the fellows he worked with. Danny was a fun guy; she and Tony had doubled with him and his girl a couple of times. But standing in the doorway of her second-floor apartment, Danny looked not only serious but ill.

"Danny?" she said. "What—"

"Liz," he said. "Liz, you've got to hold on to yourself. You've . . . *ah, God!*" He pounded the jamb of the door with one big-knuckled, dirty hand, and she saw he was crying.

"Danny, is it Tony? Is something—"

"Tony's dead," Danny said. "He was—" But he was talking to air. She had fainted.

The next week passed in a kind of dream. The story pieced itself together from the woefully brief newspaper account and from what Danny told her over a beer in the Harbor Inn.

They had been repairing drainage culverts on Route 16. Part of the road was torn up, and Tony was flagging traffic. A kid driving a red Fiat had been coming down the hill. Tony had flagged him, but the kid never even slowed. Tony had been standing next to a dump truck, and there was no place to jump back. The kid in the Fiat had sustained head lacerations and a broken arm; he was hysterical and also cold sober. The police found several holes in his brake lines, as if they had overheated and then melted through. His driving record was A-1; he had simply been unable to stop. Her Tony had been a victim of that rarest of automobile mishaps: an honest accident.

Her shock and depression were increased by guilt. The fates had taken out of her hands the decision on what to do about Tony. And a sick, secret part of her was glad it was so. Because she hadn't wanted to marry Tony . . . not since the night of her dream.

She broke down the day before she went home.

She was sitting on a rock outcropping by herself, and after an hour or so the tears came. They surprised her with their fury. She cried until her stomach hurt and her head ached, and when the tears passed, she felt not better but at least drained and empty.

And that was when Ed Hamner said, "Beth?"

She jerked around, her mouth filled with the copper taste of fear, half-expecting to see the snarling wolf of her dream. But it was only Ed Hamner, looking sunburned and strangely defenseless without his fatigue jacket and blue jeans. He was wearing red shorts that stopped just ahead of his bony knees, a white T-shirt that billowed on his thin chest like a loose sail in the ocean breeze, and rubber thongs. He wasn't smiling and the fierce sun glitter on his glasses made it impossible to see his eyes.

"Ed?" she said tentatively, half-convinced that this was some grief-induced hallucination. "Is that really—"

"Yes, it's me."

"How—"

"I've been working at the Lakewood Theater in Skowhegan. I ran into your roommate . . . Alice, is that her name?"

"Yes."

"She told me what happened. I came right away. Poor Beth." He moved his head, only a degree or so, but the sun glare slid off his glasses and she saw nothing wolfish, nothing predatory, but only a calm, warm sympathy.

She began to weep again, and staggered a little with the unexpected force of it. Then he was holding her and then it was all right.

They had dinner at the Silent Woman in Waterville, which was twenty-five miles away; maybe exactly the distance she needed. They went in Ed's car, a new Corvette, and he drove well—neither showily nor fussily, as she guessed he might. She didn't want to talk and she didn't want to be cheered up. He seemed to know it, and played quiet music on the radio.

And he ordered without consulting her—seafood. She thought she wasn't hungry, but when the food came she fell to ravenously.

When she looked up again her plate was empty and she laughed nervously. Ed was smoking a cigarette and watching her.

"The grieving damsel ate a hearty meal," she said. "You must think I'm awful."

"No," he said. "You've been through a lot and you need to get your strength back. It's like being sick, isn't it?"

"Yes. Just like that."

He took her hand across the table, squeezed it briefly, then let it go. "But now it's recuperation time, Beth."

"Is it? Is it really?"

"Yes," he said. "So tell me. What are your plans?"

"I'm going home tomorrow. After that, I don't know."

"You're going back to school, aren't you?"

"I just don't know. After this, it seems so . . . so trivial. A lot of the purpose seems to have gone out of it. And all the fun."

"It'll come back. That's hard for you to believe now, but it's true. Try it for six weeks and see. You've got nothing better to do." The last seemed a question.

"That's true, I guess. But . . . Can I have a cigarette?"

"Sure. They're menthol, though. Sorry."

She took one. "How did you know I didn't like menthol cigarettes?"

He shrugged. "You just don't look like one of those, I guess."

She smiled. "You're funny, do you know that?"

He smiled neutrally.

"No, really. For you of all people to turn up . . . I thought I didn't want to see anyone. But I'm really glad it was you, Ed."

"Sometimes it's nice to be with someone you're not involved with."

"That's it, I guess." She paused. "Who are you, Ed, besides my fairy godfather? Who are you really?" It was suddenly important to her that she know.

He shrugged. "Nobody much. Just one of the sort of funny-looking guys you see creeping around campus with a load of books under one arm—"

"Ed, you're not funny-looking."

"Sure I am," he said, and smiled. "Never grew all the way out of my high-school acne, never got rushed by a big frat, never made any kind of splash in the social whirl. Just a dorm rat making grades, that's all. When the big corporations interview on campus next spring, I'll probably sign on with one of them and Ed Hamner will disappear forever."

"That would be a great shame," she said softly.

He smiled, and it was a very peculiar smile. Almost bitter.

"What about your folks?" she asked. "Where you live, what you like to do—"

"Another time," he said. "I want to get you back. You've got a long plane ride tomorrow, and a lot of hassles."

The evening left her relaxed for the first time since Tony's death, without that feeling that somewhere inside a mainspring was being wound and wound to the breaking point. She thought sleep would come easily, but it did not.

Little questions nagged.

Alice told me . . . poor Beth.

But Alice was summering in Kittery, eighty miles from Skowhegan. She must have been at Lakewood for a play.

The Corvette, this year's model. Expensive. A backstage job at Lakewood hadn't paid for that. Were his parents rich?

He had ordered just what she would have ordered herself. Maybe the only thing on the menu she would have eaten enough of to discover that she was hungry.

The menthol cigarettes, the way he had kissed her good night, exactly as she had wanted to be kissed. And—

You've got a long plane ride tomorrow.

He knew she was going home because she had told him. But how had he known she was going by plane? Or that it was a long ride?

It bothered her. It bothered her because she was halfway to being in love with Ed Hamner.

I know what you need.

Like the voice of a submarine captain tolling off fathoms, the words he had greeted her with followed her down to sleep.

He didn't come to the tiny Augusta airport to see her off, and waiting for the plane, she was surprised by her own disappointment. She was thinking about how quietly you could grow to depend on a person, almost like a junkie with a habit. The hype fools himself that he can take this stuff or leave it, when really—

"Elizabeth Rogan," the PA blared. "Please pick up the white courtesy phone."

She hurried to it. And Ed's voice said, "Beth?"

"Ed! It's good to hear you. I thought maybe . . ."

"That I'd meet you?" He laughed. "You don't need me for that. You're a big strong girl. Beautiful, too. You can handle this. Will I see you at school?"

"I . . . yes, I think so."

"Good." There was a moment of silence. Then he said, "Because I love you. I have from the first time I saw you."

Her tongue was locked. She couldn't speak. A thousand thoughts whirled through her mind.

He laughed again, gently. "No, don't say anything. Not now. I'll see you. There'll be time then. All the time in the world. Good trip, Beth. Good-bye."

And he was gone, leaving her with a white phone in her hand and her own chaotic thoughts and questions.

September.
Elizabeth picked up the old pattern of school and classes like a woman who has been interrupted at knitting. She was rooming with Alice again, of course; they had been roomies since freshman year, when they had been thrown together by the housing-department computer. They had always gotten along well, despite differing interests and personalities. Alice was the studious one, a chemistry major with a 3.6 average. Elizabeth was more social, less bookish, with a split major in education and math.

They still got on well, but a faint coolness seemed to have grown up between them over the summer. Elizabeth chalked it up to the difference of opinion over the sociology final, and didn't mention it.

The events of the summer began to seem dreamlike. In a funny way it sometimes seemed that Tony might have been a boy she had known in high school. It still hurt to think about him, and she avoided the subject with Alice, but the hurt was an old-bruise throb and not the bright pain of an open wound.

What hurt more was Ed Hamner's failure to call.

A week passed, then two, then it was October. She got a student directory from the Union and looked up his name. It was no help; after his name were only the words "Mill St." And Mill was a very long street indeed. And so she waited, and when she was called for dates—which was often—she turned them down. Alice raised her eyebrows but said nothing; she was buried alive in a six-week biochem project and spent most of her evenings at the library. Elizabeth noticed the long white envelopes that her roommate was receiving once or twice a week in the mail—since she was usually back from class first but thought nothing of them. The private detective agency was discreet; it did not print its return address on its envelopes.

When the intercom buzzed, Alice was studying. "You get it, Liz. Probably for you anyway."
Elizabeth went to the intercom. "Yes?"
"Gentleman door-caller, Liz."
Oh, Lord.

"Who is it?" she asked, annoyed, and ran through her tattered stack of excuses. Migraine headache. She hadn't used that one this week.

The desk girl said, amused, "His name is Edward Jackson Hamner. *Junior*, no less." Her voice lowered. "His socks don't match."

Elizabeth's hand flew to the collar of her robe. "Oh, God. Tell him I'll be right down. No, tell him it will be just a minute. No, a couple of minutes, okay?"

"Sure," the voice said dubiously. "Don't have a hemorrhage."

Elizabeth took a pair of slacks out of her closet. Took out a short denim skirt. Felt the curlers in her hair and groaned. Began to yank them out.

Alice watched all this calmly, without speaking, but she looked speculatively at the door for a long time after Elizabeth had left.

He looked just the same; he hadn't changed at all. He was wearing his green fatigue jacket, and it still looked at least two sizes too big. One of the bows of his horn-rimmed glasses had been mended with electrician's tape. His jeans looked new and stiff, miles from the soft and faded "in" look that Tony had achieved effortlessly. He was wearing one green sock, one brown sock.

And she knew she loved him.

"Why didn't you call before?" she asked, going to him.

He stuck his hands in the pockets of his jacket and grinned shyly. "I thought I'd give you some time to date around. Meet some guys. Figure out what you want."

"I think I know that."

"Good. Would you like to go to a movie?"

"Anything," she said. "Anything at all."

As the days passed it occurred to her that she had never met anyone, male or female, that seemed to understand her moods and needs so completely or so wordlessly. Their tastes coincided. While Tony had enjoyed violent movies of the *Godfather* type, Ed seemed more into comedy or nonviolent dramas. He took her to the circus one night when she was feeling low and they had a hilariously wonderful time. Study dates were real study dates, not just an excuse to grope on the third floor of the Union. He took her to dances and seemed especially good at the old ones, which she loved. They won a fifties Stroll trophy at a Homecoming Nostalgia Dance. More important, he seemed to understand when she wanted to be passionate. He didn't force her or hurry her; she never got the feeling that she had with some of the other boys she had gone out with—that there was an inner timetable for sex, beginning with a kiss good night on Date 1 and ending with a night in some friend's borrowed apartment on Date 10. The Mill Street apartment was Ed's exclusively, a third-floor walk-up. They went there often, and Elizabeth went without the feeling that she was walking into some minor-league Don Juan's passion pit. He didn't push. He honestly seemed to want what she wanted, when she wanted it. And things progressed.

When school reconvened following the semester break, Alice seemed strangely preoccupied. Several times that afternoon before Ed came to pick her up—they were going out to dinner—Elizabeth looked up to see her roommate frowning down at a large manila envelope on her desk. Once Elizabeth almost asked about it, then decided not to. Some new project probably.

It was snowing hard when Ed brought her back to the dorm.

"Tomorrow?" he asked. "My place?"

"Sure. I'll make some popcorn."

"Great," he said, and kissed her. "I love you, Beth."

"Love you, too."

"Would you like to stay over?" Ed asked evenly. "Tomorrow night?"

"All right, Ed." She looked into his eyes. "Whatever you want."

"Good," he said quietly. "Sleep well, kid."

"You, too."

She expected that Alice would be asleep and entered the room quietly, but Alice was up and sitting at her desk.

"Alice, are you okay?"

"I have to talk to you, Liz. About Ed."

"What about him?"

Alice said carefully, "I think that when I finish talking to you we're not going to be friends anymore. For me, that's giving up a lot. So I want you to listen carefully."

"Then maybe you better not say anything."

"I have to try."

Elizabeth felt her initial curiosity kindle into anger. "Have you been snooping around Ed?"

Alice only looked at her.

"Were you jealous of us?"

"No. If I'd been jealous of you and your dates, I would have moved out two years ago."

Elizabeth looked at her, perplexed. She knew what Alice said was the truth. And she suddenly felt afraid.

"Two things made me wonder about Ed Hamner," Alice said. "First, you wrote me about Tony's death and said how lucky it was that I'd seen Ed at the Lakewood Theater . . . how he came right over to Boothbay and really helped you out. But I never saw him, Liz. I was never near the Lakewood Theater last summer."

"But . . ."

"But how did he know Tony was dead? I have no idea. I only know he didn't get it from me. The other thing was that eidetic-memory business. My God, Liz, he can't even remember which socks he's got on!"

"That's a different thing altogether," Liz said stiffly. "It—"

"Ed Hamner was in Las Vegas last summer," Alice said softly. "He came back in mid-July and took a motel room in Pemaquid. That's just across the Boothbay Harbor town line. Almost as if he were waiting for you to need him."

"That's crazy! And how would you know Ed was in Las Vegas?"

"I ran into Shirley D'Antonio just before school started. She worked in the Pines Restaurant, which is just across from the playhouse. She said she never saw anybody who looked like Ed Hamner. So I've known he's been lying to you about several things. And so I went to my father and laid it out and he gave me the go-ahead."

"To do what?" Elizabeth asked, bewildered.

"To hire a private detective agency."

Elizabeth was on her feet. "No more, Alice. That's it." She would catch the bus into town, spend tonight at Ed's apartment. She had only been waiting for him to ask her, anyway.

"At least *know*," Alice said. "Then make your own decision."

"I don't have to know anything except he's kind and good and—"

"Love is blind, huh?" Alice said, and smiled bitterly. "Well, maybe I happen to love you a little, Liz. Have you ever thought of that?"

Elizabeth turned and looked at her for a long moment. "If you do, you've got a funny way of showing it," she said. "Go on, then. Maybe you're right. Maybe I owe you that much. Go on."

"You knew him a long time ago," Alice said quietly.

"I . . . what?"

"P.S. 119, Bridgeport, Connecticut."

Elizabeth was struck dumb. She and her parents had lived in Bridgeport for six years, moving to their present home the year after she had finished the second grade. She *had* gone to P.S. 119, but—

"Alice, are you sure?"

"Do you remember him?"

"No, of course not!" But she *did* remember the feeling she'd had the first time she had seen Ed—the feeling of déjà vu.

"The pretty ones never remember the ugly ducklings, I guess. Maybe he had a crush on you. You were in the first grade with him, Liz. Maybe he sat in the back of the room and just . . . watched you. Or on the playground. Just a little nothing kid who already wore glasses and probably braces and you couldn't even remember him, but I'll bet he remembers you."

Elizabeth said, "What else?"

"The agency traced him from school fingerprints. After that it was just a matter of finding people and talking to them. The operative assigned to the case said he couldn't understand some of what he was getting. Neither do I. Some of it's scary."

"It better be," Elizabeth said grimly.

"Ed Hamner, Senior, was a compulsive gambler. He worked for a top-line advertising agency in New York and then moved to Bridgeport sort of on the run. The operative says that almost every big-money poker game and high-priced book in the city was holding his markers."

Elizabeth closed her eyes. "These people really saw you got a full measure of dirt for your dollar, didn't they?"

"Maybe. Anyway, Ed's father got in another jam in Bridgeport. It was gambling again, but this time he got mixed up with a big-time loan shark. He got a broken leg and a broken arm somehow. The operative says he doubts it was an accident."

"Anything else?" Elizabeth asked. "Child beating? Embezzlement?"

"He landed a job with a two-bit Los Angeles ad agency in 1961. That was a little too close to Las Vegas. He started to spend his weekends there, gambling heavily . . . and losing. Then he started taking Ed Junior with him. And he started to win."

"You're making all of this up. You must be."

Alice tapped the report in front of her. "It's all here, Liz. Some of it wouldn't stand up in court, but the operative says none of the people he talked with would have a reason to lie. Ed's father called Ed his 'good-luck charm.' At first, nobody objected to the boy even though it was illegal for him to be in the casinos. His father was a prize fish. But then the father started sticking just to roulette, playing only odd-even and red-black. By the end of the year the boy was off-limits in every casino on the strip. And his father took up a new kind of gambling."

"What?"

"The stock market. When the Hamners moved to L.A. in the middle of 1961, they were living in a ninety-dollar-a-month cheese box and Mr. Hamner was driving a '52 Chevrolet. At the end of 1962, just sixteen months later, he had quit his job and they were living in their own home in San Jose. Mr. Hamner was driving a brand-new Thunderbird and Mrs. Hamner had a Volkswagen. You see, it's against the law for a small boy to be in the Nevada casinos, but no one could take the stock-market page away from him."

"Are you implying that Ed . . . that he could . . . Alice, you're crazy!"

"I'm not implying anything. Unless maybe just that he knew what his daddy needed."

I know what you need.

It was almost as if the words had been spoken into her ear, and she shuddered.

"Mrs. Hamner spent the next six years in and out of various mental institutions. Supposedly for nervous disorders, but the operative talked to an orderly who said she was pretty close to psychotic. She claimed her son was the devil's henchman. She stabbed him with a pair of scissors in 1964. Tried to kill him. She . . . Liz? Liz, what is it?''

"The scar," she muttered. "We went swimming at the University pool on an open night about a month ago. He's got a deep, dimpled scar on his shoulder . . . here." She put her hand just above her left breast. "He said . . ." A wave of nausea tried to climb up her throat and she had to wait for it to recede before she could go on. "He said he fell on a picket fence when he was a little boy."

"Shall I go on?"

"Finish, why not? What can it hurt now?"

"His mother was released from a very plush mental institution in the San Joaquin Valley in 1968. The three of them went on a vacation. They stopped at a picnic spot on Route 101. The boy was collecting firewood when she drove the car right over the edge of the dropoff above the ocean with both her and her husband in it. It might have been an attempt to run Ed down. By then he was nearly eighteen. His father left him a million-dollar stock portfolio. Ed came east a year and a half later and enrolled here. And that's the end."

"No more skeletons in the closet?"

"Liz, aren't there enough?"

She got up. "No wonder he never wants to mention his family. But you had to dig up the corpse, didn't you?"

"You're blind," Alice said. Elizabeth was putting on her coat. "I suppose you're going to him."

"Right."

"Because you love him."

"Right."

Alice crossed the room and grabbed her arm. "Will you get that sulky, petulant look off your face for a second and *think!* Ed Hamner is able to do things the rest of us only dream about. He got his father a stake at roulette and made him rich playing the stock market. He seems to be able to will winning. Maybe he's some kind of low-grade psychic. Maybe he's got precognition. I don't know. There are people who seem to have a dose of that. Liz, hasn't it ever occurred to you that he's forced you to love him?"

Liz turned to her slowly. "I've never heard anything so ridiculous in my life."

"Is it? He gave you that sociology test the same way he gave his father the right side of the roulette board! He was never enrolled in any sociology course! I checked. He did it because it was the only way he could make you take him seriously!"

"Stop it!" Liz cried. She clapped her hands over her ears.

"He knew the test, and he knew when Tony was killed, and he knew you were going home on a plane! He even knew just the right psychological moment to step back into your life last October."

Elizabeth pulled away from her and opened the door.

"Please," Alice said. "Please, Liz, listen. I don't know how he can do those things. I doubt if even *he* knows for sure. He might not mean to do you any harm, but he already is. He's made you love him by knowing every secret thing you want and need, and that's not love at all. That's rape."

Elizabeth slammed the door and ran down the stairs.

She caught the last bus of the evening into town. It was snowing more heavily than ever, and the bus lumbered through the drifts that had blown across the road like a crippled beetle. Elizabeth sat in the back, one of only six or seven passengers, a thousand thoughts in her mind.

Menthol cigarettes. The stock exchange. The way he had known her mother's nickname was Deedee. A little boy sitting at the back of a first-grade classroom, making sheep's eyes at a vivacious little girl too young to understand that—

I know what you need.

No. No. No. I do love him!

Did she? Or was she simply delighted at being with someone who always ordered the right thing, took her to the right movie, and did not want to go anywhere or do anything she didn't? Was he just a kind of psychic mirror, showing her only what she wanted to see? The presents he gave were always the right presents. When the weather had turned suddenly cold and she had been longing for a hair dryer, who gave her one? Ed Hamner, of course. Just happened to see one on sale in Day's, he had said. She, of course, had been delighted.

That's not love at all. That's rape.

The wind clawed at her face as she stepped out on the corner of Main and Mill, and she winced against it as the bus drew away with a smooth diesel growl. Its taillights twinkled briefly in the snowy night for a moment and were gone.

She had never felt so lonely in her life.

He wasn't home.

She stood outside his door after five minutes of knocking, nonplussed. It occurred to her that she had no idea what Ed did or whom he saw when he wasn't with her. The subject had never come up.

Maybe he's raising the price of another hair dryer in a poker game.

With sudden decision she stood on her toes and felt along the top of the doorjamb for the spare key she knew he kept there. Her fingers stumbled over it and it fell to the hall floor with a clink.

She picked it up and used it in the lock.

The apartment looked different with Ed gone—artificial, like a stage set. It had often amused her that someone who cared so little about his personal appearance should have such a neat, picture-book domicile. Almost as if he had decorated it for her and not himself. But of course that was crazy. Wasn't it?

It occurred to her again, as if for the first time, how much she liked the chair she sat in when they studied or watched TV. It was just right, the way Baby Bear's chair had been for Goldilocks. Not too hard, not too soft. Just right. Like everything else she associated with Ed.

There were two doors opening off the living room. One went to the kitchenette, the other to his bedroom.

The wind whistled outside, making the old apartment building creak and settle.

In the bedroom, she stared at the brass bed. It looked neither too hard nor too soft, but just right. An insidious voice smirked: *It's almost too perfect, isn't it?*

She went to the bookcase and ran her eye aimlessly over the titles. One jumped at her eyes and she pulled it out: *Dance Crazes of the Fifties*. The book opened cleanly to a point some three-quarters through. A section titled "The Stroll" had been circled heavily in red grease pencil and in the margin the word BETH had been written in large, almost accusatory letters.

I ought to go now, she told herself. I can still save something.

If he came back now, I could never look him in the face again and Alice would win. Then she'd really get her money's worth.

But she couldn't stop, and knew it. Things had gone too far.

She went to the closet and turned the knob, but it didn't give. Locked.

On the off chance, she stood on tiptoe again and felt along the top of the door. And her fingers felt a key. She took it down and somewhere inside a voice said very clearly: *Don't do this.* She thought of Bluebeard's wife and what she had found when she opened the wrong door. But it was indeed too late; if she didn't proceed now she would always wonder. She opened the closet.

And had the strangest feeling that this was where the real Ed Hamner, Jr., had been hiding all the time.

The closet was a mess—a jumbled rickrack of clothes, books, an unstrung tennis racket, a pair of tattered tennis shoes, old prelims and reports tossed helter-skelter, a spilled pouch of Borkum Riff pipe tobacco. His green fatigue jacket had been flung in the far corner.

She picked up one of the books and blinked at the title. *The Golden Bough.* Another. *Ancient Rites, Modern Mysteries.* Another. *Haitian Voodoo.* And a last one, bound in old, cracked leather, the title almost rubbed off the binding by much handling, smelling vaguely like rotted fish: *Necronomicon.* She opened it at random, gasped, and flung it away, the obscenity still hanging before her eyes.

More to regain her composure than anything else, she reached for the green fatigue jacket, not admitting to herself that she meant to go through its pockets. But as she lifted it she saw something else. A small tin box . . .

Curiously, she picked it up and turned it over in her hands, hearing things rattle inside. It was the kind of box a young boy might choose to keep his treasures in. Stamped in raised letters on the tin bottom were the words "Bridgeport Candy Co." She opened it.

The doll was on top. The Elizabeth doll.

She looked at it and began to shudder.

The doll was dressed in a scrap of red nylon, part of a scarf she had lost two or three months back. At a movie with Ed. The arms were pipe cleaners that had been draped in stuff that looked like blue moss. Graveyard moss, perhaps. There was hair on the doll's head, but that was wrong. It was fine white flax, taped to the doll's pink gum-eraser head. Her own hair was sandy blond and coarser than this. This was more the way her hair had been—

When she was a little girl.

She swallowed and there was a clicking in her throat. Hadn't they all been issued scissors in the first grade, tiny scissors with rounded blade, just right for a child's hand? Had that long-ago little boy crept up behind her, perhaps at nap time, and—

Elizabeth put the doll aside and looked in the box again. There was a blue poker chip with a strange six-sided pattern drawn on it in red ink. A tattered newspaper obituary—Mr. and Mrs. Edward Hamner. The two of them smiled meaninglessly out of the accompanying photo, and she saw that the same six-sided pattern had been drawn across their faces, this time in black ink, like a pall. Two more dolls, one male, one female. The similarity to the faces in the obituary photograph was hideous, unmistakable.

And something else.

She fumbled it out, and her fingers shook so badly she almost dropped it. A tiny sound escaped her.

It was a model car, the sort small boys buy in drugstores and hobby shops and then assemble with airplane glue. This one was a Fiat. It had been painted red. And a piece of what looked like one of Tony's shirts had been taped to the front.

She turned the model car upside down. Someone had hammered the underside to fragments.

"So you found it, you ungrateful bitch."

She screamed and dropped the car and the box. His foul treasures sprayed across the floor.

He was standing in the doorway, looking at her. She had never seen such a look of hate on a human face.

She said, "You killed Tony."

He grinned unpleasantly. "Do you think you could prove it?"

"It doesn't matter," she said, surprised at the steadiness of her own voice. "I know. And I never want to see you again. Ever. And if you do . . . anything . . . to anyone else, I'll know. And I'll fix you. Somehow."

His face twisted. "That's the thanks I get. I gave you

everything you ever wanted. Things no other man could have. Admit it. I made you perfectly happy.''

"You killed Tony!" She screamed it at him.

He took another step into the room. "Yes, and I did it for you. And what are you, Beth? You don't know what love is. I loved you from the first time I saw you, over seventeen years ago. Could Tony say that? It's never been hard for you. You're *pretty*. You never had to think about wanting or needing or about being lonely. You never had to find . . . other ways to get the things you had to have. There was always a Tony to give them to you. All you ever had to do was smile and say please.'' His voice rose a note. *"I* could never get what I wanted that way. Don't you think I tried? It didn't work with my father. He just wanted more and more. He never even kissed me good night or gave me a hug until I made him rich. And my mother was the same way. I gave her her marriage back, but was that enough for her? She hated me! She wouldn't come near me! She said I was unnatural! I gave her nice things but . . . Beth, don't do that! Don't . . . *dooon't—*''

She stepped on the Elizabeth doll and crushed it, turning her heel on it. Something inside her flared in agony, and then was gone. She wasn't afraid of him now. He was just a small, shrunken boy in a young man's body. And his socks didn't match.

"I don't think you can do anything to me now, Ed," she told him. "Not now. Am I wrong?''

He turned from her. "Go on," he said weakly. "Get out. But leave my box. At least do that.''

"I'll leave the box. But not the things in it.'' She walked past him. His shoulders twitched, as if he might turn and try to grab her, but then they slumped.

As she reached the second-floor landing, he came to the top of the stairs and called shrilly after her: "Go on then! But you'll never be satisfied with any man after me! And when your looks go and men stop trying to give you anything you want, you'll wish for me! You'll think of what you threw away!''

She went down the stairs and out into the snow. Its coldness felt good against her face. It was a two-mile walk back to the campus, but she didn't care. She wanted the walk, wanted the cold. She wanted it to make her clean.

In a queer, twisted way she felt sorry for him—a little boy with a huge power crammed inside a dwarfed spirit. A little boy who tried to make humans behave like toy soldiers and then stamped on them in a fit of temper when they wouldn't or when they found out.

And what was she? Blessed with all the things he was not, through no fault of his or effort of her own? She remembered the way she had reacted to Alice, trying blindly and jealously to hold on to something that was easy rather than good, not caring, not caring.

When your looks go and men stop trying to give you anything you want, you'll wish for me! . . . I know what you need.

But was she so small that she actually needed so little?

Please, dear God, no.

On the bridge between the campus and town she paused and threw Ed Hamner's scraps of magic over the side, piece by piece. The red-painted model Fiat went last, falling end over end into the driven snow until it was lost from sight. Then she walked on.

THE MIRACLE WORKERS

by Jack Vance

Noted for his style and unique combinations of fantasy, science fiction, and mystery, Jack Vance (born in 1920) has won the Edgar, Hugo, and Nebula awards. He has produced many interesting novels, but is at his very best with slightly shorter lengths such as the novella below.

I

The war party from Faide Keep moved eastward across the downs: a column of a hundred armored knights, five hundred foot soldiers, a train of wagons. In the lead rode Lord Faide, a tall man in his early maturity, spare and catlike, with a sallow dyspeptic face. He sat in the ancestral car of the Faides, a boat-shaped vehicle floating two feet above the moss, and carried, in addition to his sword and dagger, his ancestral side weapons.

An hour before sunset a pair of scouts came racing back to the column, their club-headed horses loping like dogs. Lord Faide braked the motion of his car. Behind him the Faide kinsmen, the lesser knights, and the leather-capped foot soldiers halted; to the rear the baggage train and the high-wheeled wagons of the jinxmen creaked to a stop.

The scouts approached at breakneck speed, at the last instant flinging their horses sidewise. Long shaggy legs kicked out, padlike hooves plowed through the moss. The scouts jumped to the ground, ran forward. "The way to Ballant Keep is blocked!"

Lord Faide rose in his seat, stood staring eastward over the gray-green downs. "How many knights? How many men?"

282

"No knights, no men, Lord Faide. The First Folk have planted a forest between North and South Wildwood."

Lord Faide stood a moment in reflection, then seated himself and pushed the control knob. The car wheezed, jerked, moved forward. The knights touched up their horses; the foot soldiers resumed their slouching gait. At the rear the baggage train creaked into motion, together with the six wagons of the jinxmen.

The sun, large, pale and faintly pink, sank in the west. North Wildwood loomed down from the left, separated from South Wildwood by an area of stony ground, only sparsely patched with moss. As the sun passed behind the horizon, the new planting became visible: a frail new growth connecting the tracts of woodland like a canal between two seas.

Lord Faide halted his car, stepped down to the moss. He appraised the landscape, then gave the signal to make camp. The wagons were ranged in a circle, the gear unloaded. Lord Faide watched the activity for a moment, eyes sharp and critical, then turned and walked out across the downs through the lavender and green twilight. Fifteen miles to the east his last enemy awaited him: Lord Ballant of Ballant Keep. Contemplating the next day's battle, Lord Faide felt reasonably confident of the outcome. His troops had been tempered by a dozen campaigns; his kinsmen were loyal and singlehearted. Head jinxman to Faide Keep was Hein Huss, and associated with him were three of the most powerful jinxmen of Pangborn: Isak Comandore, Adam McAdam, and the remarkable Enterlin, together with their separate troupes of cabalmen, spellbinders, and apprentices. Altogether, an impressive assemblage. Certainly there were obstacles to be overcome: Ballant Keep was strong; Lord Ballant would fight obstinately; Anderson Grimes, the Ballant head jinxman, was efficient and highly respected. There was also this nuisance of the First Folk and the new planting which closed the gap between North and South Wildwood. The First Folk were a pale and feeble race, no match for human beings in single combat, but they guarded their forests with traps and deadfalls. Lord Faide cursed softly under his breath. To circle either North or South Wildwood meant a delay of three days, which could not be tolerated.

Lord Faide returned to the camp. Fires were alight, pots bubbled, orderly rows of sleep holes had been dug into the moss. The knights groomed their horses within the corral of wagons; Lord Faide's own tent had been erected on a hummock, beside the ancient car.

Lord Faide made a quick round of inspection, noting every detail, speaking no word. The jinxmen were encamped a little distance apart from the troops. The apprentices and lesser spellbinders prepared food, while the jinxmen and cabalmen worked inside their tents, arranging cabinets and cases, correcting whatever disorder had been caused by the jolting of the wagons.

Lord Faide entered the tent of his head jinxman. Hein Huss was an enormous man, with arms and legs heavy as tree trunks, a torso like a barrel. His face was pink and placid, his eyes were water-clear; a stiff gray brush rose from his head, which was innocent of the cap jinxmen customarily wore against the loss of hair. Hein Huss disdained such precautions; it was his habit, showing his teeth in a face-splitting grin, to rumble, "Why should any hoodoo me, old Hein Huss? I am so inoffensive. Whoever tried would surely die, of shame and remorse."

Lord Faide found Huss busy at his cabinet. The doors stood wide, revealing hundreds of manikins, each tied with a lock of hair, a bit of cloth, a fingernail clipping, daubed with grease, sputum, excrement, blood. Lord Faide knew well that one of these manikins represented himself. He also knew that should he request it Hein Huss would deliver it without hesitation. Part of Huss's *mana* derived from his enormous confidence, the effortless ease of his power. He glanced at Lord Faide and read the question in his mind. "Lord Ballant did not know of the new planting. Anderson Grimes has now informed him, and Lord Ballant expects that you will be delayed. Grimes has communicated with Gisborne Keep and Castle Cloud. Three hundred men march tonight to reinforce Ballant Keep. They will arrive in two days. Lord Ballant is much elated."

Lord Faide paced back and forth across the tent. "Can we cross this planting?"

Hein Huss made a heavy sound of disapproval. "There are many futures. In certain of these futures you pass. In others you do not pass. I cannot ordain these futures."

Lord Faide had long learned to control his impatience at what sometimes seemed to be pedantic obfuscation. He grumbled, "They are either very stupid or very bold planting across the downs in this fashion. I cannot imagine what they intend."

Hein Huss considered, then grudgingly volunteered an idea. "What if they plant west from North Wildwood to Sarrow Copse? What if they plant west from South Wildwood to Old Forest?"

"Then Faide Keep is almost ringed by forest."

"And what if they join Sarrow Copse to Old Forest?"

Lord Faide stood stock-still, his eyes narrow and thoughtful. "Faide Keep would be surrounded by forest. We would be imprisoned. . . . These plantings, do they proceed?"

"They proceed, so I have been told."

"What do they hope to gain?"

"I do not know. Perhaps they hope to isolate the keeps, to rid the planet of men. Perhaps they merely want secure avenues between the forests."

Lord Faide considered. Huss's final suggestion was reasonable enough. During the first centuries of human settlement, sportive young men had hunted the First Folk with clubs and lances, eventually had driven them from their native downs into the forests. "Evidently they are more clever than we realize. Adam McAdam asserts that they do not think, but it seems that he is mistaken."

Hein Huss shrugged. "Adam McAdam equates thought to the human cerebral process. He cannot telepathize with the First Folk, hence he deduces that they do not 'think.' But I have watched them at Forest Market, and they trade intelligently enough." He raised his head, appeared to listen, then reached into his cabinet and delicately tightened a noose around the neck of one of the manikins. From outside the tent came a sudden cough and a whooping gasp for air. Huss grinned, twitched open the noose. "That is Isak Comandore's apprentice. He hopes to complete a Hein Huss manikin. I must say he works diligently, going so far as to touch its feet into my footprints whenever possible."

Lord Faide went to the flap of the tent. "We break camp early. Be alert, I may require your help." He departed the tent.

Hein Huss continued the ordering of his cabinet. Presently he sensed the approach of his rival, Jinxman Isak Comandore, who coveted the office of head jinxman with all-consuming passion. Huss closed the cabinet and hoisted himself to his feet.

Comandore entered the tent, a man tall, crooked, and spindly. His wedge-shaped head was covered with coarse russet ringlets; hot red-brown eyes peered from under his red eyebrows. "I offer my complete rights to Keyril, and will include the masks, the headdress, the amulets. Of all the demons ever contrived he has won the widest public acceptance. To utter the name Keyril is to complete half the work of a possession. Keyril is a valuable property. I can give no more."

But Huss shook his head. Comandore's desire was the full simulacrum of Tharon Faide, Lord Faide's oldest son, complete with clothes, hair, skin, eyelashes, tears, excrement, sweat, and sputum—the only one in existence, for Lord Faide guarded his son much more jealously than he did himself. "You offer convincingly," said Huss, "but my own demons suffice. The name Dant conveys fully as much terror as Keyril."

"I will add five hairs from the head of Jinxman Clarence Sears; they are the last, for he is now stark bald."

"Let us drop the matter; I will keep the simulacrum."

"As you please," said Comandore with asperity. He glanced out the flap of the tent. "That blundering apprentice. He puts the feet of the manikin backward into your prints."

Huss opened his cabinet, thumped a manikin with his finger. From outside the tent came a grunt of surprise. Huss grinned. "He is young and earnest, and perhaps he is clever, who knows?" He went to the flap of the tent, called outside. "Hey, Sam Salazar, what do you do? Come inside."

Apprentice Sam Salazar came blinking into the tent, a thickset youth with a round florid face, overhung with a rather untidy mass of straw-colored hair. In one hand he carried a crude potbellied manikin, evidently intended to represent Hein Huss.

"You puzzle both your master and myself," said Huss. "There must be method in your folly, but we fail to perceive it. For instance, this moment you place my simulacrum backward into my track. I feel a tug on my foot, and you pay for your clumsiness."

Sam Salazar showed small evidence of abashment. "Jinxman

Comandore has warned that we must expect to suffer for our ambitions.''

"If your ambition is jinxmanship," Comandore declared sharply, "you had best mend your ways."

"The lad is craftier than you know," said Hein Huss. "Look now." He took the manikin from the youth, spit into its mouth, plucked a hair from his head, thrust it into a convenient crevice. "He has a Hein Huss manikin, achieved at very small cost. Now, Apprentice Salazar, how will you hoodoo me?"

"Naturally, I would never dare. I merely want to fill the bare spaces in my cabinet."

Hein Huss nodded his approval. "As good a reason as any. Of course you own a simulacrum of Isak Comandore?"

Sam Salazar glanced uneasily at Isak Comandore. "He leaves none of his traces. If there is so much as an open bottle in the room, he breathes behind his hand."

"Ridiculous!" exclaimed Hein Huss. "Comandore, what do you fear?"

"I am conservative," said Comandore dryly. "You make a fine gesture, but someday an enemy may own that simulacrum; then you will regret your bravado."

"Bah. My enemies are all dead, save one or two who dare not reveal themselves." He clapped Sam Salazar a great buffet on the shoulder. "Tomorrow, Apprentice Salazar, great things are in store for you."

"What manner of great things?"

"Honor, noble self-sacrifice. Lord Faide must beg permission from the First Folk to pass Wildwood, which galls him. But beg he must. Tomorrow, Sam Salazar, I will elect you to lead the way to the parley, to deflect deadfalls, scythes, and nettle traps from the more important person who follows."

Sam Salazar shook his head and drew back. "There must be others more worthy; I prefer to ride in the rear with the wagons."

Comandore waved him from the tent. "You will do as ordered. Leave us; we have had enough apprentice talk."

Sam Salazar departed. Comandore turned back to Hein Huss. "In connection with tomorrow's battle, Anderson Grimes is especially adept with demons. As I recall, he has developed and successfully publicized Pont, who spreads sleep; Everid, a being of wrath; Deigne, a force of fear. We must take care that in countering these effects we do not neutralize each other."

"True," rumbled Huss. "I have long maintained to Lord Faide that a single jinxman—the head jinxman, in fact—is more effective than a group at cross-purposes. But he is consumed by ambition and does not listen."

"Perhaps he wants to be sure that should advancing years overtake the head jinxman other equally effective jinxmen are at hand."

"The future has many paths," agreed Hein Huss. "Lord Faide is well-advised to seek early for my successor, so that I may train him over the years. I plan to access all the subsidiary jinxmen, and select the most promising. Tomorrow I relegate to you the demons of Anderson Grimes."

Isak Comandore nodded politely. "You are wise to give over responsibility. When I feel the weight of my years I hope I may act with similar forethought. Good night, Hein Huss. I go to arrange my demon masks. Tomorrow Keyril must walk like a giant."

"Good night, Isak Comandore."

Comandore swept from the tent, and Huss settled himself on his stool. Sam Salazar scratched at the flap. "Well, lad?" growled Huss. "Why do you loiter?"

Sam Salazar placed the Hein Huss manikin on the table. "I have no wish to keep this doll."

"Throw it in a ditch, then." Hein Huss spoke gruffly. "You must stop annoying me with stupid tricks. You efficiently obtrude yourself upon my attention, but you cannot transfer from Comandore's troupe without his express consent."

"If I gain his consent?"

"You will incur his enmity; he will open his cabinet against you. Unlike myself, you are vulnerable to a hoodoo. I advise you to be content. Isak Comandore is highly skilled and can teach you much."

Sam Salazar still hesitated. "Jinxman Comandore, though skilled, is intolerant of new thoughts."

Hein Huss shifted ponderously on his stool, examined Sam Salazar with his water-clear eyes. "What new thoughts are these? Your own?"

"The thoughts are new to me, and for all I know new to Isak Comandore. But he will say neither yes nor no."

Hein Huss sighed, settled his monumental bulk more

comfortably. "Speak then, describe these thoughts, and I will assess their novelty."

"First, I have wondered about trees. They are sensitive to light, to moisture, to wind, to pressure. Sensitivity implies sensation. Might a man feel into the soul of a tree for these sensations? If a tree were capable of awareness, this faculty might prove useful. A man might select trees as sentinels in strategic sites, and enter into them as he chose."

Hein Huss was skeptical. "An amusing notion, but practically not feasible. The reading of minds, the act of possession, televoyance, all similar interplay, require psychic congruence as a basic condition. The minds must be able to become identities at some particular stratum. Unless there is sympathy, there is no linkage. A tree is at opposite poles from a man; the images of tree and man are incommensurable. Hence, anything more than the most trifling flicker of comprehension must be a true miracle of jinxmanship."

Sam Salazar nodded mournfully. "I realized this, and at one time hoped to equip myself with the necessary identification."

"To do this you must become a vegetable. Certainly the tree will never become a man."

"So I reasoned," said Sam Salazar. "I went alone into a grove of trees, where I chose a tall conifer. I buried my feet in the mold, I stood silent and naked—in the sunlight, in the rain; at dawn, noon, dusk, midnight. I closed my mind to man-thoughts, I closed my eyes to vision, my ears to sound. I took no nourishment except from rain and sun. I sent roots forth from my feet and branches from my torso. Thirty hours I stood, and two days later another thirty hours, and after two days another thirty hours. I made myself a tree, as nearly as possible to one of flesh and blood."

Hein Huss gave the great inward gurgle that signalized his amusement. "And you achieved sympathy?"

"Nothing useful," Sam Salazar admitted. "I felt something of the tree's sensations—the activity of light, the peace of dark, the coolness of rain. But visual and auditory experience—nothing. However, I do not regret the trial. It was a useful discipline."

"An interesting effort, even if inconclusive. The idea is by no means of startling originality, but the empiricism—to use an archaic word—of your method is bold, and no doubt antagonized Isak Comandore, who has no patience with the superstitions of our ancestors. I suspect that he harangued you against frivolity, metaphysics, and inspirationalism."

"True," said Sam Salazar. "He spoke at length."

"You should take the lesson to heart. Isak Comandore is sometimes unable to make the most obvious truth seem credible. However, I cite you the example of Lord Faide, who considers himself an enlightened man, free from superstition. Still, he rides in his feeble car, he carries a pistol sixteen hundred years old, he relies on Hellmouth to protect Faide Keep."

"Perhaps—unconsciously—he longs for the old magical times," suggested Sam Salazar thoughtfully.

"Perhaps," agreed Hein Huss. "And you do likewise?"

Sam Salazar hesitated. "There is an aura of romance, a kind of wild grandeur to the old days—but of course," he added quickly, "mysticism is no substitute for orthodox logic."

"Naturally not," agreed Hein Huss. "Now go; I must consider the events of tomorrow."

Sam Salazar departed, and Hein Huss, rumbling and groaning, hoisted himself to his feet. He went to the flap of his tent, surveyed the camp. All now was quiet. The fires were embers, the warriors lay in the pits they had cut into the moss. To the north and south spread the woodlands. Among the trees and out on the downs were faint flickering luminosities, where the First Folk gathered spore-pods from the moss.

Hein Huss became aware of a nearby personality. He turned his head and saw approaching the shrouded form of Jinxman Enterlin, who concealed his face, who spoke only in whispers, who disguised his natural gait with a stiff stiltlike motion. By this means he hoped to reduce his vulnerability to hostile jinxmanship. The admission carelessly let fall of failing eyesight, of stiff joints, forgetfulness, melancholy, nausea might be of critical significance in controversy by hoodoo. Jinxmen therefore maintained the pose of absolute health and virility, even though they must grope blindly or limp doubled up from cramps.

Hein Huss called out to Enterlin, lifted back the flap to the tent. Enterlin entered; Huss went to the cabinet, brought forth a flask, poured liquor into a pair of stone cups. "A cordial only, free of overt significance."

"Good," whispered Enterlin, selecting the cup farthest from him. "After all, we jinxmen must relax into the guise of men from time to time." Turning his back on Huss, he introduced the cup through the folds of his hood, drank. "Refreshing," he whispered. "We need refreshment; tomorrow we must work."

Huss issued his reverberating chuckle. "Tomorrow Isak Comandore matches demons with Anderson Grimes. We others perform only subsidiary duties."

Enterlin seemed to make a quizzical inspection of Hein Huss through the black gauze before his eyes. "Comandore will relish this opportunity. His vehemence oppresses me, and his is a power which feeds on success. He is a man of fire, you are a man of ice."

"Ice quenches fire."

"Fire sometimes melts ice."

Hein Huss shrugged. "No matter. I grow weary. Time has passed all of us by. Only a moment ago a young apprentice showed me to myself."

"As a powerful jinxman, as head jinxman to the Faides, you have cause for pride."

Hein Huss drained the stone cup, set it aside. "No. I see myself at the top of my profession, with nowhere else to go. Only Sam Salazar the apprentice thinks to search for more universal lore; he comes to me for counsel, and I do not know what to tell him."

"Strange talk, strange talk!" whispered Enterlin. He moved to the flap of the tent. "I go now," he whispered. "I go to walk on the downs. Perhaps I will see the future."

"There are many futures."

Enterlin rustled away and was lost in the dark. Hein Huss groaned and grumbled, then took himself to his couch, where he instantly fell asleep.

II

The night passed. The sun, fickering with films of pink and green, lifted over the horizon. The new planting of the First Folk was silhouetted, a sparse stubble of saplings, against the green and lavender sky. The troops broke camp with practiced efficiency. Lord Faide marched to his car, leapt within; the machine sagged under his weight. He pushed a button, the car drifted forward, heavy as a waterlogged timber.

A mile from the new planting he halted, sent a messenger

back to the wagons of the jinxmen. Hein Huss walked ponderously forward, followed by Isak Comandore, Adam McAdam, and Enterlin. Lord Faide spoke to Hein Huss. "Send someone to speak to the First Folk. Inform them we wish to pass, offering them no harm, but that we will react savagely to any hostility."

"I will go myself," said Hein Huss. He turned to Comandore, "Lend me, if you will, your brash young apprentice. I can put him to good use."

"If he unmasks a nettle trap by blundering into it, his first useful deed will be done," said Comandore. He signaled to Sam Salazar, who came reluctantly forward. "Walk in front of Head Jinxman Hein Huss that he may encounter no traps or scythes. Take a staff to probe the moss."

Without enthusiasm Sam Salazar borrowed a lance from one of the foot soldiers. He and Huss set forth, along the low rise that previously had separated North from South Wildwood. Occasionally outcroppings of stone penetrated the cover of moss; here and there grew bayberry trees, clumps of tarplant, ginger tea, and rosewort.

A half-mile from the planting Huss halted. "Now take care, for here the traps will begin. Walk clear of hummocks, these often conceal swing-scythes; avoid moss which shows a pale blue; it is dying or sickly and may cover a deadfall or a nettle trap."

"Why cannot you locate the traps by clairvoyance?" asked Sam Salazar in a rather sullen voice. "It appears an excellent occasion for the use of these faculties."

"The question is natural," said Hein Huss with composure. "However, you must know that when a jinxman's own profit or security is at stake his emotions play tricks on him. I would see traps everywhere and would never know whether clairvoyance or fear prompted me. In this case, that lance is a more reliable instrument than my mind."

Sam Salazar made a salute of understanding and set forth, with Hein Huss stumping behind him. At first he prodded with care, uncovering two traps, then advanced more jauntily; so swiftly indeed that Huss called out in exasperation, "Caution, unless you court death!"

Sam Salazar obligingly slowed his pace. "There are traps all around us, but I detect the pattern, or so I believe."

"Ah, ha, you do? Reveal it to me, if you will. I am only head jinxman, and ignorant."

"Notice. If we walk where the spore-pods have recently been harvested, then we are secure."

Hein Huss grunted. "Forward then. Why do you dally? We must do battle at Ballant Keep today."

Two hundred yards farther, Sam Salazar stopped short. "Go on, boy, go on!" grumbled Hein Huss.

"The savages threaten us. You can see them just inside the planting. They hold tubes which they point toward us."

Hein Huss peered, then raised his head and called out in the sibilant language of the First Folk.

A moment or two passed, then one of the creatures came forth, a naked humanoid figure, ugly as a demonmask. Foamsacs bulged under its arms, orange-lipped foam-vents pointed forward. Its back was wrinkled and loose, the skin serving as a bellows to blow air through the foam-sacs. The fingers of the enormous hands ended in chisel-shaped blades, the head was sheathed in chitin. Billion-faceted eyes swelled from either side of the head, glowing like black opals, merging without definite limit into the chitin. This was a representative of the original inhabitants of the planet, who until the coming of man had inhabited the downs, burrowing in the moss, protecting themselves behind masses of foam exuded from the underarm sacs.

The creature wandered close, halted. "I speak for Lord Faide of Faide Keep," said Huss. "Your planting bars his way. He wishes that you guide him through, so that his men do not damage the trees, or spring the traps you have set against your enemies."

"Men are our enemies," responded the autochthon. "You may spring as many traps as you care to; that is their purpose." It backed away.

"One moment," said Hein Huss sternly. "Lord Faide must pass. He goes to battle Lord Ballant. He does not wish to battle the First Folk. Therefore, it is wise to guide him across the planting without hindrance."

The creature considered a second or two. "I will guide him." He stalked across the moss toward the war party.

Behind followed Hein Huss and Sam Salazar. The autochthon, legs articulated more flexibly than a man's, seemed to weave and wander, occasionally pausing to study the ground ahead.

"I am puzzled," Sam Salazar told Hein Huss. "I cannot understand the creature's actions."

"Small wonder," grunted Hein Huss. "He is one of the First Folk, you are human. There is no basis for understanding."

"I disagree," said Sam Salazar seriously.

"Eh?" Hein Huss inspected the apprentice with vast disapproval. "You engage in contention with me, Head Jinxman Hein Huss?"

"Only in a limited sense," said Sam Salazar. "I see a basis for understanding with the First Folk in our common ambition to survive."

"A truism," grumbled Hein Huss. "Granting this community of interests with the First Folk, what is your perplexity?"

"The fact that it first refused, then agreed to conduct us across the planting."

Hein Huss nodded. "Evidently the information which intervened, that we go to fight at Ballant Keep, occasioned the change."

"This is clear," said Sam Salazar. "But think—"

"You exhort me to think?" roared Hein Huss.

"—here is one of the First Folk, apparently without distinction, who makes an important decision instantly. Is he one of their leaders? Do they live in anarchy?"

"It is easy to put questions," Hein Huss said gruffly. "It is not as easy to answer them."

"In short—"

"In short, I do not know. In any event, they are pleased to see us killing one another."

III

The passage through the planting was made without incident. A mile to the east the autochthon stepped aside and without formality returned to the forest. The war party, which had been marching in single file, regrouped into its usual formation. Lord Faide called Hein Huss and made the unusual gesture of inviting him up into the seat beside him. The ancient car dipped and sagged; the power-mechanism whined and chattered. Lord Faide, in high good spirits, ignored the noise. "I feared that we might be forced into a time-consuming wrangle. What of Lord Ballant? Can you read his thoughts?"

Hein Huss cast his mind forth. "Not clearly. He knows of our passage. He is disturbed."

Lord Faide laughed sardonically. "For excellent reason! Listen now, I will explain the plan of battle so that all may coordinate their efforts."

"Very well."

"We approach in a wide line. Ballant's great weapon is of course Volcano. A decoy must wear my armor and ride in the lead. The yellow-haired apprentice is perhaps the most expendable member of the party. In this way we will learn the potentialities of Volcano. Like our own Hellmouth, it was built to repel vessels from space and cannot command the ground immediately under the keep. Therefore, we will advance in dispersed formation, to regroup two hundred yards from the keep. At this point the jinxmen will impel Lord Ballant forth from the keep. You no doubt have made plans to this end."

Hein Huss gruffly admitted that such was the case. Like other jinxmen, he enjoyed the pose that his power sufficed for extemporaneous control of any situation.

Lord Faide was in no mood for niceties and pressed for further information. Grudging each word, Hein Huss disclosed his arrangements. "I have prepared certain influences to discomfit the Ballant defenders and drive them forth. Jinxman Enterlin will sit at his cabinet, ready to retaliate if Lord Ballant orders a spell against you. Anderson Grimes undoubtedly will cast a demon—probably Everid—into the Ballant warriors; in return, Jinxman Comandore will possess an equal or a greater number of Faide warriors with the demon Keyril, who is even more ghastly and horrifying."

"Good. What more?"

"There is need for no more, if your men fight well."

"Can you see the future? How does today end?"

"There are many futures. Certain jinxmen—Enterlin, for instance—profess to see the thread which leads through the maze; they are seldom correct."

"Call Enterlin here."

Hein Huss rumbled his disapproval. "Unwise, if you desire victory over Ballant Keep."

Lord Faide inspected the massive jinxman from under his black saturnine brows. "Why do you say this?"

"If Enterlin foretells defeat, you will be dispirited and

fight poorly. If he predicts victory, you become overconfident and likewise fight poorly."

Lord Faide made a petulant gesture. "The jinxmen are loud in their boasts until the test is made. Then they always find reasons to retract, to qualify."

"Ha, ha!" barked Hein Huss. "You expect miracles, not honest jinxmanship. I spit—" He spat. "I predict that the spittle will strike the moss. The probabilities are high. But an insect might fly in the way. One of the First Folk might raise through the moss. The chances are slight. In the next instant there is only one future. A minute hence there are four futures. Five minutes hence, twenty futures. A billion futures could not express all the possibilities of tomorrow. Of these billion, certain are more probable than others. It is true that these probable futures sometimes send a delicate influence into the jinxman's brain. But unless he is completely impersonal and disinterested, his own desires overwhelm this influence. Enterlin is a strange man. He hides himself, he has no appetites. Occasionally his auguries are exact. Nevertheless, I advise against consulting him. You do better to rely on the practical and real uses of jinxmanship."

Lord Faide said nothing. The column had been marching along the bottom of a low swale; the car had been sliding easily downslope. Now they came to a rise, and the power-mechanism complained so vigorously that Lord Faide was compelled to stop the car. He considered. "Once over the crest we will be in view of Ballant Keep. Now we must disperse. Send the least valuable man in your troupe forward— the apprentice who tested out the moss. He must wear my helmet and corselet and ride in the car."

Hein Huss alighted, returned to the wagons, and presently Sam Salazar came forward. Lord Faide eyed the round, florid face with distaste. "Come close," he said crisply. Sam Salazar obeyed. "You will now ride in my place," said Lord Faide. "Notice carefully. This rod impels a forward motion. This arm steers—to right, to left. To stop, return the rod to its first position."

Sam Salazar pointed to some of the other arms, toggles, switches, and buttons. "What of these?"

"They are never used."

"And these dials, what is their meaning?"

Lord Faide curled his lip, on the brink of one of his quick

furies. "Since their use is unimportant to me, it is twenty times unimportant to you. Now. Put this cap on your head, and this helmet. See to it that you do not sweat."

Sam Salazar gingerly settled the magnificent black and green crest of Faide on his head, with a cloth cap underneath.

"Now this corselet."

The corselet was constructed of green and black metal sequins, with a pair of scarlet dragon-heads at either side of the breast.

"Now the cloak." Lord Faide flung the black cloak over Sam Salazar's shoulders. "Do not venture too close to Ballant Keep. Your purpose is to attract the fire of Volcano. Maintain a lateral motion around the keep, outside of dart range. If you are killed by a dart, the whole purpose of the deception is thwarted."

"You prefer me to be killed by Volcano?" inquired Sam Salazar.

"No. I wish to preserve the car and the crest. These are relics of great value. Evade destruction by all means possible. The ruse probably will deceive no one; but if it does, and if it draws the fire of Volcano, I must sacrifice the Faide car. Now—sit in my place."

Sam Salazar climbed into the car, settled himself on the seat.

"Sit straight," roared Lord Faide. "Hold your head up! You are simulating Lord Faide! You must not appear to slink!"

Sam Salazar heaved himself erect in the seat. "To simulate Lord Faide most effectively, I should walk among the warriors, with someone else riding in the car."

Lord Faide glared, then grinned sourly. "No matter. Do as I have commanded."

IV

Sixteen hundred years before, with war raging through space, a group of space captains, their home bases destroyed, had taken refuse on Pangborn. To protect themselves against vengeful enemies, they built great forts armed with weapons from the dismantled spaceships.

The wars receded, Pangborn was forgotten. The newcomers drove the First Folk into the forests, planted and harvested the river valleys. Ballant Keep, like Faide Keep, Castle Cloud, Boghoten, and the rest, overlooked one of these valleys. Four squat towers of a dense black substance supported an enormous parasol roof, and were joined by walls two-thirds as high as the towers. At the peak of the roof a cupola housed Volcano, the weapon corresponding to Faide's Hellmouth.

The Faide war party advancing over the rise found the great gates already secure, the parapets between the towers thronged with bowmen. According to Lord Faide's strategy, the war party advanced on a broad front. At the center rode Sam Salazar, resplendent in Lord Faide's armor. He made, however, small effort to simulate Lord Faide. Rather than sitting proudly erect, he crouched at the side of the seat, the crest canted at an angle. Lord Faide watched with disgust. Apprentice Salazar's reluctance to be demolished was understandable; if his impersonation failed to convince Lord Ballant, at least the Faide ancestral car might be spared. For a certainty Volcano was being manned; the Ballant weapon-tender could be seen in the cupola, and the snout protruded at a menacing angle.

Apparently the tactic of dispersal, offering no single tempting target, was effective. The Faide war party advanced quickly to a point two hundred yards from the keep, below Volcano's effective field, without drawing fire; first the knights, then the foot soldiers, then the rumbling wagons of the magicians. The slow-moving Faide car was far outdistanced; any doubt as to the nature of the ruse must now be extinguished.

Apprentice Salazar, disliking the isolation and hoping to increase the speed of the car, twisted one of the other switches, then another. From under the floor came a thin screeching sound; the car quivered and began to rise. Sam Salazar peered over the side, threw out a leg to jump. Lord Faide ran forward, gesturing and shouting. Sam Salazar hastily drew back his leg, returned the switches to their previous condition. The car dropped like a rock. He snapped the switches up again, cushioning the fall.

"Get out of that car!" roared Lord Faide. He snatched away the helmet, dealt Sam Salazar a buffet which toppled him head over heels. "Out of the armor; back to your duties!"

Sam Salazar hurried to the jinxmen's wagons where he helped erect Isak Comandore's black tent. Inside the tent a black carpet with red and yellow patterns was laid; Comandore's cabinet, his chair, and his chest were carried in, and incense set burning in a censer. Directly in front of the main gate Hein Huss superintended the assembly of a rolling stage, forty feet tall and sixty feet long, the surface concealed from Ballant Keep by a tarpaulin.

Meanwhile, Lord Faide had dispatched an emissary, enjoining Lord Ballant to surrender. Lord Ballant delayed his response, hoping to delay the attack as long as possible. If he could maintain himself a day and a half, reinforcements from Gisborne Keep and Castle Cloud might force Lord Faide to retreat.

Lord Faide waited only until the jinxmen had completed their preparations, then sent another messenger, offering two more minutes in which to surrender.

One minute passed, two minutes. The envoys turned on their heels, marched back to the camp.

Lord Faide spoke to Hein Huss. "You are prepared?"

"I am prepared," rumbled Hein Huss.

"Drive them forth."

Huss raised his arm; the tarpaulin dropped from the face of his great display, to reveal a painted representation of Ballant Keep.

Huss retired to his tent and pulled the flaps together. Braziers burnt fiercely, illuminating the faces of Adam McAdam, eight cabalmen, and six of the most advanced spellbinders. Each worked at a bench supporting several dozen dolls and a small glowing brazier. The cabalmen and spellbinders worked with dolls representing Ballant men-at-arms; Huss and Adam McAdam employed simulacra of the Ballant knights. Lord Ballant would not be hoodooed unless he ordered a jinx against Lord Faide—a courtesy the keep-lords extended each other.

Huss called out: "Sebastian!"

Sebastian, one of Huss's spellbinders, waiting at the flap to the tent, replied, "Ready, sir."

"Begin the display."

Sebastian ran to the stage, struck fire to a fuse. Watchers inside Ballant Keep saw the depicted keep take fire. Flame erupted from the windows, the roof glowed and crumbled. Inside the tent the two jinxmen, the cabalmen, and the spellbinders methodically took dolls, dipped them into the heat of the braziers, concentrating, reaching out for the mind of the

man whose doll they burnt. Within the keep men became
uneasy. Many began to imagine burning sensations, which
became more severe as their minds grew more sensitive to the
idea of fire. Lord Ballant noted the uneasiness. He signaled to
his chief jinxman, Anderson Grimes. "Begin the counterspell."

Down the front of the keep unrolled a display even larger
than Hein Huss's, depicting a hideous beast. It stood on four
legs and was shown picking up two men in a pair of hands,
biting off their heads. Grimes's cabalmen meanwhile took up
dolls representing the Faide warriors, inserted them into models of the depicted beast, and closed the hinged jaws, all the
while projecting ideas of fear and disgust. And the Faide
warriors, staring at the depicted monster, felt a sense of
horror and weakness.

Inside Huss's tent the braziers reeked and dolls smoked.
Eyes stared, brows glistened. From time to time one of the
workers gasped—signaling the entry of his projection into an
enemy mind. Within the keep warriors began to mutter, to
slap at burning skin, to eye each other fearfully, noting each
other's symptoms. Finally one cried out and tore at his armor.
"I burn! The cursed witches burn me!" His pain aggravated
the discomfort of the others; there was a growing sound
throughout the keep.

Lord Ballant's oldest son, his mind penetrated by Hein
Huss himself, struck his shield with his mailed fist. "They
burn me! They burn us all! Better to fight than burn!"

"Fight! Fight!" came the voices of the tormented men.

Lord Ballant looked around at the twisted faces, some
displaying blisters, scaldmarks. "Our own spell terrifies them;
wait yet a moment!" he pleaded.

His brother called hoarsely, "It is not your belly that Hein
Huss toasts in the flames, it is mine! We cannot win a battle
of hoodoos; we must win a battle of arms!"

Lord Ballant cried desperately, "Wait, our own effects are
working! They will flee in terror; wait, wait!"

His cousin tore off his corselet. "It's Hein Huss! I feel
him! My leg's in the fire, the devil laughs at me. Next my
head, he says. Fight or I go forth to fight alone!"

"Very well," said Lord Ballant in a fateful voice. "We go
forth to fight. First—the beast goes forth. Then we follow
and smite them in their terror."

The gates to the keep swung suddenly wide. Out sprang

what appeared to be the depicted monster: legs moving, arms waving, eyes rolling, issuing evil sounds. Normally the Faide warriors would have seen the monster for what it was: a model carried on the backs of three horses. But their minds had been influenced; they had been infected with horror; they drew back with arms hanging flaccid. From behind the monster the Ballant knights galloped, followed by the Ballant foot soldiers. The charge gathered momentum, tore into the Faide center. Lord Faide bellowed orders; discipline asserted itself. The Faide knights disengaged, divided into three platoons, and engulfed the Ballant charge while the foot soldiers poured darts into the advancing ranks.

There was the clatter and surge of battle; Lord Ballant, seeing that his sally had failed to overwhelm the Faide forces and thinking to conserve his own forces, ordered a retreat. In good order the Ballant warriors began to back up toward the keep. The Faide knights held close contact, hoping to win to the courtyard. Close behind came a heavily loaded wagon pushed by armored horses, to be wedged against the gate.

Lord Faide called an order; a reserve platoon of ten knights charged from the side, thrust behind the main body of Ballant horsemen, rode through the foot soldiers, fought into the keep, cut down the gate-tenders.

Lord Ballant bellowed to Anderson Grimes, "They have won inside; quick with your cursed demon! If he can help us, let him do so now!"

"Demon possession is not a matter of an instant," muttered the jinxman. "I need time."

"You have no time! Ten minutes and we're all dead!"

"I will do my best. Everid, Everid, come swift!"

He hastened into his workroom, donned his demonmask, tossed handful after handful of incense into the brazier. Against one wall stood a great form: black, slit-eyed, noseless. Great white fangs hung from its upper palate; it stood on heavy bent legs, arms reached forward to grasp. Anderson Grimes swallowed a cup of syrup, paced slowly back and forth. A moment passed.

"Grimes!" came Ballant's call from outside. "Grimes!"

A voice spoke. "Enter without fear."

Lord Ballant, carrying his ancestral side arm, entered. He drew back with an involuntary sound. "Grimes!" he whispered.

"Grimes is not here," said the voice. "I am here. Enter."

Lord Ballant came forward stiff-legged. The room was dark except for the feeble glimmer of the brazier. Anderson Grimes crouched in a corner, head bowed under his demon-mask. The shadows twisted and pulsed with shapes and faces, forms struggling to become solid. The black image seemed to vibrate with life.

"Bring in your warriors," said the voice. "Bring them in five at a time, bid them look only at the floor until commanded to raise their eyes."

Lord Ballant retreated; there was no sound in the room.

A moment passed; then five limp and exhausted warriors filed into the room, eyes low.

"Look slowly up," said the voice. "Look at the orange fire. Breathe deeply. Then look at me. I am Everid, Demon of Hate. Look at me. Who am I?"

"You are Everid, Demon of Hate," quavered the warriors.

"I stand all around you, in a dozen forms. . . . I come closer. Where am I?"

"You are close."

"Now I am you. We are together."

There was a sudden quiver of motion. The warriors stood straighter, their faces distorted.

"Go forth," said the voice. "Go quietly into the court. In a few minutes we march forth to slay."

The five stalked forth. Five more entered.

Outside the wall the Ballant knights had retreated as far as the gate; within, seven Faide knights still survived, and with their backs to the wall held the Ballant warriors away from the gate mechanism.

In the Faide camp Huss called to Comandore, "Everid is walking. Bring forth Keyril."

"Send the men," came Comandore's voice, low and harsh. "Send the men to me. I am Keyril."

Within the keep twenty warriors came marching into the courtyard. Their steps were cautious, tentative, slow. Their faces had lost individuality; they were twisted and distorted, curiously alike.

"Bewitched!" whispered the Ballant soldiers, drawing back. The seven Faide knights watched with sudden fright. But the twenty warriors, paying them no heed, marched out the gate. The Ballant knights parted; for an instant there was a lull in the fighting. The twenty sprang like tigers. Their swords glistened, twinkling in water-bright arcs. They crouched, jerked, jumped; Faide arms, legs, heads were hewed off. The twenty were cut and battered, but the blows seemed to have no effect.

The Faide attack faltered, collapsed. The knights, whose armor was no protection against the demoniac swords, retreated. The twenty possessed warriors raced out into the open toward the foot soldiers, running with great strides, slashing and rending. The Faide foot soldiers fought for a moment, then they too gave way and turned to flee.

From behind Comandore's tent appeared thirty Faide warriors, marching stiffly, slowly. Like the Ballant twenty their faces were alike—but between the Everid-possessed and the Keyril-possessed was the difference between the face of Everid and the face of Keyril.

Keyril and Everid fought, using the men as weapons, without fear, retreat, or mercy. Hack, chop, cut. Arms, legs, sundered torsos. Bodies fought headless for moments before collapsing. Only when a body was minced, hacked to bits, did the demoniac vitality depart. Presently there were no more men of Everid, and only fifteen men of Keyril. These hopped and limped and tumbled toward the keep where Faide knights still held the gate. The Ballant knights met them in despair, knowing that now was the decisive moment. Leaping, leering from chopped faces, slashing from tireless arms, the warriors cut a hole into the iron. The Faide knights, roaring victory cries, plunged after. Into the courtyard surged the battle, and now there was no longer doubt of the outcome. Ballant Keep was taken.

Back in his tent Isak Comandore took a deep breath, shuddered, flung down his demonmask. In the courtyard the twelve remaining warriors dropped in their tracks, twitched, gasped, gushed blood, and died.

Lord Ballant, in the last gallant act of a gallant life, marched forth brandishing his ancestral side arm. He aimed across the bloody field at Lord Faide, pulled the trigger. The weapon spewed a brief gout of light; Lord Faide's skin prickled and hair rose from his head. The weapon crackled, turned cherry-red, and melted. Lord Ballant threw down the weapon, drew his sword, marched forth to challenge Lord Faide.

Lord Faide, disinclined to unnecessary combat, signaled to

his soldiers. A flight of darts ended Lord Ballant's life, saving him the discomfort of formal execution.

There was no further resistance. The Ballant defenders threw down their arms and marched grimly out to kneel before Lord Faide, while inside the keep the Ballant women gave themselves to mourning and grief.

V

Lord Faide had no wish to linger at Ballant Keep, for he took no relish in his victories. Inevitably, a thousand decisions had to be made. Six of the closest Ballant kinsmen were summarily stabbed and the title declared defunct. Others of the clan were offered a choice: an oath of lifelong fealty together with a moderate ransom, or death. Only two, eyes blazing hate, chose death and were instantly stabbed.

Lord Faide had now achieved his ambition. For over a thousand years the keep-lords had struggled for power; now one, now another gaining ascendancy. None before had ever extended his authority across the entire continent—which meant control of the planet, since all other land was either sun-parched rock or eternal ice. Ballant Keep had long thwarted Lord Faide's drive to power; now—success, total and absolute. It still remained to chastise the lords of Castle Cloud and Gisborne, both of whom, seeing opportunity to overwhelm Lord Faide, had ranged themselves behind Lord Ballant. But these were matters that might well be assigned to Hein Huss.

Lord Faide, for the first time in his life, felt a trace of uncertainty. Now, what? No real adversaries remained. The First Folk must be whipped back, but here was no great problem; they were numerous, but no more than savages. He knew that dissatisfaction and controversy would ultimately arise among his kinsmen and allies. Inaction and boredom would breed irritability; idle minds would calculate the pros and cons of mischief. Even the most loyal would remember the campaigns with nostalgia and long for the excitement, the release, the license, of warfare. Somehow he must find means to absorb the energy of so many active and keyed-up men. How and where, this was the problem. The construction of roads? New farmland claimed from the downs? Yearly tournaments-at-arms? Lord Faide frowned at the inadequacy of his solutions, but his imagination was impoverished by the lack of tradition. The original settlers of Pangborn had been warriors and had brought with them a certain amount of practical rule-of-thumb knowledge, but little else. The tales they passed down the generations described the great spaceships which moved with magic speed and certainty, the miraculous weapons, the wars in the void, but told nothing of human history or civilized achievement. And so Lord Faide, full of power and success, but with no goal toward which to turn his strength, felt more morose and saturnine than ever.

He gloomily inspected the spoils from Ballant Keep. They were of no great interest to him. Ballant's ancestral car was no longer used, but displayed behind a glass case. He inspected the weapon Volcano, but this could not be moved. In any event it was useless, its magic lost forever. Lord Faide now knew that Lord Ballant had ordered it turned against the Faide car, but that it had refused to spew its vaunted fire. Lord Faide saw with disdainful amusement that Volcano had been sadly neglected. Corrosion had pitted the metal, careless cleaning had twisted the exterior tubing, undoubtedly diminishing the potency of the magic. No such neglect at Faide Keep! Jambart the weapon-tender cherished Hellmouth with absolute devotion. Elsewhere were other ancient devices, interesting but useless—the same sort of curios that cluttered shelves and cases at Faide Keep. (Peculiar, these ancient men, thought Lord Faide: at once so clever, yet so primitive and impractical. Conditions had changed; there had been enormous advances since the dark ages sixteen hundred years ago. For instance, the ancients had used intricate fetishes of metal and glass to communicate with each other. Lord Faide need merely voice his needs; Hein Huss could project his mind a hundred miles to see, to hear, to relay Lord Faide's words.) The ancients had contrived dozens of such objects, but the old magic had worn away and they never seemed to function. Lord Ballant's side arm had melted, after merely stinging Lord Faide. Imagine a troop armed thus trying to cope with a platoon of demonpossessed warriors! Slaughter of the innocents!

Among the Ballant trove Lord Faide noted a dozen old books and several reels of microfilm. The books were worthless, page after page of incomprehensible jargon; the microfilm was equally undecipherable. Again Lord Faide wondered skeptically about the ancients. Clever, of course, but to look at the hard facts, they were little more advanced than the First Folk: neither had facility with telepathy or voyance or demoncommand. And the magic of the ancients: might there not be a great deal of exaggeration in the legends? Volcano, for instance. A joke. Lord Faide wondered about his own Hellmouth. But, no—surely Hellmouth was more trustworthy; Jambart cleaned and polished the weapon daily and washed the entire cupola with vintage wine every month. If human care could induce faithfulness, then Hellmouth was ready to defend Faide Keep!

Now there was no longer need for defense. Faide was supreme. Considering the future, Lord Faide made a decision. There should no longer be keep-lords on Pangborn; he would abolish the appellation. Habitancy of the keeps would gradually be transferred to trusted bailiffs on a yearly basis. The former lords would be moved to comfortable but indefensible manor houses, with the maintenance of private troops forbidden. Naturally they must be allowed jinxmen, but these would be made accountable to himself—perhaps through some sort of licensing provision. He must discuss the matter with Hein Huss. A matter for the future, however. Now he merely wished to settle affairs and return to Faide Keep.

There was little more to be done. The surviving Ballant kinsmen he sent to their homes after Hein Huss had impregnated fresh dolls with their essences. Should they default on their ransoms, a twinge of fire, a few stomach cramps would more than set them right. Ballant Keep itself Lord Faide would have liked to burn—but the material of the ancients was proof to fire. But in order to discourage any new pretenders to the Ballant heritage, Lord Faide ordered all the heirlooms and relics brought forth into the courtyard, and then, one at a time, in order of rank, he bade his men choose. Thus the Ballant wealth was distributed. Even the jinxmen were invited to choose, but they despised the ancient trinkets as works of witless superstition. The lesser spellbinders and apprentices rummaged through the leavings, occasionally finding an overlooked bauble or some anomalous implement. Isak Comandore was irritated to find Sam Salazar staggering under a load of the ancient books. "And what is your purpose with these?" he barked. "Why do you burden yourself with rubbish?"

Sam Salazar hung his head. "I have no definite purpose. Undoubtedly there was wisdom—or at least knowledge—among the ancients; perhaps I can use these symbols of knowledge to sharpen my own understanding."

Comandore threw up his hands in disgust. He turned to Hein Huss, who stood nearby. "First he fancies himself a tree and stands in the mud; now he thinks to learn jinxmanship through a study of ancient symbols."

Huss shrugged. "They were men like ourselves, and though limited, they were not entirely obtuse. A certain simian cleverness is required to fabricate these objects."

"Simian cleverness is no substitute for sound jinxmanship," retorted Isak Comandore. "This is a point hard to overemphasize; I have drummed it into Salazar's head a hundred times. And now, look at him."

Huss grunted noncommittally. "I fail to understand what he hopes to achieve."

Sam Salazar tried to explain, fumbling for words to express an idea that did not exist. "I thought perhaps to decipher the writing, if only to understand what the ancients thought, and perhaps to learn how to perform one or two of their tricks."

Comandore rolled up his eyes. "What enemy bewitched me when I consented to take you as apprentice? I can cast twenty hoodoos in an hour, more than any of the ancients could achieve in a lifetime."

"Nevertheless," said Sam Salazar, "I notice that Lord Faide rides in his ancestral car and that Lord Ballant sought to kill us all with Volcano."

"I notice," said Comandore with feral softness, "that my demon Keyril conquered Lord Ballant's Volcano, and that riding on my wagon I can outdistance Lord Faide in his car."

Sam Salazar thought better of arguing further. "True, Jinxman Comandore, very true. I stand corrected."

"Then discard that rubbish and make yourself useful. We return to Faide Keep in the morning."

"As you wish, Jinxman Comandore." Sam Salazar threw the books back into the trash.

VI

The Ballant clan had been dispersed, Ballant Keep was despoiled. Lord Faide and his men banqueted somberly in the great hall, tended by silent Ballant servitors.

Ballant Keep had been built on the same splendid scale as
Faide Keep. The great hall was a hundred feet long, fifty feet
wide, fifty feet high, paneled in planks sawn from pale native
hardwood, rubbed and waxed to a rich honey color. Enormous black beams supported the ceiling; from these hung
candelabra, intricate contrivances of green, purple, and blue
glass, knotted with ancient but still bright light-motes. On the
far wall hung portraits of all the lords of Ballant Keep—one
hundred five grave faces in a variety of costumes. Below, a
genealogical chart ten feet high detailed the descent of the
Ballants and their connections with the other noble clans.
Now there was a desolate air to the hall, and the one hundred
five dead faces were meaningless and empty.

Lord Faide dined without joy and cast dour side glances at
those of his kinsmen who reveled too gladly. Lord Ballant, he
thought, had conducted himself only as he himself might
have done under the same circumstances; coarse exultation
seemed in poor taste, almost as if it were disrespect for Lord
Faide himself. His followers were quick to catch his mood,
and the banquet proceeded with greater decorum.

The jinxmen sat apart in a smaller room to the side.
Anderson Grimes, erstwhile Ballant head jinxman, sat beside
Hein Huss, trying to put a good face on his defeat. After all,
he had performed creditably against four powerful adversaries,
and there was no cause to feel a diminution of *mana*. The five
jinxmen discussed the battle, while the cabalmen and spellbinders listened respectfully. The conduct of the demonpossessed troops occasioned the most discussion. Anderson Grimes
readily admitted that his conception of Everid was a force
absolutely brutal and blunt, terrifying in its indomitable vigor.
The other jinxmen agreed that he undoubtedly succeeded in
projecting these qualities; Hein Huss, however, pointed out
that Isak Comandore's Keyril, as cruel and vigorous as Everid,
also combined a measure of crafty malice, which tended to
make the possessed soldier a more effective weapon.

Anderson Grimes allowed that this might well be the case
and that in fact he had been considering such an augmentation
of Everid's characteristics.

"To my mind," said Huss, "the most effective demon
should be swift enough to avoid the strokes of the brute
demons, such as Keyril and Everid. I cite my own Dant as
example. A Dant-possessed warrior can easily destroy a Keyril

or an Everid, simply through his agility. In an encounter of this sort the Keyrils and Everids presently lose their capacity to terrify, and thus half the effect is lost."

Isak Comandore pierced Huss with a hot russet glance. "You state a presumption as if it were fact. I have formulated Keyril with sufficient craft to counter any such displays of speed. I firmly believe Keyril to be the most fearsome of all demons."

"It may well be," rumbled Hein Huss thoughtfully. He beckoned to a steward, gave instructions. The steward reduced the light a trifle. "Behold," said Hein Huss. "There is Dant. He comes to join the banquet." To the side of the room loomed the tiger-striped Dant, a creature constructed of resilient metal, with four terrible arms and a squat black head which seemed all gaping jaw.

"Look," came the husky voice of Isak Comandore. "There is Keyril." Keyril was rather more humanoid and armed with a cutlass. Dant spied Keyril. The jaws gaped wider, it sprang to the attack.

The battle was a thing of horror; the two demons rolled, twisted, bit, frothed, uttered soundless shrieks, tore each other apart. Suddenly Dant sprang away; circled Keyril with dizzying speed, faster, faster; became a blur, a wild coruscation of colors that seemed to give off a high-pitched wailing sound, rising higher and higher in pitch. Keyril hacked brutally with his cutlass, then seemed to grow feeble and wan. The light that once had been Dant blazed white, exploded in a mental shriek; Keyril was gone and Isak Comandore lay moaning.

Hein Huss drew a deep breath, wiped his face, looked about him with a complacent grin. The entire company sat rigid as stones, staring, all except the apprentice Sam Salazar, who met Hein Huss's glance with a cheerful smile.

"So," growled Huss, panting from his exertion, "you consider yourself superior to the illusion; you sit and smirk at one of Hein Huss's best efforts."

"No, no," cried Sam Salazar, "I mean no disrespect! I want to learn, so I watched you rather than the demons. What could they teach me? Nothing!"

"Ah," said Huss, mollified. "And what did you learn?"

"Likewise, nothing," said Sam Salazar, "but at least I do not sit like a fish."

Comandore's voice came soft but crackling with wrath. "You see in me the resemblance to a fish?"

"I except you, Jinxman Comandore, naturally," Sam Salazar explained.

"Please go to my cabinet, Apprentice Salazar, and fetch me the doll that is your likeness. The steward will bring a basin of water, and we shall have some sport. With your knowledge of fish you perhaps can breathe underwater. If not—you may suffocate."

"I prefer not, Jinxman Comandore," said Sam Salazar. "In fact, with your permission, I now resign your service."

Comandore motioned to one of his cabalmen. "Fetch me the Salazar doll. Since he is no longer my apprentice, it is likely indeed that he will suffocate."

"Come now, Comandore," said Hein Huss gruffly. "Do not torment the lad. He is innocent and a trifle addled. Let this be an occasion of placidity and ease."

"Certainly, Hein Huss," said Comandore. "Why not? There is ample time in which to discipline this upstart."

"Jinxman Huss," said Sam Salazar, "since I am now relieved of my duties to Jinxman Comandore, perhaps you will accept me into your service."

Hein Huss made a noise of vast distaste. "You are not my responsibility."

"There are many futures, Hein Huss," said Sam Salazar. "You have said as much yourself."

Hein Huss looked at Sam Salazar with his water-clear eyes. "Yes, there are many futures. And I think that tonight sees the full amplitude of jinxmanship. . . . I think that never again will such power and skill gather at the same table. We shall die one by one and there shall be none to fill our shoes. . . . Yes, Sam Salazar. I will take you as apprentice. Isak Comandore, do you hear? This youth is now of my company."

"I must be compensated," growled Comandore.

"You have coveted my doll of Tharon Faide, the only one in existence. It is yours."

"Ah, ha!" cried Isak Comandore, leaping to his feet. "Hein Huss, I salute you! You are generous indeed! I thank you and accept!"

Hein Huss motioned to Sam Salazar. "Move your effects to my wagon. Do not show your face again tonight."

Sam Salazar bowed with dignity and departed the hall.

The banquet continued, but now something of melancholy filled the room. Presently a messenger from Lord Faide came to warn all to bed, for the party returned to Faide Keep at dawn.

VII

The victorious Faide troops gathered on the heath before Ballant Keep. As a parting gesture Lord Faide ordered the great gate torn off the hinges, so that ingress could never again be denied him. But even after sixteen hundred years the hinges were proof to all the force the horses could muster, and the gates remained in place.

Lord Faide accepted the fact with good grace and bade farewell to his cousin Renfroy, whom he had appointed bailiff. He climbed into his car, settled himself, snapped the switch. The car groaned and moved forward. Behind came the knights and the foot soldiers, then the baggage train, laden with booty, and finally the wagons of the jinxmen.

Three hours the column marched across the mossy downs. Ballant Keep dwindled behind; ahead appeared North and South Wildwood, darkening all the sweep of the western horizon. Where once the break had existed, the First Folk's new planting showed a smudge lower and less intense than the old woodlands.

Two miles from the woodlands Lord Faide called a halt and signaled up his knights. Hein Huss laboriously dismounted from his wagon, came forward.

"In the event of resistance," Lord Faide told the knights, "do not be tempted into the forest. Stay with the column and at all times be on your guard against traps."

Hein Huss spoke. "You wish me to parley with the First Folk once more?"

"No," said Lord Faide. "It is ridiculous that I must ask permission of savages to ride over my own land. We return as we came; if they interfere, so much the worse for them."

"You are rash," said Huss with simple candor.

Lord Faide glanced down at him with black eyebrows raised. "What damage can they do if we avoid their traps? Blow foam at us?"

"It is not my place to advise or to warn," said Hein Huss.

"However, I point out that they exhibit a confidence which does not come from conscious weakness; also, that they carried tubes, apparently hollow grasswood shoots, which imply missiles."

Lord Faide nodded. "No doubt. However, the knights wear armor, the soldiers carry bucklers. It is not fit that I, Lord Faide of Faide Keep, choose my path to suit the whims of the First Folk. This must be made clear, even if the exercise involves a dozen or so First Folk corpses."

"Since I am not a fighting man," remarked Hein Huss, "I will keep well to the rear and pass only when the way is secure."

"As you wish." Lord Faide pulled down the visor of his helmet. "Forward."

The column moved toward the forest, along the previous track, which showed plain across the moss. Lord Faide rode in the lead, flanked by his brother, Gethwin Faide, and his cousin, Mauve Dermont-Faide.

A half-mile passed, and another. The forest was only a mile distant. Overhead the great sun rode at zenith; brightness and heat poured down; the air carried the oily scent of thorn and tarbush. The column moved on, more slowly; the only sound the clanking of armor, the muffled thud of hooves in the moss, the squeal of wagon wheels.

Lord Faide rose up in his car, watching for any sign of hostile preparation. A half-mile from the planting the forms of the First Folk, waiting in the shade along the forest's verge, became visible. Lord Faide ignored them, held a steady pace along the track they had traveled before.

The half-mile became a quarter-mile. Lord Faide turned to order the troops into single file and was just in time to see a hole suddenly open into the moss and his brother, Gethwin Faide, drop from sight. There was a rattle, a thud, the howling of the impaled horse; Gethwin's wild calls as the horse kicked and crushed him into the stakes. Mauve Dermont-Faide, riding beside Gethwin, could not control his own horse, which leapt aside from the pit and blundered upon a trigger. Up from the moss burst a tree trunk studded with foot-long thorns. It snapped, quick as a scorpion's tail; the thorns punctured Mauve Dermont-Faide's armor, his chest, and whisked him from his horse to carry him suspended, writhing and screaming. The tip of the scythe pounded into

Lord Faide's car, splintered against the hull. The car swung groaning through the air. Lord Faide clutched at the windscreen to prevent himself from falling.

The column halted; several men ran to the pit, but Gethwin Faide lay twenty feet below, crushed under his horse. Others took Mauve Dermont-Faide down from the swaying scythe, but he, too, was dead.

Lord Faide's skin tingled with a gooseflesh of hate and rage. He looked toward the forest. The First Folk stood motionless. He beckoned to Bernard, sergeant of the foot soldiers. "Two men with lances to try out the ground ahead. All others ready with darts. At my signal spit the devils."

Two men came forward, and marching before Lord Faide's car, probed at the ground. Lord Faide settled in his seat. "Forward."

The column moved slowly toward the forest, every man tense and ready. The lances of the two men in the vanguard presently broke through the moss, to disclose a nettle trap—a pit lined with nettles, each frond ripe with globes of acid. Carefully they probed out a path to the side, and the column filed around, each man walking in the other's tracks.

At Lord Faide's side now rode his two nephews, Scolford and Edwin. "Notice," said Lord Faide in a voice harsh and tight. "These traps were laid since our last passage; an act of malice."

"But why did they guide us through before?"

Lord Faide smiled bitterly. "They were willing that we should die at Ballant Keep. But we have disappointed them."

"Notice, they carry tubes," said Scolford.

"Blowguns possibly," suggested Edwin.

Scolford disagreed. "They cannot blow through their foam-vents."

"No doubt we shall soon learn," said Lord Faide. He rose in his seat, called to the rear. "Ready with the darts!"

The soldiers raised their crossbows. The column advanced slowly, now only a hundred yards from the planting. The white shapes of the First Folk moved uneasily at the forest's edges. Several of them raised their tubes, seemed to sight along the length. They twitched their great hands.

One of the tubes was pointed toward Lord Faide. He saw a small black object leave the opening, flit forward, gathering speed. He heard a hum, waxing to a rasping, clicking flutter.

He ducked behind the windscreen; the projectile swooped in pursuit, struck the windscreen like a thrown stone. It fell crippled upon the forward deck of the car—a heavy black insect like a wasp, its broken proboscis oozing ocher liquid, horny wings beating feebly, eyes like dumbbells fixed on Lord Faide. With his mailed fist, he crushed the creature.

Behind him other wasps struck knights and men; Corex Faide-Battaro took the prong through his visor into the eye, but the armor of the other knights defeated the wasps. The foot soldiers, however, lacked protection; the wasps half-buried themselves in flesh. The soldiers called out in pain, clawed away the wasps, squeezed the wounds. Corex Faide-Battaro toppled from his horse, ran blindly out over the heath, and after fifty feet fell into a trap. The stricken soldiers began to twitch, then fell on the moss, thrashed, leapt up to run with flapping arms, threw themselves in wild somersaults, forward, backward, foaming and thrashing.

In the forest, the First Folk raised their tubes again. Lord Faide bellowed, "Spit the creatures! Bowmen, launch your darts!"

There came the twang of crossbows, darts snapped at the quiet white shapes. A few staggered and wandered aimlessly away; most, however, plucked out the darts or ignored them. They took capsules from small sacks, put them to the end of their tubes.

"Beware the wasps!" cried Lord Faide. "Strike with your bucklers! Kill the cursed things in flight!"

The rasp of horny wings came again; certain of the soldiers found courage enough to follow Lord Faide's orders and battered down the wasps. Others struck home as before; behind came another flight. The column became a tangle of struggling, crouching men.

"Footmen, retreat!" called Lord Faide furiously. "Footmen back! Knights to me!"

The soldiers fled back along the track, taking refuge behind the baggage wagons. Thirty of their number lay dying, or dead, on the moss.

Lord Faide cried out to his knights in a voice like a bugle. "Dismount, follow slow after me! Turn your helmets, keep the wasps from your eyes! One step at a time, behind the car! Edwin, into the car beside me, test the footing with your lance. Once in the forest there are no traps! Then attack!"

The knights formed themselves into a line behind the car. Lord Faide drove slowly forward, his kinsman Edwin prodding the ground ahead. The First Folk sent out a dozen more wasps, which dashed themselves vainly against the armor. Then there was silence . . . cessation of sound, activity. The First Folk watched impassively as the knights approached, step by step.

Edwin's lance found a trap, the column moved to the side. Another trap—and the column was diverted from the planting toward the forest. Step by step, yard by yard—another trap, another detour, and now the column was only a hundred feet from the forest. A trap to the left, a trap to the right: the safe path led directly toward an enormous heavy-branched tree. Seventy feet, fifty feet, then Lord Faide drew his sword.

"Prepare to charge, kill till your arms tire!"

From the forest came a crackling sound. The branches of the great tree trembled and swayed. The knights stared, for a moment frozen into place. The tree toppled forward, the knights madly tried to flee—to the rear, to the sides. Traps opened; the knights dropped upon sharp stakes. The tree fell; boughs cracked armored bodies like nuts; there was the hoarse yelling of pinned men, screams from the traps, the crackling subsidence of breaking branches. Lord Faide had been battered down into the car, and the car had been pressed groaning into the moss. His first instinctive act was to press the switch to rest position; then he staggered erect, clambered up through the boughs. A pale unhuman face peered at him; he swung his fist, crushed the faceted eye-bulge, and roaring with rage, scrambled through the branches. Others of his knights were working themselves free, although almost a third were either crushed or impaled.

The First Folk came scrambling forward, armed with enormous thorns, long as swords. But now Lord Faide could reach them at close quarters. Hissing with vindictive joy, he sprang into their midst, swinging his sword with both hands, as if demonpossessed. The surviving knights joined him and the ground became littered with dismembered First Folk. They drew back slowly, without excitement. Lord Faide reluctantly called back his knights. "We must succor those still pinned, as many as still are alive."

As well as possible branches were cut away, injured knights drawn forth. In some cases the soft moss had cushioned the impact of the tree. Six knights were dead, another four crushed beyond hope of recovery. To these Lord Faide himself gave the *coup de grâce*. Ten minutes further hacking and chopping freed Lord Faide's car, while the First Folk watched incuriously from the forest. The knights wished to charge once more, but Lord Faide ordered retreat. Without interference they returned the way they had come, back to the baggage train.

Lord Faide ordered a muster. Of the original war party, less than two-thirds remained. Lord Faide shook his head bitterly. Galling to think how easily he had been led into a trap! He swung on his heel, strode to the rear of the column, to the wagons of the magicians. The jinxmen sat around a small fire, drinking tea. "Which of you will hoodoo these white forest vermin? I want them dead—stricken with sickness, cramps, blindness, the most painful afflictions you can contrive!"

There was general silence. The jinxmen sipped their tea.

"Well?" demanded Lord Faide. "Have you no answer? Do I not make myself plain?"

Hein Huss cleared his throat, spat into the blaze. "Your wishes are plain. Unfortunately we cannot hoodoo the First Folk."

"And why?"

"There are technical reasons."

Lord Faide knew the futility of argument. "Must we slink home around the forest? If you cannot hoodoo the First Folk, then bring out your demons! I will march on the forest and chop out a path with my sword!"

"It is not for me to suggest tactics," grumbled Hein Huss.

"Go on, speak! I will listen."

"A suggestion has been put to me, which I will pass to you. Neither I nor the other jinxmen associate ourselves with it, since it recommends the crudest of physical principles."

"I await the suggestion," said Lord Faide.

"It is merely this. One of my apprentices tampered with your car, as you may remember."

"Yes, and I will see he gets the hiding he deserves."

"By some freak he caused the car to rise high into the air. The suggestion is this: that we load the car with as much oil as the baggage train affords, that we send the car aloft and let it drift over the planting. At a suitable moment, the occupant of the car will pour the oil over the trees, then hurl down a torch. The forest will burn. The First Folk will be at least discomfited; at best a large number will be destroyed."

Lord Faide slapped his hands together. "Excellent! Quickly, to work!" He called a dozen soldiers, gave them orders; four kegs of cooking oil, three buckets of pitch, six demijohns of spirit were brought and lifted into the car. The engines grated and protested, and the car sagged almost to the moss.

Lord Faide shook his head sadly. "A rude use of the relic, but all in good purpose. Now, where is that apprentice? He must indicate which switches and which buttons he turned."

"I suggest," said Hein Huss, "that Sam Salazar be sent up with the car."

Lord Faide looked sidewise at Sam Salazar's round, bland countenance. "An efficient hand is needed, a seasoned judgment. I wonder if he can be trusted?"

"I would think so," said Hein Huss, "inasmuch as it was Sam Salazar who evolved the scheme in the first place."

"Very well. In with you, apprentice! Treat my car with reverence! The wind blows away from us; fire this edge of the forest, in as long a strip as you can manage. The torch, where is the torch?"

The torch was brought and secured to the side of the car.

"One more matter," said Sam Salazar. "I would like to borrow the armor of some obliging knight, to protect myself from the wasps. Otherwise—"

"Armor!" bawled Lord Faide. "Bring armor!"

At last, fully accoutred and with visor down, Sam Salazar climbed into the car. He seated himself, peered intently at the buttons and switches. In truth he was not precisely certain as to which he had manipulated before. . . . He considered, reached forward, pushed, turned. The motors roared and screamed; the car shuddered, sluggishly rose into the air. Higher, higher, twenty feet, forty feet, sixty feet—a hundred, two hundred. The wind eased the car toward the forest; in the shade the First Folk watched. Several of them raised tubes, opened the shutters. The onlookers saw the wasps dart through the air to dash against Sam Salazar's armor.

The car drifted over the trees; Sam Salazar began ladling out the oil. Below, the First Folk stirred uneasily. The wind carried the car too far over the forest; Sam Salazar worked the controls, succeeded in guiding himself back. One keg was empty, and another; he tossed them out, presently emptied the remaining two, and the buckets of pitch. He soaked a rag in spirit, ignited it, threw it over the side, poured the spirit after.

The flaming rag fell into leaves. A crackle, fire blazed and sprang. The car now floated at a height of five hundred feet. Salazar poured over the remaining spirits, dropped the demijohns, guided the car back over the heath, and fumbling nervously with the controls, dropped the car in a series of swoops back to the moss.

Lord Faide sprang forward, clapped him on the shoulder. "Excellently done! The forest blazes like tinder!"

The men of Faide Keep stood back, rejoicing to see the flames soar and lick. The First Folk scurried back from the heat, waving their arms; foam of a peculiar purple color issued from their vents as they ran, small useless puffs discharged as if by accident or through excitement. The flames ate through first the forest, then spread into the new planting, leaping through the leaves.

"Prepare to march!" called Lord Faide. "We pass directly behind the flames, before the First Folk return."

Off in the forest the First Folk perched in the trees, blowing out foam in great puffs and billows, building a wall of insulation. The flames had eaten half across the new planting, leaving behind smoldering saplings.

"Forward! Briskly!"

The column moved ahead. Coughing in the smoke, eyes smarting, they passed under still blazing trees and came out on the western downs.

Slowly the column moved forward, led by a pair of soldiers prodding the moss with lances. Behind followed Lord Faide with the knights, then came the foot soldiers, then the rumbling baggage train, and finally the six wagons of the jinxmen.

A thump, a creak, a snap. A scythe had broken up from the moss; the soldiers in the lead dropped flat; the scythe whipped past, a foot from Lord Faide's face. At the same time a plaintive cry came from the rear guard. "They pursue! The First Folk come!"

Lord Faide turned to inspect the new threat. A clot of First Folk, two hundred or more, came across the moss, moving without haste of urgency. Some carried wasp tubes, others thorn-rapiers.

Lord Faide looked ahead. Another hundred yards should bring the army out upon safe ground; then he could deploy and maneuver. "Forward!"

The column proceeded, the baggage train and the jinxmen's wagons pressing close up against the soldiers. Behind and to the side came the First Folk, moving casually and easily.

At last Lord Faide judged they had reached secure ground. "Forward, now! Bring the wagons out, hurry now!"

The troops needed no urging; they trotted out over the heath, the wagons trundling after. Lord Faide ordered the wagons into a close double line, stationed the soldiers between, with the horses behind and protected from the wasps. The knights, now dismounted, waited in front.

The First Folk came listlessly, formlessly forward. Blank white faces stared; huge hands grasped tubes and thorns; traces of the purplish foam showed at the lips of their under-arm orifices.

Lord Faide walked along the line of knights. "Swords ready. Allow them as close as they care to come. Then a quick charge." He motioned to the foot soldiers. "Choose a target!" A volley of darts whistled overhead, to plunge into white bodies. With chisel-bladed fingers the First Folk plucked them out, discarded them with no evidence of vexation. One or two staggered, wandered confusedly across the line of approach. Others raised their tubes, withdrew the shutter. Out flew the insects, horny wings rasping, prongs thrust forward. Across the moss they flickered, to crush themselves against the armor of the knights, to drop to the ground, to be stamped upon. The soldiers cranked their crossbows back into tension, discharged another flight of darts, caused several more First Folk casualties.

The First Folk spread into a long line, surrounding the Faide troops. Lord Faide shifted half his knights to the other side of the wagons.

The First Folk wandered closer. Lord Faide called for a charge. The knights stepped smartly forward, swords swinging. The First Folk advanced a few more steps, then stopped short. The flaps of skin at their backs swelled, pulsed; white foam gushed through their vents; clouds and billows rose up around them. The knights halted uncertainly, prodding and slashing into the foam but finding nothing. The foam piled higher, rolling in and forward, pushing the knights back toward the wagons. They looked questioningly toward Lord Faide.

Lord Faide waved his sword. "Cut through to the other side! Forward!" Slashing two-handed with his sword, he sprang into the foam. He struck something solid, hacked blindly at it, pushed forward. Then his legs were seized; he was upended and fell with a spine-rattling jar. Now he felt the grate of a thorn searching his armor. It found a crevice under his corselet and pierced him. Cursing, he raised on his hands and knees and plunged blindly forward. Enormous hard hands grasped him, heavy forms fell on his shoulders. He tried to breathe, but the foam clogged his visor; he began to smother. Staggering to his feet, he half-ran, half-fell out into the open air, carrying two of the First Folk with him. He had lost his sword, but managed to draw his dagger. The First Folk released him and stepped back into the foam. Lord Faide sprang to his feet. Inside the foam came the sounds of combat; some of his knights burst into the open; others called for help. Lord Faide motioned to the knights. "Back within; the devils slaughter our kinsmen! In and onto the center!"

He took a deep breath. Seizing his dagger, he thrust himself back into the foam. A flurry of shapes came at him: he pounded with his fists, cut with his dagger, stumbled over a mass of living tissue. He kicked the softness and stepped on metal. Bending, he grasped a leg but found it limp and dead. First Folk were on his back, another thorn found its mark; he groaned and thrust himself forward and once again fell out into the open air.

A scant fifty of his knights had won back into the central clearing. Lord Faide cried out, "To the center; mount your horses!" Abandoning his car, he himself vaulted into a saddle. The foam boiled and billowed closer. Lord Faide waved his arm. "Forward, all; at a gallop! After us the wagons—out into the open!"

They charged, thrusting the frightened horses into the foam. There was white blindness, the feel of forms underneath, then the open air once again. Behind came the wagons, and the foot soldiers, running along the channel cut by the wagons. All won free—all but the knights who had fallen under the foam.

Two hundred yards from the great white clot of foam, Lord Faide halted, turned, looked back. He raised his fist, shook it in a passion. "My knights, my car, my honor! I'll burn your forests, I'll drive you into the sea, there'll be no peace till all are dead!" He swung around. "Come," he called bitterly to the remnants of his war party. "We have been defeated. We retreat to Faide Keep."

VIII

Faide Keep, like Ballant Keep, was constructed of a black, glossy substance, half-metal, half-stone, impervious to heat, force, and radiation. A parasol roof, designed to ward off hostile energy, rested on five squat outer towers, connected by walls almost as high as the lip of the overhanging roof.

The homecoming banquet was quiet and morose. The soldiers and knights ate lightly and drank much, but instead of becoming merry, lapsed into gloom. Lord Faide, overcome by emotion, jumped to his feet. "Everyone sits silent, aching with rage. I feel no differently. We shall take revenge. We shall put the forests to the torch. The cursed white savages will smother and burn. Drink now with good cheer; not a moment will be wasted. But we must be ready. It is no more than idiocy to attack as before. Tonight I take council with the jinxmen and we will start a program of affliction."

The soldiers and knights rose to their feet, raised their cups, and drank a somber toast. Lord Faide bowed and left the hall.

He went to his private trophy room. On the walls hung escutcheons, memorials, death masks, clusters of swords like many-petaled flowers; a rack of side arms, energy pistols, electric stilettos; a portrait of the original Faide, in ancient spacefarer's uniform, and a treasured, almost unique, photograph of the great ship that had brought the first Faide to Pangborn.

Lord Faide studied the ancient face for several moments, then summoned a servant. "Ask the head jinxman to attend me."

Hein Huss presently stumped into the room. Lord Faide turned away from the portrait, seated himself, motioned to Hein Huss to do likewise. "What of the keep-lords?" he asked. "How do they regard the setback at the hands of the First Folk?"

"There are various reactions," said Hein Huss. "At Boghoten, Candelwade, and Havve there is distress and anger."

Lord Faide nodded. "These are my kinsmen."

"At Gisborne, Graymar, Castle Cloud, and Alder there is satisfaction, veiled calculation."

"To be expected," muttered Lord Faide. "These lords must be humbled; in spite of oaths and undertakings, they still think rebellion."

"At Star Home, Julian-Douray, and Oak Hall I read surprise at the abilities of the First Folk, but in the main disinterest."

Lord Faide nodded sourly. "Well enough. There is no actual rebellion in prospect; we are free to concentrate on the First Folk. I will tell you what is in my mind. You report that new plantings are in progress between Wildwood, Old Forest, Sarrow Copse, and elsewhere—possibly with the intent of surrounding Faide Keep." He looked inquiringly at Hein Huss, but no comment was forthcoming. Lord Faide continued. "Possibly we have underestimated the cunning of the savages. They seem capable of forming plans and acting with almost human persistence. Or, I should say, more than human persistence, for it appears that after sixteen hundred years they still consider us invaders and hope to exterminate us."

"That is my own conclusion," said Hein Huss.

"We must take steps to strike first. I consider this a matter for the jinxmen. We gain no honor dodging wasps, falling into traps, or groping through foam. It is a needless waste of lives. Therefore, I want you to assemble your jinxmen, cabalmen, and spellbinders; I want you to formulate your most potent hoodoos—"

"Impossible."

Lord Faide's black eyebrows rose high. " 'Impossible'?"

Hein Huss seemed vaguely uncomfortable. "I read the wonder in your mind. You suspect me of disinterest, irresponsibility. Not true. If the First Folk defeat you, we suffer likewise."

"Exactly," said Lord Faide dryly. "You will starve."

"Nevertheless, the jinxmen cannot help you." He hoisted himself to his feet, started for the door.

"Sit," said Lord Faide. "It is necessary to pursue this matter."

Hein Huss looked around with his bland, water-clear eyes.

Lord Faide met his gaze. Hein Huss sighed deeply. "I see I must ignore the precepts of my trade, break the habits of a lifetime. I must explain." He took his bulk to the wall, fingered the side arms in the rack, studied the portrait of the ancestral Faide. "These miracle workers of the old times—unfortunately we cannot use their magic! Notice the bulk of the spaceship! As heavy as Faide Keep." He turned his gaze on the table, teleported a candelabra two or three inches. "With considerably less effort they gave that spaceship enormous velocity, using ideas and forces they knew to be imaginary and irrational. We have advanced since then, of course. We no longer employ mysteries, arcane constructions, wild nonhuman forces. We are rational and practical—but we cannot achieve the effects of the ancient magicians."

Lord Faide watched Hein Huss with saturnine eyes. Hein Huss gave his deep rumbling laugh. "You think that I wish to distract you with talk? No, this is not the case. I am preparing to enlighten you." He returned to his seat, lowered his bulk with a groan. "Now I must talk at length, to which I am not accustomed. But you must be given to understand what we jinxmen can do and what we cannot do.

"First, unlike the ancient magicians, we are practical men. Naturally there is difference in our abilities. The best jinxman combines great telepathic facility, implacable personal force, and intimate knowledge of his fellow humans. He knows their acts, motives, desires, and fears; he understands the symbols that most vigorously represent these qualities. Jinxmanship in the main is drudgery—dangerous, difficult, and unromantic—with no mystery except that which we employ to confuse our enemies." Hein Huss glanced at Lord Faide to encounter the same saturnine gaze. "Ha! I still have told you nothing; I still have spent many words talking around my inability to confound the First Folk. Patience."

"Speak on," said Lord Faide.

"Listen, then. What happens when I hoodoo a man? First, I must enter into his mind telepathically. There are three operational levels: the conscious, the unconscious, the cellular. The most effective jinxing is done if all three levels are influenced. I feel into my victim, I learn as much as possible, supplementing my previous knowledge of him, which is part of my stock-in-trade. I take up his doll, which carries his traces. The doll is highly useful but not indispensable. It serves as a focus for my attention; it acts as a pattern, or a guide, as I fix upon the mind of the victim, and he is bound by his own telepathic capacity to the doll which bears his traces.

"So! Now! Man and doll are identified in my mind, and at one or more levels in the victim's mind. Whatever happens to the doll the victim feels to be happening to himself. There is no more to simple hoodooing than that, from the standpoint of the jinxman. But naturally the victims differ greatly. Susceptibility is the key idea here. Some men are more susceptible than others. Fear and conviction breed susceptibility. As a jinxman succeeds, he becomes ever more feared, and consequently the more efficacious he becomes. The process is self-generative.

"Demonpossession is a similar technique. Susceptibility is again essential; again conviction creates susceptibility. It is easiest and most dramatic when the characteristics of the demon are well-known, as in the case of Comandore's Keyril. For this reason, demons can be exchanged or traded among jinxmen. The commodity actually traded is public acceptance and familiarity with the demon."

"Demons, then, do not actually exist?" inquired Lord Faide half-incredulously.

Hein Huss grinned vastly, showing enormous yellow teeth. "Telepathy works through a superstratum. Who knows what is created in this superstratum? Maybe the demons live on after they have been conceived; maybe they now are real. This, of course, is speculation, which we jinxmen shun.

"So much for demons, so much for the lesser techniques of jinxmanship. I have explained sufficient to serve as background to the present situation."

"Excellent," said Lord Faide. "Continue."

"The question, then, is: how does one cast a hoodoo into a creature of an alien race?" He looked inquiringly at Lord Faide. "Can you tell me?"

"I?" asked Lord Faide, surprised. "No."

"The method is basically the same as in the hoodooing of men. It is necessary to make the creature believe, in every cell of his being, that he suffers or dies. This is where the problems begin to arise. Does the creature think—that is to say, does he arrange the processes of his life in the same manner as men? This is a very important distinction. Certain creatures of the universe use methods other than the human nerve-node system to control their environments. We call the human system *intelligence*—a word which properly should be restricted to human activity. Other creatures use different agencies, different systems, arriving sometimes at similar ends. To bring home these generalities, I cannot hope to merge my mind with the corresponding capacity in the First Folk. The key will not fit the lock. At least, not altogether. Once or twice when I watched the First Folk trading with men at Forest Market, I felt occasional weak significances. This implies that the First Folk mentality creates something similar to human telepathic impulses. Nevertheless, there is no real sympathy between the two races.

"This is the first and the least difficulty. If I were able to make complete telepathic contact—what, then? The creatures are different from us. They have no words for *fear, hate, rage, pain, bravery, cowardice*. One may deduce that they do not feel these emotions. Undoubtedly they know other sensations, possibly as meaningful. Whatever these may be, they are unknown to me, and therefore I cannot either form or project symbols for these sensations."

Lord Faide stirred impatiently. "In short, you tell me that you cannot efficiently enter these creatures' minds; and that if you could, you do not know what influences you could plant there to do them harm."

"Succinct," agreed Hein Huss. "Substantially accurate."

Lord Faide rose to his feet. "In that case you must repair these deficiencies. You must learn to telepathize with the First Folk; you must find what influences will harm them. As quickly as possible."

Hein Huss stared reproachfully at Lord Faide. "But I have gone to great lengths to explain the difficulties involved! To hoodoo the First Folk is a monumental task! It would be necessary to enter Wildwood, to live with the First Folk, to become one of them, as my apprentice thought to become a tree. Even then an effective hoodoo is improbable! The First Folk must be susceptible to conviction! Otherwise there would be no bite to the hoodoo! I could guarantee no success. I would predict failure. No other jinxman would dare tell you this, no other would risk his *mana*. I dare because I am Hein Huss, with life behind me."

"Nevertheless we must attempt every weapon at hand,"

said Lord Faide in a dry voice. "I cannot risk my knights, my kinsmen, my soldiers against these pallid half-creatures. What a waste of good flesh and blood to be stuck by a poison insect! You must go to Wildwood; you must learn how to hoodoo the First Folk."

Hein Huss heaved himself erect. His great round face was stony; his eyes were like bits of water-worn glass. "It is likewise a waste to go on a fool's errand. I am no fool, and I will not undertake a hoodoo which is futile from the beginning."

"In that case," said Lord Faide, "I will find someone else." He went to the door, summoned a servant. "Bring Isak Comandore here."

Hein Huss lowered his bulk into the chair. "I will remain during the interview, with your permission."

"As you wish."

Isak Comandore appeared in the doorway, tall, loosely articulated, head hanging forward. He darted a glance of swift appraisal at Lord Faide, at Hein Huss, then stepped into the room.

Lord Faide crisply explained his desires. "Hein Huss refuses to undertake the mission. Therefore, I call on you."

Isak Comandore calculated. The pattern of his thinking was clear: he possibly could gain much *mana;* there was small risk of diminution, for had not Hein Huss already dodged away from the project? Comandore nodded. "Hein Huss has made clear the difficulties; only a very clever and very lucky jinxman can hope to succeed. But I accept the challenge, I will go."

"Good," said Hein Huss. "I will go, too." Isak Comandore darted him a sudden hot glance. "I wish only to observe. To Isak Comandore goes the responsibility and whatever credit may ensue."

"Very well," said Comandore presently. "I welcome your company. Tomorrow morning we leave. I go to order our wagon."

Late in the evening Apprentice Sam Salazar came to Hein Huss where he sat brooding in his workroom. "What do you wish?" growled Huss.

"I have a request to make of you, Head Jinxman Huss."

"Head jinxman in name only," grumbled Hein Huss. "Isak Comandore is about to assume my position."

Sam Salazar blinked, laughed uncertainly. Hein Huss fixed wintry-pale eyes on him. "What do you wish?"

"I have heard that you go on an expedition to Wildwood, to study the First Folk."

"True, true. What, then?"

"Surely they will now attack all men?"

Hein Huss shrugged. "At Forest Market they trade with men. At Forest Market men have always entered the forest. Perhaps there will be change, perhaps not."

"I would go with you, if I may," said Sam Salazar.

"This is no mission for apprentices."

"An apprentice must take every opportunity to learn," said Sam Salazar. "Also you will need extra hands to set up tents, to load and unload cabinets, to cook, to fetch water and other such matters."

"Your argument is convincing," said Hein Huss. "We depart at dawn; be on hand."

IX

As the sun lifted over the heath the jinxmen departed Faide Keep. The high-wheeled wagon creaked north over the moss, Hein Huss and Isak Comandore riding the front seat, Sam Salazar with his legs hanging over the tail. The wagon rose and fell with the dips and mounds of the moss, wheels wobbling, and presently passed out of sight behind Skywatcher's Hill.

Five days later, an hour before sunset, the wagon reappeared. As before, Hein Huss and Isak Comandore rode the front seat, with Sam Salazar perched behind. They approached the keep and, without giving so much as a sign or a nod, drove through the gate into the courtyard.

Isak Comandore unfolded his long legs, stepped to the ground like a spider; Hein Huss lowered himself with a grunt. Both went to their quarters, while Sam Salazar led the wagon to the jinxmen's warehouse.

Somewhat later Isak Comandore presented himself to Lord Faide, who had been waiting in his trophy room, forced to a show of indifference through considerations of position, dignity, and protocol. Isak Comandore stood in the doorway, grinning like a fox. Lord Faide eyed him with sour dislike, waiting for Comandore to speak. Hein Huss might have stationed himself an entire day, eyes placidly fixed on Lord Faide, awaiting the first word; Isak Comandore lacked the absolute serenity. He came a step forward, "I have returned from Wildwood."

"With what results?"

"I believe that it is possible to hoodoo the First Folk."

Hein Huss spoke from behind Comandore. "I believe that such an undertaking, if feasible, would be useless, irresponsible, and possibly dangerous." He lumbered forward.

Isak Comandore's eyes glowed hot red-brown; he turned back to Lord Faide. "You ordered me forth on a mission; I will render a report."

"Seat yourselves. I will listen."

Isak Comandore, nominal head of the expedition, spoke. "We rode along the riverbank to Forest Market. Here was no sign of disorder or of hostility. A hundred First Folk traded timber, planks, posts, and poles for knife blades, iron wire, and copper pots. When they returned to their barge, we followed them aboard, wagon, horses, and all. They showed no surprise—"

"Surprise," said Hein Huss heavily, "is an emotion of which they have no knowledge."

Isak Comandore glared briefly. "We spoke to the barge-tenders, explaining that we wished to visit the interior of Wildwood. We asked if the First Folk would try to kill us to prevent us from entering the forest. They professed indifference as to either our well-being or our destruction. This was by no means a guarantee of safe-conduct; however, we accepted it as such and remained aboard the barge." He spoke on with occasional emendations from Hein Huss.

They had proceeded up the river, into the forest, the First Folk poling against the slow current. Presently they put away the poles; nevertheless the barge moved as before. The mystified jinxmen discussed the possibility of teleportation, or symbological force, and wondered if the First Folk had developed jinxing techniques unknown to men. Sam Salazar, however, noticed that four enormous water beetles, each twelve feet long with oil-black carapaces and blunt heads, had risen from the riverbed and pushed the barge from behind—apparently without direction or command. The First Folk stood at the bow, turning the nose of the barge this way or that to follow the winding of the river. They ignored the jinxmen and Sam Salazar as if they did not exist.

The beetles swam tirelessly; the barge moved for four hours as fast as a man could walk. Occasionally, First Folk peered from the forest shadows, but none showed interest or concern in the barge's unusual cargo. By midafternoon the river widened, broke into many channels, and became a marsh; a few minutes later the barge floated out into the open water of a small lake. Along the shore, behind the first line of trees appeared a large settlement. The jinxmen were interested and surprised. It had always been assumed that the First Folk wandered at random through the forest, as they had originally lived in the moss of the downs.

The barge grounded; the First Folk walked ashore, the men followed with the horses and wagon. Their immediate impressions were of swarming numbers, of slow but incessant activity, and they were attacked by an overpoweringly evil smell.

Ignoring the stench, the men brought the wagon in from the shore, paused to take stock of what they saw. The settlement appeared to be a center of many diverse activities. The trees had been stripped of lower branches, and supported blocks of hardened foam three hundred feet long, fifty feet high, twenty feet thick, with a space of a man's height intervening between the underside of the foam and the ground. There were a dozen of these blocks, apparently of cellular construction. Certain of the cells had broken open and seethed with small white fishlike creatures—the First Folk young.

Below the blocks masses of First Folk engaged in various occupations, in the main unfamiliar to the jinxmen. Leaving the wagon in the care of Sam Salazar, Hein Huss and Isak Comandore moved forward among the First Folk, repelled by the stench and the pressure of alien flesh, but drawn by curiosity. They were neither heeded nor halted; they wandered everywhere about the settlement. One area seemed to be an enormous zoo, divided into a number of sections. The purpose of one of these sections—a kind of range two hundred feet long—was all too clear. At one end a human corpse hung on a rope—a Faide casualty from the battle at the new planting. Certain of the wasps flew straight at the corpse; just before contact they were netted and removed. Others flew up and away or veered toward the First Folk who stood along the side of the range. These latter also were netted and killed at once.

The purpose of the business was clear enough. Examining

some of the other activity in this new light, the jinxmen were able to interpret much that had hitherto puzzled them.

They saw beetles tall as dogs with heavy saw-toothed pincers attacking objects resembling horses; pens of insects even larger, long, narrow, segmented, with dozens of heavy legs and nightmare heads. All these cratures—wasps, beetles, centipedes—in smaller and less formidable form were indigenous to the forest; it was plain that the First Folk had been practicing selective breeding for many years, perhaps centuries.

Not all the activity was warlike. Moths were trained to gather nuts, worms to gnaw straight holes through timber; in another section caterpillars chewed a yellow mash, molded it into identical spheres. Much of the evil odor emanated from the zoo; the jinxmen departed without reluctance and returned to the wagon. Sam Salazar pitched the tent and built a fire, while Hein Huss and Isak Comandore discussed the settlement.

Night came; the blocks of foam glowed with imprisoned light; the activity underneath proceeded without cessation. The jinxmen retired to the tent and slept, while Sam Salazar stood guard.

The following day Hein Huss was able to engage one of the First Folk in conversation; it was the first attention of any sort given to them.

The conversation was long; Hein Huss reported only the gist of it to Lord Faide. (Isak Comandore turned away, ostentatiously disassociating himself from the matter.)

Hein Huss first of all had inquired as to the purpose of the sinister preparations: the wasps, beetles, centipedes, and the like.

"We intend to kill men," the creature had reported ingenuously. "We intend to return to the moss. This has been our purpose ever since men appeared on the planet."

Huss had stated that such an ambition was shortsighted, that there was ample room for both men and First Folk on Pangborn. "The First Folk," said Hein Huss, "should remove their traps and cease their efforts to surround the keeps with forest."

"No," came the response, "men are intruders. They mar the beautiful moss. All will be killed."

Isak Comandore returned to the conversation. "I noticed here a significant fact. All the First Folk within sight had ceased their work; all looked toward us, as if they, too, participated in the discussion. I reached the highly important conclusion that the First Folk are not complete individuals but components of a larger unity, joined to a greater or less extent by a telepathic phase not unlike our own."

Hein Huss continued placidly, "I remarked that if we were attacked, many of the First Folk would perish. The creature showed no concern, and in fact implied much of what Jinxman Comandore had already induced: 'There are always more in the cells to replace the elements which die. But if the community becomes sick, all suffer. We have been forced into the forests, into a strange existence. We must arm ourselves and drive away the men, and to this end we have developed the methods of men to our own purposes!' "

Isak Comandore spoke. "Needless to say, the creature referred to the ancient men, not ourselves."

"In any event," said Lord Faide, "They leave no doubt as to their intentions. We should be fools not to attack them at once, with every weapon at our disposal."

Hein Huss continued imperturbably. "The creature went on at some length. 'We have learned the value of irrationality.' 'Irrationality,' of course, was not his word or even his meaning. He said something like 'a series of vaguely motivated trials'—as close as I can translate. He said, 'We have learned to change our environment. We use insects and trees and plants and waterslugs. It is an enormous effort for us who would prefer a placid life in the moss. But you men have forced this life on us, and now you must suffer the consequences.' I pointed out once more that men were not helpless, that many First Folk would die. The creature seemed unworried. 'The community persists.' I asked a delicate question, 'If your purpose is to kill men, why do you allow us here?' He said, 'The entire community of men will be destroyed.' Apparently they believe the human society to be similar to their own, and therefore regard the killing of three wayfaring individuals as pointless effort."

Lord Faide laughed grimly. "To destroy us they must first win past Hellmouth, then penetrate Faide Keep. This they are unable to do."

Isak Comandore resumed his report. "At this time I was already convinced that the problem was one of hoodooing not an individual but an entire race. In theory this should be no more difficult than hoodooing one. It requires no more effort to speak to twenty than to one. With this end in view I ordered the apprentice to collect substances associated with the creatures. Skinflakes, foam, droppings, all other exudations obtainable. While he did so, I tried to put myself in rapport with the creatures. It is difficult, for their telepathy works across a different stratum from ours. Nevertheless, to a certain extent I have succeeded.''

"Then you can hoodoo the First Folk?" asked Lord Faide.

"I vouchsafe nothing until I try. Certain preparations must be made."

"Go, then; make your preparations."

Comandore rose to his feet and with a sly side glance for Hein Huss left the room. Huss waited, pinching his chin with heavy fingers. Lord Faide looked at him coldly. "You have something to add?"

Huss grunted, hoisted himself to his feet. "I wish that I did. But my thoughts are confused. Of the many futures, all seem troubled and angry. Perhaps our best is not good enough."

Lord Faide looked at Hein Huss with surprise; the massive head jinxman had never before spoken in terms so pessimistic and melancholy. "Speak, then; I will listen."

Hein Huss said gruffly, "If I knew any certainties I would speak gladly. But I am merely beset by doubts. I fear that we can no longer depend on logic and careful jinxmanship. Our ancestors were miracle workers, magicians. They drove the First Folk into the forest. To put us to flight in our turn, the First folk have adopted the ancient methods: random trial and purposeless empiricism. I am dubious. Perhaps we must turn our backs on sanity and likewise return to the mysticism of our ancestors."

Lord Faide shrugged. "If Isak Comandore can hoodoo the First Folk, such a retreat may be unnecessary."

"The world changes," said Hein Huss. "Of so much I feel sure: the old days of craft and careful knowledge are gone. The future is for men of cleverness, of imagination untroubled by discipline; the unorthodox Sam Salazar may become more effective than I. The world changes."

Lord Faide smiled his sour dyspeptic smile. "When that day comes, I will appoint Sam Salazar head jinxman and also name him Lord Faide, and you and I will retire together to a hut on the downs."

Hein Huss made a heavy fateful gesture and departed.

X

Two days later Lord Faide, coming upon Isak Comandore, inquired as to his progress. Comandore took refuge in generalities. After another two days Lord Faide inquired again and this time insisted on particulars. Comandore grudgingly led the way to his workroom, where a dozen cabalmen, spellbinders, and apprentices worked around a large table, building a model of the First Folk settlement in Wildwood.

"Along the lakeshore," said Comandore, "I will range a great number of dolls, daubed with First Folk essences. When this is complete I will work up a hoodoo and blight the creatures."

"Good. Perform well." Lord Faide departed the workroom, mounted to the topmost pinnacle of the keep, to the cupola where the ancestral weapon Hellmouth was housed. "Jambart! Where are you?"

Weapon-tender Jambart, short, blue-jowled, red-nosed, and big-bellied, appeared. "My lord?"

"I come to inspect Hellmouth. Is it prepared for instant use?"

"Prepared, my lord, and ready. Oiled, greased, polished, scraped, burnished, tended—every part smooth as an egg."

Lord Faide made a scowling examination of Hellmouth—a heavy cylinder six feet in diameter, twelve feet long, studded with half-domes interconnected with tubes of polished copper. Jambart undoubtedly had been diligent. No trace of dirt or rust or corrosion showed; all was gleaming metal. The snout was covered with a heavy plate of metal and tarred canvas; the ring upon which the weapon swiveled was well-greased.

Lord Faide surveyed the four horizons. To the south was fertile Faide Valley; to the west open downs; to north and east the menacing loom of Wildwood.

He turned back to Hellmouth and pretended to find a smear of grease. Jambart boiled with expostulations and protestations; Lord Faide uttered a grim warning, enjoining less laxity, then descended to the workroom of Hein Huss. He found the head jinxman reclining on a couch, staring at the ceiling. At a bench stood Sam Salazar surrounded by bottles, flasks, and dishes.

Lord Faide stared balefully at the confusion. "What are you doing?" he asked the apprentice.

Sam Salazar looked up guiltily. "Nothing in particular, my lord."

"If you are idle, go, then, and assist Isak Comandore."

"I am not idle, Lord Faide."

"Then what do you do?"

Sam Salazar gazed sulkily at the bench. "I don't know."

"Then you are idle!"

"No, I am occupied. I pour various liquids on this foam. It is First Folk foam. I wonder what will happen. Water does not dissolve it, or spirits. Heat chars and slowly burns it, emitting a foul smoke."

Lord Faide turned away with a sneer. "You amuse yourself as a child might. Go to Isak Comandore; he can find use for you. How do you expect to become a jinxman, dabbling and prattling like a baby among pretty rocks?"

Hein Huss gave a deep sound: a mingling of sigh, snort, grunt, and clearing of the throat. "He does no harm, and Isak Comandore has hands enough. Salazar will never become a jinxman; that has been clear a long time."

Lord Faide shrugged. "He is your apprentice, and your responsibility. Well, then. What news from the keeps?"

Hein Huss, groaning and wheezing, swung his legs over the edge of the couch. "The lords share your concern, to greater or less extent. Your close allies will readily place troops at your disposal; the others likewise, if pressure is brought to bear."

Lord Faide nodded in dour satisfaction. "For the moment there is no urgency. The First Folk hold to their forests. Faide Keep, of course, is impregnable, although they might ravage the valley . . ." He paused thoughtfully. "Let Isak Comandore cast his hoodoo. Then we will see."

From the direction of the bench came a hiss, a small explosion, a whiff of acrid gas. Sam Salazar turned guiltily to look at them, his eyebrows singed. Lord Faide gave a snort of disgust and strode from the room.

"What did you do?" Hein Huss inquired in a colorless voice.

"I don't know."

Now Hein Huss likewise snorted in disgust. "Ridiculous. If you wish to work miracles, you must remember your procedures. Miracle working is not jinxmanship, with established rules and guides. In matters so complex it is well that you take notes, so that the miracles may be repeated."

Sam Salazar nodded in agreement and turned back to the bench.

XI

.Late during the day, news of new First Folk truculence reached Faide Keep. On Honeymoss Hill, not far west of Forest Market, a camp of shepherds had been visited by a wandering group of First Folk, who began to kill the sheep with thorn-swords. When the shepherds protested they, too, were attacked, and many were killed. The remainder of the sheep were massacred.

The following day came other news: four children swimming in Brastock River at Gilbert Ferry had been seized by enormous water-beetles and cut into pieces. On the other side of Wildwood, in the foothills immediately below Castle Cloud, peasants had cleared several hillsides and planted them to vines. Early in the morning they had discovered a horde of black disklike flukes devouring the vines—leaves, branches, trunks, and roots. They set about killing the flukes with spades and at once were stung to death by wasps.

Adam McAdam reported the incidents to Lord Faide, who went to Isak Comandore in a fury. "How soon before you are prepared?"

"I am prepared now. But I must rest and fortify myself. Tomorrow morning I work the hoodoo."

"The sooner the better! The creatures have left their forest; they are out killing men!"

Isak Comandore pulled his long chin. "That was to be expected; they told us as much."

Lord Faide ignored the remark. "Show me your tableau."

Isak Comandore took him into his workroom. The model was now complete, with the masses of simulated First Folk properly daubed and sensitized, each tied with a small wad of foam. Isak Comandore pointed to a pot of dark liquid. "I will explain the basis of the hoodoo. When I visited the camp I watched everywhere for powerful symbols. Undoubtedly there were many at hand, but I could not discern them. However, I remembered a circumstance from the battle at the planting: when the creatures were attacked, threatened with fire, and about to die, they spewed foam of dull purple color. Evidently this purple foam is associated with death. My hoodoo will be based upon this symbol."

"Rest well, then, so that you may hoodoo to your best capacity."

The following morning Isak Comandore dressed in long robes of black and set a mask of the demon Nard on his head to fortify himself. He entered his workroom, closed the door.

An hour passed, two hours. Lord Faide sat at breakfast with his kin, stubbornly maintaining a pose of cynical unconcern. At last he could contain himself no longer and went out into the courtyard, where Comandore's underlings stood fidgeting and uneasy. "Where is Hein Huss?" demanded Lord Faide. "Summon him here."

Hein Huss came stumping out of his quarters. Lord Faide motioned to Comandore's workshop. "What is happening? Is he succeeding?"

Hein Huss looked toward the workshop. "He is casting a powerful hoodoo. I feel confusion, anger—"

"In Comandore, or in the First Folk?"

"I am not in rapport. I think he has conveyed a message to their minds. A very difficult task, as I explained to you. In this preliminary aspect he has succeeded."

" 'Preliminary'? What else remains?"

"The two most important elements of the hoodoo: the susceptibility of the victim and the appropriateness of the symbol."

Lord Faide frowned. "You do not seem optimistic."

"I am uncertain. Isak Comandore may be right in his assumption. If so, and if the First Folk are highly susceptible, today marks a great victory, and Comandore will achieve tremendous *mana!*"

Lord Faide stared at the door to the workshop. "What, now?"

Hein Huss's eyes went blank with concentration. "Isak Comandore is near death. He can hoodoo no more today."

Lord Faide turned, waved his arm to the cabalmen. "Enter the workroom! Assist your master!"

The cabalmen raced to the door, flung it open. Presently they emerged supporting the limp form of Isak Comandore, his black robe spattered with purple foam. Lord Faide pressed close. "What did you achieve? Speak!"

Isak Comandore's eyes were half-closed, his mouth hung loose and wet. "I spoke to the First Folk, to the whole race. I sent the symbol into their minds—" His head fell limply sidewise.

Lord Faide moved back. "Take him to his quarters. Put him on his couch." He turned away, stood indecisively, chewing at his drooping lower lip. "Still we do not know the measure of his success."

"Ah," said Hein Huss, "but we do!"

Lord Faide jerked around. "What is this? What do you say?"

"I saw into Comandore's mind. He used the symbol of purple foam; with tremendous effort he drove it into their minds. Then he learned that purple foam means not death— purple foam means fear for the safety of the community, purple foam means desperate rage."

"In any event," said Lord Faide after a moment, "there is no harm done. The First Folk can hardly become more hostile."

Three hours later a scout rode furiously into the courtyard, threw himself off his horse, ran to Lord Faide. "The First Folk have left the forest! A tremendous number! Thousands! They are advancing on Faide Keep!"

"Let them advance!" said Lord Faide. "The more the better! Jambart, where are you?"

"Here, sir."

"Prepare Hellmouth! Hold all in readiness!"

"Hellmouth is always ready, sir!"

Lord Faide struck him across the shoulders. "Off with you! Bernard!"

The sergeant of the Faide troops came forward. "Ready, Lord Faide."

"The First Folk attack. Armor your men against wasps, feed them well. We will need all our strength."

Lord Faide turned to Hein Huss. "Send to the keeps, to the manor houses, order our kinsmen to join us, with all their troops and all their armor. Send to Bellgard Hall, to Boghoten, Camber, and Candelwade. Haste, haste, it is only hours from Wildwood."

Huss held up his hand. "I have already done so. The keeps are warned. They know your need."

"And the First Folk—can you feel their minds?"

"No."

Lord Faide walked away. Hein Huss lumbered out the main gate, walked around the keep, casting appraising glances up the black walls of the squat towers, windowless and proof even against the ancient miracle weapons. High on top the great parasol roof Jambart the weapon-tender worked in the cupola, polishing that which already glistened, greasing surfaces already heavy with grease.

Hein Huss returned within. Lord Faide approached him, mouth hard, eyes bright. "What have you seen?"

"Only the keep, the walls, the towers, the roof, and Hellmouth."

"And what do you think?"

"I think many things."

"You are noncommittal; you know more than you say. It is best that you speak, because if Faide Keep falls to the savages you die with the rest of us."

Hein Huss's water-clear eyes met the brilliant black gaze of Lord Faide. "I know only what you know. The First Folk attack. They have proved they are not stupid. They intend to kill us. They are not jinxmen; they cannot afflict us or force us out. They cannot break in the walls. To burrow under, they must dig through solid rock. What are their plans? I do not know. Will they succeed? Again, I do not know. But the day of the jinxman and his orderly array of knowledge is past. I think that we must grope for miracles, blindly and foolishly, like Salazar pouring liquids on foam."

A troop of armored horsemen rode in through the gates: warriors from nearby Bellgard Hall. And as the hours passed, contingents from other keeps came to Faide Keep, until the courtyard was dense with troops and horses.

Two hours before sunset the First Folk were sighted across the downs. They seemed a very large company, moving in an undisciplined clot with a number of stragglers, forerunners, and wanderers out on the flanks.

The hotbloods from outside keeps came clamoring to Lord Faide, urging a charge to cut down the First Folk; they found no seconding voices among the veterans of the battle at the planting. Lord Faide, however, was pleased to see the dense mass of First Folk. "Let them approach only a mile more— and Hellmouth will take them! Jambart!"

"At your call, Lord Faide."

"Come, Hellmouth speaks!" He strode away with Jambart after. Up to the cupola they climbed.

"Roll forth Hellmouth, direct it against the savages!"

Jambart leapt to the glistening array of wheels and levers. He hesitated in perplexity, then tentatively twisted a wheel. Hellmouth responded by twisting slowly around on its radial track, to the groan and chatter of long-frozen bearings. Lord Faide's brows lowered into a menacing line. "I hear evidence of neglect."

"Neglect, my lord, never! Find one spot of rust, a shadow of grime, you may have me whipped!"

"What of the sound?"

"That is internal and invisible—none of my responsibility."

Lord Faide said nothing. Hellmouth now pointed toward the great pale tide from Wildwood. Jambart twisted a second wheel and Hellmouth thrust forth its heavy snout. Lord Faide, in a voice harsh with anger, cried, "The cover, fool!"

"An oversight, my lord, easily repaired." Jambart crawled out along the top of Hellmouth, clinging to the protuberances for dear life, with below only the long smooth sweep of roof. With considerable difficulty he tore the covering loose, then grunting and cursing, inched himself back, jerking with his knees, rearing his buttocks.

The First Folk had slowed their pace a trifle, the main body only a half-mile distant.

"Now," said Lord Faide in high excitement, "before they disperse, we exterminate them!" He sighted through a telescopic tube, squinting through the dimness of internal films and incrustations, signaled to Jambart for the final adjustments. "Now! Fire!"

Jambart pulled the firing lever. Within the great metal barrel came a sputter of clicking sounds. Hellmouth whined, roared. Its snout glowed red, orange, white, and out poured a sudden gout of blazing purple radiation—which almost instantly died. Hellmouth's barrel quivered with heat, fumed, seethed, hissed. From within came a faint pop. Then there was silence.

A hundred yards in front of the First Folk a patch of moss burnt black where the bolt had struck. The aiming device was inaccurate. Hellmouth's bolt had killed perhaps twenty of the First Folk vanguard.

Lord Faide made feverish signals. "Quick! Raise the barrel. Now! Fire again!"

Jambart pulled the firing arm, to no avail. He tried again, with the same lack of success. "Hellmouth evidently is tired."

"Hellmouth is dead," cried Lord Faide. "You have failed me. Hellmouth is extinct."

"No, no," protested Jambart. "Hellmouth rests! I nurse it as my own child! It is polished like glass! Whenever a section wears off or breaks loose, I neatly remove the fracture and every trace of cracked glass."

Lord Faide threw up his arms, shouted in vast, inarticulate grief, ran below. "Huss! Hein Huss!"

Hein Huss presented himself. "What is your will?"

"Hellmouth has given up its fire. Conjure me more fire for Hellmouth, and quickly!"

"Impossible."

"Impossible!" cried Lord Faide. "That is all I hear from you! Impossible, useless, impractical! You have lost your ability. I will consult Isak Comandore."

"Isak Comandore can put no more fire into Hellmouth than can I."

"What sophistry is this? He puts demons into men, surely he can put fire into Hellmouth!"

"Come, Lord Faide, you are overwrought. You know the difference between jinxmanship and miracle working."

Lord Faide motioned to a servant. "Bring Isak Comandore here to me!"

Isak Comandore, face haggard, skin waxy, limped into the courtyard. Lord Faide waved peremptorily. "I need your skill. You must restore fire to Hellmouth."

Comandore darted a quick glance at Hein Huss, who stood solid and cold. Comandore decided against dramatic promises that could not be fulfilled. "I cannot do this, my lord."

"What! You tell me this, too?"

"Remark the difference, Lord Faide, between man and metal. A man's normal state is something near madness; he is at all times balanced on a knife-edge between hysteria and apathy. His senses tell him far less of the world than he thinks they do. It is a simple trick to deceive a man, to possess him with a demon, to drive him out of his mind, to kill him. But metal is insensible; metal reacts only as its shape and condition dictates, or by the working of miracles."

"Then you must work miracles!"

"Impossible."

Lord Faide drew a deep breath, collected himself. He

walked swiftly across the court. "My armor, my horse. We attack."

The column formed, Lord Faide at the head. He led the knights through the portals, with armored footmen behind.

"Beware the foam!" called Lord Faide. "Attack, strike, cut, draw back. Keep your visors drawn against the wasps! Each man must kill a hundred! Attack!"

The troop rode forth against the horde of First Folk, knights in the lead. The hooves of the horses pounded softly over the thick moss; in the west the large pale sun hung close to the horizon.

Two hundred yards from the First Folk the knights touched the club-headed horses into a lope. They raised their swords and, shouting, plunged forward, each man seeking to be first. The clotted mass of First Folk separated: black beetles darted forth and after them long segmented centipede creatures. They dashed among the horses, mandibles clicking, snouts slashing. Horses screamed, reared, fell over backward; beetles cut open armored knights as a dog cracks a bone. Lord Faide's horse threw him and ran away; he picked himself up, hacked at a nearby beetle, lopped off its front leg. It darted forward, he lopped off the leg opposite; the heavy head dipped, tore up the moss. Lord Faide cut off the remaining legs, and it lay helpless.

"Retreat," he bellowed. "Retreat!"

The knights moved back, slashing and hacking at beetles and centipedes, killing or disabling all which attacked.

"Form into a double line, knights and men. Advance slowly, supporting each other!"

The men advanced. The First Folk dispersed to meet them, armed with their thorn-swords and carrying pouches. Ten yards from the men they reached into the pouches, brought dark balls which they threw at the men. The balls broke and spattered on the armor.

"Charge!" bawled Lord Faide. The men sprang forward into the mass of First Folk, cutting, slashing, killing. "Kill!" called Lord Faide in exultation. "Leave not one alive!"

A pang struck him, a sting inside his armor, followed by another and another. Small things crawled inside the metal, stinging, biting, crawling. He looked about: on all sides were harassed expressions, faces working in anguish. Sword arms

fell limp as hands beat on the metal, futilely trying to scratch,
rub. Two men suddenly began to tear off their armor.

"Retreat," cried Lord Faide. "Back to the keep!"

The retreat was a rout, the soliders shedding articles of
armor as they ran. After them came a flight of wasps—a
dozen or more, and half as many men cried out as the poison
prongs struck into their backs.

Inside the keep stormed the disorganized company, casting
aside the last of their armor, slapping their skin, scratching,
rubbing, crushing the ferocious red mites that infested them.

"Close the gates," roared Lord Faide.

The gates slid shut. Faide Keep was besieged.

XII

During the night the First Folk surrounded the keep, forming a ring fifty yards from the walls. All night there was
motion, ghostly shapes coming and going in the starlight.

Lord Faide watched from a parapet until midnight, with
Hein Huss at his side. Repeatedly, he asked, "What of the
other keeps? Do they send further reinforcements?" to which
Hein Huss each time gave the same reply: "There is confusion and doubt. The keep-lords are anxious to help but do not
care to throw themselves away. At this moment they consider
and take stock of the situation."

Lord Faide at last left the parapet, signaling Hein Huss to
follow. He went to his trophy room, threw himself into a
chair, motioned Hein Huss to be seated. For a moment he
fixed the jinxman with a cool, calculating stare. Hein Huss
bore the appraisal without discomfort.

"You are head jinxman," said Lord Faide finally. "For
twenty years you have worked spells, cast hoodoos, performed auguries—more effectively than any other jinxman of
Pangborn. But now I find you inept and listless. Why is
this?"

"I am neither inept nor listless. I am unable to achieve
beyond my abilities. I do not know how to work miracles.
For this you must consult my apprentice Sam Salazar, who
does not know either, but who earnestly tries every possibility
and many impossibilities."

"You believe in this nonsense yourself! Before my very
eyes you become a mystic!"

Hein Huss shrugged. "There are limitations to my knowledge. Miracles occur—that we know. The relics of our ancestors lie everywhere. Their methods were supernatural, repellent to our own mental processes—but think! Using these same methods the First Folk threaten to destroy us. In the place of metal they use living flesh—but the result is similar. The men of Pangborn, if they assemble and accept casualties, can drive the First Folk back to Wildwood—but for how long? A year? Ten years? The First Folk plant new trees, dig more traps—and presently come forth again, with more terrible weapons: flying beetles, large as a horse; wasps strong enough to pierce armor; lizards to scale the walls of Faide Keep."

Lord Faide pulled at his chin. "And the jinxmen are helpless?"

"You saw for yourself. Isak Comandore intruded enough into their consciousness to anger them, no more."

"So, then—what must we do?"

Hein Huss held out his hands. "I do not know. I am Hein Huss, jinxman. I watch Sam Salazar with fascination. He learns nothing, but he is either too stupid or too intelligent to be discouraged. If this is the way to work miracles, he will work them."

Lord Faide rose to his feet. "I am deathly tired. I cannot think, I must sleep. Tomorrow we will know more."

Hein Huss left the trophy room, returned to the parapet. The ring of First Folk seemed closer to the walls, almost within dart-range. Behind them and across the moors stretched a long pale column of marching First Folk. A little back from the keep a pile of white material began to grow, larger and larger as the night proceeded.

Hours passed, the sky lightened; the sun rose in the east. The First Folk tramped the downs like ants, bringing long bars of hardened foam down from the north, dropping them into piles around the keep, returning into the north once more.

Lord Faide came up on the parapet, haggard and unshaven. "What is this? What do they do?"

Bernard the sergeant responded. "They puzzle us all, my lord."

"Hein Huss! What of the other keeps?"

"They have armed and mounted; they approach cautiously."

"Can you communicate our urgency?"

"I can, and I have done so. I have only accentuated their caution."

"Bah!" cried Lord Faide in disgust. "Warriors they call themselves! Loyal and faithful allies!"

"They know of your bitter experience," said Hein Huss. "They ask themselves, reasonably enough, what they can accomplish which you who are already here cannot do first."

Lord Faide laughed sourly. "I have no answer for them. In the meantime we must protect ourselves against the wasps. Armor is useless; they drive us mad with mites. . . . Bernard!"

"Yes, Lord Faide."

"Have each of your men construct a frame two-feet square, fixed with a short handle. To these frames should be sewed a net of heavy mesh. When these frames are built we will sally forth, two soldiers to guard one half-armored knight on foot."

"In the meantime," said Hein Huss, "the First Folk proceed with their plans."

Lord Faide turned to watch. The First Folk came close up under the walls carrying rods of hardened foam. "Bernard! Put your archers to work! Aim for the heads!"

Along the walls bowmen cocked their weapons. Darts spun down into the First Folk. A few were affected, turned, and staggered away; others plucked away the bolts without concern. Another flight of bolts, a few more First Folk were disabled. The others planted the rods in the moss, exuded foam in great gushes, their back-flaps vigorously pumping air. Other First Folk brought more rods, pushed them into the foam. Entirely around the keep, close under the walls, extended the mound of foam. The ring of First Folk now came close and all gushed foam; it bulked up swiftly. More rods were brought, thrust into the foam, reinforcing and stiffening the mass.

"More darts!" barked Lord Faide. "Aim for the heads! Bernard—your men, have they prepared the wasp nets?"

"Not yet, Lord Faide. The project requires some little time."

Lord Faide became silent. The foam, now ten feet high, rapidly piled higher. Lord Faide turned to Hein Huss. "What do they hope to achieve?"

Hein Huss shook his head. "For the moment I am uncertain."

The first layer of foam had hardened; on top of this the First Folk spewed another layer, reinforcing again with the rods, crisscrossing, horizontal and vertical. Fifteen minutes later, when the second layer was hard, the First Folk emplaced and mounted rude ladders to raise a third layer. Surrounding the keep now was a ring of foam thirty feet high and forty feet thick at the base.

"Look," said Hein Huss. He pointed up. The parasol roof overhanging the walls ended only thirty feet above the foam. "A few more layers and they will reach the roof."

"So, then?" asked Lord Faide. "The roof is as strong as the walls."

"And we will be sealed within."

Lord Faide studied the foam in the light of this new thought. Already the First Folk, climbing laboriously up ladders along the outside face of their wall of foam, were preparing to lay on a fourth layer. First—rods, stiff and dry; then great gushes of white. Only twenty feet remained between roof and foam.

Lord Faide turned to the sergeant. "Prepare the men to sally forth."

"What of the wasp nets, sir?"

"Are they almost finished?"

"Another ten minutes, sir."

"Another ten minutes will see us smothering. We must force a passage through the foam."

Ten minutes passed, and fifteen. The First Folk created ramps behind their wall: first, dozens of the rods, then foam, and on top, to distribute the weight, reed mats.

Bernard the sergeant reported to Lord Faide. "We are ready."

"Good." Lord Faide descended into the courtyard. He faced the men, gave them their orders. "Move quickly, but stay together; we must not lose ourselves in the foam. As we proceed, slash ahead and to the sides. The First Folk see through the foam; they have the advantage of us. When we break through, we use the wasp nets. Two foot soldiers must guard each knight. Remember, quickly through the foam, that we do not smother. Open the gates."

The gates slid back, the troops marched forth. They faced an unbroken blank wall of foam. No enemy could be seen.

Lord Faide waved his sword. "Into the foam." He strode forward, pushed into the white mass, now crisp and brittle and harder than he had bargained for. It resisted him; he cut and hacked. His troops joined him, carving a way into the foam. First Folk appeared above them, crawling carefully on the mats. Their back-flaps puffed, pumped; foam issued from their vents, falling in a cascade over the troops.

Hein Huss sighed. He spoke to Apprentice Sam Salazar. "Now they must retreat, otherwise they smother. If they fail to win through, we all smother."

Even as he spoke the foam, piling up swiftly, in places reached the roof. Below, bellowing and cursing, Lord Faide backed out from under, wiped his face clear. Once again, in desperation, he charged forward, trying at a new spot.

The foam was friable and cut easily, but the chunks detached still blocked the opening. And again down tumbled a cascade of foam, covering the soldiers.

Lord Faide retreated, waved his men back into the keep. At the same moment First Folk, crawling on mats on the same level as the parapet over the gate, laid rods up from the foam to rest against the projecting edge of the roof. They gushed foam; the view of the sky was slowly blocked from the view of Hein Huss and Sam Salazar.

"In an hour, perhaps two, we will die," said Hein Huss. "They have now sealed us in. There are many men here in the keep, and all will now breathe deeply."

Sam Salazar said nervously, "There is a possibility we might be able to survive—or at least not smother."

"Ah?" inquired Hein Huss with heavy sarcasm. "You plan to work a miracle?"

"If a miracle, the most trivial sort. I observed that water has no effect on the foam, nor a number of other liquids: milk, spirits, wine, or caustic. Vinegar, however, instantly dissolves the foam."

"Aha," said Hein Huss. "We must inform Lord Faide."

"Better that you do so," said Sam Salazar. "He will pay me no need."

XIII

Half an hour passed. Light filtered into Faide Keep only as a dim gray gloom. Air tasted flat, damp and heavy. Out from the gates sallied the troops. Each carried a crock, a jug, a skin or a pan containing strong vinegar.

"Quickly now," called Lord Faide, "but careful! Spare the vinegar, don't throw it wildly. In close formation now—forward."

The soldiers approached the wall, threw ladles of vinegar ahead. The foam crackled, melted.

"Waste no vinegar," shouted Lord Faide. "Forward, quickly now; bring forward the vinegar!"

Minutes later they burst out upon the downs. The First Folk stared at them, blinking.

"Charge," croaked Lord Faide, his throat thick with fumes. "Mind now, wasp nets! Two soldiers to each knight! Charge, double-quick. Kill the white beasts."

The men dashed ahead. Wasp tubes were leveled. "Halt!" yelled Lord Faide. "Wasps!"

The wasps came, wings rasping. Nets rose up; wasps struck with a thud. Down went the nets; hard feet crushed the insects. The beetles and the lizard-centipedes appeared, not so many as of the last evening, for a great number had been killed. They darted forward, and a score of men died, but the insects were soon hacked into chunks of reeking brown flesh. Wasps flew, and some struck home; the agonies of the dying men were unnerving. Presently the wasps likewise decreased in number, and soon there were no more.

The men faced the First Folk, armed only with thorn-swords and their foam, which now came purple with rage.

Lord Faide waved his sword; the men advanced and began to kill the First Folk, by dozens, by hundreds.

Hein Huss came forth and approached Lord Faide. "Call a halt."

"A halt? Why? Now we kill these bestial things."

"Far better not. Neither need kill the other. Now is the time to show great wisdom."

"They have besieged us, caught us in their traps, stung us with their wasps! And you say halt?"

"They nourish a grudge sixteen hundred years old. Best not to add another one."

Lord Faide stared at Hein Huss. "What do you propose?"

"Peace between the two races, peace and cooperation."

"Very well. No more traps, no more plantings, no more breeding of deadly insects."

"Call back your men. I will try."

Lord Faide cried out, "Men, fall back, Disengage."

Reluctantly the troops drew back. Hein Huss approached the huddled mass of purple-foaming First Folk. He waited a moment. They watched him intently. He spoke in their language.

"You have attacked Faide Keep; you have been defeated. You planned well, but we have proved stronger. At this moment we can kill you. Then we can go on to fire the forest, starting a hundred blazes. Some of the fires you can control. Others not. We can destroy Wildwood. Some First Folk may survive, to hide in the thickets and breed new plans to kill men. This we do not want. Lord Faide has agreed to peace, if you likewise agree. This means no more death traps. Men will freely approach and pass through the forests. In your turn you may freely come out on the moss. Neither race shall molest the other. Which do you choose? Extinction—or peace?"

The purple foam no longer dribbled from the vents of the First Folk. "We choose peace."

"There must be no more wasps, beetles. The death traps must be disarmed and never replaced."

"We agree. In our turn we must be allowed freedom of the moss."

"Agreed. Remove your dead and wounded, haul away the foam rods."

Hein Huss returned to Lord Faide. "They have chosen peace."

Lord Faide nodded. "Very well. It is for the best." He called to his men. "Sheathe your weapons. We have won a great victory." He ruefully surveyed Faide Keep, swathed in foam and invisible except for the parasol roof. "A hundred barrels of vinegar will not be enough."

Hein Huss looked off into the sky. "Your allies approach quickly. Their jinxmen have told them of your victory."

Lord Faide laughed his sour laugh. "To my allies will fall the task of removing the foam from Faide Keep."

XIV

In the hall of Faide Keep, during the victory banquet, Lord Faide called jovially across to Hein Huss. "Now, head jinxman, we must deal with your apprentice, the idler and the waster Sam Salazar."

"He is here, Lord Faide. Rise, Sam Salazar, take cognizance of the honor being done you."

Sam Salazar rose to his feet, bowed.

Lord Faide proffered him a cup. "Drink, Sam Salazar, enjoy yourself. I freely admit that your idiotic tinkerings saved the lives of us all. Sam Salazar, we salute you and thank you. Now, I trust that you will put frivolity aside, apply yourself to your work, and learn honest jinxmanship. When the time comes, I promise that you shall find a lifetime of employment at Faide Keep."

"Thank you," said Sam Salazar modestly. "However, I doubt if I will become a jinxman."

"No? You have other plans?"

Sam Salazar stuttered, grew faintly pink in the face, then straightened himself and spoke as clearly and distinctly as he could. "I prefer to continue what you call my frivolity. I hope I can persuade others to join me."

"Frivolity is always attractive," said Lord Faide. "No doubt you can find other idlers and wasters, runaway farm boys, and the like."

Sam Salazar said staunchly, "This frivolity might become serious. Undoubtedly the ancients were barbarians. They used symbols to control entities they were unable to understand. We are methodical and rational; why can't we systematize and comprehend the ancient miracles?"

"Well, why can't we?" asked Lord Faide. "Does anyone have an answer?"

No one responded, although Isak Comandore hissed between his teeth and shook his head.

"I personally may never be able to work miracles; I suspect it is more complicated than it seems," said Sam Salazar. "However, I hope that you will arrange for a workshop where I and others who might share my views can make a beginning. In this matter I have the encouragement and the support of Head Jinxman Hein Huss."

Lord Faide lifted his goblet. "Very well, Apprentice Sam Salazar. Tonight I can refuse you nothing. You shall have exactly what you wish, and good luck to you. Perhaps you will produce a miracle during my lifetime."

Isak Comandore said huskily to Hein Huss, "This is a sad event! It signalizes intellectual anarchy, the degradation of jinxmanship, the prostitution of logic. Novelty has a way of attracting youth; already I see apprentices and spellbinders whispering in excitement. The jinxmen of the future will be sorry affairs. How will they go about demonpossession? With a cog, a gear, and a push-button. How will they cast a hoodoo? They will find it easier to strike their victim with an ax."

"Times change," said Hein Huss. "There is now the one rule of Faide on Pangborn, and the keeps no longer need to employ us. Perhaps I will join Sam Salazar in his workshop."

"You depict a depressing future," said Isak Comandore with a sniff of disgust.

"There are many futures, some of which are undoubtedly depressing."

Lord Faide raised his glass. "To the best of your many futures, Hein Huss. Who knows? Sam Salazar may conjure a spaceship to lead us back to home planet."

"Who knows?" said Hein Huss. He raised his goblet. "To the best of the futures!"

Please fill in the form below in block letters:

NAME_____

ADDRESS_____

_____

_____

_____

Send to Robinson Publishing Cash Sales,
P.O. Box 11, Falmouth, Cornwall TR10 9EN

Please enclose cheque or postal order to the value of the cover price plus:

In UK only – 55p for the first book, 22p for the second book, and 14p for each additional book to a maximum £1.75.

BFPO – 55p for the first book, 22p for the second book, and 14p for the next seven books and 8p for each book thereafter.

Overseas – £1.25 for the first book, 31p per copy for each additional book.

Whilst every effort is made to keep prices low, it is sometimes necessary to increase prices at short notice. Robinson Publishing reserve the right to show on covers, and charge, new retail prices which may differ from those advertised in text or elsewhere.

ORDER FORM

If you cannot find these titles in your bookshop, they can be obtained directly from the publisher. Please indicate the number of copies required and fill in the form overleaf in block letters.

The Mammoth Book of Short Science Fiction Novels
___ Presented by Isaac Asimov   £4.95

The Mammoth Book of Short Fantasy Novels
___ Presented by Isaac Asimov   £4.95

The Mammoth Book of Short Crime Novels
___ Edited by Bill Pronzini and Martin H. Greenberg   £4.95

The Mammoth Book of Short Spy Novels
___ Edited by Bill Pronzini and Martin H. Greenberg   £4.95

The Mammoth Book of Modern Crime Stories
___ Edited by George Hardinge   £4.95

The Mammoth Book of Classic Fantasy
___ Edited by Cary Wilkins   £4.95

The Mammoth Book of Classic Science Fiction
___ Presented by Isaac Asimov   £4.95

The Mammoth Book of Best New Science Fiction
___ Edited by Gardner Dozois   £4.95

Mythic Beasts
___ Edited by Isaac Asimov, C. Waugh and M.
Greenberg   £3.50

Supermen
___ Edited by Isaac Asimov, C. Waugh and M.
Greenberg   £2.95

Intergalactic Empires
___ Edited by Isaac Asimov, C. Waugh and M. Greenberg
                                                       £2.95